D0958280

continued on next page . . .

LAST CHANCE

Rachel McKenna shocked everyone when she danced with legendary gunfighter Lane Cassidy. But she knew he could be her last chance for happiness . . .

"Readers who loved *After All* . . . will be overjoyed with this first-rate spin-off."
—*Publishers Weekly*

AFTER ALL

The passionate and moving story of a dance hall girl trying to change her life in the town of Last Chance, Montana . . .

"Historical romance at its very best." —*Publishers Weekly*

UNTIL TOMORROW

A soldier returning from war shows a backwoods beauty that every dream is possible—even the dream of love . . .

"Landis does what she does best by creating characters of great dimension, compassion, and strength." —*Publishers Weekly*

PAST PROMISES

She was a brilliant paleontologist who came west in search of dinosaurs. But a rugged cowboy poet was determined to unearth the beauty and passion behind her bookish spectacles . . .

"Warmth, charm, and appeal . . . *Past Promises* is guaranteed to satisfy romance readers everywhere." —Amanda Quick

COME SPRING

WINNER OF THE ROMANCE WRITERS OF AMERICA'S
"RITA AWARD FOR FAVORITE NOVEL OF 1993"

Snowbound in a mountain man's cabin, beautiful Annika learned that unexpected love can grow as surely as the seasons change . . .

"A beautiful love story." —Julie Garwood

JADE

Her exotic beauty captured the heart of a rugged rancher. But could he forget the past—and love again?

"Guaranteed to enthrall . . . an unusual, fast-paced love story."
—*Romantic Times*

ROSE

Across the golden frontier, her passionate heart dared to dream . . .

"A gentle romance that will warm your soul."
—*Heartland Critiques*

WILDFLOWER

Amidst the untamed beauty of the Rocky Mountains, two daring hearts forged a perilous passion . . .

"A delight from start to finish!"
—*Rendezvous*

SUNFLOWER

WINNER OF THE ROMANCE WRITERS OF AMERICA'S
"GOLDEN MEDALLION FOR BEST HISTORICAL ROMANCE"

Jill Marie Landis's stunning debut novel, this sweeping love story astonished critics, earning glowing reviews including a FIVE STAR rating from Affaire de Coeur . . .

"A truly fabulous read! The story comes vibrantly alive, making you laugh and cry . . ."
—*Affaire de Coeur*

Blue Moon

Jill Marie Landis

JOVE BOOKS, NEW YORK

BLUE MOON

A Jove Book / published by arrangement with
the author

PRINTING HISTORY
Jove edition / July 1999

The Penguin Putnam Inc. World Wide Web site address is
http://www.penguinputnam.com

ISBN: 0-515-12527-X

A JOVE BOOK®
Jove Books are published by The Berkley Publishing Group,
a member of Penguin Putnam Inc.,
375 Hudson Street, New York, New York 10014.
JOVE and the ''J'' design
are trademarks belonging to Penguin Putnam Inc.

PRINTED IN THE UNITED STATES OF AMERICA

10 9 8 7 6 5 4 3 2 1

To Rex and Betsy Wright,
the ultimate southern Illinois research tour guides.

To the Davis, Scott, and Wettaw families
in southern Illinois and Indiana.

To Virginia Murillo . . . university graduate.
Congratulations!

To Phyllis Ruffin . . . you can do it!

To Hoby "What a guy!" Parks.

Dear Reader,

Hearing from so many of you is one of the joys of being a writer, especially when your letters are about secondary characters you would like to see again in the role of hero or heroine. Noah LeCroix, the hero in *Blue Moon*, made his first appearance in *Just Once* as a reclusive, mysterious man who lived in a treehouse in a swamp in Kentucky. Half-Cherokee, half–French Canadian, Noah met with an accident while piloting a flatboat down the Mississippi, one that left him scarred. At the end of *Just Once,* Noah stood alone in woodland shadows watching his best friend's wedding ceremony, lifted his hand in a silent salute, and then blended into the forest alone.

After receiving many requests for Noah's story, I decided that his tale just had to be told—and so for all of you who asked for it, here's *Blue Moon*. It's the love story of Olivia Bond and Noah LeCroix—a heroine who has faced unspeakable hardships and is trying to find her way home, and a reluctant hero who comes to cherish the commitment and ties that bind a man to home and family. For those of you who are meeting Noah for the first time, I hope you fall in love with him as did so many others.

I enjoy hearing from readers and can be reached at Nancy Berland Public Relations, 7209 Lancelot Place, Oklahoma City, Oklahoma 73132, or at my homepage: *http://www.nettrends.com/jillmarielandis.*

Enjoy!

"*Yf they say the mone is belewe,*
We must beleve that it is true."

Wm. Roy and J. Barlow
REDE ME AND BE NOT WROTHE
1528.

From *The Dictionary of Cliches,* James Rogers, 1987,
Ballantine.

prologue

She would be nineteen tomorrow. If she lived.

In the center of a faint deer trail on a ribbon of dry land running through a dense swamp, a young woman crouched like a cornered animal. The weak gray light from a dull, overcast sky barely penetrated the bald cypress forest as she wrapped her arms around herself and shivered, trying to catch her breath. She wore nothing to protect her from the elements but a tattered, rough, homespun dress and an ill-fitting pair of leather shoes that had worn blisters on her heels.

The primeval path was nearly obliterated by lichens and ferns that grew over deep drifts of dried twigs and leaves. Here and there the ground was littered with the larger rotting, fallen limbs of trees. The fecund scent of decay clung to the air, pressed down on her, stoked her fear and gave it life.

Breathe. Breathe.

The young woman's breath came fast and hard. She squinted through her tangled black hair, shoved it back, her fingers streaked with mud. Her hands shook. Terror born of being lost was heightened by the knowledge that night was going to fall before she found her way out of the swamp.

Not only did the encroaching darkness frighten her, but so did the murky, silent water along both sides of the trail. As she realized she would soon be surrounded by night and water both, a strangled cry escaped her. Behind her, from somewhere deep amid the cypress trees wrapped in rust-colored bark, came the sound of a splash as some unseen creature dropped into the watery ooze.

She rose, spun around and scanned the surface of the swamp. Frogs and fish, venomous copperheads, and turtles big as frying pans thrived beneath the lacy emerald carpet of duckweed that floated upon the water. As she knelt there wondering whether she should continue on in the same direction or turn back, she watched a small knot of fur skim over the surface of the water toward her.

A soaking-wet muskrat lost its grace as soon as it made land and lumbered up the bank in her direction. Amused yet wary, the girl scrambled back a few inches. The creature froze and stared with dark beady eyes before it turned tail, hit the water, and disappeared.

Getting to her feet, the girl kept her eyes trained on the narrow footpath, gingerly stepping through piles of damp, decayed leaves. Again she paused and lifted her head, listening for the sound of a human voice, the pounding footsteps that would mean someone was in pursuit of her along the trail.

When all she heard was the distant knock of a woodpecker, she let out a sigh of relief. Determined to keep moving, she trudged on, ever vigilant, hoping that the edge of the swamp lay just ahead.

Suddenly, the sharp, shrill scream of a bobcat set her heart pounding. With a fist pressed against her lips, she squeezed her eyes closed and froze, afraid to move, afraid to even breathe. The cat screamed again and the cry echoed across the haunting silence of the swamp until it seemed to stir the very air around her.

She glanced up at dishwater-gray patches of weak afternoon light, nearly obliterated by cypress trees that grew so close together in some places that not even a small child could pass between them. The thought that a wildcat might be looming somewhere above her in the tangled limbs, crouched and ready to pounce, sent her running down the narrow, winding trail.

She had not gone a hundred steps when the toe of her shoe caught beneath an exposed tree root. Thrown forward, she began to fall and cried out.

As the forest floor rushed up to meet her, she put out her hands to break the fall. A shock of pain shot through her wrist an instant before her head hit a log.

And then her world went black.

chapter
1

Noah LeCroix walked to the edge of the wide wooden porch surrounding the one-room cabin he had built high in the sheltering arms of an ancient bald cypress tree and looked out over the swamp. Twilight gathered, thickening the shadows that shrouded the trees. The moon had already risen, a bright silver crescent riding beneath a faded blue sphere. He loved the magic of the night, loved watching the moon and stars appear in the sky almost as much as he loved the swamp. The wetlands pulsed with life all night long. The darkness coupled with the still, watery landscape settled a protective blanket of solitude around him. In the dense, liquid world beneath him and the forest around his home, all manner of life co-existed in a delicate balance. He likened the swamp's dance of life and death to the way good and evil existed together in the world of men beyond its boundaries.

This shadowy place was his universe, his sanctuary. He savored its peace, was used to it after having grown up in almost complete isolation with his mother, a reclusive Cherokee woman who had left her people behind when she chose to settle in far-off Kentucky with his father, a French Canadian fur trapper named Gerard LeCroix.

Living alone served Noah's purpose now more than ever.

He had no desire to dwell among "civilized" men, especially now that so many white settlers were moving across the Ohio into the new state of Illinois in droves.

Noah turned away from the smooth log railing that bordered the wide, covered porch cantilevered out over the swamp. He was about to step into the cabin, where a single oil lamp cast its circle of light, when he heard a bobcat scream. He would not have given the sound a second thought if not for the fact that a few seconds later the sound was followed by a high-pitched shriek, one that sounded human enough to stop him in his tracks. He paused on the threshold and listened intently. A chill ran down his spine.

It had been so long since he had heard the sound of another human voice that he could not really be certain, but he thought he had just heard a woman's cry.

Noah shook off the ridiculous, unsettling notion and walked into the cabin. The walls were covered with the tanned hides of mink, bobcat, otter, beaver, fox, white-tailed deer, and bear. His few other possessions—a bone-handled hunting knife with a distinctive wolf's head carved on it, various traps, some odd pieces of clothing, a few pots and a skillet, four wooden trenchers and mugs, and a rifle—were all neatly stored inside. All he owned and needed in the world, save the dugout canoe secured outside near the base of the tree.

But even the sight of the familiar surroundings, sparse but comfortable, could not help him shake the feeling that something unsettling was about to happen, that all was not right in his world.

Pulling a crock off a high shelf, Noah poured a splash of whiskey into a cup and drank it down, his concentration intent on the deepening gloaming and the sound of the swamp. An unnatural stillness lingered in the air after the puzzling scream, almost as if, like him, the wild inhabitants of Heron Pond were collectively waiting for something to happen. Unable to deny his curiosity any longer, Noah sighed in resignation and walked back to the door.

He lingered there for a moment staring out at the growing shadows. Something was wrong. *Someone* was out there. He reached for the primed and loaded Hawken rifle that stood just inside the door and stepped out into the gathering dusk.

He climbed down the crude ladder of wooden strips nailed to the trunk of the massive, prehistoric cypress that supported his home and stepped into the dugout pirogue tied to a cypress tree that poked out of the water. Noah paddled the shallow wooden craft toward a spot where the land met the deep dark water with its camouflage net of duckweed, a natural boundary all but invisible to anyone unfamiliar with the swamp.

He reached a rise of land that supported a trail, carefully stepped out of the pirogue, and secured it to a low-hanging tree branch. Walking through thickening shadows, Noah breathed in his surroundings, aware of every subtle nuance of change, every depression on the path that might really be a footprint on the trail, every tree and stand of switch cane.

The sound he thought he heard had come from the southeast. Noah headed in that direction, head down, staring at the trail although it was almost too dark to pick up any sign. A few hundred yards from where he'd left the pirogue, he paused, raised his head, sniffed the air and listened to the silence.

Instinctively, he swung his gaze in the direction of a thicket of slender cane stalks and found himself staring across ten yards of low undergrowth into the eyes of a female bobcat on the prowl. Slowly he raised his rifle to his shoulder and waited to see what the big cat would do. The animal stared back at him, her eyes intense in the gathering gloaming. Finally, she blinked and with muscles bunching beneath her fine, shiny coat, the cat turned and padded away.

Noah lowered the rifle and shook his head. He decided the sound he'd heard earlier must have been the bobcat's cry and nothing more. But just as he stepped back in the direction of the pirogue, he caught a glimpse of ivory on the trail ahead that stood out against the dark tableau. His leather moccasins did not make even a whisper of sound on the soft earth. He closed the distance and quickly realized that what he was seeing was a body lying across the path.

His heart was pounding as hard as Chickasaw drums when he knelt beside the young woman stretched out upon the ground. Laying his rifle aside, he stared down at the unconscious female, then looked up and glanced around in every direction. The nearest white settlement was beyond the swamp to the northeast. There was no sign of a companion or fellow traveler nearby, something he found more than curious.

Noah took a deep breath, let go a ragged sigh and looked down at the girl again. She lay on her side, as peacefully as if she were napping, so very still that the only evidence that she was alive was the slow, steady rise and fall of her breasts. Although there was no visible sign of injury, she lay on the forest floor with her head beside a fallen log. One of her arms was outstretched, the other tucked beneath her. What he could see of her face was filthy. So were her hands, but they were beautifully shaped, her fingers long and tapered. Her dress, nothing but a rag with sleeves, was hiked up to her thighs. Her shapely legs showed stark ivory against the decayed leaves and brush beneath her.

He reached out tentatively to touch her, noticed that his hand shook, and balled it into a fist. He clenched it tight, then opened his hand and gently touched the tangled black hair that hid the side of her face. She did not stir when he moved the silken skein nor when he brushed it back and looped it over her ear.

Her face was stained with mud streaks. Her lashes were long and dark, her full lips tinged pink. The sight of her beauty took his breath away. Noah leaned forward and gently reached beneath her. Rolling her to her back, he straightened her arms and noted her injuries. Her wrist appeared to be swelling. She had an angry lump on her forehead near her hairline. When she moaned as he lightly probed her injured wrist, he realized he was holding his breath. Noah expected her eyelids to flutter open, but they did not.

He scanned the forest once again. With night fast closing

in, he saw no alternative except to take her home with him. If he was going to get her back to the treehouse before dark, he would have to hurry. Gently he cradled her in his arms, reached for his rifle and then straightened. Even then the girl did not awaken, although she did whimper and turn her face against his buckskin jacket, burrowing against him. It felt strange carrying a woman in his arms, but he had no time to dwell on that as he quickly carried her back to the pirogue, set her inside, and untied the craft. He climbed in behind her, holding her upright, then gently drew her back until she leaned against his chest.

As the paddle cut silently through water black as pitch, he tried to concentrate on guiding the dugout canoe home, but was distracted by the way the girl felt pressed against him, the way she warmed him. As his body responded to a need he had long tried to deny, he felt ashamed at his lack of control. What kind of a man was he, to become aroused by a helpless, unconscious female?

Overhead, the sky was tinted deep violet, an early canvas for the night's first stars. During the last few yards of the journey, the swamp grew so dark that he had only the yellow glow of lamplight shining from his home high above the water to guide him.

Run. Keep running.

The dream was so real that Olivia could feel the leaf-littered ground beneath her feet and the faded chill of winter that lingered on the damp April air. She suffered, haunted by memories of the past year, some still so vivid they turned her dreams into nightmares. Even now, as she lay tossing in her sleep, she could feel the faint sway of the flatboat as it moved downriver long ago. In her sleep the fear welled up inside her.

Her dreaming mind began to taunt her with palpable memories of new sights and scents and dangers.

Run. Run. Run, Olivia. You're almost home.

Her legs thrashed, startling her awake. She sat straight up and felt a searing pain in her right wrist and a pounding in her head that forced her to quickly lie back down. She kept her eyes closed until the stars stopped dancing behind them, then she slowly opened them and looked around.

The red glow of embers burning in a fireplace illuminated the ceiling above her. She lay staring up at even log beams that ran across a wide planked ceiling, trying to ignore the pounding in her head, fighting to stay calm and let her memory come rushing back. Slowly she realized she was no longer lost on the forest trail. She had not become a bobcat's dinner, but was indoors, in a cabin, on a bed.

She spread her fingers and pressed her hands, palms down, against a rough, woven sheet drawn over her. The mattress was filled with something soft that gave off a tangy scent. A pillow cradled her head.

Slowly Olivia turned her aching head, afraid of who or what she might find beside her, but when she discovered she was in bed alone, she thanked God for small favors.

Refusing to panic, she thought back to her last lucid memory, a wildcat's scream. She recalled running through the cypress swamp, trying to make out the trail in the dim light before she tripped. She lifted her hand to her forehead and discovered a swelling there. After testing it gingerly, she was thankful that she had not gashed her head open and bled to death.

She tried to lift her head again but intense pain forced her to lie still. Olivia closed her eyes and sighed. A moment later, an unsettling feeling came over her. She knew by the way her skin tingled, the way her nerve endings danced, that someone was nearby. Someone was watching her. An instinctive, intuitive sensation warned her that the someone was a man.

At first she peered through her lashes, but all she could make out was a tall, shadowy figure standing in the open doorway across the room. Her heart began to pound so hard that she was certain the sound would give her consciousness away.

The man started to walk into the room, and she bit her lips together to hold back a cry. She watched him move about purposely. Instead of coming directly to the bed, he walked over to a small, square table. She heard him strike a piece of flint, smelled lamp oil as it flared to life.

His back was to her as he stood there at the table; Olivia opened her eyes wider and watched. He was tall, taller than most men, strongly built, dressed in buckskin pants topped by a buff shirt with billowing sleeves. Despite the coolness of the evening, he wore no coat, no jacket. Indian moccasins, not shoes, covered his feet. His hair was black as pitch, cut straight and worn long enough to hang just over his collar. She watched his bronzed, well-tapered hands turn up the lamp wick and then set the glass chimney in place.

Olivia sensed he was about to turn and look at her. She wanted to close her eyes and pretend to be unconscious, thinking that might be safer than to let him catch her staring at him, but as he slowly turned toward the bed, she knew she had to see him. She *had* to know what she was up against.

Her gaze swept his body, taking in his great height, the length of his arms, the width and breadth of his shoulders before she dared even look at his face.

When she did, she gasped.

Noah stood frozen beside the table, shame and anger welling up from deep inside. He was unable to move, unable to breathe as the telling sound of the girl's shock upon seeing his face died on the air. He watched her flinch and scoot back into the corner, pressing close to the wall. He knew her head pained her, but obviously not enough to keep her from showing her revulsion or from trying to scramble as far away as she could.

He had the urge to walk out, to turn around and leave. Instead, he stared back and let her look all she wanted. It had been three years since he had lost an eye to a flatboat accident on the Mississippi. Three years since another woman had laughed in his face. Three years since he had moved into southern Illinois to put the past behind him.

When her breathing slowed and she slowly calmed, he held his hands up to show her that they were empty, hoping to put her a little more at ease.

"I'm sorry," he said as gently as he could. "I don't mean you any harm."

She stared up at him as if she did not understand a blessed word.

Louder this time, he spoke slowly. "Do—you—speak—English?"

The girl clutched the sheet against the filthy bodice of her dress and nodded. She licked her lips, cleared her throat. Her mouth opened and closed like a fish out of water, but no sound came out.

"Yes," she finally croaked. "Yes, I do." And then, "Who are you?"

"My name is Noah. Noah LeCroix. This is my home. Who are you?"

The lamplight gilded her skin. She looked to be all eyes, soft green eyes, long black hair, and fear. She favored her injured wrist, holding it cradled against her midriff. From the way she carefully moved her head, he knew she was fighting one hell of a headache, too.

Ignoring his question, she asked one of her own. "How did I get here?" Her tone was wary. Her gaze kept flitting over to the door and then back to him.

"I heard a scream. Went out and found you in the swamp. Brought you here—"

"The wildcat?"

"Wasn't very hungry." Noah tried to put her at ease, then shrugged and stared down at his moccasins. Could she tell how nervous he was? Could she see his awkwardness, know how strange it was for him to be alone with a woman? He had no idea what to say or do. When he looked over at her again, she was staring at the scarred side of his face.

"How long have I been asleep?" Her voice was so low that he had to strain to hear her. She looked as if she expected him to leap on her and attack her at any moment, as if he might be coveting her scalp.

"You slept around two hours. You must have hit your head very hard."

She reached up and felt the bump. "I guess I did."

He decided not to get any closer, not with her acting as if she were going to come out of her skin. He backed up, pulled a stool out from under the table, and sat down.

"You going to tell me your name?" he asked.

The girl hesitated, glanced toward the door, then looked back at him. "I'm Olivia Bond. Where am I?"

"Heron Pond."

Her attention shifted to the door once again as recollection dawned. "The swamp," she whispered. Her eyes widened as if she expected a bobcat or a cottonmouth to come slithering in.

"You're fairly safe here. I built this cabin over the water."

"*Fairly?*" She looked as if she were going to try to stand up again. "Did you say—"

"Built in a cypress tree. About fifteen feet above the water."

"How do I get down?"

"There are wooden planks nailed to the trunk."

"Am I anywhere near Illinois?"

"You're in it."

She appeared a bit relieved.

"Are you hungry? I figure anybody with as little meat on her bones as you ought to be hungry."

What happened next surprised the hell out of him. It was a little thing, one that another man might not have even noticed, but he had lived alone so long that he was used to concentrating on the very smallest of details: the way an iridescent dragonfly looked with its wings backlit by the sun, the sound of cypress needles whispering on the wind.

Someone else might have missed the smile that hovered at the corner of her lips when he had said she had little meat on her bones, but he did not. How could he, when that slight, almost-smile had him holding his breath?

"I've got some jerked venison and some potatoes around here someplace." He started to smile back, until he felt the pull of the scar at the left corner of his mouth and stopped. He stood up, turned his back on the girl, and headed for the long wide plank tacked to the far wall where he stored his larder.

He kept his back to her while he found what he was looking for, dug some strips of dried meat from a hide bag, unwrapped a checkered rag with four potatoes inside, and set one on the plank where he did all his stand-up work. Then he took a trencher and a wooden mug off a smaller shelf high on the wall and turned them over to knock any unwanted creatures out. He was headed for the door, intent on filling the cookpot with water from a small barrel he kept out on the porch, when the sound of her voice stopped him cold.

"Perhaps an eye patch," she whispered.

"What?"

"I'm sorry. I was thinking out loud."

She looked so terrified he wanted to put her at ease.

"It's all right. What were you thinking?"

Instead of looking at him when she spoke, she looked down at her hands. "I was just thinking . . ."

Noah had to strain to hear her.

"With some kind of an eye patch, you wouldn't look half bad."

His feet rooted themselves to the threshold. He stared at her for a heartbeat before he closed his good eye and shook his head. He had no idea what in the hell he looked like anymore. He had no reason to care.

He turned his back on her and stepped out onto the porch, welcoming the darkness.

A little while later, Olivia lay in the stranger's bed, trying to make herself small, trying to fade into the bedclothes so that he might not notice her, but as they were the only two people in the treehouse, that was impossible. Noah LeCroix was careful to keep his face turned away from her as she watched him move back and forth. He stoked the fire in the fireplace and then buried a potato in the hot ash. When she thought of how he must have carried each stone up the tree in order to build the small fireplace, she wondered at his accomplishment and marveled at the craftsmanship.

Since he seemed to have dismissed her, she studied him freely, thankful that he had not asked any prying questions. She would not relish volunteering anything about herself, so she asked him nothing about himself, either.

Now that she had recovered from the shock of seeing the deep indentation and puckered skin of his eye socket, the ragged line that ran from below his eye to the corner of his mouth, she had to admit he was not a bad-looking man. In fact, she could see he had been extremely handsome. His looks were dark, exotic. His build rugged.

He had kept his distance, had not forced his company or any questions on her, had not pried. For that she was grateful. Still, she knew enough of men from raw firsthand experience to know not to let down her guard. Not even for an instant. She would remain wary, ready to flee if necessary, no matter how badly her head throbbed or her wrist ached. She would never let a soft-spoken, well-mannered man fool her again.

Now as she waited while her host prodded the coals in the fireplace and then poured her a cup of steaming coffee, she tried to remain alert. Her condition prevented her from making any kind of swift exit. Not that she would relish going back out into the swamp anyway. For now, though she found herself alone with a complete stranger, she was happy to be out of the dark, high and dry above the watery wilderness.

When the potato was cooked, he left her alone while she ate it, sipped strong coffee, and nibbled on jerked venison. She decided he must have been watching her from the porch while she ate, for as soon as she took the last bite, he immediately appeared, collected the trencher and mug, and set them on the crude sideboard. Then he turned to her again, took a deep breath and let out a long sigh.

"Just out of curiosity, what were you doing out there in the swamp alone?"

"I'd rather not talk about it right now."

Half expecting him to question her further, Olivia waited, but all Noah LeCroix did was nod. He appeared terribly uneasy as his gaze scanned the small interior of his tidy cabin. The pained expression on his face gave her pause. Because he was unlike any of the men she had dealt with lately, she did not know what to make of Noah LeCroix and no idea what to expect. That in itself made her feel vulnerable.

"I'm sorry to have to impose upon you like this, but—"

"No need to be sorry. There is no way you can leave tonight."

Olivia glanced around the room and wondered if she should make some effort to vacate the only bed.

As if he could read her tumultuous thoughts, he shifted his stance, cleared his throat and volunteered, "I'll bed down on the porch."

"Thank you. That would be kind of you."

An awkward stillness lengthened between them.

"If you don't need anything else, I'll put out the lamp," he said, reminding her that he was still there, still watching her.

She could not face the dark. "If . . . if you could just turn the lamp low, but leave it burning?"

Noah nodded and did as she had asked. As the darkness slowly thickened, he once again became the illusive, mysterious figure she had first glimpsed upon awakening. The glow from the fire expanded his shadow until the elongated black shape wavered over the log walls, following Noah as he walked out and was quickly swallowed by the night.

chapter
2

IT WAS LATE IN THE SEASON, TOO WARM TO SNOW, BUT there was a heaviness and a damp chill in the air. The stars appeared faded and thin, indicating rain before morning. Noah closed the front of his buckskin jacket and sat down on the floor of the covered porch. With his back pressed to the outside wall, he was impervious to the cool air.

He could hear the dried moss in the mattress rustle each time the girl moved restlessly in his bed. Strange, he thought, so strange having someone else here, in his house. Strange to listen to the sounds of another person moving about where a few hours ago only his own footsteps and the pulse of the swamp marked the passing of time. Intrigued by her, knowing she was lying there awake, he found himself holding his breath, listening for the slightest sound.

His mother had passed on when he was fourteen, and for sixteen years now Noah had lived alone. Not long before his mother died, his father had come to them and said he was too old to endure the rigors of the life of a fur trapper any longer. Gerard LeCroix told them he was leaving forever to return to his legal wife and family in Canada. His white family.

Because it was his father's habit to disappear for months at a time on hunting forays into the western territories and Canada, they missed his infrequent involvement in their lives very little. The son of a recluse, Noah was used to the solitude of the forest, to living off the land and dwelling in isolation. His mother, a mystic who claimed she heard voices in the wind, had segregated herself from her own people and brought him up outside the tribal community because the voices forewarned her of the coming of the whites. She saw no future for the Cherokee people, nor for any of the other native tribes, and so she became a recluse, intent upon raising Noah to survive off the land alone and escape the onslaught from the east.

When his mother suddenly died of fever, Noah left the small cabin in northern Kentucky that they had inhabited for most of his life and moved west, closer to the Mississippi. He built his first treehouse in a swampy marshland near Sandy Shoals, Kentucky, an experimental, smaller version of this one on Heron Pond. He had grown to love that first, odd house, one intended to be only temporary at best, but he had ended up living there thirteen years.

It was during his time living in Kentucky that he met the one and only man to whom he had ever grown close enough to call friend, a white settler named Hunter Boone, the owner of a tavern and trading post on the Mississippi.

As soon as Hunter found out that Noah felt at home on water, that he could navigate the rivers with ease, he encouraged him to try his hand at piloting settlers' flatboats through the Mississippi's dangerous shoals.

Hesitant at first, Noah soon realized he had a natural talent for the job, which paid two dollars a boatload; he found the challenge exhilarating. Although he never became comfortable around the flatboat passengers, he loved navigating the wild waters.

His skills became much sought after, especially during the spring when the rivers often ran high and fast. Because he was used to living off his fur trades, he saw no need for the white man's money and so he never fell into a routine. Instead, he began to pick and choose the occasional boat to pilot and continued to live alone in the swamp until three years ago when, one fateful day on a trip downriver to New Orleans with Hunter, their flatboat ran into a log.

Hanging over the bow while guiding the boat, Noah lost his footing and was launched into the water. A partially submerged log floating downstream hit him in the head, tore the side of his face and took his eye. It was Hunter who saved him from certain death when he pulled him, torn and bleeding, from the raging Mississippi.

Certain that with the loss of his eye, his talent would be diminished, Noah never went back to river piloting. Nor did he stay in Kentucky long, for shortly after the accident, Hunter decided to marry and settle down, and began urging Noah to do the same.

His friend told him it was not natural for a grown man not to want a woman and even went so far as to persuade Noah to look for a wife. "Go on down to New Orleans and look around," Hunter had suggested. "At least down there, if you don't find a wife, you can buy some time with a woman."

Noah had no need for a wife, but thought maybe it was time he had a woman, so he took Hunter's advice and went to New Orleans to buy himself a night with a whore.

The plan proved to be a disaster. The first woman he tentatively approached at a riverside tavern stared long and hard at the new, still-raw side of his face, threw back her head and laughed.

"You think I want to take on a half-breed with half a face? Honey, even *I* ain't that desperate," she had said.

He damned her for laughing, damned himself for being fool enough to have listened to Hunter in the first place, and headed back to Kentucky without looking back.

Now, as Noah sat outside listening to the sound of Olivia Bond's gentle, rhythmic breathing, he wondered how and why a man would make a choice that would put an end to the dream in his heart—a choice like the one his own father had made when he returned to his white wife and children in Canada. Even as Gerard LeCroix had sworn to Noah's mother that she and Noah would always hold a piece of his heart, he left them to spend his old age with his first wife, to die among people of his own kind. Family.

As for dreams of his own future, Noah had had none

since the accident and his ill-fated trip to New Orleans. Even before he had lost his eye, he had lived day by day, waiting to see what each new sunrise would bring into his life. He had always been uncomfortable around people, had never imagined himself married. He had been content with keeping up his home in the swamp, hunting and trapping to survive, living in solitude. He knew nothing but isolation. Extended family, ties of the heart, were for others, not him. He did not miss what he had never known.

Inside the cabin, Olivia Bond was finally asleep. He could tell by the steady, even cadence of her breathing and was relieved. Without making a sound, he walked back indoors, paused beside the bed to make certain she was tucked in, then picked up the lamp and carried it back outside along with a burlap sack filled with some of his mother's old things. The sack had been ignored so long it was dusty.

He opened the sack and searched through its contents. Finally his fingers identified the object he was looking for and he pulled out a small, round hand mirror. He purposely kept the reflective side down so that he saw only the ivory back and not his image on the shiny surface.

The mirror had been a gift his father brought home to his mother when Noah was no more than seven or eight years old. As he traced the streaked, yellowed ivory back with his fingertips, he recalled the way his mother had smiled up at his father when he had presented her with the treasure. After she looked into the mirror and studied her own reflection, his mother had laughed and pressed it close to her heart. Then she remembered Noah, smiled and handed him the mirror. For the first time ever he had been able to clearly see his own face.

His eyes had been dark as pitch, his nose straight, his skin brown. His thick black hair shone with glints of blue-black highlights where the sunlight that shimmered through the trees touched it. He recalled being disappointed when he discovered he did not resemble his father at all. His mother's Cherokee blood was predominant in his build, his coloring, and features.

Gerard LeCroix had been of medium height, portly, heavily bearded, and always jovial. He loved to sing and play his concertina. Whenever he was with them, the woods were filled with music and the sound of his deep baritone laugh. During cold spells in winter when they were closeted indoors, sometimes his father would appear and weather out the storm with them, teach them to speak English and French, and sing many, many songs.

That music and laughter came back to haunt Noah now as he took care to hold the old mirror upside down. He found himself smiling, enjoying the brief sojourn into the past, until the girl inside the house stirred and murmured in her sleep.

Noah straightened, looking into the halo radiating from the lamp. He turned the mirror over in his hands, taking a deep breath before he leaned close to the light and looked at his reflection.

The lamplight was not kind. The unmarked right side of his face had not changed much in three years, but on the left there was the empty eye socket, deep and puckered. A jagged red streak ran down his cheek from the outside edge of the depression, almost as if a molten tear had seared a path down his face. It ended near the corner of his mouth. He traced the scar with his fingertip.

All things considered, the damage was not as bad as he remembered. He held the mirror between his knees, put a hand over his ruined eye, and studied himself objectively. The girl was right, he decided. An eye patch would definitely help.

He remembered the way Olivia Bond had stared, the panic in her expression, and he found himself wishing he had given her some warning before he walked in on her, but he was rusty as an old nail when it came to using the manners he had learned by mimicking Hunter and the others at Sandy Shoals.

Unlike him, Olivia Bond was physically perfect: flawless, except for the minor injuries that would heal, the dirt on her milky skin, and the fact that she was so thin. But her weight was really no concern of his. Come morning he would take her to the edge of the swamp. From there, the nearest settler's cabin was a good hour's walk. All he really had to do was point her on her way.

Tomorrow Olivia Bond would be gone, but Noah reckoned it would be a long, long time before he forgot her. He set the mirror down and picked up a soft piece of cured hide, spread it on the plank flooring of the porch near the oil lamp, and with a small piece of charred wood from the fire, he began to draw a pattern on the leather.

She was dreaming again. The old, familiar nightmare. No escape. She is almost eighteen. The flatboat. Her father. His young second wife, Susanna. Her half-brothers: Payson Junior, five, and Freddie, three years old.

The bearded stranger, Colonel Sullivan. Asking her father for a ride downriver. Shifty and suspicious. Must warn him. "No, Daddy. Don't take him aboard."

Suddenly, a hole in the boat. Taking on water. Pulling into shore. Other men. The colonel's men. Thieves. No, no, it's a trap. Run. Run. Fight off the darkness. It's only a nightmare. Struggling to awaken. Still no escape.

"They don't have much." The colonel's voice. "Ought to get somethin' for that silver teapot."

Payson Bond reaching for a rifle. How, Daddy? How can you hold off five men?

"You think you can kill us all?" Sullivan laughing. "Try it, farmer."

"I can kill one of you." Her father's voice. His fear so evident. "Which one will it be?"

The leader leers at her. "Give us the girl. We'll leave you alone."

Run. Run. Her father's shock. Susanna's cry. The little boys clinging to their mother's skirts.

"Give us the girl. Give us the girl."

Freddie wailing. Little Pay terrified. Susanna's sobs. Her father frozen. His long, tapered fingers white-knuckled on the rifle. Helpless. He cannot kill. He can only teach. The pirates with broken teeth. Tobacco-stained beards.

"Give us the girl." Sullivan's demand. Two men step toward Payson.

"No!" Her own voice screaming. Her father turns, looks at her. Considering. Her hope dies.

"We'll spare you. Spare the rest of your brood," Sullivan promises. *"Give up the girl. Nothing else we want. Give her up. Save four lives and that babe on the way."*

Susanna wails. *"Oh, God. Listen. Please listen to him, Payson."*

"Susanna, no!" Her own voice again. Desperate. Disbelief. Betrayal.

"Olivia, think of the boys . . ." Susanna pleads. *"I can't let them harm my boys."* Susanna reaches for Payson. Grabs his sleeve. Begs. *"Payson, please. Give her to them."*

Indecision in her father's eyes. Her heart shatters like spun glass.

"I'm so sorry." Payson whispers, lowers the rifle. Submits. *"What else can I do?"*

"But what about me, Daddy?" She screams. *"What about me?"* Shamed by her selfishness.

Run, run.

She tries to run. The river pirates are on her, dragging her past her father. Payson's silent surrender. He sheds tears, but cannot fight. Susanna on her knees, sobbing, her arms around the boys. Freddie wailing uncontrollably. Little Pay the only one to plead for her. He breaks away from his mother. Runs to Colonel Sullivan.

"Don't take my sister, sir. Please, let her go." The man laughs, cuffs Little Pay. The boy turns to Payson. *"Papa, don't make Livvie go!"*

The men shove and pull her. Fight, run! She tries. Scratches them, kicks, twists. But they are too strong. She screams until her throat is raw.

"No, Daddy! No! Don't let them take me! Don't let them take me! . . ."

"Don't let them take me!"

Shocked awake by the sound of Olivia's screams, Noah

shot to his feet and ran inside. The sun was dawning, filling the cabin with misty blue light, just enough illumination for him to make out her form in the middle of the bed. Her hair was a wild black mane that hid most of her face. She cradled her wounded wrist as she rocked back and forth sobbing uncontrollably. The sheet and blanket were wadded together. The hem of her frayed gown rode up to reveal her thighs. The neck of the dress hung open, exposing her shoulder and the rise of her breast.

Noah's breath caught in his throat. Suddenly he felt as if his moccasins had been nailed to the floor. He couldn't move. He couldn't speak. Even if he had some inkling of what to say to calm her, the words would not have come. He had never been alone with a strange woman—not under any circumstances. Now here he stood before one who was not only hysterical, but half-naked. He was helpless and appalled, not at her, but at himself, for he had no idea how to console her.

Whether it was hours or seconds that passed as he stood there, he could not be certain, but soon Olivia stopped rocking. Her head came up and she blinked and looked around, as if she had no recollection of where she was or how she got there. When she turned and stared at him, he knew she was trying to place him, to remember where she was.

He watched her expression change from one of acute anguish to one of fear. She did not flinch or take her eyes off him, but slowly, ever so slowly, she slipped one hand across the bed until her fingers came in contact with the bedclothes. She hastily covered herself.

She did not say a word as she pressed back against the wall, almost as if she was waiting for him to pounce.

Noah took a deep breath, willed himself to speak. Despite the fact that she was a stranger, that she was just passing through his life for a night, he found himself involuntarily reacting to her. "If you're all right," he said, barely able to put words together, "then I'll go back outside."

Ashamed of his physical reaction to her, of his inability to help her, he turned and left her alone again.

• • •

With relief, Olivia watched him go. As soon as he was out of the room she realized she was trembling violently. The old nightmare had left her exhausted, sweaty and shaken, unable to stop her tears. But more than the horrible dream, it was the raw desire on her host's face that left her terrified.

So, he is human after all.

Last night, when he had kept his distance—and his hands to himself—Olivia had wondered if perhaps Noah LeCroix was different than other men; if—thankfully—she inspired no lust in him.

But this morning when she finally realized where she was, when she saw him standing there watching her, even the dawning sunlight in the room could not disguise the raw desire on his face or the way his body had responded to the sight of her. He had just been waiting.

She truly feared him in that moment and braced herself, ready to fight, fully expecting him to cross the room and try to take her, then and there. But Noah LeCroix had surprised her. Again.

Even though lust showed plainly on his face, he had not acted on it. Instead, he had turned and virtually run out of the cabin.

Her hands shook as she swiped at her tears and tried to stop quaking. She hated this inability to control herself after the recurring nightmare as much as she hated having to relive it all, over and over—the rending separation from her family, her father's betrayal, the boys' terror. Susanna's face when she had said, "Olivia, think of the boys." Most of all her own guilt. Her inability to sacrifice herself for them and go willingly. Her shame over the need for self-preservation that had made her cry out, "But what about *me*?"

"*What about me?*"

It had been a little over a year since that day. She had been an innocent girl of seventeen, a girl with her whole life ahead of her, a life that held the promise of many happy tomorrows in their new home in Illinois.

Yesterday, at long last, she had thought she was finally

close to being reunited with her family—until her life once again took an ill-fated turn and suddenly she had been forced to take refuge in the swamp. Her head still ached from the knock against the log, and her wrist was still swollen and tender, but not nearly as bad as it had been last night. When she thought of how she felt a score older than she had a year ago, she remembered that today was her birthday. Amazingly, she had lived long enough to see nineteen, but there would be no celebration. She would pass this day as she had most every day since she had been taken from her family. She would see to her immediate needs, do whatever it took to survive, try to find a way to get back home to them again.

But now, the fragile illusion that she might be safe here in Noah LeCroix's treehouse had just been shattered. She had to get away. She looked out the window above the bed, out at the cloudy sky beyond the lattice of leaves. She was literally up a tree and there was no way down, no way out of the swamp without LeCroix's help. All she could do was hope and pray that when he came back in, he would not give in to temptation and desire, that he would continue to keep his need in check.

chapter
3

To the casual observer, everything in Darcy Lankanal's world was perfect. As sole owner of a thriving house of chance, liquor, and prostitution, he had a fortune piled up in the bank of New Orleans as well as in a metal box hidden in the wall behind the headboard on his bed. The establishment, inherited from his mother, was named the Palace of Angels and boasted the best gaming tables, the finest liquor, and the most beautiful women in the entire South. His clothing was tailored in France and, despite his usually less than respectable occupation, he was admired by those who deemed themselves the upper crust of Creole society—so much so that he was often invited to their soirées and fêtes.

But all was not right in Darcy's world, nor had it been since Olivia Bond disappeared more than a month ago.

Darcy took a pull on his cigar, blew out a lazy blue smoke ring and watched it fade into the haze of the salon's smoke-filled air. Then he reached up and ran his palm over his neat blond hair. As he smoothed his hand down the striped waistcoat beneath his double-breasted cutaway jacket, he easily hid his frustration and turmoil, smiled his most charming, carefree smile, and perused the salon.

His mother, Nicolette, God rest her soul, had taught him that the secret of a well-run establishment of any kind was the ever-vigilant, constant presence of its owner. Darcy always took his mama's advice to heart.

During what appeared to be nothing more than a casual stroll around the huge salon and gaming room, Darcy greeted familiar customers, sized up strangers, flashed eye contact to his many well-paid and therefore very loyal dealers and bartenders, and calculated exactly how much liquor was leaving the bar. His patrons included riverboat captains, wealthy foreign travelers, and plantation owners, and all of them considered themselves lucky to be able to sit elbow to elbow, hunched over cards and dice at his nearly twenty tables. Thieves and cutthroats were not allowed.

Upstairs, the whores known as "Darcy's ladies" were busy making him almost as much money as he would clear downstairs. He had hand-picked and personally trained each and every one of them since he'd inherited the Palace. Each one had been his own special "property" at one time or another, his alone to savor and enjoy, to pamper and coddle while she remained ensconced in his personal suite until a new, virginal initiate came along.

Two or three months spent with a new girl had been his routine until Olivia Bond entered his life. Now, despite the noise in the smoky salon, even as he wandered about observing the proceedings, Darcy could still see Olivia's face, hear her voice, smell her, taste her on his lips.

Somehow the stubborn little witch with coal-black hair and fern-green eyes had gotten under his skin more than any woman before her. Somehow she had unwittingly enchanted him to the point of igniting an obsession. No matter how much the other girls complained about her, teased him, tried to tempt him away, or openly pouted about Olivia's unprecedented length of special status, Darcy had not been able to cut her loose and launch her in the business of whoring for his customers.

She had lived with him over a year in his private suite, surrounded by luxury, at his beck and call morning, noon, and night. Just when he thought that she was finally warming to him, that she had come to accept her place, she had somehow managed to escape, slipping out onto the streets of New Orleans and disappearing without a trace. He was fast becoming convinced that she was no longer in the city. He had already spent a small fortune on a search and even now men were out combing the streets and waterfront for her, questioning soldiers, slavers, even the nuns at the Ursuline convent.

Darcy snubbed out the cigar in a crystal dish set out on the table for that very purpose. Across the room, one of his most requested ladies of the night, Marcella Champion, made eye contact and smiled at him, then began to weave her way through the maze of tables. Her eyes were as clear as a cloudless blue sky, and her long, blond hair bounced with a vibrant sheen. Whenever one of the patrons stopped her, either by word or touch, Marcella would pause and smile at him as if he were the only man in the world. Then the two would share a laugh and before she moved on, she whispered into his ear and convinced him that he just might be lucky enough to have her tonight.

Marcella, like Darcy's other whores, had taken to selling her body like a swan takes to water. If only the same could have been said of Olivia. For some reason, even though he tried long and hard, Darcy could never reach Olivia's heart and soul, never convince her that she would be far better off leaving her old life behind to live like a queen under his protection. He could not charm her, beguile her, bribe her, or tempt her into accepting that she would eventually be working for him. Her body might have been entirely in his possession, but she had never totally surrendered.

He sensed from the first that he would have a hard time convincing Olivia that working for him would give her a percentage of the money she earned and, in turn, give her power in her own right, far more money and power than any man's wife would ever have, certainly. His girls wore the finest clothes. They had carriages at their disposal and elegant furnishings in their rooms. They used their own money in any way they wished. Not one of them had ever tried to run away, at least not after a few weeks with him. Even the girls who came to him against their will, just as Olivia had, were eventually charmed by him after he had separated them from everyone but himself, made them dependent and spoiled and tutored them in the fine art of pleasing a man, thus taking pleasure himself.

Once he deemed a girl ready for work, once she agreed to his terms, she was no longer a prisoner in any sense of the word. And he was no slaver. When the time came for a girl to retire, or if she was offered a position as some wealthy man's exclusive mistress, he would let her patron, or the woman herself, pay back his initial investment in her, and then he would bid her fond *adieu*. Some women down on their luck had even come to him voluntarily, begging to be added to his stable of whores.

Eventually, when he was ready to give her up, Olivia would have been afforded all of the same generous opportunities. But no matter how well he taught her, no matter how deftly he had manipulated her body, no matter how often he had coaxed a physical response out of her, he had never been able to persuade her to leave the past behind. She never did become convinced that he and the Palace of Angels were the keys to her future.

But no matter how much she wished it otherwise, no matter how much she tried to deny or hide it, Olivia was very, very good in bed. For that reason alone, no amount of tears or pleading on her part would ever convince him that she would never become what he wanted her to be.

He knew one thing for certain that she did not. Olivia Bond was a sensual, erotic woman, perhaps the most alluring woman he had ever known—but she hated him with a singular passion he had never seen in a woman before, which made her not only tantalizing but unforgettable.

Marcella had finally reached his side. The light scent of her perfume, just enough to entice but not overwhelm, made him aware of her presence even before she said a word to him as he kept his eyes trained on the room.

"Quite the crowd tonight." Her voice had a husky edge to it, one that her regulars often admired.

"Rainy nights always bring them in," he said offhandedly.

"Darcy, look at me."

Slowly, he turned, partially dismissing all the action that pulsed around him. Concentrating on anything was an effort lately. He looked down into Marcella's kohl-accented eyes.

"The other girls wanted me to talk to you. Tonight."

"It'll have to wait until tomorrow morning," he told her, shifting positions, watching a beefy doorman hoist an unwanted troublemaker and discreetly remove him from the room.

"Tomorrow you will come up with some other excuse not to listen. It must be *now*, Darcy, while I have at least half of your attention."

He sighed.

She stepped closer. "You've got to forget her and move on. Find someone to replace her. Send your men to scout out another new girl, and do it quickly. None of us can stand the way you've been moping around here like a whipped hound."

"I don't think," he said, pulling another cigar out of his vest pocket, "that it is any of your business what I do or how I act. You all answer to me, not the other way around."

When Marcella laid her hand on his coat sleeve, he let his gaze slide to where she touched him. She immediately let go.

"She's gone, Darcy. She's slipped back down whatever rabbit hole it was she crawled out of. Forget her. Lord knows, the way you kept her to yourself for so long did not sit well with the others. You made a pet out of that one. A damned pet, singling her out like that. Before Olivia, you never kept any of us more than a few months. You never *had* to."

"As I recall, you lasted five months. Didn't you, Marcella?"

She ignored his remark. "What I want to know," she said, pressing closer, lowering her voice, "was what *she* had that none of *us* ever had. What little trick, or should I say *tricks*, did she use to get you to keep her as your exclusive property so long? What in the hell did a virgin know that none of *us* knew, Lankanal?"

That very question had been running through his own mind for weeks. Darcy suddenly pictured Olivia lying naked in his bed, remembered what it felt like to run his hands over her unblemished skin, what it did to him every time he took her. He could not forget what she had looked like the day the ruffians from upriver sold her to him. Seventeen years old, terrified, defeated, too frightened to talk, submissive only because she was too weak to fight. Her huge eyes were swollen from crying, her plain but once-adequate gown torn and filthy—but despite it all, she was still lovely and guaranteed to be a virgin.

What he remembered most was the black hatred that smoldered in her eyes, a hatred for him that even her fear did not hide. He saw it there each and every time he opened the door to his suite and went to her. It never faded, was never replaced by submission or even weary resignation. He started to believe it was that very obvious scorn that fired his need for her, stoked his interest and kept it alive. Perhaps it was the challenge in that very hatred that fueled this obsession.

"Well, Darce?"

He had almost forgotten that Marcella was still standing there waiting for an answer. She and the others might just as well keep on waiting. Let them gossip in the private parlor where they waited for their patrons to call for them.

Darcy leaned down to light the cigar off the sulfur match a waiter had hurried to offer him. He held the tip of the tobacco over the flame and inhaled until the end of the cigarillo glowed red. Then he slowly blew another smoke ring and watched it fade before he looked down into Marcella's eyes again and remembered the way Olivia had felt beneath his hands.

"What did she do to me? You know, Marcella, darlin', I really couldn't say. I really couldn't say at all."

Heron Pond

Every time Olivia heard a noise outside she held her breath and focused on the door, but so far Noah LeCroix had not reappeared. She had no idea where he had gone, but she had watched through the open door as he disappeared over the edge of the porch, and she assumed he had climbed down the ladder. Deciding to explore, she discovered that it took most of her strength just to throw back the cover, crawl to the edge of the bed, and swing her legs over. Each time she moved, her head would spin, forcing her to take it very, very slowly. When her head continued to pound just as hard as it had yesterday, she decided she was hurt more seriously than she had realized. Finally, she gave up, lay back down, and fell asleep.

When she awoke, she was determined to ignore her pain. She tried to marshal her strength and perched on the edge of the bed. She cradled her injured wrist in her lap and kept her ankles primly pressed together. She could not bear to think of putting on her shoes and having to suffer the burn of the blisters on her heels where they were rubbed raw.

Before she could move, there was a thump outside and within seconds, Noah came striding through the door. A pair of dead mallards dangled from his right hand; his rifle was in the other. He set it stock down and leaned it against the wall.

At some point, he had tied a buckskin eye patch over his scar. She tried not to stare overmuch as he slapped the ducks down on the table and pulled a knife out of the leather sheath strapped to his waist.

Olivia forced herself to breathe. "Would you mind taking me to the edge of the swamp so that I can be on my way?"

He turned around slowly and stared at her, his forehead marred by a frown. Although he had given her no reason to fear him, experience had taught her to be wary. Self-preservation was a hard habit to break. If she had to fight her way out, she would lose. Not only was he a foot taller and physically stronger, but it was taking a concerted effort for her just to hold up her head.

"Where were you headed?" he asked.

"Shawneetown. Is it far?"

"About sixty miles from here as the crow flies. You still thinking of traveling alone?"

She had not intended to—but after trusting a man named Stanley Marlborough to help her get home, she instead found herself running from his lust and his roving hands, and ended up alone. She raised her chin a notch and looked Noah square in the eye.

"Yes. I intend to go on by myself."

"You didn't just fall out of the sky and land here in the middle of the swamp. Why don't you tell me what you're doing by yourself in the first place?"

"I prefer to find my own way."

"Like you did yesterday?"

"I'll definitely be more careful this time." She refused to think about the bobcat. Or the snakes. Not with Noah watching her with such undisguised desire again. She saw him press his open palms against his thighs, ball his hands into fists and then open them.

Now, she thought, *now he'll try to touch me. He'll put his hands on me and try to make me do things I don't want to do and he'll succeed because I'm so weak. So terribly weak.*

He took a step toward her.

Olivia braced herself.

He said, "If you want to head off alone through the countryside, go right ahead. There are bears out there, and hunters' traps, and plenty of wolves and coyotes beyond the swamp. You want to go right now?" He ignored the sad, limp duck carcasses, crossed the room, and waited by the door for her to make the next move. "Let's go."

For a moment she could not believe her luck had changed. Despite the way he looked at her, he was clearly not going to attack her. He was not refusing to take her out of the swamp. He was actually going to send her on her way without argument. The bears, wolves, snakes, and bobcats collectively did not frighten her as much as the thought of what might happen if he acted on his desire.

When Olivia pushed herself up with her good arm, her legs started to shake. Stars danced in front of her eyes.

The next thing she knew, she was lying on the bed again, looking up into Noah's concerned face.

"You all right?" he asked softly.

Her mouth had suddenly gone dry. She ran her tongue over her lips and tried to swallow. Immediately he disappeared and seconds later came back with a long-handled ladle of water. He gently cradled the back of her head in his hand and pressed the ladle to her lips. She took a few sips. When she was through, he lowered her head to the pillow.

"Looks like you'll have to put off leaving for a while."

His voice was so soft, so matter-of-fact that she sighed.

"But you *will* take me out of here, won't you? You *will* let me go when I'm able?"

"Why wouldn't I?"

Olivia looked up into his face. Couldn't she tell a man's lie from the truth anymore? Could he possibly be feigning such a puzzled expression? Could it be that here was a truly honorable man, one who would not harm her? A man who would ignore his own desire and see her safely out of here?

She did not even realize she had shed a tear until he reached out and wiped it off her cheek with his thumb. His hand, where it cupped her face, felt warm and dry and gentle, so caring that she was tempted to let down her guard. When she met his gaze, he quickly turned his head so that she saw only the perfect side of his face.

"You don't need to worry. Say the word and I'll point you in the direction of Shawneetown," he whispered, concentrating on the scene outside the window. "But until you feel up to it, you'd best stay put."

"I hate to impose on you like this, but I have no choice."

She turned her head and looked through the window. The shutters were open, and weak sunlight was shining through the canopy of cypress. Outside, a woodpecker worked for his meal, and the hushed sound of leaves rustled on a slight breeze. It smelled like rain. Spring had shaken off winter's final embrace.

The air in the small cabin was permeated with the scent of wood smoke even though the fire had died sometime during the night. She knew that in a few minutes he would have it burning again, that the mallards would be roasting on a spit over the coals. Her mouth watered, thinking of what a luscious meal the fowl with iridescent feathers would make.

It had been weeks since she had eaten a hearty, substantial meal. Stanley Marlborough's hunting skill would not have filled a powder horn. On the journey north, more often than not they had been forced to eat johnnycakes that his wife, Polly, had directed Olivia to make out of corn flour and water.

She blinked back another tear and stared up at the ceiling. The unusual cabin was warm and snug, and for the time being she was apparently safe. She had found herself in far worse circumstances and discovered the world was not a gentle place, that some men had no honor, so Olivia told herself to be grateful and tried to relax—but it was difficult with Noah sitting on the edge of the bed. His weight dragged the mattress down on one side. He was not touching her, but his nearness was unsettling. She could feel his intent gaze, meeting it as she turned to look up at him again.

"I guess I'll have to stay on for a little while longer." She half expected to see a sign of triumph on his face, but all he did was nod before he stood and quickly turned away.

Could it be, she wondered, that Noah LeCroix was more afraid of their tentative arrangement than she?

Noah left her alone except to offer her more water and then to help her recline against the pillow to eat. That meant touching her, leaning over her, catching his breath when he felt her hair brush against his cheek.

He kept busy with his daily routine, taking pride in his cooking when she complimented the roast duck. His feelings were all jumbled. He was as thankful that she was not able to leave just yet as he was disturbed by the knowledge she was staying on.

He could not have known that having companionship after all this time would prove so unsettling. He hoped she could not see his confusion, hoped she was unaware of his reaction to her nearness, the sound of her voice, her beauty. Although he had done nothing to indicate he would ever, could ever harm her, he sensed that she was still very wary, almost frightened of him. He tried to keep his distance, wondering what kind of men she had known, what kind of man could have instilled such fear in her.

He ate alone at the table, keeping the ruined side of his face turned away even though she did not seem to have an aversion to his scar. After his experience in New Orleans, he was uncomfortable having her look at it any more than she had to.

He cleaned up and put the trenchers and utensils away before looking at her again. He noticed she had fallen asleep; he was free to take refuge alone on the porch.

Below him the frogs sang in a harmonious chorus. Noah stood close to the rail, where the rain dripped over the eaves. He looked through the treetops, staring out at patches of gray sky framed in the small spaces between the interwoven branches, and felt the kiss of spring in the rain and on the night air. Beyond the wetlands the trees were budding. The dogwood and redbud would soon bloom. Another long winter was over. Spring meant that new life would soon be in evidence everywhere. The animals of the forest, plains, and woodlands were choosing mates, making nests, digging burrows. It was the natural course of things.

Noah sighed. Spring fever. Maybe that was why having a female in his home made him so jumpy. He was all too aware of Olivia as a woman, as a soft, gentle, mysterious creature so very different from himself.

By the time he turned away from the railing, Noah had convinced himself that he must be dwelling on Olivia Bond day and night because she had intruded so suddenly into his well-ordered world. He even went so far as to admit that he was curious because he was ignorant of a woman's nature. He was not used to having one around, especially one who was so very lovely.

And although it momentarily entered his mind, he flatly refused to believe that her nearness stirred him so because he was the oldest living male virgin in the state of Illinois.

chapter
4

IT RAINED FOR TWO DAYS AND A NIGHT. OLIVIA AT-tempted to make herself invisible, or as least as unobtrusive as humanly possible in the one-room cabin while Noah was forced to remain inside with her. Although he never once gave her reason to worry, she remained ever vigilant and grew more and more curious because he seemed as wary of her as she was of him.

They engaged in stilted, polite exchanges whenever nec-essary, but most of the time the air was rife with tension. Noah went about the business of his life, repairing a stool with a wobbly leg, cutting out pieces of tanned hide to construct a new pair of moccasins. Olivia stayed on the bed, not so much because she still felt weak, but because there was no place else to sit except beside him at the table.

It was still raining early on the morning of the second day of foul weather when she scratched her head, caught her fingers in the tangled mass, and then looked down at the dirt beneath her nails.

"I need a bath." She sighed the words aloud without thinking.

Startled when the sound of her voice fractured the si-lence, Noah quickly came to his feet, knocking the stool to the floor. He straightened it carefully before he looked over at her.

"You need a bath?"

There was such a look of intense concern and confusion on his face that Olivia found herself smiling.

"I'm sorry," she said, quickly sobering as she crossed her arms beneath her breasts. "I was just thinking aloud."

He hovered, immobilized by indecision. "You need a bath," he repeated.

"I know."

"A bath." He was still half a room away, one hand on the tabletop, his work forgotten.

"Water. Soap. You know." She had not actually ever seen him wash up, but she had heard water splash outside and saw the evidence of his clean face and hands and the dampness on the collar of his shirt. Not once had he offered to bring her soap and water. Not once had she had the courage to ask for anything that would make her feel any more beholden.

He nodded, looked her over slowly from head to toe, and walked out.

She had seen more of the back of Noah LeCroix than the front, for he spent most of his time trying to get away from her. The concept of a man running from her was not only welcome, but very, very curious. This man was fast proving too good to be true. He had shown her nothing but kindness, albeit a guarded, standoffish sort of kindness. With nothing to do but sit on his comfortable bed and contemplate her life and her circumstances, she realized with no little trepidation that here in the strange treehouse built over the swamp, she had actually started to feel safe. But her experience thus far had taught her that feeling secure with a stranger was a very bad sign.

Could this have been his plan, then? To take her in, make her feel confident, even secure with him, only to realize later that she had become his prisoner after all? She glanced around at the four walls covered with the hides and furry skins of dead animals, looked out the window and saw only the sky, the branches and leaves of trees. She was completely at his mercy, dependent upon him, imprisoned by the swamp.

A sharp thump in the doorway made her start. Noah was

headed her way with a bulky half-barrel in his arms. He negotiated the open doorway, crossed the room, and set the barrel down near the bed. His straight black hair sparkled with raindrops. Across his shoulders, his shirt was spotted with dampness. After hanging a caldron over the fire, he made a good five trips in and out again carrying bucketfuls across the room, pouring them into the caldron while Olivia watched in stunned silence.

Next, he rummaged through the goods he kept on the far side of the room—a collection of tins and sacks, stoneware crocks, and stacks of hides. Soon he walked back carrying a hunk of soap, a small, clean rag, a larger piece of white muslin for a towel, and a thick, folded piece of doeskin.

Neither of them spoke as he pulled a stool near the half-barrel and slowly, precisely laid out the soap, rag, and towel on the seat. Then he carefully filled the barrel with warm water from the caldron.

"There." He stood with the doeskin in his hand, waiting. Hell would freeze over before she stripped down and plunged in with him standing there.

She eyed the barrel. "I . . . I'll never fit in that," she blurted.

He looked startled. His face turned red as fire. "Yes. I mean, no, you won't. I mean . . . that is . . . I thought that you could . . . stand in it. Or lean over it. Maybe."

Olivia thought he might choke before he finished. For a long moment, the awkward silence stretched between them and then, Noah's eye widened and he blinked.

"I'm going out to see to my traps. It's high time. Past time. I'll be back in a while."

"It's raining. You'll get wet." There was no way she could bathe with him in the room, but she hated to run him out of his own house into the rain.

He was spreading out the buckskin on the end of the bed. As he unfolded it, she saw that it was a gown with fringe across the bodice and along the hem. Inside of that was a beautiful turquoise and violet silk shawl covered with fanciful embroidery. When she looked up, he was beside the door, shrugging into his own knee-length buckskin coat.

"The rain has almost stopped. In a little while the sun will break through."

Outside the window, water was still streaming in rivulets off the roof.

"Are you sure?"

"Sure as anyone can be about the weather. The drops are getting bigger. It will stop soon."

He slipped the rawhide strap of a powder horn over his shoulder, then tightened the knife sheath on his hip. A black hat hung on a peg near the door. He took it down and put it on, then picked up the long rifle. He thrust his chin in the direction of the dress on the bed.

"You can put that on when you get through." His gaze touched on the filthy gown she was wearing. Stunned by both the offer and his understanding, she swallowed her shame.

"Noah?"

"What?" He was almost outside.

It was the first time she had said his name aloud. It conjured memories of bible stories, of floods and animals walking two by two. This man, unless he was doing a fine job of acting, seemed gentle enough to charm wild animals into following him aboard an ark.

"Thank you." It had been so long since she had anything to be thankful for that the words felt foreign on her tongue.

He nodded, easily dismissing her gratitude. Through the open door behind him, the curtain of rain had become a heavy, silent gray mist.

"Will you be all right?" He shifted his weight as if he were uncomfortable, impatient to be away.

They were such small things, his offering her the gown and the lovely shawl, being kind enough to ask if she would be all right while he was gone. Without warning, her eyes smarted. When hot tears filled them and his image wavered, she tried to hide how much his show of concern had moved her. Instead of looking at him, she concentrated on the surface of the clear water shimmering in the tub.

"I'll be fine," she said softly. She listened for him to leave before she remembered that his footsteps rarely made a sound. Looking up, she found him still there, framed in the open doorway.

"I won't be far off. If anything . . . if you should need any help, just holler and I'll hear you."

Her throat was too thick for words. All she could do was nod as he left her alone. The door closed with a hollow sound behind him. Olivia sat there staring and found herself picturing him there, tall and silent, watching, always watching her as if she were some strange, exotic creature he had found in the swamp, one that he had absolutely no idea what to do with. That in itself astounded her and kept her thinking of him long after he was gone.

Noah shared his pirogue with two beaver carcasses and a green-winged teal that had landed to rest and preen on the bow.

"So, duck," he whispered, "would you like to hear about a man who keeps making a fool of himself?"

The duck looked over at him, took wing and left the pirogue bobbing just enough to barely ripple the water.

"Not interested?"

Noah stretched but made no move to pick up the paddle, content to sit in the shelter of the trees, close enough to the treehouse to hear Olivia should she call for help. As he had predicted, the rain had stopped shortly after he left but he still tarried in the open, unwilling to return before his guest had a chance to finish bathing. If he walked in and found her even in the slightest state of undress he was certain that his heart would stop and he would keel over. That, or explode.

Since she was feeling up to bathing, he reckoned she was one step closer to traveling. As soon as he went back, he was determined to bring up the subject of her leaving, one she had not broached since the morning she'd demanded he take her out of the swamp and then fainted dead away.

He sighed and stared down at the dead beavers. One had drowned in the trap on the edge of the swamp. The other had nearly been cut clean in half when the sharp jaws of the trap slammed closed. He hated killing but he did it in order to survive, never taking more than he needed for food and trade. Today he was just thankful to have caught something. Now, having the beavers to skin and new pelts to cure would keep him busy. He could only hope that the work would help keep his mind off Olivia.

She had been with him almost four days and he still knew next to nothing about her or how she came to be on Heron Pond. He was beginning to think he never would. There was a hunted wariness in her eyes, one he had seen often enough in the creatures he tracked and trapped. She seemed content to keep her silence, and he suspected it was most likely to protect herself from whoever or whatever had driven her into the swamp in the first place.

He could not help wondering what she was running from or why she was headed to Shawneetown. Was she going home or running away? Would anyone welcome her? Was anyone searching for her?

He had been to Shawneetown once, picked up a flatboat and piloted it down the Ohio to Cairo. Not much to the town then except the saline mines that were nearby.

A water moccasin swam toward the boat, leaving a spiraling trail behind it through the duckweed before it veered off. Not enough to take his mind off Olivia.

Could she sense the hunger she aroused in him? Was that why she was so cautious and kept so very quiet? Was that why the wary, haunted look never left her eyes? Or was it his face? Did the long scar and the eye patch keep her ill at ease?

She was disrupting his life. He could not think of anything but her. Nor could he sleep or eat more than a few bites. She filled him up, his mind, his senses. Her smallest movement had him sitting bolt upright out of a deep sleep, listening to see if she was having another nightmare, waiting until she settled back down, wondering what he should do if she did not. Her softest sigh claimed his complete attention.

He had to send her on her way before he went insane. It was past time. She was on the mend. Her color was better now. Her cheeks had flushed bright pink when he brought in the bath. The glow had made her green eyes sparkle. How much more beautiful would she be once she was clean and dressed?

Noah took a deep breath, blew it out again and picked up the paddle. He had given her more than enough time to bathe. The storm had passed and the sun had broken through the remaining clouds. He bent at the waist and pulled the paddle through the water toward him. Poking the long paddle into the water to steer the light craft was second nature to him. The pirogue moved along, creating barely a ripple and hardly more than a soft splash. As he headed back home, Noah was sure the pounding of his heart was making more noise than his paddle.

Noah drifted the last few yards to the base of the huge tree, slipped a rope around a knobby cypress knee that grew two feet out of the water and climbed out of the pirogue. He was reaching in for the beaver when he paused, arrested by the sound of Olivia humming a song. The tune drifted down through the leaves and branches of the tree, light and charming as a caress, teasing him, coaxing him to hurry back.

He held onto his hat and leaned back far enough to look up, and then he saw her—sitting on a stool she had carried out to the porch, perched near the railing in a stream of sunlight, wearing his mother's old dress and the shawl his father had brought from a place far, far away. She was bent over brushing her dark, heavy hair with her fingers, stroking it over and over, untangling the wet curls, letting the warm spring sun dry it. Noah's breath caught. The sight held him, made him feel like a thief as he stood there stealing more than a glimpse of her private moment.

The melody of the song teased his memory. His mind searched for remnants of the notes hidden somewhere in a corner of his mind where bits and pieces of his childhood lingered. Shaking off the urge to watch until her hair was dry and she went back inside, he forced himself to move instead.

Noah tied the beavers together by the legs, slung his burden over his shoulder and let the animals hang against his back. He took his rifle in the same hand as the rope and then started up the crude wooden steps nailed to the tree. When he was halfway up she sang the chorus aloud and the words came rushing back to him along with the rest of the tune. Without thinking, he began to whistle along.

"Fa-la-la-la, Fa-la-la-la-la, Fa-la-la-la, Fa-la-la-la."

He whistled all the way up the ladder as the words flowed merrily through his head, their meaning nonsense at first; a miracle really, that his mind could recall them from so very long ago.

"Soldier, O soldier, a-comin' from the plain / Courted a lady through honor and through fame / Her beauty shone so bright that it never could be told / She always loved the soldier because he was so bold / Fa-la-la-la-la . . ."

When his head cleared the edge of the porch, Noah stopped abruptly. Olivia was no longer singing. She was still seated on the stool, her dark hair clean and partially damp, flowing around her shoulders. His mother's butterscotch doeskin dress covered her completely except where the open neck skimmed her collarbone and her forearms showed at the ends of the short sleeves. Her bare toes and ankles were revealed beneath the fringed hem. The shawl had slipped, draped itself over the crooks of her arms.

He pulled himself up until he was standing on the porch. She grimaced when he dropped the beaver carcasses on the wooden deck, so he picked them up again and carried them around the corner out of sight. When he came back, she was standing with one hand braced against the rail that surrounded the porch. Her slight figure was almost lost inside the dress. He took in the rest of her. Dirty, she had been lovely. Clean, she was the most beautiful woman he had ever laid eyes on.

In that moment he knew that he could stand there forever just for the privilege of watching the sunlight shimmer on her hair, to see the soft breeze lift the ends of her flowing curls and tease them around her shoulders. To see her stand there and look back at him made his head swim and his mouth go dry. Surely his physical reaction had nothing to do with her. Surely there was something else wrong with him, something behind this strange surge of longing, the overwhelming need for something elusive and far more than he had ever wanted out of life before.

Olivia seemed hesitant to step away from the rail. Why *would* she dare move, he wondered, with him standing there staring at her with his one good eye like some kind of a madman? The only way to break the spell was to concentrate on anything but her.

"The dress and shawl were my mother's," he said abruptly.

She ran a hand over the smooth doeskin. "It's beautiful."

"Not fancy." He felt as if his throat were closing up and could not get more than two words out.

"Still, it's very nice. It feels like velvet. The shawl is wonderful."

"You look better."

He almost told her she looked beautiful.

He was no saint, just a flesh-and-blood man, and right now his flesh and blood were taking over his rational thought. If the whore down in New Orleans had not laughed in his face, if he had ever had a woman, maybe he would not be standing here salivating over Olivia Bond, wondering what it would feel like to take her in his arms and make love to her. As it was, he could only imagine how it would be to run his hands over her smooth skin, to wrap himself in her long hair, to bury himself inside her.

His heart was thundering in his chest, his blood hammering at his temples. He was either going stark raving mad with desire or coming down with some terrible disease.

He forced himself to concentrate. Her color had faded except for two bright spots high across her cheeks. It was a moment or two before he realized she was starting to weave. Without thinking, he went to her, slipped his arm around her waist, felt her sag against him.

She smelled of soap and sunlight and fresh air. Her hair was as soft as down. Holding her, he felt weightless, as if moving through a dream. A glance at her face, suddenly so near, and he saw her thick sable lashes flutter.

He held her as they walked back into the cabin, kept his arm tight around her waist. They stepped around the wash-tub. Near it there were still small puddles of water on the floor. He imagined her standing naked in the barrel, splashing water over herself, kneeling with water beaded on her skin as she washed her long hair. There was a tightness in his loins, a very loud pounding in his ears. He did not release her until she was lying on the bed again. He drew away from her slowly and stood back. His arms felt empty. Quickly he turned away and went back outside to get her some water; he came back in with a mugful.

He waited until she had taken a few sips and then asked, "Are you all right?"

Olivia nodded, frowning with concern. "I got a little dizzy all of a sudden."

"You're still weak on your feet, is all."

"Surely I should be feeling better by now."

"You're moving about more every day."

She laced her fingers together, looking at them, then back up at him. "Why are you being so kind to me? I can't possibly repay you."

"Why?" He was confused by her question.

She sighed. "You have been nothing but kind and I . . . well, I don't—" Huge tears welled up in her eyes and spilled down her cheeks. She quickly brushed them away, but not before one plopped on the bodice of the doeskin.

Noah watched the droplet widen into a small circle as it soaked into the soft leather.

"Don't cry." He didn't mean for the words to come out as harsh as they sounded.

Immediately she looked over at him and whispered, "I'm sorry."

"Don't be sorry." That, too, came out as a harsh command. At a complete loss, he paced over to the table and sat down on a stool and watched her, wishing he knew something, anything of dealing with women.

•　　•　　•

Olivia tried to stop her tears. She was unused to such kindness. Noah LeCroix was quickly proving to be more honorable than any man she had ever known.

She put her hand to her temple and rubbed it slowly. Her head no longer ached as badly as before, and she really had felt stronger until the light and woozy feeling had come upon her so suddenly, surprising her as much as Noah's rush to her side.

She had expected him to grab the stool she had carried out to the porch and shove it under her, but he had slipped his arm around her. Instead of recoiling in fear of his touch, she had experienced a breathtaking sense of security, a quiet sense of peace, almost as if she no longer had to battle alone to protect herself. The comfort of such a feeling had reduced her to tears.

And more, she had known the flush of desire, the need to be held by Noah LeCroix, which had come as more than a shock. After what she had been through, physical attraction to a man was something she had been sure she would never, ever feel.

Confused, frightened by her feelings, she knew she had to get away from here, from him, from what being alone with him was beginning to do to her.

"I shouldn't be here. I have to go—"

"You're safe here," he assured her.

Her throat closed. She choked back a sob. Being safe was a dream that had evaded her for so very, very long.

"Don't do that!" For the first time, he raised his voice and spoke to her sharply. Noah stood up and began to pace, tracking through the water she had splashed on the floor.

She tried to stop crying, to wipe away tears as fast as they could fall.

She licked a tear off the corner of her mouth and watched him grow more and more uncomfortable until finally he turned to her again.

"Look, I'm sorry. I'm no good at this." He ran his hand through his hair and sighed. Then he stopped pacing and stood beside the bed. "You want more water or something?"

She shook her head.

"Are you hungry?"

She began to hiccup down sobs. Olivia buried her face in her hands and shook her head no. She held her breath as she tried to pull herself together. He was getting more agitated the more she cried. Finally, when she thought she had herself under control, she looked up at Noah. He was still there at her bedside, his hands clenched into fists. She tried to smile, managed half of one, and saw him relax a bit.

"That's better," he muttered, sounding more perturbed than relieved. "Listen, I've got those beavers to clean."

She knew she would be seeing the back of him soon. He had the look on his face she had come to recognize, the one he always wore right before he walked out.

"You've been so good to me. I wish there were something I could do to repay you." She had nothing to give. No coin, no worldly goods. Nothing but herself, her body. Certain that the idea came from some dark, soiled corner of her soul, she was appalled at herself for even thinking it, knowing full well that before she had been torn from her family, she had been so innocent that such a thought would never have crossed her mind.

"I can cook for you," she said, recalling her old life. "I can clean and sweep and straighten things for you." It was a meaningless offer, for he appeared to be quite self-sufficient.

"You don't owe me anything. I wasn't about to leave you out there alone to die in the swamp. Anyone would do the same."

"No." She shook her head, quite certain of it. "Not everyone would help a stranger, especially a woman alone. Not everyone would be so kind. I've never met anyone like you."

He turned away. "I don't guess you've run into too many half-breeds with one eye."

"That's not what I meant."

He still looked as if he wanted to leave, and yet he tarried.

"What is it?" Olivia asked.

"You could clear up one thing for me, if you would."

She nodded, knowing what he was going to say. When he spoke, the request came as no surprise.

"You can tell me what you were doing lost out here in the first place. You didn't just fall out of the sky."

There was so much to tell, mostly things she did not want anyone else to know, but she could tell him some of it; she owed him that much.

"I was traveling to Illinois from Louisiana with an English family, Stanley and Polly Marlborough, and their baby daughter. I met them in New Orleans and in exchange for the privilege of traveling north with them, I cared for their little girl."

As her story slowly unfolded, her tears were replaced by her lingering outrage at Stanley Marlborough. Noah walked to the table and pulled out the remaining stool, sat down and continued to give her his attention.

"Around noon of the day you found me, we stopped the oxcart along the trail and had taken our midday meal and rest. Polly and the baby were asleep in the shade of a hickory tree and I had decided to walk to a nearby stream to wash up a bit and clean the eating utensils."

Olivia paused long enough to reach up and tuck her hair back behind her ears, then she gathered the shawl close. Outside, the birds seemed to be pouring out all the singing they had been denied during the rainstorm. The gentle breeze was still blowing the last of the clouds away, but inside the cabin the air was still. Noah watched her in silence and waited patiently to hear what she had to say.

"I had just wandered down to the stream when Mr. Marlborough came up behind me, grabbed me by the arms, turned me around and pulled me up against him." Remembering, she reached up and touched her fingertips to her mouth. "Before I could scream, he covered my mouth with his. I tried to pull away."

Lost in the memory, she fell silent, seeing it all over again. Then she shook herself and continued. "Finally, I managed to pull away from him and started running, through the water at first, right through the streambed. I ran up the bank on the other side and did not look back. I didn't notice the forest growing more dense until it was too late and I had turned down a trail that led into the swamp. I was afraid to look back, afraid Mr. Marlborough might be searching for me.''

Stanley Marlborough was young and able, not yet twenty-five, with the fine features of an English aristocrat: clear blue eyes, ruddy skin, sandy hair. Used to having everything he wanted, he was so angry that he chased her at first. She heard his footsteps pounding close behind her, his breath coming in ragged bursts. When he slowed and fell behind, she reckoned he was more afraid of Polly than he was determined to catch his quarry. Still, she raced on, long after she could not hear him anymore.

''By the time I realized I was lost, I was too confused to find my way out. I wandered down one path after another until dusk, and then I was terribly frightened that I was going to have to spend the night alone in the swamp. I heard a bobcat scream, started running and hit my head on a fallen log. That's the last thing I remember before I woke up here.''

Noah had not moved. He sat so still that she thought he was not listening for a moment, until she looked hard into his face and what she saw there made her shiver. His expression had darkened to one of barely suppressed anger, one she would not have guessed him capable of.

''That explains it.'' He was looking at the floor now, his voice so soft she barely heard.

''What?''

He lifted his head and looked directly at her. ''Now I know why I saw all that fear in your eyes when you awakened.''

''I didn't know where I was.''

''It was more than that. You were afraid of me, because of the way I look.'' He gestured toward his eye patch and scar. ''But it was also because of what that man tried to do to you.''

She felt the sting of tears again, and reminded herself

that Noah would become upset if she cried again. She blinked the tears away.

"What that man tried to do to you was not your fault."

She wiped her face, smearing tears down her cheeks. Could he really understand? Would anyone ever understand how confused she had been without the faintest idea why he had attacked her? She had done nothing to deserve his unwanted attention. What if there was some flaw in her? Something that she unwittingly did that encouraged the worst in a man?

"Thank you for saying that," she said softly, still in doubt. "Especially since you really don't know me at all."

"I know enough." Noah got to his feet, nudging the stool back under the table with his foot.

She knew he was eager to tend to the grisly task of skinning the beavers, but he lingered at the foot of the bed.

"You let me know as soon as you feel up to heading out of here and I'll take you to the edge of the swamp."

He walked out without a second glance and, oddly, Olivia felt a wave of regret. She wished she had not told him anything about her experience with Stanley Marlborough. She wished she had simply made up some story about becoming separated from her traveling companions, but she owed him the truth—it was the least she could do for him. He had shown her only kindness, asked nothing else of her. She would not hide the truth from him, as she would have to from so many others for the rest of her life.

But now that he knew, did he seem more anxious than before to be rid of her?

Noah walked around the porch to the back of the cabin, pulled his skinning knife out of its sheath, raised it high and plunged it into the wooden railing. Then he braced his hands, one on either side of the knife, and tightened his fingers around the smooth cypress. He had no idea what Stanley Marlborough looked like, but he could easily imagine an Englishman's mush-colored face and the feel of a scrawny neck between his hands.

Still, it was easy for him to understand the desire that

drove a man to put his hands on Olivia, the hunger that had pushed her employer to attack her. He had felt that same desire, experienced that raw hunger himself. What he could not understand, or ever condone, was the man's lack of honor. How could Marlborough have succumbed to such base, animal instinct?

He did not have to imagine what it was like to lie wide awake no more than a few feet away from her every night and think about slipping into bed with Olivia, of taking her into his arms. He knew the torture of such thoughts first-hand—and he had only been with her for a few days. What would it be like to have to be with her for weeks on end? How long could he ignore the wanting that grew stronger with each and every encounter?

How long could he hide his desire?

He knew with utmost certainty that Olivia had done nothing to encourage his longing, and yet it was inspired. She probably had no notion what she did to a man just by looking his way. No notion at all.

He took a deep breath and prayed that she would mend quickly.

chapter
5

Payson Bond stared down at the broken plow handle in his
filthy hand. Once his hands had been smooth and white
except where his fingertips had been stained with ink. They
were a teacher's hands, a poet's hands, but now they were
chapped and cracked, his palms callused, his nails ragged
and backed with dirt.

Once he had had lofty goals and a dream, a vision of
moving his family to the Illinois frontier so that he would
be out from under the control of his wealthy father-in-law.
He would clear the land, set down roots, teach the children
of his neighbors, and prosper. He had wanted to become a
part of history, to be among the brave and hardy souls who
left homes and family behind to conquer new lands much
romanticized in the East, a place of noble savages and
stouthearted planters and farmers, of pioneers who followed
their dreams into a West newly opened after the Louisiana
Purchase.

Once he had been happy. The whole family had been
happy. Susanna; Payson Junior; Frederick, his youngest.

Olivia.

Just thinking of her nearly bent him double with pain.
Olivia, his lovely daughter born of his first wife, Margaret.

None of them could bear to mention Olivia's name anymore, not even the little boys. At first his sons were forever asking when she would come home, at least until the day Susanna had burst into tears and run from the house screaming, scaring them all half to death. After that, Olivia's name slowly faded from their conversations, as if speaking it aloud would dredge up all the horror and memories of the day she was taken from them.

Payson laid the broken plow handle on the ground beside the heavy blade and unfastened the lines on the brown cob mare. He gave her a swat on the rear and she ambled off in the direction of the cabin, toward her feed trough, moving faster than he had been able to get her to pull the plow all morning.

As he headed for the cabin, he reached into the back pocket of his wool pants and pulled out a soiled kerchief, lifted his hat and wiped the cloth across his brow. It came away sweat-stained and streaked with dirt. He shoved it back into his pocket, wishing away the circumstances of his life, wishing with every step and every heartbeat that when he opened the door of the cabin that life would be the way it used to be, that Susanna's big blue eyes would light up and she would greet him with a smile or a tender touch. He wished the boys would run to him with shouts of joy, their faces shining, their spirits light, their life as innocent and free as all children's lives should be.

The cabin was already on the tract of land he had purchased. His acres backed up to the woods, and on the south side he had begun to clear another field. Built by a settler intent upon moving on to a bigger piece of land with his profit, the cabin was small and crudely made, but it had provided the immediate shelter his family needed. There were rough shelves for dishes and for his many books, two long benches, a table and a bedframe, a packed dirt floor, and a loft for the boys.

Early on he had purchased some chickens, but the wolves had gotten most of them. He had the mare, a milk cow, a plow, and a neighbor who would loan him an ox and cart when he needed them.

He knew that inside, Susanna had retreated to her rocker, silent and forlorn. She sat there for hours, staring at the bare dirt floor or the empty hearth. Day after day she rocked back and forth, her hands lying idle in her lap, her hair knotted, her clothing unwashed. More often than not she let the fire grow cold while she spent her time dwelling on the child she had lost shortly after their arrival, the lifeless baby girl who had died without ever having wakened to life.

His sons had taken to escaping the cabin to play somewhere at the edge of the wood—sweaty, barefoot, faces always streaked with dirt, noses runny, hair standing out in all directions. Slowly they were losing all touch with the ordered, civilized life they had once known. They had grown so much that their clothes no longer fit them. Their wrists and arms and their knobby little ankles hung out of the ends of cuffs and hems.

Payson dreaded every step he took toward the log cabin that he could see across the open land. The field he had struggled to clear himself was still peppered with the stumps of hickory, sycamore, and maple trees he could not pull out even with the horse and plow. His crop of corn had yet to be planted.

He was no farmer. He knew that now, too late, now that he faced this hard land where brute strength was glorified and a man was judged more by the rows he could plow in a day and the amount of whiskey he could hold than by education or wealth.

He had what his neighbors called "book larnin'." He was a teacher, a poet, a man of letters—not a farmer nor a hunter, not a drinker, not even a dreamer anymore. His dreams were long gone. Shattered. Vanished as all visions eventually do, but his had gone not little by little, but all at once. His dreams had vanished with Olivia.

For Susanna's sake, for all their sakes, he should have listened to his father-in-law and stayed in Virginia. But instead, he had stubbornly clung to the idea that he would be able to carve a home out of the raw, fertile land available in Illinois. He had been too pigheaded to take the money and small plantation that Susanna's father offered them, one that would enable him to keep Susanna in the style in which she had always lived.

Her father was a rich man, one who had felt sorry for a near-penniless, widowed teacher and had hired him to tutor his only child, not to steal her heart. Richard Morrison had fought their marriage every step of the way. He had argued until the bitter end, tried to dissuade Susanna from marrying a poor widower with a daughter very near her own age. But Morrison's objections only made headstrong Susanna more determined.

After trying to be the husband Susanna deserved for six long years, Payson finally convinced his wife that if they moved away from her father's constant ridicule and were settled on their own homestead in Illinois, they would truly be happy. Instead, he had turned her life into a living hell.

As he walked over the heavy clods of dirt in the field, his steps began to drag the closer he came to the cabin. There was not a wisp of smoke curling out of the chimney, but at least spring was here, and now whenever Susanna let the fire go out the boys were not threatened with frostbite.

She had let things go so far during the winter that he had been forced to take in a poor Scots girl who had come begging to help fetch and carry in exchange for room and board. He offered her sleeping space in the loft with the boys and gave her bed and board in exchange for help, but Molly MacKinnon was a wild, outspoken girl with no notion of responsibility. She had up and disappeared toward the middle of March. Now the boys had no supervision at all while he was in the fields or out hunting.

On the threshold, Payson paused and looked at the planks of the rough-hewn door. Although he felt as if the weight of the world were on his shoulders, he straightened them anyway and tried to summon a smile. The expression felt unnatural, more like a grimace. He set the broken plow handle against the outer wall.

Swinging the door open, he stepped into the close, dark interior of the cabin. His gaze immediately went to Susanna and once more he was filled with dread. She was in the rocker, just as he had known she would be, staring into the cold, ash-filled hearth. Her slim, tapered fingers were knotted together in her lap, her head bowed. Long tendrils of her light brown hair straggled along the sides of her face. She did not even look up when he walked in and quietly closed the door behind him. He was scared to death for her, scared of what would become of them all.

"Susanna?"

His wife did not respond. Payson walked over to the rocker, stood behind her, reached out and laid his hand on her shoulder. He closed his eyes, wishing he could will his strength into her. She was only twenty-four, too young to dwell in the depths of despair for the rest of her life. That was what scared him most of all, the idea that one day she would tire of being so very miserable and take her own life. There was so much he could not forgive himself for already, that he doubted he could exist under such a burden, even for his boys.

If there were only something he could do to bring her back, he would gladly do it to save her, but he had no notion what that might be anymore. There was no way to change the past.

"Where are the boys, Susanna?"

He wished she would shrug her shoulder at least, or give him some sign that she had heard him, but Susanna did not stir. Payson sighed. He walked past the shelves where his collection of books gathered dust. How long had it been since he had an hour to himself? Since he had been able to luxuriate in reading or work on one of his own poems? He ignored the books and went to the long trestle table that took up far too much space in the small room. He sat down, thirsting for a cup of coffee, too tired to make one for himself.

He had barely hit the bench when the door flew open and banged against the wall behind it.

"Little Pay'th cut hith head off!" Freddie, his younger son, yelled at the top of his lungs as he came flying through the door.

Susanna did not even flinch. Payson got to his feet, concerned but not panicked. Little Pay had had an accident nearly every other day since they had moved to Illinois, and four-year-old Freddie was always happy to exaggerate every one of them.

Payson was on his way to the door when Little Pay walked in with his hand pressed to his forehead. A trickle of blood showed between his fingers.

"I cut myself down by the crick." Little Pay, not having noticed Payson yet, was calling out to Susanna.

"I'll get a rag," Payson said, stepping over the bench.

Little Pay swung his gaze across the room, looking at Payson and then at his mother, who had not moved at all.

"I didn't know you were here, Pa."

Disheartened, the boy started across the room to get his own rag. On the way he bumped into the elegant carved sideboard shoved up against a wall, a remnant of their former life. It was a lasting piece of luxury, a wedding gift from Susanna's father, one that looked as out of place in the crude cabin as a tinker at a governor's ball.

"Ouch!" Little Pay bellowed when he connected with the sideboard. "I hit my head again. I think it's bleedin' worse."

"He'th bleedin' worthe!" Freddie echoed.

The rocker started to creak.

Picking up a dishtowel on the way across the room, Payson went directly to his older son. By now, Freddie had climbed up on Payson and Susanna's bed, his dirty bare feet adding another contribution to an already soiled quilt. Payson inspected Little Pay's wound and slipped his arm around the boy's shoulder as he held the dishtowel against the superficial cut. Beneath his worn cotton shirt, Little Pay felt bone thin. All of them had lost weight during the long hard winter when there was little food put by because Payson had discovered too late that his hunting skills were lacking, but his elder son seemed to have suffered most of all.

"Maybe Mama could wipe it off." Little Pay sounded doubtful as he looked over at his mother.

"Let's not bother your mama." Payson glanced toward his young wife and felt the rip in his heart tear a little more. He bit his lips and concentrated on his boy.

"You're all right, son," Payson told the child as he pressed the rag to the wound. He sat down on the edge of the bed and pulled Little Pay between his knees and asked, "How did you manage to do this?"

He dabbed at the cut until it stopped bleeding.

Little Pay shrugged. "Just fell."

"You've got to be more careful," Payson warned. "There's not an inch left of you that's not bruised or battered."

Freddie was trying to climb up the cabin wall by inserting his bare toes into the cracks between the wood where the chinking was missing. Payson ignored him.

"Freddie's climbin' the wall, Pa," Little Pay told him.

Payson sighed. "I know, son. Freddie, get down, please."

"Papa, you need help putting in those seeds yet?" His wound forgotten for the moment, Little Pay volunteered so earnestly that Payson felt ashamed.

"The field isn't ready yet, son. Besides, the plow handle broke this morning. I'll have to fix it and finish plowing before I can start the planting."

The boy said nothing. He looked over at his mother and Payson followed his gaze. The rocker had stopped moving, but his wife held her silence and did not turn around.

Susanna could hear her boys and Payson across the room, but she felt as if she were trapped in another world where she could not reach them. They had begun to talk around her as if she were not there, and in a very real sense, she wasn't. Just her body and a corner of her mind that still clung to a thread of her old life, her old self.

She was too young to feel so old, but she did. Old and helpless, the life draining out of her a little more each day. She imagined it seeping into the dirt floor beneath her feet, draining right through the soles of her shoes, right down into the soil of this cursed Illinois ground.

Little Pay seemed to scratch or bruise or skin something constantly. She wondered if perhaps it made the hurt inside go away if you hurt bad enough on the outside. She ached for Payson and the boys, but she could do nothing. The pain she already bore went so deep she was numb, paralyzed with it.

She could still hear everything, though. Even earlier, when Payson had said something about a broken plow, she was screaming inside, but the sound would not come out. How could it, when it took every ounce of strength she had in her just to breathe?

Didn't Payson know they were cursed now and always would be? When would he stop trying? When would he admit that he had been wrong and simply give up?

Not until he was dead, she reckoned. Not until then, when they might all be dead and buried.

He was beside her now, hunkered down on one knee, his hand atop hers. She knew if she turned her head very slightly that she would see him looking up at her as if he wanted to cut his heart out and lay it on a platter and give it to her, if that would make her happy. The flat light of guilt would be there in his blue eyes, along with the beaten-down hopelessness that had taken up residence inside of him in the same way that pain had made a permanent home in her heart.

She could not worry about the boys' aches and complaints, or a broken plow, or anything else. Not when it was only a matter of time before the devil came to take her away the way he had her little baby girl.

She was damned as that little unnamed baby, damned for all eternity, and sitting here in Illinois she felt one step closer to hell. Bears still roamed the deep woods, and snakes crawled inside the cabin to sleep in warm corners. Their homestead was covered with tree stumps that fought the plow. Last summer they had been swarmed by plagues of mosquitoes and then Payson, like so many of the other settlers, had been hit by a terrible quaking sickness and fever. Once the ague came upon a body, it never left, just kept reappearing without the slightest warning. They had met some of the neighbors, all of them friendly, none of them their equal in education or social graces. Payson had worked himself to the bone in the field that still lay un-planted. He had tried to hunt, but mostly all he brought home were squirrels that he and the boys trapped. Life was more than a struggle,—it was a disaster.

It was safer to let her world dwindle to the rocking chair than to move about in it. The perfect place to sit and await the devil until he came to collect the rest of his due was right here in front of this cold hearth. The baby would not be enough. One by one, he would take them all.

Susanna was sure he would, for she still had to pay for what she had done to Olivia.

New Orleans

The air had grown still, gathering itself into the thick, chok-ing humidity that was as oppressive as a wool blanket in summer. In two more months all but the hearty would leave the city and take up residence in country homes and on outlying plantations where they would not have to fear the yellow fever brought on by the heat.

Closeted in a private office downstairs, Darcy leaned back in his chair and squinted at the slovenly figure across the expanse of rich mahogany.

"I would appreciate it greatly if you would get your fat ass off my desk, Leonard," he said without a trace of ran-cor. The lackey slid his bulk up and off the corner of the desk. Darcy squelched the urge to take out a handkerchief and wipe the spot where the man had sat. Instead he picked up a small pair of silver scissors he trimmed his cigars with and began to turn them over and over in his hands.

Miles Leonard scratched the bald spot that stood out like an island in a sea of matted brown hair. "Like I was saying, I don't think you're gonna find her anyplace. If she was in New Orleans, my boys would've picked up her scent."

Darcy fought the urge to close his eyes and recall Oli-via's scent himself, telling himself not now, certainly not in front of this idiot. He said nothing as he waited for more of Miles Leonard's excuses as to why he had found no trace of Olivia.

"Somehow she left the city, probably the very day she disappeared, from all I can gather. There's no one who even claims to recollect seeing her."

The fact that right now, at this very minute, someone might be using her for his own was a notion that infuriated Darcy more than the idea that he might never see her again. It was one thing to lose her before he was finished with her, but it was quite another to think that someone else might be enjoying her instead.

He imagined Olivia escaping the house, being approached by someone offering to help her, being too naive to realize she might be stepping into a trap that was not silk-lined this time. Someone may have taken her off the streets and into his own possession. She could be anywhere. Used, abused, cast aside already. With her ebony hair, someone might have tried to sell her as a slave to collect a high bounty. Even though she was white, there was no way she could prove otherwise, not in a city where high-yellow octoroons who could pass for white were greatly valued.

His mind tried to take him down a path he wanted to avoid, flashing dark images of another man, in another room somewhere. The man's hands on Olivia. What if this time she gave in easily, gave herself without hostility, without the same silent, simmering anger she always showed him?

When he realized he was close to breaking the delicate, embossed silver scissors, Darcy set them down.

"Someone might be hiding her." He voiced the disturbing thought aloud.

"If they are, it's the best kept secret in N'awlins," Leonard told him. "I haven't heard a thing from any of my sources. With all the house slaves and servants around, someone is bound to talk sooner or later."

There were dozens of men like Miles Leonard in New Orleans, men willing to do anything for a bit of coin that would buy them their next jug of whiskey, their next whore. Men like Miles Leonard were not welcome through the front doors of the Palace of Angels. The type of whore this man could afford would never work here. But he needed Leonard, and his strict policy of maintaining a certain level of clientele did not extend to the back door, to the men who brought him new girls on occasion, men who would carry out other, less respectable tasks that a man in his business might need to have taken care of.

"If she did leave town, she had to go upriver. Keep asking around the waterfront. See if any of the boatmen who just came down might have seen her along the way."

The corner of Leonard's mouth curved into a lurid smile. "You said she'd be pretty hard to miss."

As beautiful as she was, Olivia would be *very* hard to miss, Darcy thought, but he wasn't about to elaborate. It was his habit not to engage in conversation with imbeciles any longer than he had to.

"I gave you a full description," he reminded the other man.

"I'll need a few more dollars to pass around, something to prime the pump." Leonard scratched again, this time it was his crotch.

Darcy stood to signal the end of the meeting. Miles Leonard hovered like a stubborn hound unwilling perform without a bone. Darcy had no inclination to open his desk and withdraw any money while the man stood there watching. Instead he leaned across the desk, picked up his pen, and dipped the nib into an inkwell. He scrawled a few words and a figure on a sheet of paper and shoved it at Leonard.

"Give this to the barkeep downstairs and he'll give you the cash."

With the promise of more money secure, Leonard finally moved toward the door.

"And Miles?"

The big man paused and turned around. "Yeah?"

"Take the money and leave. Do your drinking someplace else and get back to me the minute you hear anything."

chapter
6

Heron Pond

Olivia knew she was in trouble the moment she started to feel safe. It was not something that came over her all of a sudden, but slowly, the way the colors of sunset tinted the sky as she watched it from a wooden stool near the window. Gradually nature added a hint of color here, a pure ray of light there, until the sky was awash with all the colors of the rainbow. Very soon, the first star would appear on a deep indigo sky.

Her feeling of security was not something that had happened in an instant. It had come over her so gradually that it was too late now to guard against it.

In the week since she had been living with him, Noah had not once spoken a single word or made any gesture that gave her cause to fear him. Certainly, there was undisguised hunger in his expression, the same sort of hot intensity she had seen in a man before, one she had learned to recognize, but there was also something more powerful in Noah, a stubborn strength of will that she wished she possessed. He refused to bend, even to his own deep desires.

The colored sky was beginning to fade, so Olivia stood up and walked outside where the evening air felt cool on her skin. She walked to the railing and looked down into the swamp. She rubbed her arms and then let her hands slide over the soft doeskin of the dress Noah had given her.

Even in the dwindling light, she could still see a huge blue heron standing one-legged in shallow water, as still as one of the cypress. With Noah's help she had come to know the names of some of the birds of Heron Pond. Watching their comings and goings helped fill the long, quiet hours she spent alone recuperating whenever he was out hunting, much needed hours of peace and solitude that had given her time to regain her strength, not only in body, but in mind.

Cicadas started a noisy hum that seemed to vibrate through and around her. Olivia closed her eyes and took a deep breath. No longer did she find the close, damp air cloying. Instead, the now-familiar, fecund scent of the swamp calmed her, just as did the chorus of birds and insects, the spatter of rain on the trees and the roof, the way the ribbons of sunlight cut through the foliage and shifted whenever a breeze touched the leaves of the trees.

Such serenity was so foreign to her that she had fought it at first. She had been so certain that Noah was not what he seemed, that he might pose a threat, that it had been hard to relax. But he never came close to her. Never touched her, hardly even looked her way. Slowly the peace of the quiet swamp seeped into her soul, calming her, lulling her into a contented quiescence.

She was no longer afraid of the dark water below the huge cypress. Instead she saw it as more of a moat, a protective barrier between this lush world and the outside, and she knew why Noah LeCroix had chosen to dwell here.

On Heron Pond he was safe from the prying eyes of those who might shun him because of his scarred face. Here he was master of his own world, content to come and go as he pleased, living off the land with no one to answer to, nothing to fear except perhaps the natural predators who shared his world with him.

Darcy would never find me here.

Standing alone in the gathering dusk, she dared to remember Darcy Lankanal, what he had done, what she had become at his hands. Those memories never lingered far from her mind. The still-vivid images were always there, always lurking. She had struggled to keep them at bay since her escape, afraid that dwelling on them might somehow link her to Darcy again, might somehow conjure him up and bring him back into her life.

If she hid here in the swamp forever, she would never have to worry about Darcy finding her. Nor would she have to face her father or worry that he would find out what she had become. It was a nice dream, but she could not stay here forever. She loved her family and missed them all, especially the boys. They were her kin. She belonged with them.

Besides, this was Noah's home, *his* retreat. Not hers. He had taken her in only until she was well, and that day had come.

Noah.

Noah was as different from Darcy as night from day. Darcy with his blond hair and fair looks, the angelic smile that most women found devastating. Lankanal was as selfish and arrogant as he was handsome. He was obsessed with bending her to his will, and because he was always so successful at making her body, if not her mind, respond to him, she hated him more than she ever thought she could hate anyone or anything.

She would never forget the day the colonel and his river pirates drove her into New Orleans. They surrounded her, pushed and shoved her through the streets, past apathetic strangers who gave the filthy riverboat crew no more than a second glance. Exhausted, her spirit and heart broken, she had stood unprotesting, her tears spent, hungry, filthy, not caring whether she lived or died.

One of Darcy's dealers had ushered them through the walled garden and hurried them into a stable area where a shining, black lacquered carriage was stored. The man left them and soon after, Darcy had come sauntering in. She had straightened at the sight of him, daring to hope that the handsome, well-dressed gentleman would save her.

She waited for him to blast the pirates for what they had

done to her, to her family. She expected him to call the authorities. Everything would soon be straightened out. She would be sent home. But appearances are deceiving. Darcy asked Sullivan if she was a virgin. When the colonel said he could guarantee it with his life, Darcy counted out five twenty-dollar pieces and handed them over to Sullivan.

She had stood there confused and uncomprehending, clinging to a slim thread of hope that quickly unraveled as Darcy led her into the Palace of Angels. He kept his hand on her arm as he walked her upstairs to his opulent suite and locked the door. He summoned house slaves, ordered a hot bath.

She shed tears of embarrassment and humiliation when he made her strip out of her filthy clothes right there in front of him. She futilely tried to cover herself with her hands while he inspected every inch of her and then told her to get into the tub. He knelt on the floor beside her, took up perfumed soap and scented oil and a washrag, then washed her all over. She sat there and cried silent tears of shame. He washed her hair, rinsed it with clear, warm water that he poured out of a beautiful cloisonné pitcher. He held her hand, pulled her from the tub, towel-dried and combed her hair.

Then he led her to his bed. He told her that life as she knew it was over and that she was his until he was satisfied she was well versed in the art of lovemaking. Then, she would join the other girls who worked for him. He told her that there was no hope of escape, that she should not even consider it, for that would be a foolish waste of time.

Dazed and brokenhearted, she did not fight him when he finally took her. Over the next few days he used her in every way a man could use a woman's body; by the end of her first week with him, she had lost both her virginity and her innocence and hated herself for what she had become.

From that day on she could not bear to look into a mirror, which was a challenge because his suite was filled with them. Darcy told her she was beautiful, more so than any of the others. He swore she would soon fall in love with him and with her new profession. He tried to convince her that she would eventually accumulate her own wealth, tried to explain that wealth meant power.

She knew that by then it would be too late—that she could never truly be free, no matter how much money she had, for she would never be able to buy back her virginity or her soul.

His words fell upon deaf ears, but his touch was charismatic. Her body responded while her heart lay cold and dead inside. Her mind shut down whenever he took her. It was the only way she could stay sane.

For months she watched and planned and looked for a way to escape. But even now that she was free of Darcy and New Orleans, she could not escape the memories, the old nightmare, or herself.

Now she sighed and turned away from the rail. There was a pot of beans on the hearth. He never failed to leave food for her when he went out hunting. Lately he had taken to avoiding her altogether, returning late at night to bed down outside without disturbing her.

Inside, she lit the oil lamp and replaced the chimney. She looked around the small cabin, knowing it was time to leave and dreading the future. Would her family accept her if they found out what she had become? Could she face her father without hating him for giving her up to the colonel and his men?

Life would be so much easier if she could just stay here in Noah's treehouse, hidden away from the world and everyone in it, but she sensed that his control was stretched to the limit, and he had made no move to alter their relationship. She had begun to wonder how she would react if he did. They were locked in an impossible situation. It was time to leave.

Noah cleared the opening in the floor of the porch. He was dog-tired from rising early and staying out late, tired of sleeping on the hard floor outside, sick of fighting the demons inside him. He was a man, not a priest. Not an hour of the day went by when he did not think of Olivia Bond, of the way she moved, of the sound of her sigh, of the whisper of her bare feet against the floor.

He was confused, befuddled by the intense need that her nearness ignited in him, hated wanting something he had never thought he would need so badly. He ached with the sheer power of it.

Now he made his footsteps silent as he walked across the porch toward the glow of lamplight from within the cabin. Olivia was already asleep, yet tossing fitfully in his bed. Though she had not dreamed it for days, her nightmare was upon her again and he wished there were some way he could keep her from having to suffer it yet again. At the foot of the bed he looked down at her. As if she sensed him there, she calmed and settled back into deep, even breathing.

He turned around and walked out of the cabin. Shoved up against the outside wall, his hard pallet looked cold and uninviting.

Crying. She was crying in a dark, damp place where she did not want to be, but could not escape. Walls of stone surrounded and imprisoned her. Firelight writhed and danced against the rock. Darcy stepped out of the shadows and came toward her. She tried to run but her feet did not move. Something held her. Something made her stay. Kept her from running.

"It took a while, Olivia," he drawled, "but I knew I'd find you. You're mine, you know. Only mine. Did you think otherwise?"

He walked toward her, arms open wide, wanting to embrace her.

"No!" A dry scream was torn from her throat. "I won't go back again. I can't do it, Darcy. I'll die first."

He reached out, grabbed her by the shoulders, shook her hard.

"Let me go!" she screamed. Terror ricocheted through her. "Please, no more. No more," she sobbed. "Let me go!"

Suddenly there was a presence in the cave with them,

one that came from behind Darcy. One that made her feel safe. It grew closer, stronger, until she began to calm and felt surrounded by that calm. She heard a man's voice, but did not recognize the words. Her fear slowly dissolved as his warmth spread through her. As the angel of the darkness wrapped his arms around her and began to take on reality, Darcy's image diminished until it finally faded away.

"Shh, Olivia. Shush," the comforting presence whispered in her ear. "You're all right. You're safe now, Olivia. Wake up."

When she opened her eyes it was still dark. She was no longer in a cold, dark place surrounded by impenetrable stone walls, but wrapped in a man's strong embrace. The warmth she had experienced, the intense feeling of protection, was very, very real.

"Shh. You're all right, Olivia." Noah was rubbing her back, patting her like a child. Then, as his palm began to move in slow circles, she let his warmth seep into her and settled against him, cherished, protected. Safe. New.

He reached up and brushed her hair off the side of her face. His fingers were tentative, soothing. He held her as tenderly as one might a precious gem. His touch demanded nothing, and yet she felt the need to embrace him. When she slipped her arms around him, she expected Noah to pull away. He stiffened, but did not run from her this time.

They sat unmoving, eyes closed, arms around each other, seconds passing swift and silent, fast as a hummingbird's heartbeat. She could feel his arousal strong and hard where their bodies met, felt herself slowly melting inside, remembering the tempting opiate of sexual release. More than that, she wondered if being with Noah and giving of herself freely might not cleanse her heart and soul of Darcy.

Her own need began to fill her up, tempt her, make her heart beat faster. Aware of the male hardness of his chest where her breasts pressed against him, she caught his outdoor scent, felt the hush of his warm breath against her cheek. He was a mystery, an enigma, this man of honor. She wanted to taste him. She lifted her chin slightly, just enough so that she could see his mouth. Clinging to him, she raised herself until their lips met. She traced the seam of his mouth with her tongue and when she felt him shudder, she realized a power that was foreign to the overwhelming helplessness she had experienced for so long. Such heady knowledge made her dizzy.

Slowly, hesitantly, he opened to her kiss and gradually began to imitate the movement of her tongue against his, darting, tasting, delving. She pulled her arms away long enough to be able to reach up and cup his face between her hands as she kissed him long and deep, wishing she could crawl inside him where no one could ever hurt her again.

His arms had tightened around her; his hands no longer moved with the innocence of giving comfort. Now they explored, tentatively, almost as if he were waiting for her to guide him. His hesitancy made her body ache all the more. She wanted his hands on her, wanted him to erase all that Darcy had ever done to her.

When the kiss ended they clung to one another, breathing as hard as befit young animals racing toward freedom. She took his hand in hers, cradled it against her palm, drew it to her breast and molded him until he cupped her with his fingers. She pressed against the heat of his hand, stretched upward again so she could savor his taste, feel his mouth moving upon hers.

She led the way, encouraging him with soft sighs. Whispering against his lips. Shifting in his embrace, she placed one hand upon his thigh, let it inch slowly upward, toward his manhood. He moaned, a choked sound that might have been a sigh of pleasure or a weak protest. She could not resist. She brushed his buckskin pants where they strained across his arousal, heard him moan, felt him shudder.

Noah's heart was pounding, beating with such intensity that he thought it might explode. Her light, explorative touch set his blood thrumming through his veins. She tantalized him everywhere at once. Her lips were exquisite, her kiss indescribable. He was consumed with her. With touching her, kissing her. He was exhilarated by her.

The world had narrowed to the two of them. Time had stopped when her lips touched his for the first time. He was certain there had been nothing before and there would be nothing after her and this golden, explosive moment in time.

Brazenly she cupped him, and he nearly jumped out of the bed. She gently cradled his pulsing, aching manhood in her hand and when he felt the heat of her palm through the leather of his pants, he moaned again. All rational thought left him and he acted on instinct as he pressed her back against the pillow and covered her with his body. She slid her hands up to the front of his shirt, tore at the hem as she pulled it out of his pants, exposed his chest and ran her hands up and down his ribs.

Curiosity did not guide him. It was need, pure and simple, need and an intense hunger for this woman who had slipped into his life, into his home—invading his senses, stirring up his world, his desire, igniting him.

His hands found their way to the hem of the doeskin dress. He slipped his hand onto her leg beneath the butter-soft fabric. Her skin was smooth and white as starlight. As he slid his palm up her leg, the dress rose with his hand. When he reached her thigh, he was shaking with need. Touching her intimately was nearly his undoing. He was trembling violently, fighting to hold back, expecting her to come to her senses and push him away.

Instead, Olivia surprised him by rocking her hips, pressing against him in invitation, urging him on with soft cries and whispers. He froze when she frantically untied his pants and shoved them down around his hips. Guiding him, she gently urged him to lie down alongside her. He pressed close to her and felt his throbbing erection against her thigh.

In a dreamlike state, he rose up and over her. Afraid he would reach a climax before he entered her, he watched starbursts explode in his mind's eye. Exquisite pleasure-pain pulsed through him until he wanted to scream. There would be no turning back now.

Olivia ignored his scar and framed his face with her hands as she kissed him deeply. Where his cheek brushed against hers it became moist with the heat of her tears.

He nudged her legs apart with his knee, wrapped her in his arms, mounted her. Inexperience made him brave. Excitement made him hurry. His heart and mind were focused on only her, on Olivia and his pulsing need. He could not think past his next heartbeat, his next breath. Sliding into her moist, slick passage, he buried himself to the hilt.

Acute awareness hit him. He was inside Olivia, sheathed and surrounded by her. He could feel her sliding up and down around him, taking him in, stretching to admit all of him. She lunged up and up against him, as her hips bucked frantically.

She called out his name, urging him on. Unable to control himself any longer, he climaxed.

Olivia's breath came in ragged tears. Noah collapsed against her, his cheek against hers, his breath hot against her ear. Shock overwhelmed her so that she could not move or think or speak.

What in the world had she just done?

When had the nightmare ended and the dream begun—the comforting dream that she now realized with terrifying clarity was indeed reality?

She whispered his name.

Looking dazed, he sat up and shoved a hand through his hair.

"Are you all right?" He leaned back on his elbow, staring down at her, watching her closely.

She could see his face clearly in the moonlight filtering through the open window. His expression was clouded by confusion and doubt, as if, like her, he had no explanation of how things had gone so far. As if he, too, doubted the reality of what had just happened.

Oh, my God. What have I done? What have I become?

He had been so strong over the past days. She was well aware that Noah would never have crossed the line if she had not led him over it. She had recognized the desire in his eyes and knew that he wanted her, and he had kept his need under control and never made a move toward her, and probably never would have if she had not wantonly seduced him in the dark.

Reeling, she closed her eyes, thinking back over the last few moments, trying to sort out the tumultuous upheaval inside her. At the end of her nightmare when she awoke in his embrace, she had wanted the safety and security of his arms to go on and on.

She could not blame Noah for what happened, for she had initiated their lovemaking. She had kissed him first, touched him first, urged him on, prompted him until he had acted on his desire. She had used him, used his desire to get what she had wanted so desperately—freedom from the memory of Darcy Lankanal, to feel cherished and protected and safe from her past, if only for a few stolen moments.

He reached out and touched her cheek where her tears had dried, and he smiled at her for the first time since she had met him. The smile transformed him, lit up his face.

"You are mine now, Olivia. You belong to me." He sounded so certain, so sure. As if she were a treasure he had been searching for his whole life long.

Ashamed of what she had become, of what she had done and was about to do to him, she pressed her hands over her eyes. "Oh, Noah, I'm so sorry."

Beside her, he stiffened. "Sorry?"

She dropped her hands. Looked over at him again. "I never meant for this to happen. I . . . I was confused."

"Confused?"

"Yes, the nightmare . . ."

What could she tell him that would not make her sound like a madwoman? That she had used him to help her forget her past, and her fear, and Darcy? That she had wanted to feel him inside her, hoping to experience a rebirth as well as release? That she wanted to erase the memory of Darcy, and carry only thoughts of Noah with her when she left?

Could she tell him that something inside her hoped that what was so very good and so very honorable in him might take root in her, that his goodness might cancel out the sordid months she had spent in New Orleans?

Now he lay beside her waiting for explanations she could not give without telling him everything. She was about to hurt him, but there was no other way.

"At dawn I want you to take me to the edge of the swamp. I can't stay here any longer."

She buried her face in her hands and as she did, she felt him climb over her and leave the bed. She heard his clothing rustle.

"I understand," he said. There was a new hardness to his tone, one she had not heard him use before. She looked up and saw the fury on his face, but more than that, the hurt and betrayal.

"Noah, you don't understand at all."

He nodded. "Oh, but I do. You didn't mean to make love to a one-eyed half-breed. Now you're sorry." He turned around and tied the waistband of his pants.

"That's not true," she cried. "That's not the way of it at all. I don't think of you that way."

A cold, silent tension filled the air until he turned around again. "Don't worry, Olivia. It was nothing to me either."

She stood up and went to him, trying to grab his sleeve, but he jerked his arm away. "Don't say that, please. I know you wanted me and I wanted *you*, Noah, truly I did, and it was beautiful. But I never meant for this to happen. I never meant for things to go that far."

She clasped her hands together, then pulled them apart, trying to put her feelings into words. "I'm not worthy of a man like you."

He laughed, but there was a hollow, bitter ring to it.

"Really, Noah, you have no idea. You deserve so much better. You deserve someone with a clear conscience, someone with an unblemished soul."

"I don't know what you're talking about."

"Because you don't know me or what I have done. I have to find my family, Noah. I have to find out what happened to them. I have a past, Noah. I have much to settle inside myself, and it wouldn't be fair to drag you into any of this."

"What if you don't find them?"

She took a deep breath. The same question had entered her mind and given her pause often enough. Beyond finding her family, she had no future.

"I honestly don't know what I'll do then. I just know that we can't be together. Things are not that simple, Noah."

"Why not?"

"Because of where I've been and what I've done. If you knew, you would never want me again."

"Tell me."

"I'm too ashamed."

"What are you saying, Olivia?"

She shook her head. "I'm asking you to let me go, Noah. Take me to the edge of the swamp and let me go."

"I can't do that. Not until I know why."

He stared down at her, solid and immovable, his arms folded across his chest. There was no hunger in his eyes now, only anger and betrayal, but most of all confusion.

He had taken her in and shown her only kindness and respect. She had done this to him, tempted him beyond reason, drawn him into her arms, into her body—and used him in a frantic, misguided effort to heal herself. She had succeeded in hurting him, her savior, the one man who had shown her only kindness.

Sick at heart, empty inside, she walked back to the bed and sat down. There was no going back or denying what had just passed between them, not with the scent of their lovemaking still heavy in the air. The sheets were tangled. The intensity of her release still pulsed faintly at her core.

Wrapping her arms around her midriff, Olivia hugged herself and rocked back and forth, cursing Darcy Lankanal for what he had made her. He had taught her too long and too well. She was as dirty as he was now, her blood just as hot, her soul just as tainted.

She shoved her hand through her hair, pushing it back off her face. She sighed. "Sit down, Noah. It's a long story and not a pretty one."

• • •

Olivia lost herself in the telling, becoming caught up in it so much that it was as if she had slipped back in time, over a year, to that very day on the Ohio River.

It was a beautiful, terrible day. The little boys, her half-brothers, had needed her constant attention. They were understandably restless and bored after days of confining travel. Neither the flatboat nor the river fascinated them anymore.

She felt uneasy when a man calling himself Colonel Sullivan had hailed them from the shore. Her father agreed to give him a ride downriver so that he could meet up with some companions. After watching the man closely, Olivia thought him too shifty. There was nothing he had actually done to alarm her; it was just a feeling that she had. He made her skin crawl.

She took her father aside and tried to persuade him not to allow Sullivan aboard, but Payson Bond would not consider leaving a man stranded; he told Olivia so before assuring her that she need not worry. He sent her to mind the boys and keep them from upsetting her stepmother, Susanna.

While she spoke, Noah kept moving, stoked the fire, made a pot of coffee. She waited while he filled two cups and brought her one.

"You father saw nothing wrong with the man?" He stood over her until she took the first sip and then sat down on a stool near the table.

Olivia wiped away a tear as she shook her head. "My father prides himself on trying to live the golden rule. He welcomed the 'colonel' aboard, even though he was shabbily dressed and crude-talking. Sullivan went back among the boxes and crates and made himself comfortable and we pulled back out into the river."

"I know what happened next," Noah said. "He started shouting that the flatboat was leaking and you had to pull into shore."

She was shocked. "How did you know?"

"It's an old trick," he told her, ignoring his coffee. "A man will beg passage and while aboard, drill a hole in the bottom of the flatboat. He times it so that the pilot will have to pull into shore at a place where the rest of the thieves are waiting.''

"We were so naive," she whispered. "Does it happen often?"

"More than most folks know," he assured her. "River pirates prey on the settlers. There are caves and hideouts up and down the rivers."

Olivia wanted this over with, so she began again. "As soon as we landed, four more of the bandits stepped out of the woods and hailed Colonel Sullivan. He drew a gun and demanded we all disembark." She tried to swallow the taste of fear as she relived the memory aloud for the first time.

"My father was able to get to his rifle, but when he tried to hold them all off, the colonel said that he'd never succeed. He told my father that if he handed me over to them, that he would let the rest of the family go."

"Your half-brothers, their mother, your father," Noah clarified.

She nodded. "Yes. Susanna was carrying another child. She was upset, begging my father to listen to them, to give me up. I am certain they would have killed us all. I was surprised when they kept their word and didn't kill the rest of my family anyway." She fell silent, remembering the river, the terrible grief brought on by the separation, the fact that Susanna could not meet her eyes just before the men dragged her away.

Noah's hand tightened on the coffee cup. "You father did not fight?"

"No. He isn't a fighting man."

"The pirates took you to New Orleans." He leaned forward, resting his forearms on his knees.

"They did not touch me. A virgin was worth more." She answered the question hanging between them. "They sold me to a gambler who owns a whorehouse. A man named Darcy Lankanal. He locked me in his suite, kept me for his own personal use for a year."

Noah was watching her so intently that she could not

bear to meet his gaze. Her shame was heavy as she looked down at her hands folded in her lap.

"Finally, I found a way to escape and ran."

"And met up with Stanley Marlborough."

She was surprised he had remembered the name. "Yes." She thought she heard him say, "No wonder."

"What's that?" she asked.

"No wonder you were so frightened of me."

Olivia nodded. "I have not met any honorable men of late."

He walked over to her and took the untouched coffee. She thanked him and waited while he set the cup on the table and came back to her side. She was exhausted, but somehow felt as if some of the burden of the past had lifted. She watched him reach for her and did not shrug away. He brushed away a tear on her cheek, lifted the bedclothes for her, and waited while she climbed back in. Then he took a step back. She could not read his expression; somehow he had wiped all signs of emotion off his face.

"Noah?"

"At dawn I'll take you to the edge of the swamp."

A sleepless night left Noah wrung out, but an hour before dawn he was on his feet, ready to take Olivia away. He paced the porch waiting for the sun's first rays to wash the sky with light. Anger had been his constant companion since her story had ended and he had left her alone—and wonder at what had passed between them, and confusion, but most of all anger. Anger at the man who had made her suffer, anger at himself for being fool enough to give in to his own lust.

He knew now why she had to leave and why he could not ask her to stay. More than anything, she wanted to find her family, and as much as he wished she would turn her back on them and stay, he knew she could not. From the very first he knew that she would never be his to keep, but he did not know the depths of why until she finished her story last night.

Now he not only had to give her up, but he would have

to live with the lingering pain of emotions he never wanted to feel, live knowing what it was to need a woman. Wondering what woman could ever compare to Olivia?

He had sat up all night, staring out at the swamp, trying to understand as he recalled every detail. After her nightmare, Olivia had seemed confused and disoriented. She told him that she had needed him, needed the feeling of peace and security he gave her. She said she had used him in an effort to forget Darcy Lankanal, the man who had imprisoned her in his whorehouse.

"Oh, Noah. I'm so sorry."

He could not get the taste or the scent of her out of his mind. If he lived to be one hundred he would never forget last night or Olivia.

Yes, he had known from the first that she was not his to keep, but when he went to her and took her in his arms, when she kissed him, put her hands on him and urged him on, he had lost all of his resolve. There was no turning back. He had not thought beyond the moment or his need. Somewhere in the back of his mind, in the farthest corner of his heart, he had assumed that after they made love, she would want to stay with him forever.

He had been a naive, simpleminded fool.

With the memory of what they had done haunting him, he knew that if he was forced to spend another night here with her and not have her again, he would surely go insane.

Inside the cabin, she finally stirred. He heard her feet when they hit the floor, knew she was walking to the hearth to warm her bare toes. She had convinced him that he need only take her to the edge of the swamp and point her on her way.

His pack was ready. It lay on the porch near the opening to the steps and his rifle. He found what he was looking for and then walked into the cabin. When she saw him there in the doorway she blushed and looked down at her hands.

"There's some hoecake if you're hungry." He spoke without looking at her and walked over to the table. She did not answer, so he took her lack of response as a refusal. He could not eat a crumb.

He slammed around, started tasks, forgot why he had begun and left them, started others, noticed that his hands were not steady. He walked away from the table. Coffee went unmade, the hoecake uneaten. Even without looking in her direction, he could tell Olivia had not moved a step.

He had taken refuge in the swamp in part because solitude was what he knew, but also because here no one would stare at his scars. Here he would never be reminded of the world he had left behind or of its mysteries. He would never have to face all the things he barely understood: towns and settlements, homes and hearths, obligations and families. After his accident, he never dreamed that one day he would take pleasure in a woman's body. Now that he had, how was he to keep the memories from rushing back again and again?

"Noah?"

Not expecting her to be standing close, he spun around and nearly collided with Olivia. Her deep green eyes were ravaged with shadows. There were dark smudges beneath them. Sleep had eluded her the way it had him.

"*What?*"

She flinched slightly at his harsh tone, so he softened it and repeated, "What?"

He could not stop a surge of anger as he looked into her upturned face. It would be a long time before he could forgive her for what she had done, for what she had given him and then taken away.

"Where is my other dress?"

"Your dress?"

"The dress I had on when I got here. If you will give it back, I'll change and we can leave." She pressed her lips together, worried with her hands, did everything but look directly at him.

"I burned it."

Quickly, her eyes touched his face again. "You did what?"

"It was a rag." Rough and raveled. Not worthy of her flawless skin.

"It was all I had," she whispered.

"You have another now."

"I can't take this one."

"Because it is not good enough?" It was made in the style of his mother's people. She had fashioned it with her own hands.

"Because it is too fine."

"Take it. And the shawl. Or would you go back to your people naked?"

He could see that the question hurt her, even though he had not meant it to. He picked up the bundle he had carried in, thrust it at her.

"What is this?"

He watched her unfold the packet wrapped in a cornmeal sack until its contents were revealed. Inside lay a pair of moccasins made out of one of his finest pieces of tanned leather. He had decorated them the way his mother taught him. Beading was woman's work, he knew that, but the skill helped fill the long, empty hours.

She held the shoes close, tracing the starburst pattern with her fingertip. He wished she would look up again so that he might look into her eyes, see his scarred reflection there and remember why he had to let her go.

"These are beautiful."

"Put them on and then we will leave."

Part of him wanted her to linger over them, to prolong the inevitable, but she went directly to a stool, sat down and slipped one on. He saw it was nearly a perfect fit and turned away so that when she lifted the hem of the dress to put on the other, he would not glimpse her ankles again.

There was nothing to argue, no pretty speech to make that might persuade her to stay. What had happened between them last night was a mistake. She had told him so. Certainly once was not enough to keep them together. He knew that now.

Wordless, Noah walked outside and waited. She joined him shortly and he went first down the steps nailed into the tree trunk. At the base of the giant tree he waited in the pirogue, balancing the shallow craft so that it would not tip over. Morning had broken, bringing the swamp to life.

The fringed hem of the dress swayed around her ankles as she hung on the last step and searched for a foothold with her toes. Finally, tentative and hesitant, she waited for him to help.

"Slowly put one foot in and keep your hands on the step until you are steady," he advised.

Looking wide-eyed and scared, she took a seat in front of him. Noah pushed off and they drifted over the deceptively still surface of the water. Beneath the duckweed, several feet below the surface, a current carried life-sustaining fresh water through the swamp.

Neither of them spoke as he wove the craft between the trees, ever north and east. Where no path seemed to exist, he read the bark on the trees, watched the direction of the breeze on the shimmering surfaces of the leaves. He wished things between them were different, that he could tell her of the things she was seeing, teach her about the swamp, but she was leaving. Why bother?

Olivia remained silent as they floated along, staring off into the distance. Unlike the day he had brought her to the house unconscious, she did not lean against him. Instead she held herself stiffly erect and did not allow herself to touch him at all. For the last time, he took in her hair, the brave set of her shoulders.

Finally they reached the edge of Heron Pond. Where the water met the land, a new settler had cleared a few acres in the fall. The sun-drenched, freshly plowed open space that stood ready for planting was a shock to look upon after months of the close confines of the swamp, where the sky was only visible in bits and pieces.

The open expanse left Noah feeling vulnerable. How many more acres of forest would fall to settlers' axes? This was what his mother had foreseen in her visions, what the voices on the wind had warned of. The whites were coming. The first people, the native people of these lands, would fall like the trees of the forest before the newcomers finished clearing the land.

He pulled the canoe up to the shore, cradled his long rifle, and stepped out. Even though it tore at his soul to have to touch her again, he reached for Olivia's hand.

There was a moment of hesitation when she stared at his fingers and he thought that she might refuse his help, but then she slipped her hand into his and let him pull her to her feet.

At the touch of her flesh upon his, his heart started to pound. When she walked past him, she came so close to him that he had to close his eyes, take a deep breath and try to still his erratic heartbeat. She stood aside waiting while he dragged the canoe up onto dry land and began walking toward the treeline. Olivia hurried up behind him, dogging his heels.

At the edge of the clearing he stopped and pointed across the newly plowed field.

"If you cut directly across there and keep heading toward the rise, you will come to a cabin where you can ask directions to Shawneetown. Perhaps someone there will take you the rest of the way."

She kept her eyes trained in that direction, then nodded, but did not look over at him.

"You should be fine. It's still early. There is no one around for miles," he said.

She nodded again.

"The sun is shining. You will be warm enough." He felt like an idiot. He could not seem to stop talking.

He thought she was going to change her mind and tell him that she would stay when she suddenly took one step and then another and began to head across the field. Two yards away, she stopped and turned around. Her fingers worried a strand of her long, dark hair. He had to strain to hear her.

"Thank you, Noah. I owe you my life. I will never forget you. I only hope that someday you can forgive me for what I did last night. If you ever think of me, I hope it will be kindly."

Before he could say anything, she turned around and was on her way, picking her steps carefully as she negotiated the plowed rows. He took a step in her direction, then another before a cold sweat broke out along his spine and he halted in his tracks. He walked over to the nearest tree and leaned back against it, the rifle in his arms forgotten as he watched her go.

Olivia did not look back, nor did it appear that she was going to. Instead she pressed on with a determined stride as she crossed the settler's field alone. Noah had never met or spoken to the man who had claimed this land, but he had watched him from afar. One day last year when he was checking his traps, he had seen the man's wife bring the farmer his noon meal. There had been children, too, running and frolicking around the trees.

By rights, Noah thought, shouldn't a man with children be a kind man? A caring one? Then he remembered Stanley Marlborough, who had agreed to take Olivia up the Mississippi but then attacked her. A married man could be just as much a scoundrel as one who was not.

Olivia was farther away now, almost halfway across the clearing. Distance appeared to have made her shrink. Small and vulnerable, no longer was she a temptation confined within his four walls. No longer was she the young woman whose very scent aroused him. Out in the open, she was nothing more than a young, defenseless woman in his mother's doeskin dress and silk shawl, crossing a field alone toward an unknown fate.

If he was not there to protect her from harm, anything could happen.

She was headed toward the one place he never thought to be again, the confusing world of white men, where owning land and goods, building more and bigger houses, and amassing possessions seemed to be an all-consuming pastime. Perhaps she knew how to navigate that world, but he did not. Nor did he care to learn.

He pushed away from the tree when he saw her stumble. She righted herself quickly and he let out a sigh of relief.

Olivia knew plenty about the world. That much had been apparent last night, but had she learned to judge a man? Was she still naive enough to be taken in by someone like Stanley Marlborough again? Was she strong enough, cunning enough to avoid men like Darcy Lankanal?

Unable to leave, he continued to watch her and could not believe it when he saw her slowly drift off course. He had told her to head toward the rise in the land. Couldn't she see that it was more to the left than the right? Had she no sense of direction at all? Suddenly it came to him that he had found her in the first place because she had gotten lost. Without him, it looked like she was going to wander off course.

"Damn." Noah pushed off the hickory tree. He hurried over to the pirogue and reached for his pack.

chapter
7

HE WALKED UP BEHIND HER WITHOUT A SOUND AND scared her within an inch of her life.

"*What* are you *doing*?" With her feet planted wide on the plowed hunks of rich soil, Olivia frowned at Noah. Although she had found herself secretly wishing he were with her, she had no idea he had been walking behind her until she caught a glimpse of him out of the corner of her eye.

"You're going the wrong way," he informed her coolly, looking off toward the horizon. "I told you to walk toward that rise." He pointed far left of where she was headed.

Olivia squinted. From the edge of the swamp the gentle sweep of the land had been easy to see. From where she stood now, things looked entirely different.

"Well. Thank you." She turned in the right direction. "Thank you very much."

He did not head back to the swamp as she expected. Instead, he stood there looking decidedly uncomfortable, staring off in the direction of the homesteaders' cabin. In the open sunlight, the thin, jagged red scar down the side of his face was more noticeable, but certainly not offensive. The leather eye patch gave him a rugged, daring appearance. His buckskin coat and pants, his red shirt, the rifle he handled so naturally—all of it only added to his mystique.

She was such a harlot that she had a sudden urge to reach

out to him, to cup his cheek, to raise herself on tiptoe and kiss him. Her breasts ached. Her nipples throbbed, teased by memory alone. She cursed such thoughts, cursed her traitorous body, closed her eyes and forced herself to turn away.

"I'll take you to Shawneetown," he said, surprising her with the unsolicited offer.

To go out among people again, to show his scars—she knew what that would cost him, and she could not let him suffer any more on her account.

"I can get there on my own."

He made a sound, somewhere between a snort and a laugh.

"I will," she assured him.

"You lead the way. I'll just go along to make sure."

There was still no sign of any cabin from where they stood on the open land.

"Noah—"

"Start walking so we don't drag this out any longer than we have to, all right?"

Unwilling to let him see her relief, Olivia stopped arguing and started walking. When he fell in beside her, the safe, secure feeling was back.

Twenty times—she knew because she counted—twenty times she had thought of starting up a conversation to keep the silence from growing more strained than it already was, but then she would stop herself. What could she say that had not already been said?

They reached the cabin, the log walls rough and obviously new, for they were barely weathered. Two dogs jumped up when they caught their scent and came running across the field barking, ears flapping. Olivia moved closer to Noah and realized it had already become instinctive to look to him for protection.

The matching pair of spotted brown-and-white setters proved to be harmless. They began running in circles and wagging their tails, jumping up and down. In the shadow of the overhanging roof of the cabin up ahead, Olivia noticed a woman framed in the open doorway. Wearing a calico dress covered by a threadbare apron, the homesteader awaited their arrival with a rifle aimed in their direction. Her light brown hair was pulled back in a severe style, her features set in a harsh scowl. Before they moved another yard closer, she hollered at them.

"You two get on, now, you hear? Jest keep moving. I don't cotton to no Indians around here and I don't give handouts to the likes of you."

Without giving Noah a chance to comment, Olivia yelled back, "My name is Olivia Bond and I'm looking for my family in Shawneetown. I was wondering if you might have heard of Payson Bond, or know where he might have settled?" She tried to keep her tone light and friendly, but it was hard with a shotgun pointed directly at her.

"Never heard of him." The woman made no move to invite them closer.

Olivia whispered to Noah, "Do you think she is out here alone?"

"More than likely her man is off hunting."

"What should we do?"

"*We?*"

Olivia put one hand up to shade her eyes. The woman gestured with the gun, waving it in indication that they should keep walking. "I said I don't want none of your kind around here. Jest get a move on, now. Go on, get?"

Olivia took a step in the direction of the cabin. "I've a good mind to tell her a thing or two."

Noah reached out, put his hand on her shoulder. "Don't waste your time."

The resignation in his voice nearly broke her heart. If this was the type of reception he received everywhere he went, no wonder he wanted nothing to do with civilization. She looked down at the doeskin gown and moccasins and realized that with her long black hair she might be taken for an Indian, too. She wondered what kind of welcome they would get in Shawneetown.

Circumventing the cabin, they walked across the field, toward a wooded bluff. Soon they were out of sight of the cabin and standing on what appeared to be the head of a trail that started through the woods. After a sudden dark thought, Olivia turned to him. She didn't know what straits she might be reduced to if they could not find her family at all.

Noah shifted the pack slung over his shoulder, his mouth set in a hard line. With his brows slammed together he looked as if he would rather be anywhere else in the world.

"I'm sorry I got you into this, Noah."

His scar had made him so awkward around her that she hated to think of him having to face a town full of strangers or take more abuse from someone like the woman who had just run them off her land.

"The decision was mine," he said without looking at her.

"I just hope we can find my family sooner than later." She wanted to spare him as much as she could, even though she did not want to think about telling him good-bye. When the time came, she only hoped she would be able to watch him walk away without letting him know how much he had come to mean to her already.

Shawneetown

As Noah stood with Olivia on the outskirts of Shawnee-town, he had the urge to turn tail and run. Self-imposed isolation had not prepared him to face a large settlement of whites whose values and customs were so foreign to the way he had been raised.

He had realized as much the first time he had come across the much smaller community where Hunter lived in Kentucky. For days before he spoke to the tall white man who would eventually become his friend, Noah had watched the comings and goings of the settlers dwelling in a few cabins on a bluff above the river. If it had not been for Hunter Boone, who was somewhat of a loner himself, Noah would never have learned even the rudiments of the manners of white society.

He had never considered himself white, even though his

father's blood ran in his veins equal to his mother's. Now he was about to enter another settlement, this one with five times as many dwellings and more people than he could count milling around the ferry and the boat on the water-front. He would rather walk through a swamp full of cottonmouth snakes.

"*This* is Shawneetown?" There was disappointment, not to mention hesitation, in Olivia's voice.

"This is it." Maybe she would change her mind now that she had seen the place and would want to go back to Heron Pond.

"This isn't a town," she mumbled.

"What is it then?" How much bigger was the place she had come from in the East? He couldn't even fathom it.

"A brick hotel and a boat landing don't make this a town."

"Kaskaskia is the only other place in southern Illinois that has this many people," he assured her.

"It's so . . . muddy," she whispered. "So raw and new."

The spring floods were over, but the main thoroughfare was covered with thick mud churned by horses' hooves and wagon wheels. A dark, dirty waterline stained the ground floors of the cabins along the street, cabins that housed stores, shops, and families. When the river left its banks, the inhabitants moved to the upper floors until the water receded.

"What was my father thinking?" she whispered.

Noah looked at the woman beside him. They had been alone on the trail for two days. He had spent the night sitting beside a campfire watching over her while she slept. He had not minded the task in the least, for it meant that he could watch her the way he had longed to during the day, without her knowledge. He could take his fill of looking at her, memorize the way she lay with her hands folded together beneath her cheek, the soft sound of her sigh, the dark bow of her lashes.

While she slept unaware, he could let his gaze wander where his hands longed to, down the tempting line of her throat, over her breasts, along the swell of her hip, down her thigh. He could imagine the feel of her lying beneath him, recall the way her body gave and took him into her, the way they fit together as if they had been created specifically for one another.

But unlike him, she was not inexperienced. She had known another man's touch, another's body. She had grudgingly told him how, despite her abhorrence, she had responded to Lankanal time and again.

She had slept more peacefully last night than any night since he had found her. He had not slept at all. Noah wondered if he had somehow helped banish her nightmares, or if she had merely been too exhausted to dream. He would never know.

"Maybe we should go back," he thought aloud.

Olivia slowly turned and looked into his face, her eyes haunted by shadows and distant memories. "Noah, surely you know I can't. I have to find out what happened to my family."

He knew nothing of the sort. He had no connections, no family ties.

"And if they're not here?"

She searched his face with her gaze, her forehead marred by a frown. "I will cross that bridge when I come to it."

He had offered her a place in his life, but even if she could not find her family, she was still refusing to take it.

Walk away, he told himself. *Leave before you make a complete fool of yourself.*

But he could not leave without knowing that she would be safe, that she would have a place to lay her head without worrying about becoming some man's victim again.

He surveyed the town, willing to let her make the first move, to conduct a search for her family on her own terms. He was nothing more than her guide, her bodyguard. A casual observer. They were among her people now. He had to tread carefully, to follow their rules, their laws. He had to draw on his memory and recall the things Hunter had told him.

He reminded himself that his father's blood ran in his veins, too. That he was half white and he could bear to live among them for as long as it took to see Olivia settled.

He could set aside his own discomfort for her in order to do what he had to do.

They walked into town together; if Olivia was ashamed of the dress he had given her or disturbed by the stares of the townsfolk, she did not let on. Instead, she walked with her head high, her expression set, daring anyone to comment. At the river landing she asked after her family, but everyone there was emigrating and had barely any knowledge of Illinois, let alone the names of all the settlers in the area.

Noah heard the whispers, felt the curious stares of the easterners and foreign-born folk speaking odd-sounding words who were headed farther west, to Kaskaskia. He stared them down, daring them to look him in the face, never the first to turn away.

Olivia suggested they try the hotel and taverns, which looked to be crowded gathering places, but before they reached the first establishment they were approached by a woman carrying a basket of eggs down the street.

"I'm Faye Matheson. I run the Nu Way Dry Goods store." The bespectacled woman in a drab serge gown stood no taller than five feet. Although she was smiling broadly, Noah could not help but notice that Mrs. Matheson was studying Olivia. As yet, she had not given him a second glance.

"My husband, Ern, is the keeper of the peace in Shawneetown. You two just passing through, or do you intend to stay around and put down roots?"

Olivia introduced herself and then got directly to the point. "I'm here searching for my family. I . . . we were separated during the move to Illinois and I lost touch with them. They were supposed to have settled around this area."

Faye shoved her spectacles up the bridge of her nose and shifted the basket on her arm. "Well you're talking to the right person, that's for sure. Ern and I know near to everybody in these parts. If your kin settled anywhere close by, I'll know 'em."

Noah's gut tightened. Olivia went very still, so still that he sensed she was deeply hesitant before she went on.

"My father is Payson Bond and my stepmother is—"

"Susanna." Faye Matheson finished for her.

Olivia reached over and grabbed Noah's hand, holding on as if he were a lifeline. He shifted uncomfortably and looked around to see if anyone on the street had taken any notice besides Mrs. Matheson.

"You know them?" Olivia's eyes widened in disbelief.

Faye nodded, but her smile dimmed. "I do, but not well. They don't get into town, but I sure do know *of* them, and I know they'll be right happy to see you." She was still watching Olivia closely. "Why don't you come on over to my place? You can sit a spell and have a cup of coffee and I'll tell you how to find the place."

Olivia glanced up at him. Noah nodded.

"I'll go down to the ferry crossing and wait for you there," he said.

"*Will* you wait?"

She looked as if she doubted she would ever see him again. They had found her family. He should walk away while there was nothing left between them but a night of memories. Another man could leave her now with a clear conscience, knowing she was safe, that he had taken her as far as he needed.

But he wasn't another man, and he could no more walk away from her yet than he could fly.

"I'll see you in a while." He started to leave.

"Noah, wait." Olivia turned to the peacekeeper's wife. "I would love to sit and chat over a cup of coffee with you, Mrs. Matheson, but I would really like to find my father's homestead before dark."

Noah looked over at the Matheson woman and found her staring intently at him, squinting hard behind her spectacles. He started to turn the scarred side of his face away from her, then caught himself and stopped.

"Do I know you?" She folded her arms, forgetting Olivia entirely as she focused on him.

"You were going to tell her how to find her father," he reminded her.

Faye Matheson shook her head. "It's the darnedest thing. I feel like I ought to know you for some reason. You're not from around here?"

A farmer driving an empty cart drew up beside them. "Mornin', Miz Matheson. How you doin' this mornin'?" He nodded to Olivia and then turned his attention on Noah.

"We really have to be going." Olivia tried to excuse them again. "If you could just tell me the way, ma'am?"

Both the farmer and Faye Matheson were staring at him now. Noah's hand tightened on his rifle. Sweat broke out on his forehead and he had a sudden urge to scratch under his eye patch.

The farmer, with a blank expression not unlike that of his ox, stood by expectantly. Faye Matheson continued to try to place Noah.

"What's your name?" she finally asked.

Noah said absolutely nothing. The farmer smiled.

"His name is Noah." Olivia sounded frustrated. "Noah LeCroix."

"Well, I'll be hog-tied and pickled." The farmer took off his hat and slapped his knee with it and whistled. "Wait 'til the boys down at the tavern hear this. They're gonna have to see it with their own eyes, I'm afraid, or they're never gonna believe I saw Noah LeCroix in the flesh."

"What are you talking about?" Noah was barely able to unclench his jaw and get the words out.

"Why, last I heard, you was *dead*."

For the life of him, Noah could not figure out why this man he had never met from a town he had passed through but once—and that more than five years before—should have heard anything about him, let alone that he was dead.

"I'm standing right here," Noah told him coolly before he turned to Mrs. Matheson. "Lady, we need to be on our way. If you won't tell us where Miss Bond's father lives, then we'll find someone who will."

He felt Olivia's hand touch his sleeve. "Please, Noah."

"Noah LeCroix. Noah LeCroix." Faye Matheson muttered. Far from showing any offense, she shook her head and continued to repeat his name over and over.

"The flatboat pilot," the farmer said, nudging Faye with his elbow. "*The* flatboat pilot. The Prince of the Ohio. The half-breed who made a deal with the devil and guided near on to a thousand flatboats safely down to New Orleans, 'fore the devil took his due and turned the river on him, ripped off half his face and swallowed him up without a belch afterward."

Tall and lanky as a scarecrow, the farmer looked Noah up and down, from the toes of his moccasins to his black felt hat.

Faye declared, "That's it! I knew he reminded me of somebody. I heard the river took off half his face. One of the survivors of the accident claimed he saw your eye float past while he was swimming to shore."

Now Olivia was staring at him too. She stepped closer and said in a hushed whisper, "Oh, Noah, I'm so sorry."

As the farmer chuckled and congratulated himself for spotting Noah first, Faye started to hum a little ditty and tap her foot. Olivia looked appalled and anxious. It was bad enough he stood out because of his mixed blood, but now, somehow, while he had been hiding in the swamp, he had become a legend. The Prince of the Ohio.

Then right there in the middle of the muddied thoroughfare, Faye Matheson started humming louder and with more enthusiasm until the farmer joined in and they started singing.

> "*Devil had the river,*
> *A-flowin' fast and wild,*
> *Until he saw the half-breed,*
> *Said, 'I have to have that child.'*
> *Walked up to make a bargain,*
> *As the devil often do,*
> *Tapped the half-breed on the shoulder*
> *Said, 'I gotta talk to you.'*

> *"Oh, Noah LeCroix, Noah LeCroix,*
> *Prince of the Ohio.*
> *Oh, Noah LeCroix, Noah LeCroix,*
> *Prince of the Ohio!"*

Noah turned to Olivia. "Make them *stop*."

"Let's go. Surely someone else knows where my father lives." She tugged on his hand.

A crowd was gathering. Faye and the farmer sang on.

> *"Oh, I'll give you more than fame*
> *For your trouble if you dare.*
> *Everyone will speak your name,*
> *And talk about your bravery.*
> *All you have to do is give me,*
> *The right to claim your soul. . . ."*

The farmer suddenly noticed their chagrin and stopped in mid-verse. Over Faye's off-key warbling, he said to Olivia, "Did you say you're looking for the Bonds?"

Two steps away, trying to outrun his humiliating notoriety, Noah stopped in his tracks and swung around.

"We are." He tried to intimidate the farmer with a one-eyed stare.

"I'd be mightily honored if you would let me lead the way. Payson Bond's land butts up to mine. I'm Bob Carver."

"Which way?" Noah demanded to know over a rousing chorus of *"Oh, Noah LeCroix, Noah LeCroix."*

The farmer pointed northeast. "Right through there, past the land office and the Cake and Beef store."

Noah turned to Olivia. "You ride along with him on the oxcart. I'll go on ahead and wait for you at the edge of the woods."

Olivia's heart went out to him as she watched Noah pull his hat low on his brow and stare at the ground as he jogged a few yards down the muddy road. He quickly disappeared

between two log buildings, one sporting a fancy shingle
that read CAKES N BEEF.

When she turned around again, Faye had finally stopped
singing and was hurriedly explaining to three newcomers
what the fuss was all about.

". . . so I stood here thinking to myself that I knew him
from somewheres, and then Bob come along and recognized the name and sure enough, it was Noah LeCroix."

"*The* Noah LeCroix?" A bearded gent in a tall crowned
hat and a cutaway coat leaned into the center of the crowd
toward Faye. "*Oh, I'll give you more than fame . . .*" he
sang. "*That* Noah LeCroix?"

"One and the same. Half-breed with a missing eye."
Bob nodded. "How many of *them* you think are running
around here?"

"Where's he been all these years?" A squat, fat hunter
in the back of the crowd shouted. "Has he made another
deal with the devil?"

A hush fell over the crowd. They all looked at Olivia.
Part of her was tempted to fabricate a whopping tale to
satisfy their curiosity, but she quickly decided that would
only add fuel to the fire. She envisioned Noah's beautiful
treehouse sanctuary and his peaceful life before she had
turned it upside down.

"He's been away."

It was all they would ever hear from her. Her patience
at an end, she drew the farmer aside. "If you don't mind,
sir, I'd like to get to my father's homestead before dark."
More than that, she wanted to leave Shawneetown behind
and join Noah at the edge of the woods.

The center of attention, Bob Carver immediately straightened his shoulders and offered her his arm. "Right this
way, miss. Any friend of Noah LeCroix is a friend of
mine." He actually shouted so those in the back row could
hear.

As he helped her up onto the narrow seat of the oxcart,
Olivia tried to tell herself that she was anxious because she
could not wait to be reunited with her family. But her heart

kept reminding her that what she really wanted was to re-
assure herself that Noah had not disappeared and left her
without a good-bye.

It was hard to ignore her heart.

chapter
8

Bond Homestead

Payson had Little Pay and Freddie to live for, which should have been enough for any man. But on days like this, when a dense gray mood of lethargy and heavy sorrow settled over him, he seriously thought that his boys might have been better off raised by their Grandfather Morrison in Virginia.

He wrapped a rag around his hand and pulled a Dutch oven out of the fire. Turnip-and-squirrel pie was a habit he wouldn't mind breaking, but turnips and some corn flour were all they had left until he could bring down something other than the squirrels the boys had practically tamed.

"That smell good to you, Susanna?" He lifted the lid of the pot and waved his hand over the steaming contents, hoping to tempt his wife.

The rocker never even slowed, nor did the off-key tune she hummed almost continually now. The steady creak of the wooden rocker was enough to drive him as crazy as she appeared to be.

"Have you seen the boys?" He had vowed weeks ago that he would not give up talking to her. He would not be reduced to silence, driven to hide behind it the way she did. Not as long as the boys still depended on him. Not until he had given up altogether.

"It sure looks good," he lied. It looked downright watery, the crust lumpy. The piddling bit of squirrel meat was hardly enough for a single man, let alone a family of four.

"You know where the boys are?" Payson crossed the room and put his hand on Susanna's shoulder. He had not touched her any more intimately in almost a year. She did not even look up.

"Susanna?" He gave her a gentle shake. "Where are the boys?"

The humming stopped, but she continued to pump the rocker back and forth.

"Outside, I suppose. Playing outside someplace," she barely whispered.

He swallowed the anger and frustration that he seldom gave in to and wondered if she would notice if he walked out and never came back. Would she eventually get up? Fix some food for the boys and herself?

If he thought his leaving would force her back to life, he would go this very minute. But what father could take that chance? He could not afford to be wrong. Susanna had locked herself deep into the dungeon of suffering she had built for herself. The boys did not deserve to lose both of them.

"I'm going out to look for them."

He knew that she would eventually shuffle over to the table and sit waiting for him to return. Mealtimes were the few times of day she would get out of the rocking chair, and that was only because he had demanded she sit with the boys while they ate.

"We're still a family," he had insisted not long ago. The words had sounded hollow and false the day he threatened and cajoled her into sitting down with the boys for meals. He had never raised his voice to her before, nor had he again. After that, she went to the table for meals, but she rarely ate more than a few bites.

The boys had to be found while the pie cooled. Payson opened the door, squinting against the setting sun. Across the half-plowed field, an oxcart bumped and rumbled over the furrowed ground. Beside it, lanky as a beanpole, walked

Bob Carver, his nearest neighbor. The man had been more than willing to befriend Payson when they first settled. He and his family had even brought some of the other Shawneetown folk to help the newcomers clear out the old cabin and shed, but after the baby was stillborn and Susanna began to curl up inside herself, the Carvers and the rest of them had stopped coming by.

The callers were still too far away for him to recognize the tall, broad-shouldered man in buckskins walking beside Carver or the woman seated on the oxcart. He did not really care who they were, for he would have welcomed the devil if he walked up to the door offering a momentary diversion.

''Bob Carver's crossing the field with an oxcart, Susanna.'' He looked over his shoulder. ''Hear that, honey? Someone's coming to call.''

Virginia came to mind, and with it the days when they had lived with her father, existing on the man's charity. At the plantation, whenever callers were seen riding up the long drive, house slaves would begin fixing refreshments. Susanna and Olivia's laughter would echo up the stairwell as they speculated on who might be calling.

Payson shook his head, refusing to let the past spoil the present.

He looked outside again, where a blazing sunset fired the sky above the treeline. He raised his hand in salute, although all he could make out against the bloodred sky were the dark silhouettes of the two men walking beside the oxcart, and the woman riding high on the swaying seat. Bob Carver waved back. Payson calculated just how far the turnip-and-squirrel pie might stretch as he stepped over the threshold and waited to welcome the visitors.

Noah heard Olivia's quick intake of breath, saw her scoot to the edge of the seat and grip the wood until her knuckles whitened. She leaned forward, straining to get a better look at the man who had suddenly appeared in the open doorway of the small cabin up ahead of them. Her face went pale, her eyes unusually bright. She nearly flew over the front of the cart when the right wheel hit a particularly deep rut and the vehicle bounced a mile high. Noah reached up to steady her, drew her attention and earned himself a nervous smile.

"That's my father." Her voice was strained, unsteady.

Although he could not imagine any father turning away a daughter who had suffered so much, and none of it her fault, he knew she would be hesitant to tell her family about Lankanal and the whorehouse. He did not know Payson Bond, and therefore did not know what the man might do.

He was already in too deep. He was not about to walk away until he knew that she would fare well here.

The man in the doorway waved. His brown hair was shot through with blond highlights. As they drew closer, Noah could see that Payson Bond was not a very big man, slight of build, wiry. He wore sturdy, coarse wool trousers and a white cambric shirt. He still had a full head of hair, but his shoulders were already beginning to stoop.

"Please, stop the cart. Let me down, Mr. Carver," Olivia begged.

Carver stopped the huge ox and stood by its head while Noah helped Olivia down. Concentrating on her father, she did not notice when Noah held her too close for a breath too long. She clung to his sleeve while she gathered courage to go the rest of the way alone. She was trembling.

"Do you want me to go with you?" He spoke softly, for her ears alone. Bob Carver was watching them closely, alternately shifting his view from them to the cabin and back again.

Olivia shook her head no. "I have to do this by myself," she told him, searching his face with her gaze as if looking for strength. He could not give her that, only encouragement.

"He is your father, Olivia."

She let go of his arm and took another step toward her future and all the doubt that plagued her.

Olivia tried to swallow around the lump in her throat. As she neared the house, she could see her father more clearly but as yet, he had not recognized her. He was thin, much thinner than she recalled. Hatless, his receding hairline etched pale coves on his forehead. His eyes were stark blue, and the planes and angles of his face stood out in sharp relief. Only thirty-eight years old, he looked much older.

For a while after her mother died there had been only the two of them. Versed in scholarly pursuits, he had taken work where he could get it, traveling Virginia, hiring on to tutor rich planters' children.

Seeing him so slight and looking so vulnerable all alone in the doorway of the little cabin made her heart ache for him. Where were Susanna and the boys? Where was the family he had sacrificed her in order to save? She hoped to God he had not lost them, too. Not now.

All the resentment she had harbored during her long months of captivity shifted, not as far as forgiveness, but away from resentment. He still was and always would be her father.

She knew the moment he recognized her, for his whole demeanor changed. He straightened, gave a cry she could not hear, then started running across the field, arms open wide as if he wanted to embrace not only her, but the woods and trees and the fiery sunset sky.

Tears were streaming down the hollows of his cheeks by the time he reached her. They fell into each other's arms, rocking side to side without a word, for there were no words. There was nothing that anyone had ever said before that would express all they needed to say.

He held her close, his shoulders heaving with silent, soul-wrenching sobs, and when he finally pulled back he did not let go. Payson ran his hands over her face, tracing it like a blind man, his fingers shaking so hard she had to close her eyes.

"Are you all right?" The words were strained, furtive, demanding only because he needed to know. "Are you all right?"

No, Daddy. I will never be the same.

I will never be that young or carefree or innocent again.

I am nineteen now and I am old inside.

My soul is tarnished and I am afraid to love.

Olivia hugged him close, patting his back as she would

have one of the little boys. All the things she might have said, all the things she had thought of saying to him in the middle of those long and terribly desperate nights in New Orleans, all of those things she could not say now. Not with his tears of joy still wet upon his cheeks.

"Yes, Daddy," Olivia lied. "I'm all right."

"Oh, Livvie, we thought you were dead."

I was, Daddy.

"I'm here now, Daddy."

"Oh, God, Olivia. Why are you dressed that way? Where have you been? I've been so worried." He tried to read her face the way he read his books.

Olivia whispered, "Please, don't ask me that now, Daddy. I'll tell you someday."

He went very still. Finally he said, "I'm just so happy to have you home."

"Where are the boys? Where is Susanna?"

"The boys are fine. They're off playing someplace." He looked down at the ground he had tilled. "Susanna . . . Susanna's been sick."

"Dearest Lord in heaven!"

Payson's strangled cry had slowly sifted through the haze, intruding into Susanna's carefully woven web of isolation and retreat. Something in his voice had sent a chill down her spine, one as cold and sharp as a knife, so much so that she winced. She looked up from where her hands lay idle in her lap. The door was open and a shaft of burnt-umber light streamed into the room, forcing her to squint against the unaccustomed brightness.

There was no sign of Payson, only the fading sound of his cry lingering on the still, close air inside the cabin.

Susanna pushed herself up out of the rocker. Every bone creaked, every muscle screamed. She was stiff and sore from sitting—how long had it been? She could not fathom time anymore, nor did she care to try. Her gait was no more than a slow, uneven shuffle as she hobbled toward the open door, drawn not by the light, but by the cry torn from her husband's throat.

She flung her arm over her eyes to shield them from the intense light before she stood in the open door and took the brunt of the sun's last rays. As she finally dared look out across the field, what was left of the sun ducked below the horizon and Susanna could see clearly. She dropped her arm away from her eyes, using her hand to brace herself in the doorway.

While she was in the safe haven of her rocking chair, time had moved on and left her behind. Where trees had once surrounded the field, Payson had cleared more land. Row upon uneven row of tilled soil fanned out around the cabin, but then abruptly halted. A plow missing a handle stood off to the side of the tilled soil, in silent explanation of why the furrowed rows stopped.

She watched Payson run across the field with his arms open wide, staggering, righting himself, running again straight toward the slight, fragile figure of a young woman in an Indian gown of doeskin standing a few yards in front of an oxcart and two men.

A cry was building inside Susanna, too, one that she was powerless to stop, and yet when it bubbled up into her throat and her mouth opened to let it out, not a sound issued forth. The searing pain of that suffocated scream brought her to her knees.

She knelt in the dirt outside the cabin while the past slammed into the present, and watched Payson race across his land, reach for the ebony-haired girl and pull her into his arms. She watched them rock back and forth in each other's embrace. Then he ran his hands over her face, making certain it was truly his girl come back to him again, back from whatever horrors might have befallen her, back from the grave.

The scream inside Susanna finally found its way out and the word that the sound wrapped itself around was *"Olivia!"*

Noah sat in the evening glow of twilight resting on a stump outside the cabin, engaged in a silent staring contest with two little boys. They had come tearing around the corner of the log house jabbering and shoving at one another until they saw him sitting there and stopped dead in their tracks. Their eyes popped and they froze to the spot.

Finally, the taller boy glanced at the closed cabin door. He screwed up enough courage to speak.

"You an injun or something?"

Noah nodded. "Partly."

"What happened to your eye?" The little one took a step toward Noah, but his older brother put his hand on the boy's shirt and yanked him back.

"Accident," Noah said.

He hadn't been around many children, just the ones who happened to be on board flatboats he was hired to pilot downriver. Hunter Boone had a passel of nieces and nephews down in Sandy Shoals and Noah had taken meals with them sometimes. One Christmas he had even carved some wooden animals for them to play with, but on the whole, children were a different breed of animal he knew nothing about.

The older one looked as if he had thought things through. He straightened his shoulders and puffed out his narrow chest. He scrutinized Noah carefully. He seemed particularly attracted to the skinning knife.

"You gonna scalp our ma and pa with that?"

Noah took his time wiping his hand over his mouth to hide a smile. "No."

"Well, I heard a thcream," the shorter one said, eyeing him suspiciously.

"What's a thcream?" Noah frowned. He thought he knew most of the English words there were to know, but *thcream* was a new one.

"Freddie talks funny," the older boy informed him. "He said, he heard a *scream*."

"That was your ma," Noah obliged.

"Did you hurt her or thomthing?" The little one, Freddie, was on the verge of tears, which made Noah extremely nervous.

"No. I guess she was excited."

"Why?"

Noah sighed. "Listen, somebody else ought to be along to tell you why. Sit down. Don't ask me anything else."

"You talk funny." It was the little one again.

"You do, too." Noah nodded. *There.*

"It's getting dark. We're supposed to be eatin' supper." The older boy began to pick at a scab on his elbow.

"I wouldn't do that, if I were you," Noah warned.

"It's all right. I bleed all the time."

"What's your name?" The stump was biting into Noah's butt. He shifted around.

"Little Pay. It's really Payson Bond Junior, but nobody ever calls me that because of my pa's name is Payson, too, so they call me Little Pay." He tipped his head toward his brother. "This here minnow is Freddie."

Freddie saluted Noah, then wiped his nose on the back of his hand. "Pa thaid we were having thquirrel pie for thupper. You can eat my turnipth," he offered.

"Eat them yourself," Noah said. Both boys looked as if they had not had a good meal in years. Their pants were too short, showing their bony little ankles and dirty feet.

Just then the door opened and Olivia stepped out into the waning light. Little Pay called her name and ran directly over to her. Freddie hung back until she went down on her knees to hug his brother, then he crept forward and stepped into the same hug.

"You came back, Livvie." Little Pay clung to her neck and kissed her cheek. "I thought you were never coming home again after those men took you away. Did you sail down the river to a pirate ship?"

"No, nothing like that."

Noah watched her fight back tears as she hugged the dirty little ruffians, her half-brothers.

Little Pay's tone was accusatory. "Where were you, Livvie? Why did you stay away so long? Why didn't you find us before now?"

"Where did you get that injun dreth, Livvie? Did you join the red thkinned thavageth?" Freddie yelled.

Noah stood up to put a stop to the questions that were

obviously disturbing Olivia. He walked over to the trio and stood over them.

"Now, let go of her. I need to talk to her." Noah had no idea his words would produce such immediate action. Both of the boys jumped toward their sister and flanked her.

Olivia got to her feet and dusted off the front of the doeskin gown.

"Thank you," she whispered with a smile that made his heart stumble.

"Your father's wife, is she all right?"

Olivia looked down at the boys. "Why don't you two get along and wash up for supper." They left somewhat reluctantly, but after she promised she would join them in a minute or two, they went inside. She waited until the door closed behind them before she started to walk away from the cabin. Noah fell into step behind her.

"Oh, Noah, I can't believe the straits my father is in. Susanna lost the child she was carrying shortly after they settled in here and she hasn't been the same since. Daddy said she sits all day, mourning a little girl baby that died at birth."

Noah scanned the edge of the woods that bordered the field. Darkness had deepened there. Long black shadows cloaked the tall hickory and maple trees. Lost in thought, Olivia had headed off in that direction. He took her arm and turned her back toward the cabin without her even noticing the change in direction. She walked on, talking out her feelings, more to herself than him.

"The cabin is a mess. I don't think they have had a decent meal in days, maybe weeks. My father never was good at hunting and now that he has the land almost cleared, he has no time to try, if he wants to get the corn in. Susanna does nothing, so he has been forced to take care of the boys, the cooking, the fields. Their clothes and bedding are filthy. He said they had a Scottish girl that worked for room and board, but she ran off and they haven't seen her since."

Noah tried to fathom a man who could not hunt. It was

a man's duty, one that ensured survival, one every man should know, but whites were different. Some of them hunted while some refined other skills.

"What did your father do before he came here?"

"He was a teacher."

"But not of hunting."

She laughed and shook her head. "No. Not of hunting. He taught poetry and literature. Other men hired him to teach their children how to read books, to write, to study."

Noah knew of books, but he could not read.

"A man can't eat books, nor can he feed them to his children."

She stopped pacing and looked over at him. The light was almost gone. "But a man can learn about hunting by reading a book."

He thought of the lethal traps his father had taught him to use, the look of the dead animals caught in them. The blood and the skinning, the curing of hides, the butchering of the meat. His mother had taught him to make and use a bow and arrows. His father had given him his long rifle. No book could ever prepare a man for the bloody tasks he had learned from his parents, just as no words could prepare a man for the way a woman's warm breath felt on his skin, or the way it felt to slide inside a woman's body.

He stopped walking. "Reading about something is not the same as doing it, is it?"

She shook her head. "No. You're right. It isn't."

Olivia made no move to go back inside the cabin, although it was dark now and the only light they had to see by was the glow from the lamp inside. The little boys' voices filtered out through the window. They were asking their father about Olivia, where would she sleep, if she was home to stay.

Noah knew of no reason to linger save one—he was loath to leave her. He had brought her home again. She was with her family. But was she safe? Could Payson Bond put enough food on the table for another mouth? The man could not even feed or clothe the others very well. Could he protect Olivia if he had to? He had already failed once.

A shaft of light cut across the ground at their feet as the door opened and Payson stepped outside. He walked over to Noah and held out his hand. Noah shook it.

"Mr. LeCroix, I would like to thank you for seeing my daughter home safely. She told me that you helped her make the journey from New Orleans."

He glanced over at Olivia. She shook her head, the gesture barely noticeable. She still had not told her father about where she had spent the past year. Noah wondered if this man of books had ever read anything that would shock him as much as what Olivia was keeping from him.

Noah nodded in understanding and to Payson he merely said, "My pleasure."

"You'll have some supper with us." Payson was watching them both closely. "Stay the night."

Turnip-and-thquirrel pie. Noah started to refuse until Olivia reached for his hand.

"Please stay, Noah," Olivia begged. There was such quiet desperation in her voice that he reconsidered.

Turnip-and-thquirrel pie.

He thought of the dirty, skinny little boys. Probably no more than a spoonful of pie for each. Susanna Bond was sick in heart and mind. Why would *any* man want to stay here, even for dinner?

Olivia's hand was warm in his. She was standing close beside him, this woman who did not want his love to keep, but could not seem to send him away.

Noah sighed.

Turnip-and-thquirrel pie.

And Olivia.

"I'll stay."

chapter
9

OLIVIA KNELT BESIDE THE BED WHERE SUSANNA LAY UN-conscious. She reached out and touched the young woman's forehead, smoothed back Susanna's golden hair. If she had encountered her stepmother in town earlier, she would not have recognized her. Susanna's usually bright cheeks were sallow, her mouth pinched. The once-shining, light brown curls that Olivia had so admired were lank and matted, stuck to her head.

"Oh, Susanna," Olivia whispered, wondering what could have laid the vibrant woman so low. She reached out for Susanna's hand and enfolded it in her own. When Payson walked up beside her, Olivia turned to look over her shoulder at him.

"Daddy, what happened to her? How long has she been like this?"

Her father seemed to curl in on himself. He rubbed his hand over his face and stared at nothing. His helplessness frightened Olivia, shook her to the core. All throughout her captivity, she had imagined them whole and healthy and happy. The thought that her suffering had ensured their survival had given her a reason not to give up. No matter how much her father's decision had shocked and hurt her, she had hung on to hope by making plans to escape and return to them.

Her father stepped closer. "She was never the same after

the robbery and kidnapping. She begged me to turn back then and move us all home to her father's plantation again, but I refused. I told her that if you somehow managed to escape those men, you would come here looking for us. She thought you were dead. I refused to believe it, but as time went on, Livvie, I began to think that we would never see you again. Then the baby came, a little girl. Born dead. After that, Susanna might as well have been dead, too. She was too broken up inside to go on.''

He looked into Olivia's eyes and quoted one of his favorite passages from Milton's *Samson Agonistes.*

''The Sun to me is dark / And silent as the Moon / When she deserts the night / Hid in her vacant interlunar cave. / . . . To live a life half dead, a living death . . .''

''Oh, Daddy.'' He still took refuge in the poets. She did not know what to tell him.

Only twenty-four now, Susanna had been eighteen when Payson married her. To Olivia, she had always been more like a sister or best friend than a stepmother. Seeing her now made Olivia feel guilty for each and every time she had hated her for begging Payson to give her to the pirates.

As she clung to Susanna's hand, she asked, ''What can we do for her, Daddy?'' She heard his soft sigh.

''I'm hoping now that you've come back, maybe she'll brighten up.''

Olivia leaned forward and whispered softly. ''Susanna, please wake up.'' She did not expect a response and was surprised when Susanna's eyelids slowly fluttered open and she looked around, disoriented as she focused on Olivia's face.

''Livvie? Is that really you?'' Her voice sounded thick and unused.

Olivia's eyes smarted. ''It's me,'' she whispered, knowing she was not the Olivia they had lost, but she was here all the same.

''Am I dreaming? You aren't dead?''

''No,'' Olivia shook her head. ''You are not dreaming. I'm not dead. I'm really and truly here, Susanna.''

"We kept all your things, Livvie. Your trunk is up in the loft."

"Thank you," she whispered.

"You don't have to stay here." Susanna spoke so softly that Olivia had to lean closer to hear.

"What do you mean, Susanna?"

"I won't blame you . . . if you don't want to stay around me. But I don't think . . . that I'll be here much longer."

"What are you saying, Susanna?" Olivia cupped her face, felt for fever. Susanna's face was not overly warm, but her skin had the pallor of a tallow candle.

"I'm so tired. I just want to sleep forever. Payson and the boys . . . they need you, Livvie. They need someone to look after them."

"I'm here now. I'll stay and get you on your feet in no time. You'll see."

Olivia looked up at her father and found him defeated, his hands hanging loose at his sides. She could not ever recall seeing him so lost, not even when her own mother had died. Nor had she expected to find him in such dire straits. The boys were filthy, their clothes torn. The old cabin was not only poorly made compared to Noah's, but it was dirty as a sty. Obviously her father was not only out of money, but out of dreams.

There was no one else who knew them as she did, no one else who could help.

"I'm home. I'll help you, Daddy. I'll take care of Susanna and the boys. Things will be better soon. For all of us."

Susanna sighed and closed her eyes. Olivia took her hand and tucked it beneath the covers. Then she got to her feet.

Noah and the two boys were still seated at the table, which was now littered with dirty dishes and an empty black Dutch oven. She hurried to Noah's rescue. He looked as if he had been alone long enough with Little Pay and Freddie, especially since they kept asking him all manner of questions.

Her father walked over to the table, straddled the bench and sat down. Beside Noah, he looked dwarfed and pale.

When Olivia reached them, Noah looked up at her and smiled. Despite her resolve, she felt herself quicken as his dark gaze roamed over her, touching her body as surely as his hands. Her thoughts began to stumble down a path so fraught with sensual memories that she quickly looked away and forced herself to concentrate on the boys.

Freddie was acting the clown by tapping on his head with a wooden spoon. She walked up behind Little Pay and ruffled his hair.

"You need a good bath, young man. You and Freddie both look like a couple of mud hens. Tomorrow morning we'll get out a washtub and work on every inch of you."

"You gotta watch out for my elbow." Little Pay's expression sobered. He rolled up the too-short sleeve of his shirt and almost proudly displayed an arm covered with bruises, scabs, and scars. His elbow hosted the freshest of the wounds.

Olivia grabbed Little Pay, gently turned him toward the light, and inspected both arms. "What in the world happened to you?" She tenderly touched each wound. "Daddy, did you see his arms?"

"You ought to thee hith kneeth," Freddie volunteered.

"He's accident prone," Payson told her.

"Since when?" Olivia sat down heavily, glanced over at Noah, and caught him frowning at Little Pay.

"Oh, I guess since we first got here. Or maybe it was after the baby. I can't recall exactly when he started having so many falls and bumps."

Despite the dirt all over him, Olivia pulled Little Pay into the circle of her arms. Freddie demanded her attention too, and climbed up beside her on the bench, where he threw his arms around her neck.

"Time you two went to bed," she laughed. "Before you squeeze me to death."

"Will you sleep in the loft with us, Livvie?"

Her decision was easy. There was no place else for her to bed down.

"Yes. But only if you go up quietly without waking your mother. I'll be up after I wash the supper things."

Reluctantly, the boys let her go. Freddie crawled under the table and popped up on the other side next to Noah.

"You want to thleep in the loft with uth?"

Noah did not answer the boy. Instead, he stared directly into her eyes until Olivia had to look away.

"No."

"But you're going to thtay here. Where will you thleep?"

"Outside."

Freddie stood on the bench, where he was shoulder-to-shoulder with Noah. "Then I'll thleep with you outthide."

"Me, too!" Little Pay hollered. "I'll get a blanket."

Olivia grabbed the waistband of his pants as he started to scoot off the bench. "Hold on, Little Pay. You and Freddie are sleeping in the loft with me. Noah doesn't want company, do you, Noah?"

Too late she realized her mistake. Noah smiled a lazy, slow smile.

"Get to bed, boys," Payson sounded tired. "You can talk to Mr. LeCroix tomorrow."

With much grumbling and shoving, the two little boys left the table and climbed the ladder to the loft. When they did not even glance over at Susanna, who was in bed asleep, Olivia could not help but think of the many times she had envied her stepmother being the one they begged to tuck them in and sing them to sleep. They were good boys. They still loved their mother, but Susanna was suffering and lost to them.

As she left the men to finish their coffee, Olivia stood up and began to gather the things off the table. Something had gone terribly wrong with her family in her absence and she meant to find out what and why. Besides, worrying about them would help take her mind off Noah.

Payson took a sip of coffee and then leaned forward on his elbows. He watched the striking half-breed's gaze surreptitiously follow Olivia's every move. Noah LeCroix was not the kind of man he would have ever imagined for his daughter—but he was the man who had brought her home to them, a gift beyond measure.

"I owe you more than my thanks for bringing Olivia home, Mr. LeCroix. I wish I could reward you in some way."

Noah shook his head to decline the gratitude, just as Payson suspected he would. The big man of few words seemed to be an honest sort, and the admiration on his face whenever he looked at Olivia told Payson all he wanted to know. Whatever had passed between his daughter and this man had not stemmed from malice of any kind. Noah LeCroix, whether he knew it himself or not, was head over heels in love with Olivia.

As for his daughter, Payson could not fathom her thoughts the way he did before she was taken from them. Although Livvie seemed the same, so loving and giving, already willing to help with Susanna and the boys, there was a strained nervousness about her, coupled with a sad detachment. Her eyes revealed a deep torment that he wished he could deny. A girl had been taken from him. A woman had returned. He decided to take the coward's way out, refusing to force her to tell him what she had been through in the past year. She could not tell him yet, and he could not bring himself to hear. Not with his own life in such a shambles, his wife all but lost to him, his fields still lying fallow.

His heart and mind cried out, *No more. Not yet.*

It was blessing enough to know that she was home safe and sound. Noah LeCroix was the man responsible for bringing her back and because of that, the man was more than welcome at his table.

"You plan on staying in the area long, Mr. LeCroix?"

Payson could not help but notice his guest's discomfort. LeCroix seemed to concentrate on keeping the scarred side of his face turned away from everyone.

"No." Noah shifted on the bench. He picked up his empty coffee cup, looked inside, set it down.

Payson watched Olivia carry away another pile of dirty dishes. LeCroix had not let the girl out of his line of vision since he had entered the cabin with her. His Livvie had always been a good girl. The good Lord had seen fit to give her back. Her help was sorely needed here.

From the way LeCroix was watching Olivia, he didn't appear in any hurry to leave, which spurred Payson to ask, "You do much hunting, LeCroix?"

Noah finally looked away from Olivia and at Payson. "That's about all I do."

"I'm not much of a hunter, I'm afraid."

"Olivia said that you are a teacher. A man of books." Noah glanced over at the collection of volumes on the shelves that lined the front wall.

"That's right. Unfortunately, what I have discovered, Mr. LeCroix, is that there is not much call for a man of letters on the Illinois frontier."

"I don't expect so." Noah's dark eyes flashed Olivia's way and then back to Payson.

"The day I arrived, a man in town told me that he was of the opinion if a person could speak and be understood, then what was the use of learning grammar. He went on to remind me that with most goods being bartered, what farmer needs to know arithmetic?" He shook his head and smiled. "That's not to say a teacher won't be needed in the not-too-distant future, but right now people are concentrating on settling in, hunting and clearing the land for farming, and putting up cabins. I know firsthand that they don't have much time to worry about what they call 'book larnin',' for themselves or their children. Do you read and write, Mr. LeCroix?"

"Just my name." The man was not the least uncomfortable or embarrassed with his admission.

Payson's stomach churned. He had never been one to beg, but life had brought him to the lowest point he had ever known. Now, right here at his very table, sat a man who could, if he was willing, help see him through the spring. The boys', Susanna's, and now Olivia's very lives might depend on LeCroix's willingness to help.

Payson set aside his empty coffee mug and leaned across the table toward Noah. He glanced over to where Susanna lay motionless in bed. Up in the loft, Olivia was whispering softly to the boys, tucking them in. Payson lowered his voice.

"Mr. LeCroix, I already owe you far more than I can ever repay for bringing my girl home." He looked down at his hands, so cracked and raw. Hands that should be writing poems, putting thoughts down on paper, penning his observations of the new land and people of Illinois for eastern periodicals. "You'll never know how hard it is to ask any more of you, a stranger, but I might not have another chance. Right now, you're just about the only hope I've got of keeping this family together."

The big man across the table watched him closely with a shuttered expression that gave nothing away.

Payson swallowed. There was nothing for him to do but lay his cards on the table. "I was wondering if you could see your way clear to stay on for a while, lend a hand by doing some hunting for my family. At least until I can get the corn in and a vegetable garden going. In exchange, I could teach you to read."

Noah stared at Olivia's father, a man not yet forty years old, but already worn and beaten down by life. He did not know Payson Bond well enough to know what the man was feeling, but he knew himself and what it would cost him to admit defeat, to have to beg for help. Bond was in over his head and sinking fast. For whatever reasons, he had dragged his family miles away from their home and settled here without the slightest inclination of what was in store.

Bond had already lost Olivia once. Now the man had all but admitted he could not provide for her or the rest of his family.

Noah thought about the snare in front of him. It was well baited with the one thing that he could not resist right now—Olivia.

Bond was leaning forward, focusing on him directly as if trying to read Noah's thoughts. "Well, Mr. LeCroix?"

"I am no hero." Noah almost winced, thinking of his

reception today in town. Olivia chose that moment to climb down from the loft and catch his eye. The material of the doeskin gown molded over her hips. As her feet moved down the rungs of the ladder, the fringe swayed, rewarding him with a glimpse of her shapely calves. He felt himself quicken and turned his attention back to Payson Bond, which was a mistake. Olivia's father was watching him so closely that he almost looked down in shame, afraid the man knew what he had been thinking.

"I don't need book-reading lessons. I can read trails, animal signs, rivers." He didn't see the need to know how to recognize more letters than the ones in his name. He had gotten along his whole life without knowing how to read, and he figured that with one eye gone he'd have a harder time learning than before.

Olivia walked over to the table. She stood at her father's shoulder, watching Noah closely. He had the urge to put all of this behind them, to grab her and run out the door, carry her back to Heron Pond and hold the world at bay. She was his now. She did not belong here with this weak, pale man. She did not deserve to work like a slave for a father who could not guard and protect or provide for her the way he could.

"What's this about reading lessons?" She laid her hand on her father's shoulder and smiled over at Noah.

He felt his damned heart turn over and silently cursed its weakness.

"I've asked Noah if he would stay and do some hunting for us in exchange for reading lessons." The disappointment was already thick in Payson's tone, as if he could sense that Noah was about to refuse.

"Oh, Daddy." Olivia addressed her father, but the look she sent Noah told her that she was speaking directly to him. "Noah can't stay here. He never wanted to come to Shawneetown in the first place. He has to leave." Their eyes met across the table. Regret, guilt, and something more—something that mirrored the riot of feelings tumbling around inside him—echoed in her eyes.

He can't stay here.

There was really no reason on earth why he had to go back to Heron Pond any time soon. Since the accident, his days had passed without incident, virtually the same morning, noon, and night, until he found Olivia and she turned his neatly ordered world upside down.

"You need a smokehouse," Noah told Payson. "For the meat."

The man appeared startled, as if his thoughts had already wandered elsewhere.

"Well, yes, I do. I just haven't gotten around to building one yet."

"I'd have to build it to smoke and store the meat."

Payson sat up straighter, his face suddenly as animated as it had been when he first saw Olivia. His eyes lit up.

"Are you saying you'll stay?"

"Noah, you can't," Olivia said, quickly stepping away from her father. "I know how much you want to get home. Especially after the reception you got in town today."

"What happened in town today?" Payson asked.

Both Olivia and Noah ignored his question. The thought of his residing with them apparently terrified her.

"You can't stay here," she said again.

"I'll be the judge of that."

"You mean you would actually consider it?" Payson was on his feet. Noah thought the man was going to jump up and down with joy.

"I have. I'll stay long enough to build you a smokehouse and put in enough provisions to see you through the winter."

Payson rounded the end of the table, thanking Noah for his good heart, for his kindness. He even began to pound him on the back.

As Noah sat there wondering what had come over him, he tried to dismiss Payson's overwhelming gratitude with a shrug. He was more concerned with Olivia, with the look of distress on her face. He waited for her to continue to object. Instead, she turned on her heel and ran out the door.

• • •

Olivia was afraid to walk too far away from the cabin and the light that issued from the window, so she paced the open field not far away. When more light streamed from the cabin, she knew someone had opened the door and stepped outside, but she did not turn around. If it was her father, he would have questions. If it was Noah, she would have to face the riot of emotion roiling inside her. She wasn't ready for either.

When someone walked up behind her, she knew without looking that it was Noah, for he moved as silently as the light breeze that set the fringe around the hem of her gown whispering.

Besides, her father would have spoken by now, but not Noah. Noah would be content to stand there until she acknowledged him, no matter how long that might take. Wrapping her arms around herself, she rubbed her hands up and down, ignoring the bright stars tangled across the sky, the scent of fertile soil still warm from the day's sunshine. Ignoring Noah for as long as she dared.

If he stayed, how could she trust herself around him day in and day out? It was growing impossible not to seek him out with her eyes. Yesterday as they crossed the open Illinois landscape, walking through woods and fields, meadows and hills together, she found herself wishing that she could be the woman he thought she was, that she could be everything that Noah deserved and more. Last night when they had bedded down on the trail, she thought it would be their last night together. The memories of what they had shared in his cabin, the way his hands had felt on her skin, the way he had made her body sing, were still too raw and new. Even her homecoming had been made bittersweet, knowing that once she and Noah parted, more than likely they would never cross paths again.

"Even if you stay, Noah, I can never be what you want me to be."

Without turning around, she sensed him when he stepped closer. She was tempted to lean back against him, to have him enfold her in his strong arms.

"My mother used to claim that she knew what the future

would bring." His voice was melodic, lyrical, almost as if he were telling her a story about someone else's life. "That was why she preferred to live away from others and why she moved with my father and never went back. She said it hurt her too much to know what was going to befall her family, her friends, her people. She heard voices in the wind, voices that warned her of the white settlers moving in and that the Cherokee would become fewer and fewer until they disappeared. Do you have such a talent, Olivia, to see the future?"

"No." Olivia shook her head. If she had, she would never have let her father move across the Ohio, never been Darcy's captive. But then she would never have met the man standing behind her now.

"I am staying because your father asked, because he cannot put meat on your table and I can."

She wished she could believe that was the only reason he was still here, but she suspected it was really because of what had happened between them three nights ago. She wished with all her heart that she was free to love him, that she could be the good and perfect woman he deserved.

"Olivia, turn around."

Even as she shook her head no, to refuse, she turned to him.

"Tell me that you want me to leave and I will."

"You know that I can't do that. My father needs your help. You saw the boys. They are nearly starving. I am not that cruel, Noah. I can't tell you to leave knowing that they will all suffer for it."

He put his hand beneath her chin and tilted her head until she was forced to look up at him.

"When you first came to me, I would not have wanted you to look so closely at my face. Now I want that and more. I want you to look at me so I can see your eyes when you tell me that you don't ever want me again."

"Don't make me do this, Noah."

"Because you can't."

"If you agreed to stay because you think that you can buy time to persuade me to go back with you, you should know right now that's not going to happen. But I won't send you away, because my family will suffer.''

''You *can't* send me away because you still want me.''

''No.'' She shook her head, trying to deny it.

''Don't lie, Olivia. I have seen the truth in your eyes when you thought I was not looking.''

She tried to turn away but he would not let her. ''Don't do this to me, Noah.''

He let go of her chin. Before she could react, he pulled her into the circle of his embrace. ''You are mine, Olivia. No matter what has gone before. Another man may haunt your nightmares, but he is your past and nothing but a bad dream. I'll wait, Olivia, until you know what your body already knows so well—that you're mine.''

She put her hands against his chest and tried to hold him off, but he was stronger, more determined than her weak will would ever be.

When he lowered his head, her breath caught in her throat. So did her words of protest, and they died there. His heart was beating fast and hard beneath her hands, like a river running wild and free. He drew her up against him until their lips met. His full mouth was not gentle, nor was it cruel. She knew no fear, only the same tearing anguish and confusion she had known after they made love. Clearly she wanted him, more now than before because this time she was not driven by a nightmare or its aftermath. Nor was she urged only by a need to feel secure in his arms.

No, this time she wanted Noah LeCroix, not some name-less, faceless dark angel hovering on the edge of her conscience. She was aware of every pulsing, beat of desire thrumming through her just as surely as she was convinced that giving in to that need again was wrong. Before Darcy had trained her so long and so well, she would not have known such need existed. She would not have been tempted to abandon all and give in to such longing.

Before her will failed entirely and her traitorous body persuaded her to give in again, she pulled back with such force that the kiss ended abruptly.

Between uneven breaths she cried softly. "Noah, please. Please let me go."

He did not force her. As she knew he would, he let her go and suddenly stepped back. She felt as if she had been wrenched from his arms and stripped naked, so bereft was she of his warmth. When his reaction finally came, his words cut through her as swift and sure as his sheathed knife might cut through a silken web.

"Have it your way then, Olivia. You don't want me. You think yourself unworthy. I'll stop trying to convince you otherwise."

His words hung heavy on the air between them as she stood looking up at him, silhouetted against the night sky. The breeze lifted the ends of his uneven hair. Even though he had not bothered to turn the wounded side of his face away from her, his scar was invisible in the dark. He was so handsome. Tall and proud, more noble than she could ever hope to be. He turned and walked away without a word. She could not call him back. She could never let him know he had been right. She wanted him more than she wanted to take her next breath.

chapter
10

DECADENCE WAS NOT A DEROGATORY WORD IN DARCY Lankanal's opinion. Like his mother before him, he made it a habit to surround himself with luxurious objects, beautiful people, and the finest in clothes, liquor, food, and wine. He never settled for less than the very best.

Stupid people annoyed him even more than ugly ones. So did unctuous ones, which is why for the life of him he did not know why he was sitting across the desk from Telford Betts, an ingratiating land agent with lily-white hands and a too-soft belly.

Ensconced in a wing chair in the room downstairs that served as both office and his private parlor, Darcy absently ran his fingers up and down the satin lapel of a formal cutaway jacket. Tonight he would be dining in one of the finest homes in the French Quarter, the guest of a Creole family of long standing in the city. He always liked to make an entrance, but if he tarried much longer, he would be more than fashionably late.

Telford's arrival had been unscheduled. After the last time the man was here, Darcy had decided never to agree to meet with him again. Later tonight, when he found out which of his people had admitted Betts without coming to him first, heads would roll, for this bothersome individual was continually trying to convince him that he should diversify and acquire land outside Louisiana.

Just now though, Betts assured him, he had some news of the utmost interest.

"Why don't you get to the point, Betts? I have a pressing engagement."

"I think you're going to like what I have to say, Mr. Lankanal. I think you are going to like it very much."

"Talk."

"I've been up to Illinois. Fastest-growing new state in the union. One hundred and sixty acres of land can be had for two dollars an acre. Folks are moving into Illinois from all over, but mostly from the South, so they see things our way politically, if you take my meaning."

Darcy started to push himself up out of the chair. "Even so, I think I've made it more than abundantly clear that I'm not interested in investing in land, nor do I want to set up any kind of establishment unless the clientele is of a certain social standing. Now, if you'll excuse me, Betts, I'd like you to leave." Darcy was sure he had made his wishes perfectly clear, but when Betts did not move, he decided he might have to call one of the bodyguards in the salon.

"Oh, I didn't come here just to persuade you to buy land, although that's always a part of it." Betts chuckled. "No, sir. I came because of what I heard when I stepped off the keelboat an hour ago."

The man looked so puffed up and sure of himself that Darcy was intrigued. "And what might that be?"

"That you have a reward out for information about that jade-eyed little whore I saw you with last time I was here."

Betts's words almost stopped Darcy's heart.

"And?"

"I've seen her."

Darcy's hands went cold. He felt the blood rush out of his head, straight to his loins. Just when he had almost given up hope of ever laying eyes on Olivia again, she had been sighted. Sweat broke out on his upper lip. He turned his back on Betts, hating to give the man any satisfaction that he had brought him to such a show of weakness. He walked over to a bookshelf full of books he had never read, took down a leather-bound book with gilt binding, and studied it, feigning nonchalance.

Finally, he looked up at Betts again. "Where do you think you saw her?"

"I don't think. I know. She was in Illinois."

Illinois. If fate had not led Betts to that place, Darcy knew he never would have found Olivia. But she had been seen. That was all the proof he needed that she was meant to be his. Now it was just a matter of time.

"Who was she with?"

"Now that's the interesting part." Betts smiled and waited for a reaction.

"How so?" Darcy wanted to leap across the room, grab Betts by the throat and shake the story out of him. Instead, he tamped down his excitement, forced himself to stay calm.

"The man she's hooked up with is some kind of a legend around those parts. A flatboat pilot."

Olivia was with a man. Black rage threatened to blot out all else. The notion agitated Darcy even though it made sense. No woman, especially one as young and unsophisticated as Olivia, could have left New Orleans on her own.

"There was a crowd gathered in front of a tavern. I heard somebody singing and walked over to see what was going on. For a minute I didn't recognize her because she was dressed like a squaw, so I didn't pay her any mind. Then she looked up and I saw all that curly black hair and those unforgettable green eyes and knew I had seen her somewhere before. Then I remembered it was right here in this room."

Dressed like a squaw. Darcy's head pounded. Olivia was *his* exclusive property. No other man had laid eyes on her while she was here with him, at least not that he could recall, not even Betts. He thought back, trying to remember a meeting with the land agent when Olivia might have been present. The man had come around once trying to persuade him to invest in the newly opened territories. Darcy had been with Olivia in his suite when Betts was announced. Always looking for a good investment, Darcy agreed to meet the man. Olivia had surprised him by asking if she could accompany him downstairs. He recalled how, at the time, he had been pleased and tried to fool himself into thinking that she must have wanted to be with him. Lately she had been taking more of an interest in the Palace and the goings-on downstairs; since he was loath to leave her, he had taken her along.

That day she had said nothing, making herself unobtrusive by sitting in the corner with a book open on her lap the entire time he talked with Betts. After Betts walked out, Darcy took Olivia's place in the wing chair, pulled her onto his lap, and eventually persuaded her to ride him where he sat.

Aroused and shaken by the now vivid memory, Darcy quickly sat down behind his desk. He ran a hand over his eyes and asked Betts, "Did she see you?"

"No. I was in the back of the crowd. I didn't think much of it. I thought she had probably quit this place and somehow got tied up with the half-breed."

"*What* half-breed?"

"The one she was with. The one with an eye patch. That's part of the talk about him—how he sold his soul to the devil and lost an eye." Betts looked pleased as punch as he dropped each bit of information.

It was worse than Darcy could have imagined. How in the hell had Olivia ended up with a half-breed? All kinds of scenarios entered his mind. She might have been captured while wandering the streets of New Orleans. After all, she had been taken once, by the river brigands who knew he was in the market for beautiful girls. All manner of men crowded the avenues and waterfront—immigrants, Creoles, soldiers, trappers, sailors, Indians, slaves, and slavers. With Olivia's bad luck, she might have run into the worst of the lot.

His thoughts kept flashing to the day she had been with him here in the office. She had been so docile, so willing to do whatever he asked. He had shown her the entire first floor, had proudly taken her into the gaming hall, the kitchen, the private dining room where the other girls took their meals. Quite a few times afterward she had expressed an offhanded interest in the place that he never questioned. Not too many weeks later, she disappeared.

Now her absorption with the inner workings of the Palace became perfectly clear. While he had been a fool to think that she was finally resigning herself to a life here, she had really been plotting her escape. Darcy stared down at his hands where they gripped the edge of the desk. His knuckles were white.

"So." Telford Betts sighed. "How much money do I get for a reward?"

"When I find Olivia, I'll give you your reward, Betts. Where exactly did you say she was? Indiana?"

If Betts had mentioned the name of the town, Darcy did not remember hearing it. All he could think of was Olivia, dressed like a squaw, wandering around with a one-eyed half-breed.

"Illinois. But I didn't say where exactly." Betts looked like a fat cat stuck in a pot of cream. "I'll be more than happy to take you there."

Darcy pushed away from the desk and stood up so fast that Betts flinched and paled. "Look, *after* I find her, I'll pay you good money for the information."

Darcy was surprised by the usually mild-mannered man's temerity. "I stand to make a lot more if I lead you to her," Betts told him. "That way I'll also have a chance to show you some of that land which I can't seem to interest you in any other way."

Darcy splayed his hands palms down on the desk and leaned toward Betts. "I don't give a good goddamn about any land up the Mississippi or any place else. *Where is Olivia?*"

"You ever stop to think she might not want to be found?"

"Did you ever stop to think what it would feel like to have your tongue ripped out of your throat?"

Betts stood, brushed off the front of his wool coat, picked

up the tall hat he had propped on his knee, and cleared his throat.

"She looked perfectly happy with the man she was with. You may need help getting her back."

"I don't need you or your help."

"If you want her, you'll have to let me take you there. Otherwise, how do I know you'll ever pay me a damn cent if I have to sit here on my hands waiting?"

Darcy hated Betts for holding all the cards. The man stood there smug and stubborn, his pale jowls hanging, his small, bespectacled eyes unflinching in the face of a rage he could not even imagine, for if Betts had, he would have shouted out the name of the town and run screaming from the room without looking back. The only thing Darcy could do right now was give in.

"Fine. Come back tomorrow, ready to leave for Illinois," Darcy said.

As Betts stood to depart, there was a knock at the office door.

"What next?" Darcy groused as he whipped the door open.

Romello, his personal butler, had a pained look on his dark face. "A man to see you in the stables, sir. With a delivery."

Darcy asked Romello to escort Betts out through the salon as he made his way through the house toward the stables in back. A "delivery" meant that one of his more unsavory associates had arrived with another girl.

Although he found himself thinking he would rather be on his way to the dinner party, Darcy walked into the stables where Miles Leonard and two of his river scum companions waited for him. Beside Miles stood a girl whose head was bowed. With her long dark hair hanging over her shoulders, hiding the side of her face, Darcy thought for a moment it was Olivia. His heartbeat accelerated. His hands itched to touch her, to hold her. Oddly enough, he wanted to comfort her. The moment he stepped closer, she looked up, staring at him with huge brown eyes. Not Olivia's eyes at all. Not Olivia.

The girl's shoulders were thin, her complexion wan. Confused and disoriented, she made no sound, nor did she even cry. No doubt in shock, she simply stood there looking back at him.

Darcy walked over to her and put his hand beneath her chin, raising her head so that she was forced to look into his eyes.

"Damn it, Miles. This one doesn't even look thirteen." Disgusted, he let go of the girl and brushed his hands together. "Where did you find her?"

"Bought her from her father down on Bayou Lafourche. He swore she was fourteen."

As Darcy stared down the girl, an uncomfortable, edgy feeling came over him. He looked over his shoulder, into the brick-lined courtyard beside the Palace where a fountain bubbled in the twilight.

"How old are you, girl?"

"Twelve, sir."

Darcy sighed. "How much, Leonard?"

"A hunnert, Mr. Lankanal."

Darcy figured the girl's no-account father probably sold her for twenty-five. "Go around to the back of the salon. Tell Peters what I owe you this time and tell the truth. He'll give you the money." Without touching her, Darcy looked down at the girl. "What's your name?"

"Annette, sir."

"Come with me, Annette."

He led her back across the courtyard, past the fountain, to the back door of the kitchen. Romello was there waiting, watching, a dour expression of disapproval on his face. If the man had not waited attendance on him for so long and so well, Darcy would have sold him. He didn't need a conscience at this point in his life. He needed Olivia back.

He strode through the door with Annette behind him, stopped in front of Romello and indicated the girl with a wave of his hand.

"Take her over to the convent and give her to the Ursulines. Tell them I'll send over a healthy donation in the morning so that they can see to her education."

Romello hid his surprise well, Darcy noted. The man-servant bowed and indicated to the girl that she should follow him. They quickly slipped out of the kitchen without another word.

As Darcy watched them leave, he wondered if perhaps he was coming down with something.

Bond Homestead

Greeting the day with his face uplifted to the rising sun, Noah stood alone outside the lean-to he had built to sleep in over the past few weeks. He had set up camp just inside the woods on the edge of the Bond property, where the breeze kept down the mosquitoes and there was plenty of fresh water for bathing and fishing in a nearby stream.

The weather had been warm and dry except for an afternoon shower now and again and as the days lengthened toward summer, the first shoots in the fields began to show. The morning sun inspired the birds to sing from the highest branches of the maple trees as Noah headed toward the stream, stripping off his red cotton shirt as he walked along. From the narrow foot trail worn into the grass between his campsite and the stream, he paused to look over at the Bond cabin. The only sign of life was the wisp of smoke that curled up out of the chimney.

If he had to guess, he would say that Olivia was probably the only one up and about. He could say with all honesty that he did not think Payson Bond would ever make a good farmer. Even working alone, Noah had already built a smokehouse as well as a new shed for the Bonds' milk cow and mare. As far as he was concerned, Payson Bond's head was in the clouds; when it wasn't, Bond was down with a strange ailment that gave him a fever and the shakes.

Noah kept to the woods and spent his days hunting and his nights tossing and turning, thinking of Olivia, wondering if she still had nightmares. Since she had come home, she had done nothing but work from sunup to sundown.

Throughout the day he would see her hoeing the vegetable patch, cleaning, sewing, scrubbing clothes in a halfbarrel behind the house and then hanging clothes out on a rope to dry. She played with the boys, took care of her stepmother, and cooked up the meals they all shared in the evenings. These occasions were as much a torture as they were the highlight of his day. Suppertime was the only time he really shared with her.

She was everywhere at once, helping everyone else, avoiding him. Olivia was so preoccupied that she wasn't even aware that he watched her whenever he was working nearby. What he saw worried him. She still jumped at unexpected noises and every now and again he would see her scan the edge of the property as if she were watching, waiting for the man from New Orleans, the man who had used her and made her feel unworthy of love.

Noah would give anything to take her fear away.

Tossing his shirt at his feet, Noah sat down, took off his moccasins, and stripped off his pants. He set them aside before he waded into the stream buck naked.

Olivia stepped outside the cabin door, careful not to spill the cup of hot sassafras tea in her hands. Pasting a smile on her face, she centered the cup on its saucer and walked over to the patch of morning sunlight where she had set up the rocker for Susanna. Now instead of being closeted inside, her stepmother could stare out across the fields, but at least the grieving young woman had lost some of her pallor. She would actually speak every now and again.

"I brought you some tea, Susanna." When Susanna was not in a talking mood, Olivia would still carry on a oneway conversation. "It's your favorite this time, not as strong as what I gave you yesterday. You brought quite a selection from home." There were plenty of teas in the wooden tea cabinet, but the lovely silver tea service, one of the few fine things that Susanna had brought from Virginia, had been stolen during the river raid.

Olivia set the cup and saucer on Susanna's lap, forcing her to hold it or have it spill all over, then stood beside the rocker and lifted a hand to her hair. She had taken to wearing it pulled back, tied with a ribbon to keep it out of the way while she worked.

"Daddy's ague seems a bit better today. Yesterday he shook so hard with chills that I thought the bed was going to walk across the room."

Trying to make light of her father's recurring condition was the only way Olivia could cope with this additional burden. He had told her that the strange malady was common among the Illinois settlers. It came on without warning at certain times of the year as a fever, violent shakes, and chills, and then disappeared just as quickly only to return with a vengeance again in a few days or months.

Beyond the yard in front of the cabin, the corn was coming up, thanks to the sun and an occasional shower. Trying to picture the dappled light through cypress, with lush emerald duckweed floating on water, the serenity of Noah's retreat on Heron Pond, Olivia took a deep breath of the fresh morning air and braced herself for another hard day. She wished she were stronger, that there were more hours in the day, that things were better. Then she sighed and reminded herself that if wishes were horses, beggars would ride. The only bright spot in this day would be suppertime, if and when Noah decided to join them for the evening meal.

"Susanna, did you see which way the boys went when they left the house?" She wanted to tell Freddie not to wander too far off before she had a chance to cut down a pair of Little Pay's trousers for him and turn up the hems. *"Susanna?"*

"What?" Susanna turned listless eyes her way. Olivia reminded herself that patience was supposed to be a virtue.

"The boys. Which way did they go?"

"Why, I didn't really notice."

"That's the trouble," Olivia said more harshly than she had intended.

Her stepmother had never lost her little-girl tone or the soft, honeyed Virginia drawl that so reminded Olivia of the

Morrison plantation where they had all lived for a time and where Susanna had been born.

Olivia went down on one knee beside the rocker and laid her hand on the armrest to stop the rocking. She waited until Susanna finally looked over at her.

"What is it, Livvie?"

"I think Little Pay is hurting himself on purpose, Susanna, and I'm worried about him."

"Whyever would he want to do something crazy as that?"

Olivia took a deep breath and sighed. Something had to be done to shake Susanna out of her stupor, and Olivia had decided she was the one who would have to do it. Her father claimed that Susanna was most likely suffering female maladies, that they had to comfort her and nurture her else she might lose her mind altogether and go insane.

Olivia had gone along with his wishes for four weeks now, and had taken over all the household chores, including raising the boys and trying to deal with Susanna while everyone tiptoed around her stepmother. Susanna seemed slightly better, but not much, and while she rocked her life away, the boys and Payson were suffering as much as if she had already died and left them.

"He's hurting himself to get you to notice him," Olivia told her.

"This morning I saw him walk off with Freddie. I just . . . I just don't recall which way they went." Susanna's voice trailed away. "Maybe they went around back . . ."

"He wants you to *really* see him, Susanna. He wants you to hold him and talk to him the way you used to. He and Freddie both need you, and I believe Little Pay thinks the only way he can shake you out of this sadness is by hurting himself to get your attention."

Susanna fell silent again, turned and stared off across the field of sprouting corn.

The rocker shook when she tried to move it again, but Olivia held firm, refusing to let Susanna slip away so easily. Her stepmother was not the only one suffering here. They all were. If Susanna was going to lose her mind, Olivia decided maybe she should just get on with it. Her father might not be willing to force his wife out of the black mood in which she was trapped, but something had to be done, so Olivia did not mince words.

"The boys need you. Daddy needs you, too. You can't mourn forever. Staring off into the sky won't get you home to Virginia, and it won't bring back your baby girl, either, no matter how much you wish it."

When Susanna made no response at all, Olivia's temper boiled over.

"Damn it, Susanna, come back to them. The living need you, not that baby you put into the ground."

She knew firsthand that mourning got one nowhere. Hadn't *she* mourned during those first weeks after she had been ripped from her family? Hadn't *she* cried over her fate, been utterly despondent because her father had not fought to keep her? Hadn't *she* grieved over what she thought was Susanna's betrayal? Over her stolen virginity? And on top of it all, she had even lived with the shame of hating them because they had given her up so easily.

It was not until she had finally stopped crying that she was able to start planning a way to escape Darcy.

Susanna had not yet responded. Thinking she might as well be talking to the moon, Olivia gave up. She was about to stand up and go inside when a choked, mournful sound erupted from her stepmother. Susanna slowly turned, her lips trembling, her arms locked tight around her middle.

"It hurts, Livvie. It hurts so bad. I can't make it stop," she whispered through her tears.

Forgotten, the cup and saucer in Susanna's lap tipped over. The tepid tea stained Susanna's skirt, but she did not even react to the spill. The china pieces slipped off her lap and hit the dirt. Olivia let them go, reached out, wrapped her arms around Susanna, hugged her close.

"I know. I know it hurts, but you aren't alone, Susanna."

Olivia closed her eyes against her own pain as she held the sobbing woman in her arms and let Susanna pour out all the grief she had buried inside for so long.

"Cry it out, Susanna. Cry it all out," Olivia whispered softly as she held the young woman who had been step-mother, sister, and friend, and begged God to forgive her for ever, ever blaming Susanna for her own fate.

When she felt a firm hand gripping her shoulder, Olivia started. She looked up. Her father was standing there beside her. Barefoot, in his undershirt and pants, he was clutching the quilt around his shoulders. Lines creased his skin. His blue eyes were red-rimmed with tears of his own. His receding, light brown hair stood on end. He was so thin, his clothes so worn and mended, that he looked like a poorly stuffed scarecrow.

"Let me, Livvie," he said, reaching for Susanna. The quilt fell from his shoulders and slid to the ground.

Olivia waited until he went down on his knees beside the rocker, then released Susanna into his arms. When she pulled away from them, a sorrowful loneliness swept through her, one so very powerful that she ached to her bones with it.

Looking down on her father and Susanna, seeing them wrapped in each other's arms as they shared their grief over a lost child and broken dreams, Olivia felt more trapped in her own loneliness and isolation than ever before. Her un-guarded thoughts immediately flew to Noah. Even though she hated herself for being so selfish and so unfair to him, she was thankful that he had not gone back to Heron Pond.

She needed to see him, now, this minute. She needed the solace his calm presence always gave her, needed to see the warmth of his crooked smile, to hear the cadence of his voice, to look at him and relive the memory of the night they had shared. She needed the safe, secure feeling that he gave her.

It was nothing short of selfish, depending on his concern and caring, wanting him near and yet remaining unwilling to share in the kind of relationship she knew he wanted. Until today she had kept her distance. She never sought him out for selfish reasons. Oh, she would give him mes-sages from her father or go to him when she was looking for the boys. When he was working near the cabin she would take him his meals, but she made it a point not to linger, not to tempt him or be tempted.

She was almost to his campsite before she even realized she had come this far. She paused beneath the trees and looked around, but there was no sign of him.

All of her determination to see him quickly ebbed away leaving her frustrated and even more alone. She wandered over to a stump not far from the fire ring of stones and sat down heavily. She wiped her forehead with the back of her wrist, shoved her hair back off her hairline, and looked up at the canopy of trees.

Overhead, magpies chattered to one another, and in the woods behind her, two wild turkeys called to each other as they foraged between the trees. Olivia sighed. The tears she had shed on the way to the woods had dried on her cheeks. She wished the wistful loneliness would pass as easily. A huge flock of pigeons flew overhead, so many that they looked like a dark gray cloud.

She didn't know whether to be relieved or unhappy that Noah was not here. At least now she would not have to suffer the guilt of using him again in order to make herself feel better. Olivia took a deep breath, thought of all the chores waiting for her back at the cabin, and gathered her courage to go back and face it all. She put a smile on her face and told herself to expect the best. Perhaps a good cry had lightened Susanna's soul. Perhaps now her father and his wife could rediscover the love they had once shared, one that Olivia had so envied and had hoped to find one day.

She shook out the cotton skirt of one of the gowns she had worn a lifetime ago, stood up and lifted her face to the sun. Stretching her arms high over her head, she took a deep breath of summer air alive with the scent of wildflowers.

Then she opened her eyes, turned around, and screamed.

chapter

11

NOAH'S SUDDEN APPEARANCE BEHIND HER, HALF-NAKED, nearly frightened Olivia witless. Her scream still echoed in her ears. Her heart pounded.

"I'm sorry," Noah apologized, but a slight lift at the corner of his mouth gave her the impression he was not sorry in the least. "You need to be careful. Sometimes Indians still walk these woods."

She was hard-pressed to concentrate on what he was saying, what with him standing there bare-chested, a turkey-red cotton shirt slung over his shoulder, watching her with a glint of appreciation and no little suspicion in his eye. Glistening with water, his hair was slicked back, dark as pitch. The long lashes over his eye were spiked. His eye patch was in place, the leather ties darkened by water stains.

"Why are you here, Olivia?"

"You don't waste words, do you?"

"Did Payson send you?"

She shook her head, wishing she had never come. There was no way she could admit her tremendous need to see him. She did not fully understand it herself.

"No, Daddy didn't send me."

"Then why did you come?"

Because I needed to see you.

Because you were the first one I thought of when I felt lost.

"I wondered if you had seen the boys."

He turned away and shrugged on his shirt. "They're at the stream."

Instead of going after the children, she lingered while he went about his business as if she were not there at all. Leaving her standing there in awkward silence, he ducked low and stepped into the lean-to. From where she stood Olivia could see his bedroll and, unfortunately, she found it easy to imagine lying there in the dark beside him. She wondered what it would be like to look up at the stars, listen to the call of the hoot owls in the trees with him. Did he think of her as often as she thought of him, she wondered, or had he really been able to dismiss her almost entirely?

Right now he did not particularly act as if he wanted her there at all. On the verge of complete humiliation, Olivia looked off in the direction of the stream.

"I just did something I shouldn't have," she admitted softly, feeling better already for having voiced her concern aloud. It didn't really matter whether he listened or not, she decided; she just needed to talk.

"I was sharp with Susanna. I told her that she has mourned long enough and that she needs to take care of the living." She shuddered. She had only meant to help, not hurt.

Noah had buttoned up his shirt by now, so she no longer had to avoid looking at his distracting muscles. He was on his haunches, stirring the embers of the fire, and gave no indication that he had even heard her until he straightened.

"I know nothing of families, Olivia."

With heavy sadness in her heart, she took a few steps toward a nearby bush, plucked a stem covered with leaves and fanned it back and forth. She had asked for this. She had wanted him to give up caring about her, but she had not expected it to hurt when he did. With the stem in her hand, she turned and caught Noah watching her from across the campfire.

Quickly, he looked away. She crossed the clearing to stand over him.

"Are you having supper with us tonight?"

Mentally she tallied what supplies they had. Thanks to Noah, the new smokehouse was well stocked. He had taught her father how to smoke meats and instructed him to butcher a couple of wild hogs in the fall so they would have an abundant supply of ham.

Noah stood up and appeared to be concentrating on her mouth. Then he met her eyes. His expression was so set, so determined, that she thought he was about to decline.

"I'll come, as long as I don't have to sit beside Freddie."

Her heart lightened, Olivia laughed.

"I really have to be getting back."

There was corn bread to bake, beans to boil, breakfast to clear away, clothes to wash and hang. In between she would find a little time to hoe a row or two in the vegetable patch.

They stood nearly toe to toe now. She watched the rise and fall of his chest. Knowing what it felt like to be held against his heart did not make going back any easier.

"I really do have to leave," she said lamely.

"So you said."

She needed to linger in his presence, if only for a moment longer. A few scant inches separated them. She heard him let out a long, heavy sigh. Her feet were rooted to the ground. She lifted her eyes to his face.

"Olivia," he whispered, bringing his lips closer to hers, "you really should go now."

"I know," she whispered back.

His hands never left his sides, but his mouth was so close that she could almost taste him. She closed her eyes, wishing she had the power to deny her need for this man. She did not want to hurt him for anything in the world. Half expecting him to walk away and leave her standing there like a fool, she was surprised and captivated when his mouth touched hers. He traced the seam of her lips with his tongue, tentatively, searching and exploring, tasting.

She moaned low in her throat and dropped the leafy stem

as she reached for his arms. Beneath his shirt, his forearms were corded with muscle. He had not moved, nor did she, even when she touched him. She ran her hands down his arms, and found his hands knotted into fists. He was holding himself back. She knew what it must be costing him, for it cost her, too. The temptress that Darcy had awakened in her smiled even as her conscience prodded her to stop. Her grip tightened on Noah's wrists, and then she let go. When the kiss ended, she did not step back.

He was breathing heavily and looked pained.

Unfortunately, she dropped her gaze and immediately saw that he was aroused. Quickly, she looked back up.

"Does it amuse you, Olivia, to play with me the way Freddie plays with fireflies in the evening?" His voice was rough, gravelly, as if the words had to fight their way out of him.

Each evening the boys ran along the edge of the wood catching lightning bugs, trapping them in their sweaty hands, shoving them down inside empty bottles. The insects would beat themselves against the glass, their bright yellow-green glow sadly weakening, until by morning they lay burnt out on the bottom of the bottles.

She shook her head to deny it, but before she could utter a word, a high-pitched scream came from somewhere nearby. She immediately recognized Freddie's voice.

"Noah? Noah!" The boy was coming down the trail toward the camp and although they could not see him through the trees yet, there was no denying the frantic sound in his voice.

"Over here, Freddie," Olivia yelled back as she started to run toward the trail. Suddenly the little towhead shot into the clearing, panting like a scared rabbit, his eyes wide and frantic.

"You gotta come, Livvie. You too, Noah."

"What is it? What's wrong?" She knelt down and grabbed his bony shoulders.

Freddie gulped until he finally squawked, "Little Pay'th drowned himthelf! I think he'th dead."

• • •

The words were as effective as ice water. Noah's hot blood cooled instantly. Here was trouble of a kind he could handle, not like the confusing, mysterious torment Olivia stirred in him whenever she was near.

He sidestepped both of them and ran down the trail toward the creek. The water had been running high and swift this morning, eddying in a gentle whirling motion near the rocks in the center of the stream. To him, the current was next to nothing. To a child, it would be deadly.

The path ended at the water's edge. He heard Olivia and Freddie on the trail behind him, shouting back and forth as they ran. He scanned the pool, saw no sign of the other boy.

"He wath *there*." Breathless, Freddie ran up beside him, stood against Noah's thigh and pointed to the middle of the stream. "He wath *right there*!" Then he began to wail.

Noah did not hesitate. He stepped into the stream and made a skimming dive across the surface of the water toward the center of the pool. Then he dove. His eye patch tore away as he shot through the water and swept it with his hands. Feeling around for Little Pay, he hoped to come in contact with the child's body before it was too late. He surfaced and gulped air, dove again.

Suddenly, a strange, gentle peace began to flow through him, one so calming that it was astounding. Then something most odd began to happen. In a voice not unlike the bubbling gurgle of the stream, the water itself seemed to guide him. If he had not been feeling so tranquil, he would have thought that he was going mad, but as clearly as if it could communicate in words, the water guided him ahead, then to the right. He soon felt the brush of cloth beneath his palm. His fingers closed over the fabric. He tugged Little Pay into his arms and surfaced.

Only seconds had passed, and yet it might have been hours. Once he surfaced, Noah could still hear the odd whispers, not unlike voices in the water, but upon seeing Little Pay lying so lifeless, his skin pale, his lips blue, the strange connection with the water was broken. Noah waded to the bank of the stream where Olivia stood with her fist shoved against her mouth. Above her hand, her eyes were stark with shock. Freddie was trembling, his face white as dogwood blossoms.

Little Pay dangled limp as a wet rag in Noah's arms. He looked down at the boy and then into Olivia's eyes.

"Take him home," she whispered.

The cabin was no more than a few hundred yards away from Noah's shelter in the wood and though he was certain the boy was dead, something compelled him to run the distance. Why, he could not say, except perhaps because Little Pay's body was the heaviest burden he had ever carried in his life and he wanted to be rid of it.

He wanted to lay the boy out in his home, turn tail and run. To leave the Bonds and all their heartache behind. He did not want to see Payson Bond's face when the man looked upon his lifeless son. He did not want to hear Susanna's cries or watch her go entirely insane.

And Olivia? Maybe now she would leave and go with him. Maybe now she would leave these people and all their misery and go with him back to Heron Pond.

As his legs pumped and his feet crushed the sprouting corn, the boy's lithe body bounced up and down in his arms. As he neared the cabin, his thoughts crystalized. He had been better off raised without the knowledge of family ties, or of what it meant to love more than one person at a time, to care for more than one, to lose and bury not just one, but many.

In the face of the this new, sudden tragedy of the Bonds, he was shaken by the knowledge that if the child in his arms were his own son, he did not think he could go on.

When Payson heard Olivia shouting, he walked to the corner of the cabin and looked across the field. He was weak from this latest bout of ague. Dizziness still came and went, so at first when he saw Noah racing toward the cabin, carrying what looked like a rag doll with its arms and legs flopping, with Olivia running behind him and Freddie trying to keep up, Payson thought he was hallucinating. But then he heard Olivia cry out for Noah to wait. Freddie had tripped

in a dirt trough and lay there spent, facedown in the cornfield.

When his mind cleared, Payson realized that it was no
doll in Noah's arms and he ran to meet them, ignoring the
pebbles that cut his bare feet. His legs felt as if they might
give out at any second. When he ran up to Noah and saw
Little Pay's bleached skin, the water dribbling out of the
corner of his mouth and down the side of his cheek, he
staggered, but he did not fall.

He tried to stop the big man, but Noah kept running and
passed him by, headed for the cabin. Noah dwarfed the
child so that from behind, all Payson saw were Little Pay's
bare feet and knobby ankles dangling over his arm.

Payson remembered Susanna, worn out from crying, still
seated in the rocker in her spot of warm sunshine. In a few
strides Noah would be there, tearing down the partially
mended fabric of her fragile will to go on. Payson became
frantic to reach her first, but there was no way in hell he
could overtake the taller, stronger man.

When he came around the corner of the cabin, it was too
late to do anything but watch. Noah stood there holding
Little Pay, looking as if he had just awakened from a bad
dream and wasn't quite sure of where he was. Payson saw
Susanna slowly turn around. He expected her to scream
when she saw Noah holding Little Pay.

Instead, she carefully pushed herself up out of the rocker
and slowly walked over to Noah. Payson hurried to join
them.

"Give him to me," Payson said to Noah. "Give me my
boy."

Noah did not let go.

"What happened?" As calm as death, Susanna reached
out. Her hand was steady as she brushed Little Pay's hair
back off his forehead.

"He walked into the pool in the stream." Noah's breath
was still uneven.

Susanna raised her arms. He gently lowered the boy into
them. She seemed to droop under the load, even though the
boy weighed next to nothing soaking wet. She did not falter

as she walked back to the rocking chair. Holding her son against her breast, she sat back down and cradled him as she had not done since Little Pay had grown tall and lanky and considered himself a boy, not a baby.

With his sorely tried strength ebbed to nothing, Payson watched his wife and somehow summoned the courage to stand beside her, close to the rocker, so that his thigh rubbed against her shoulder. Words lodged in his throat.

Susanna whispered to their son. "I see you now, Little Pay. I love you, baby." She bent and pressed a tender kiss to her older son's soft, suntanned cheek. Then she started rocking him gently, patting him on the back as if he were no older than an infant.

Olivia and Freddie had reached the cabin. Payson heard them behind him, heard his daughter whisper frantically to Noah, listened to Freddie as the boy hiccuped down sobs. Payson looked down upon Susanna and Little Pay with no notion of how he could go on. He was trapped between purgatory and hell. He could not return Susanna to her father and tell the man that because he, Payson, had been too stubborn to live off charity, it had cost the wealthy Virginian, Richard Morrison, two of his grandchildren and Susanna's sanity.

He squeezed his eyes closed, ran a hand over his face, and finally forced himself to move. "Let me take him." He bent toward Susanna, then paused. He felt his stomach drop to his toes. Was his mind playing tricks on him?

Had Little Pay's lashes just fluttered?

"Noah," Payson said, waving him closer, daring to hope. "Noah, come see if he's breathing," he whispered.

The other man's clothing was soaked, water dripped onto the ground around his feet, but LeCroix was there in an instant, leaning over Susanna, softly begging her pardon, pressing two fingers against the thin blue vein in Little Pay's neck. The color from the turkey-red shirt he was wearing spotted the shoulder of Susanna's faded yellow gown. It wasn't until Noah looked up at Payson that he realized LeCroix had lost his eye patch. The puckered depression on the scarred side of his face was not horrible at all. The relief in his good eye was unmistakable.

"He's alive," Noah whispered in awe. For a moment Payson thought LeCroix might actually be moved to tears.

"Let's get him inside," Payson said.

Susanna quickly handed the boy over to Payson, rose, and followed close behind her husband as he carried Little Pay in and laid him in the center of the bed.

"Livvie, help me get his clothes off." Susanna spoke in a low but firm tone, the first time she had sounded like her old self in almost a year. As she started unbuttoning the boy's shirt, Olivia hurried around to the opposite side of the bed and bent to the task of stripping off his too-short pants.

Payson stood at the foot of the bed, shoving his hands through his hair. While Susanna and Livvie worked together again with swift, silent efficiency, he watched them through a blur of tears. His world had just righted itself and settled back into place.

Standing apart from the Bonds in a pool of sunlight that streamed through the open door, Noah watched Susanna and Olivia undress Little Pay, prop his head on the pillows, and draw the covers over his bony chest. He was not aware of Freddie beside him until he felt a small, warm hand slip into his and hold on tight. He looked down. Freddie looked up.

"Whath happening?" Freddie whispered, all eyes and tousled white-blond hair. "I thought Little Pay wath dead."

The boy's hand was as fragile as a sparrow's wing. Noah could feel the tiny bones beneath the skin, so fragile that if he barely squeezed at all, he would crush them. The thought was intimidating.

"He's not dead," Noah whispered back. "I think maybe when I ran across the field, I shook the water out of him."

Freddie smiled up at him. "You did good, Noah. I would be tho lonethome if Little Pay wath really dead."

Noah knelt down until he was at eye level with the boy. "What happened at the pool, Freddie?"

The child stared back intently. "Where did your eye go?"

Noah blinked his good eye and sighed. He had forgotten until now that his eye patch had come off in the pool.

"I was in an accident and it got poked out."

"Doeth it hurt?"

Noah shook his head. "Not anymore."

"Can I touch it?"

"What?"

"Can I touch the hole?"

Noah looked over at Olivia, hoping for rescue, but she was sitting on the bed opposite Susanna. Both women were holding Little Pay's hands, talking to the boy, who was conscious again.

Noah sighed. "All right."

Freddie's eyes were round with fear, but his hand came up. With one finger, he barely touched the empty eye socket before he jerked his hand away. Then his narrow little chest swelled.

"What happened at the pool, Freddie?"

"Little Pay waded in and I hollered to him not to go too far but he juth kept walkin' until he wath up to his butt and then hith middle and then hith cheth and then he juth . . . dithappeared."

Noah stood up again, drawing Olivia's attention. When she gazed at him across the room as if he had hung the moon, his heart plummeted to his feet. Freddie let go of his hand and ran straight over to Olivia. She hugged the boy before he climbed up onto her lap, then she slipped her arm around his waist to anchor him there.

"Hey, Little Pay," Freddie spoke to his brother as conversationally as if nothing untoward had happened. "I got to put my finger in Noah'th eye hole!"

Little Pay flashed a grand smile over at Noah, then turned back to his brother. "Well that's nothing. I saw a heavenly band of angels in the pool."

Noah watched Olivia reach out and tap the end of Little Pay's nose. "Don't go telling tales, Little Pay."

"I'm not, Livvie," the boy insisted. "I really did see a

whole bunch of them. They had golden halos and the fluffiest, softest white wings you ever saw and they all talked to me.''

"What did they say, son?'' Payson was seated beside Susanna. Noah never knew so many people could fit on a bed and oddly enough, none of them looked in the least uncomfortable.

"They told me that they had plenty of angels for now and that they wanted me to go on back home.'' He looked up at his mother, whose hand rested on his chest, above his heart. "They told me I wouldn't have any more accidents.''

Susanna leaned down and hugged him close. "That's good, son. That's real good news. Isn't it, Livvie?''

Olivia squeezed Freddie so hard he yelped. "Ow, Livvie! You're thquithin' me!''

None of them noticed when Noah walked out of the cabin. Once outside, he moved away from the door and lowered himself into Susanna's rocking chair. Never having sat in one in his life, he tested it first, rocking slowly a few times before he leaned back and fell into a smooth rhythm. Directly across the field, beneath a huge old hickory, he could see a small white wooden cross and realized that Susanna must have been sitting here day after day, staring out at the grave of her stillborn child.

Angels in the pool. His father had read a story of angels from his bible once. Back then, Noah had wondered if perhaps the voices his mother heard might be the sound of angels, but when he asked, she told him that she didn't believe that they were and went on to say that she wished it were that simple. Since she had estranged herself from her people, Noah never knew his extended family, or even how to find them. If he did, he would go to them now, ask if any of them had ever heard voices in the wind or the water. Perhaps someone could explain what had happened to him.

Something had spoken to him when he dove for Little Pay. Something that guided him right to the boy—something not akin to sight, and yet stronger than intuition. It had almost seemed as if the water *spoke* to him or even _sang_ to him by sounding chords. As he searched for Little Pay he had _sensed_ the water's fluid dance, known where every rock and ripple lay hidden beneath the water's surface. He turned his head and gazed off in the direction of his camp in the wood. The stream and the pool lay beyond. He fought an intense urge to go back and dive beneath the water again just to see if the strange sensation would come back to him.

He fought the urge, pumped the rocker back and forth, and found the movement soothing. Inside, the Bonds were still talking among themselves. Now and again, he heard Olivia's voice above the others.

Someday she would want children of her own. As sure as he knew the sun would set, he knew that once she had healed, once she could let herself love and be loved, she would want a family. She deserved to be happy. She deserved a man who could give her what she wanted.

Even after all the weeks he had spent here, he was still not used to the way the Bonds dealt with each other. He had not become accustomed to the chatter and constant activity of the little boys, their scuffles, the lack of privacy. He did not know how or when Payson Bond found time to think, what with his constant work in the fields, his wife's misery, his worries about providing for all of them.

Although the boys had trailed after him as often as they could, he was still uncomfortable around them. He had no notion of how to deal with children, how to care for them, what to say to them. And after what happened today, he was certain that he could not bear to lose a child of his own, a child of his and Olivia's.

He laid his head against the back of the rocker and thought, _The Prince of the Ohio is a coward._ He wanted Olivia, but he had not stopped to think about what wanting her really entailed. Maybe she was right. Maybe it was best for him to leave her, to give up and go back to Heron Pond and the simple, unencumbered life he knew, a life where he was cut off from the world of feeling.

Mired in his dark thoughts, he did not hear her walk up beside him.

"Noah? Are you all right?"

He looked up at her, memorized the way her long, dark hair curled over her shoulders, the bright spots of color on her cheeks, the way her long lashes feathered at the corners of her eyes. Now that Little Pay was all right, a glorious, buoyant joy radiated from her, one unlike any he had seen since he found her.

"I'm fine," he assured her, slowly pushing himself to his feet.

"You saved Little Pay, Noah." She reached for his hand and held it to her cheek. "You saved his life."

He shook his head, remembered the quaking coward's heart that had sent him jogging across the field so that he could put the boy's body down and be done with the ache.

"I did nothing of the kind."

"Whether you want to believe it or not, you did. I think you really did shake the water out of him somehow," she said.

He wanted to deny it, but she went on before he could speak.

"Don't look so worried. I'm not about to go writing another verse about you." She squeezed his hand, let it go, and smoothed the front of her gown. "Noah, you can smile now, you know. Little Pay is going to be all right."

"I'm going home, Olivia. Back to Heron Pond."

c h a p t e r

12

HE HEARD HER SWIFT INTAKE OF BREATH. HER HANDS fluttered over her skirt again like two lost butterflies as she fussed with the folds. She pressed her palms together.

"You're leaving?" She sounded shocked, as if it were an impossibility. As if she had some right to dictate to him.

He nodded. "Going home." The relief, the joy he expected was missing. He was running scared, afraid of making a fool of himself over her again, afraid of the voices in the water.

"You need to go on with your life, Olivia, and so do I. Your father's corn is growing. The smokehouse is built and stocked. There are vegetables in the patch." The Bonds would not starve. He had given his word to help Payson and he had kept it. But right now he had to get away from Olivia, from all of them, from caring too much.

"I have to leave."

"But—"

"You know why I can't stay." He thought of the kiss they had shared that morning, of what might have happened again before Little Pay spoke to the angels, before he had heard the voices in the water. He wanted her still, but he refused to live with such constant, aching torment any longer.

She stared at the ground. "I'm sorry, Noah. I told you that I was no good."

Forgetting the family inside, he grabbed her by the shoulders, held her fast, forced her to look at him. Tears shimmered in her eyes.

"You are good, Olivia. You *are* good." Would she ever believe it? Would she ever feel worthy enough to let herself love anyone? He quickly dropped his hands and stepped back.

"Say good-bye, Olivia, and let me go."

"Are you leaving now? Just like this?"

He tried to ignore the guilt twisting his insides.

"I'm going to collect my things and leave from the camp. Tell your family good-bye for me."

Enough had happened already today without having to learn to say good-bye to little boys. Noah wished he had on a fine new shirt, or at least a clean one, that his hair wasn't plastered to his head and his eye patch missing. He wished he looked the best he could, so that when she thought of him, if she thought of him at all, she would remember him that way.

"Olivia—" There were many, many more things he wanted to say to her, things of his heart. Most of all, he wanted to thank her for what she had given him the night before they left Heron Pond, but he knew it would only make her upset with herself, her actions. So, there were no words he could say.

"Good-bye, Noah."

The tears shimmering in her eyes almost changed his mind.

"Good-bye, Olivia."

Before anyone came out of the cabin, he turned around and slowly ran across the unevenly plowed rows of new corn shoots, toward his campsite in the wood.

Olivia watched him go, waited to see if he would have a change of heart, but he did not look back. Noah LeCroix carried himself with more grace than any man she had ever seen. He *had* saved Little Pay, no matter how he tried to deny it. No one else could have dived into that pool and pulled him out in time. Somehow, he had been responsible for reviving the boy. Maybe Noah and the angels both.

Olivia sighed, blinking back tears. She didn't need clear vision to see the rest of her life stretched before her. What other man would want her after what she had been in New Orleans? It would be selfish to call Noah back because *he* did, which was exactly what her fickle heart wanted her to do. No doubt he wanted her because she was the only woman he had ever known. But he deserved better. And she knew it. He deserved a woman of his worth, a woman of honor unsullied by her past.

She watched him until the foliage closed in around him. Then intense dread slowly came over her.

Freddie came running out of the house.

"Whereth Noah?" He looked around expectantly. "Hey, are you cryin', Livvie?"

"Noah's gone. He's going back to his own home."

"Why?"

"He's finished helping Daddy."

"I wanna go tell him 'bye."

She put her hands on the boy's shoulders, holding him there gently but firmly.

"He said to tell you good-bye. He was in a hurry."

"Ith he coming back?"

"I don't think so."

"Why?"

"He has his own life."

She closed her eyes, momentarily letting herself sink into memories of Heron Pond, the blessed stillness, the dense cypress, the shadows and sunlight on the water. The blue heron. The white egrets against the dark forest green.

She felt the boy staring up at her. "You *are* cryin', Livvie."

"I guess I am, a little."

"I'm thure gonna mith him," Freddie said.

She started to say, "Me, too," but the words stuck in her throat.

It took Noah but a few moments to change into dry clothes and load his pack. He hastily fashioned a new eye patch out of a strip of red cloth he ripped from the hem of his shirt, tied it on like a headband, then pulled it down over his empty eye socket. He put on his black hat. Then he packed up his bedroll, shouldered his long rifle, and started the long walk home.

He had almost reached the edge of Payson Bond's land when he noticed two male riders approaching from the direction of Shawneetown. He made sure his rifle was loaded and primed and waited as the men on horseback drew closer.

Until he was certain they meant no harm to Olivia and her family, he was not about to go on.

A handsome square-jawed man in his early thirties accompanied by a boy in his teens pulled rein when they reached him. Noah sized them up and waited to hear what they had to say. The gentleman doffed his hat and dismounted. Cut out of the same hide, the two looked to be father and son.

"Are you Noah LeCroix?" There was no denying the look of excitement on the man's face. Noah winced, afraid the traveler might burst into song.

Reluctant, Noah nodded. "I am."

The man shoved out his hand. "I'm Benson Bridges, sir." He gestured toward the boy. "This is my son, Gerald. I'm headed down the river to Tennessee and you're just the man I'm looking for."

"Why is that, Mr. Bridges?" Noah guessed what the man wanted before he said the words.

"I've come to beg for your help, if I have to. The river's running high and all the best pilots are taken. I'm in quite a pickle. I'm a businessman first and foremost, so let me say right off that I'm willing to pay whatever you ask, Mr. LeCroix, within reason that is, to get me downriver right away."

"I'm out of the business." Noah shouldered his rifle, hefted his pack and prepared to walk away, even though he had to admit to a dose of excitement that had started to snake its way through his blood when he thought of piloting a craft downriver.

"Every man has a price, Mr. LeCroix."

"I don't." Noah wondered what it was about white men and money. He had not met one who did not believe a man would do just about anything for enough gold. He started to walk around Bridges, but the man smiled and blocked his way. The son, Gerald, leaned on his pommel and closely watched the exchange. His face was sunburned, as if he had already spent too much time on the river without his hat.

"Oh, come on, LeCroix. You really willing to turn down more than most of these men earn in a year just to make one trip?"

Noah paused to consider. "Money doesn't matter."

What did he need money for? The land provided all he would ever need. He shifted, looked over at the sandy-haired young man whose blue eyes missed nothing. Bridges and his kind were moving here in droves. How many years would it be before they flushed him out of his swamp? How long before the settlers cleared so much land that the fertile plains and woodlands could no longer provide for them all? That had always been his mother's prophesy, her darkest vision. White men like these would take everything and ruin the land.

"You have quite a name in these parts," Bridges told him.

"So?"

"So I want the best and I'm used to getting it. I have to be in New Orleans in a few days." The man watched him closely. Noah guessed Bridges was a shrewd trader, one sharp enough to seek out his most vulnerable spot.

"I hear you haven't been on the river since you lost your eye. Are you scared your legend might crumble?"

Noah was not about to bother telling the man he had not even known he was a legend until a few weeks ago. It wasn't a fading legend he feared, but failing the people in the boat.

"If you don't want the money, maybe you have a wife who would appreciate a fancy new dress or a new horse?"

Wife. Noah almost laughed; then he pictured Olivia in a

fancy new gown, wearing some shiny ribbons in her hair, green to match her eyes. Store-bought candy would make Little Pay and Freddie's eyes light up.

He shook his head. Impossible. He was on his way home.

"I heard down at the riverfront that you haven't been back on the water for three years. You don't look the type who would run from a challenge to me, LeCroix."

"You don't know me, so don't make judgments, Mr. Bridges." Hadn't he just run from Olivia? From what living too near her was doing to him? From the confusing notions and complications of family?

"Why don't you call me Benson?"

"Why don't you head back to Shawneetown?"

Noah didn't know what irritated him more, Benson Bridges' dogged persistence or the notion that he couldn't shake the urge to say yes and take to the river again. If he agreed, would he hear the voices in the water? Would the strange *knowing* come over him again, or had that been a once-in-a-lifetime occurrence? Accepting the offer would mean challenging the river. The waters would be running high and fast after the spring thaw and rains. How would he fare? Would his skill and not just his perception be off with only one eye?

Noah looked over at the boy and then the man. "You want to risk your family's lives, Mr. Bridges? Maybe lose your fine strong son, there?"

Benson Bridges sobered. "That's exactly why I've come to see *you*, LeCroix. You're the best there is—"

Noah cut him off. "When I had both eyes."

"I'm willing to bet you're still the best. Hell, if you are half as good as they say you were, you could take us down the Ohio and the Mississippi blindfolded."

Noah reckoned that one-eyed he *was* better than some of the piss-poor pilots he had run across.

Hell, why not? he suddenly thought. Without Olivia in his life, there was nothing to make his heart race anymore, nothing to look forward to except the monotony and solitude. Maybe the river would fill the void for a while. Maybe he could find out if the strange thing that had happened in the stream would haunt him again. He would discover if he was either blessed or cursed with the voices whispering in his head.

"I can see you're considering it, LeCroix." Bridges rocked back on his heels, already smug.

Noah looked out from beneath his hat brim, scanned the treeline, over the open land. The Bond cabin wasn't visible from where he stood, but he could see the smoke from the chimney rising above the treetops.

If he made it downriver, he could stop in at Sandy Shoals and visit Hunter Boone and his wife, Jemma. He had never felt as great a need to see his old friend as he did right now.

"I'll do it." He extended his hand to Bridges. "I'll take you all the way to Natchez. From there the worst of the river is behind you and you can hire on another man to get you to New Orleans." He had no desire to go where there were more people than a man could count in a day. Nor did he want to chance running into the man who had hurt Olivia, Darcy Lankanal.

The boy took off his hat, whipped it over his head and let out a war whoop. "Wait until folks hear this," he cried. "Noah LeCroix is taking us downriver."

"You won't be sorry," Bridges told Noah.

"I hope not."

A few new stanzas were added to his song as soon as Noah walked into Shawneetown alongside Benson Bridges and his son and they headed for the riverfront. With the red rag still tied around his head, he suffered the stares of the townsfolk, some of whom followed along at a discreet distance and stayed to hover nearby while he was introduced to the rest of the party at the river. When he met Bridges' wife and four daughters, doubt and responsibility weighed heavy on him and Noah tried to back out of the bargain until Bridges asked if he was a man of his word.

Noah studied the man's attractive, well-dressed wife as she eyed him back suspiciously. The woman openly argued with her husband against leaving. She was afraid, dead-set against challenging the river, especially after she had a look at Noah. Ranging in age from eight to fourteen, the pretty round-faced girls clung together and giggled while their brother, Gerald, walked the horses aboard.

It weighed heavy on Noah, the notion that all of their lives would be in his hands. He walked on board the flatboat, one of many made and purchased in Erie. It looked to be a sturdy enough craft. While a crowd stood by on the muddy riverbank, Noah ignored them, walked to the front of the boat, gauged the current's speed, and tried not to strain to hear the voices in the water.

It was one of the swiftest currents he had ever seen. Word around town was that a handful of boats had gone downriver over the past week and three had broken up, sending passengers and goods into the water, many to their deaths. Other boats were beached along the shoreline, their owners opting to wait for the water to recede. Noah took a deep breath. Muddy, deep water churned wildly in the midst of the current as it rushed downstream. The sound lulled him, drowning out the murmur of the onlookers who stood along the shore watching in expectation.

Beneath him, the flatboat swayed, almost as if impatient to be on its way.

"What do you think, LeCroix? Can you do it?"

Noah sensed hesitation in Bridges for the first time. Faced with both the river and his wife's concern, the man was losing his bravado.

Noah scanned the opposite bank, then looked up and down the river. Hidden sandbars, debris, rocks, and shoals lurked beneath the water. Could he do it again? Could he see this family safely through?

"LeCroix?"

He ignored Bridges and waited for some sign, some intuitive impression that would assure success. He noted the wind direction, the breeze off the river. Then slowly, as if fed by the current, his heart began to beat in time with the water's flow. A soothing calm swept through him, the same sort of settling peace he had experienced in the pool. He listened for a moment longer, completely at one with the water. Then he smiled to himself.

Finally he turned his back on the Ohio and looked over at Bridges.

"I'm ready to leave any time you are."

Olivia leaned into kneading a pile of bread dough, pressed it down with the heels of her hands, straightened, pulled it toward her, pressed it against the floured tabletop again. She blew a stray curl out of her eyes. It was another day like most, full of endless chores and challenges. Since Noah had left, the days seemed empty and the nights endless. No longer did she catch herself watching for a glimpse of him or hoping he might suddenly appear at the door. He had been gone nearly a month now and she had finally convinced herself that he wasn't coming back.

Without Noah to trail after, the boys always seemed to be underfoot. She would have found it hard to keep her spirits up if it weren't for the fact that Susanna was slowly acting more like her old self and her father seemed much happier. There was a glimmer of hope that the couple might find the love they had once shared.

She was up to her elbows in dough when the boys came running through the door, Little Pay filthy but otherwise unscathed. Since his near-drowning, his string of accidents had ended and he had been far more attentive to his mother, even a bit more patient with Freddie.

They ran over to the table, where Freddie proceeded to poke a dirty finger into the bread dough. Olivia grabbed his wrist and pretended she was going to munch his finger off.

"Why can't we go to town today, too? I never even been there oneth," Freddie whined, pulling his hand out of her grasp. He swung on the edge of the table and then disappeared beneath it.

"You have, too," Little Pay reminded him. "When we moved here."

"I wath too little to remember."

All morning long she had tried to explain to them that they would all stay home so that Susanna and their father could go into Shawneetown alone. Little Pay had not argued, but Freddie continued to wage a hard-fought campaign.

"Run out and pick some flowers for your mother, why don't you?" She looked over at Little Pay as if to say, "Please, get him out of here."

He reached under the table and started tugging on his brother's arm. "Come on, Freddie, let's go."

"Aw . . ."

"We can race to the woods."

"Mark, thet, go!" Freddie shot out from beneath the table, and ran out the door with Little Pay charging after him yelling at the top of his lungs, "Cheater! You're cheating!"

Olivia laughed and shook her head.

"Livvie, would you mind braiding my hair for me?" Susanna walked up behind her.

Olivia gathered up the dough, dropped it in a heavy crockery bowl, and covered it with a dishtowel. She dusted off her hands on her apron.

"I would love to," Olivia assured her. "It's been a long, long time, hasn't it?" She looked into Susanna's blue eyes. Her stepmother's heart was mending.

Susanna led the way outside with her brush and some pins in her hands. Olivia followed. Susanna sat down on a tree stump near the door and handed over the brush.

"Are you certain you don't want to go into town with your father?"

"Not at all. I'm too tired to go today."

"All right then," Susanna said. "If you're sure."

Olivia relaxed as she combed out Susanna's long blond hair. Since Little Pay's accident in the stream Susanna had taken to joining in more, looking out for the boys, and even taking more pride in her appearance. When Payson asked Olivia to go to Shawneetown with him, she suggested that Susanna might want to go instead. Susanna had surprised them by readily agreeing, and a while later she even requested a hot tub of water for a good soak.

"You don't seem tired, Livvie, even though I know we work you too hard."

"I'm just thankful to be here," she said. She forced herself not to let her mind wander back to Heron Pond and the man who had wanted her to stay with him.

A long silence stretched between them while Olivia brushed out Susanna's hair and then separated it into three thick sections for braiding.

"Where were you, Livvie, all that time? Can't you tell us yet? Were you with Noah?"

Olivia's hands stilled. An image of Darcy standing over her, his satin dressing gown open down the front, flashed behind her eyes. She took a deep breath and told a half-truth.

"Noah brought me to Shawneetown."

Perceptive enough to hear the evasion, Susanna did not ask for more detail. Olivia lost herself in weaving the braid, twisting skein over skein of thick hair.

When her father came around the corner of the cabin and walked up to the two of them, Olivia could not help but notice that there was an awkward nervousness about him.

He watched her braid Susanna's hair for a few seconds. "I've got all the cured pelts Noah left us and a box of tomatoes loaded," he said.

"They'll make good barter for some of the things we need," Olivia said.

"You certain you don't want to come along? You and the boys could ride along in the cart." He had borrowed Bob Carver's oxcart for the journey.

Olivia shook her head, glad Freddie wasn't around to hear the offer.

"No, Daddy, you and Susanna need a day away from us, I'm sure."

Besides, she thought, she had no intention of going into town and be reminded of the day she arrived with Noah. Nor did she want to be anywhere near so many strangers coming and going on the river. If Darcy had put out a reward for her return, the kind of river scum he dealt with would be looking high and low for her. Until a little more time passed, she didn't want to risk running into any of them in town.

Freddie and Little Pay came around the house with bunches of brown-eyed Susans clutched in their hands.

"We got you some flowers, Ma," Little Pay said, thrusting them at Susanna. She took them with much fuss. Then, almost shyly, as if she no longer had the right, she kissed each boy on the cheek and thanked them.

"What if I weave a few of these into your braid?" Olivia suggested.

Susanna agreed, and by the time Olivia was finished, the boys pronounced their mother as beautiful as a queen. Payson stepped forward, took her hand, kissed it and then made a low bow, like a courtier of old. He went inside to get his rifle. Not, he reminded them, that he could actually hit anything with it. Susanna sent the boys in after him.

When they were alone, she stood up and took Olivia's hand, blushed and dropped her gaze. Her grip tightened. She swallowed a few times, working up the courage to speak.

"Livvie, I can't leave this hanging between us any longer. I hope someday you can forgive me for what happened on the river."

"Oh, Susanna, please. It's over now. We're all here, we're all fine." Olivia spoke without thinking. She had forgotten the baby Susanna lost, until she saw Susanna's tears. "I'm sorry, I—"

"Hush," Susanna shook her head. "Let's not speak of what happened again. I can tell that you've suffered, Livvie, and if it's any consolation, I have hated myself for begging your father to send you off with those horrible men that day."

"Please, Susanna, don't." Olivia didn't want to be reminded, nor did she want to hear her stepmother beg for forgiveness she could not yet fully give.

"I thought that you were surely dead, Livvie, and when God took my baby, I was certain He was making me pay for what I said that day. I know something terrible must have happened or you would have told Payson where you were. I know it's never far from his mind."

Olivia glanced frantically toward the door, praying her father wouldn't choose that moment to come outside. "I can't talk about it, Susanna," she whispered, trying to head off her panic, the terrible memories and lingering fear that Darcy still might find her. "Not yet."

"Then we won't speak of this ever again." Susanna leaned over and kissed Olivia on the cheek. "I only hope you can find it in your heart to forgive me someday."

Susanna rode high on the swaying oxcart, looking out across the fields Payson had cleared and plowed by himself and marveled that this man of letters, this mule-headed, inexperienced husband of hers had accomplished so much while she had been so mired in mourning. Glancing over her shoulder, she surveyed the modest cabin on the edge of the wood where the boys stood in the yard waving good-bye, until they lost interest and ran off to play.

When she turned back around, the cart was passing her baby girl's grave.

"Payson, please stop."

She saw him hesitate and thought he might be about to deny her request. He drew inward and shut down at first, but then he straightened, studying her carefully. Pulling on the ox's rig, he stopped the animal in its tracks. Then he walked over to help her climb down.

Susanna had never even been close to the little mound beneath the spreading oak where her infant daughter lay buried. Payson had taken the baby from her and carried it away before she was ready to let it go. She had seen the crooked little white cross marker from the cabin, but could not bear to look at it until Livvie had come home and forced her to go outside, into the sunlight.

Tears stung her eyes as Susanna knelt beside the grave and ran her hand across the new grass that sprouted over the tiny bump in the soil, pulling up a few straggling weeds and wilted dandelions. She was ashamed that this forlorn little grave for the baby with no name had been abandoned by everyone, even her mother. Susanna reached up, pulled one brown-eyed Susan out of her braid, then another and another, until she had them all in her hands.

Then, leaning over the grave, she slowly formed the letter B for *Baby* on the grass.

Payson walked up behind her and must have sensed her need to commune with the infant she had never known, for he remained silent until she rocked back, rested on her heels and sighed.

"There'll be others, Susanna." He spoke softly, resting his hand on her shoulder.

She stared down at the yellow blossoms, so bright, so vibrant with life against the green grass, and felt her heart stir. It had been so long since she had felt any inkling of love left within her, for herself or anyone, that she was overwhelmed with the brilliant flood that began to fill her.

Hopeful, she turned to look over her shoulder at him, saw the unconditional love in his eyes. It was the first time since the day she had begged him to give Livvie away that she had seen the same enduring love that had persuaded her to marry him reflected there.

Payson knelt beside her in the grass, put his arm around her shoulders and drew her close.

"Will there, Payson? Will there be other babies?"

" 'Bid me live, and I will live / Thy Protestant to be; / Or bid me love, and I will give / A loving heart to thee.' I love you, Susanna. You and the boys and Livvie are my life. There'll be more babies, whenever you are ready."

She lifted her mouth to his, knowing his kiss would be gentle, knowing the past was slipping behind the present. Knowing that they could begin again.

chapter
13

The Prince of the Ohio walked into Hunter Boone's tavern and trading post on the Mississippi, pausing just inside the door to watch his old friend serve up beer in heavy wooden mugs to a boatload of men standing shoulder to shoulder along the bar. To the naked eye, Hunter had not changed in three years. Still a commanding figure, he stood head and shoulders above the other men, taking coin, filling mugs, and wiping down the bar while keeping up a stream of conversation.

It was early in the day, so the long trestle tables set up around the cavernous room in the log structure were mostly empty, but the aroma of baking bread filled the air. Noah's stomach rumbled at the pleasurable thought of digging into a noon meal. Hunter's sister-in-law, Hannah, and his wife, Jemma, knew how to fill a man's stomach.

He knew what would happen as soon as the men at the bar saw him, but there was nothing to be done for it, so with rifle in hand and his pack slung over his shoulder, Noah walked across the room. It didn't take long for Hunter to look up and recognize him. When he did, the big man in buckskins left the bar and strode across the room, grabbed Noah in a bear hug, and pounded him heartily on the back.

"Where in the hell have you been? I already know all about some of the Prince of the Ohio's latest exploits. Heard you not only launched in the worst current in years, but delivered the boat safely to Natchez."

Noah nodded. "That's about the size of it."

"Along the way, did you warn another pilot what was beneath the surface a half a mile up ahead, and save him from capsizing?"

The men at the bar had stopped talking and were listening intently to the exchange. Noah shifted, uncomfortable with the attention.

"Don't believe everything you hear," Noah said, careful to keep his voice low.

"You're gonna be a bigger legend than you were before. How did you do it?" Hunter clapped him on the back again, took his arm and led him over to a table near the bar and motioned for him to sit down. "Here, let me take your rifle and your pack. You'll stay the night, of course. Hell, stay a week or two. It'll be great for business Wait until Jemma sees you." Hunter glanced over at the patrons at the bar, then back at Noah. "You look good. Real good, Noah. Better than I expected."

Noah nodded. "Thanks." He hoped Hunter would eventually let him get a word in. There was so much he wanted to say to the man who had brought him back from the brink of death and then talked him into living.

At a sign of movement in the door to the cabin addition where the women did the cooking, Noah turned his head and saw Jemma Boone drying her hands on an apron tied around her burgeoning waistline. With her blond hair, blue eyes, and ready, dimpled smile, she had an angelic look about her that belied her mischievous nature. She recognized him immediately and her face lit up. Noah stood as she crossed the room to greet him.

"Noah LeCroix, you've been away far too long."

She reached up to hug him, catching him off guard. He had never put his arms around a woman carrying a child before; for an awkward moment, he did not quite know how to maneuver. Jemma made him blush when she burst out laughing.

"Hunter says he likes it when there's more of me to love, and right now there's plenty." She walked over to Hunter and sidled up close enough to slip beneath his arm.

At the easy but telling gesture, an anchor of loneliness tugged at Noah's heart.

"I hear you sold your soul to the devil," she laughed.

"You know better than that," Hunter told her. "Noah drives too hard a bargain. The devil couldn't afford to trade with him."

Noah finally laughed, thinking of the bag full of gold Bridges had paid him after he delivered the family safely down to Natchez. It had taken him two weeks to come back up the Trace as far as Sandy Shoals, but the solitude of the trail had been worth the delay.

"Where you headed?" Hunter asked as he took Noah's pack and rifle and stored them behind the bar.

"Home to a cypress swamp in southern Illinois."

"I've heard a lot about that section of Illinois. Fertile river valleys that overflow like the Nile. Didn't somebody buy a tract of land last year on the delta between the Mississippi and the Ohio and name it Cairo? I've often thought of moving up there." Hunter quickly glanced over at Jemma. Her smile had quickly faded. "Well, not until the children get older," Hunter added.

"Children?" Noah looked at Jemma and then Hunter.

"This is the second," she said proudly, smoothing her hand over the bulge beneath the apron. "We've already got a little boy."

Noah looked up at Hunter. "I can't believe it."

"Why not?"

He shrugged, embarrassed again. "I don't know. It's just that . . . well, I guess it was bound to happen."

Jemma and Hunter both laughed. "Wait until you see him," Hunter boasted. "He's the cutest little imp on both sides of the Mississippi."

"He's only saying that because Derek looks just like him," Jemma said.

Noah watched the looks they exchanged and found himself having to look away. Jemma promised him the best meal he had eaten in years and bustled off to the kitchen after telling Hunter that she would send his brother, Luther, in to tend the bar so that he and Noah could talk.

A young traveler at the bar, tall and lanky with a thin blond beard, was watching Noah with awe.

"You're really him, aren't you?" The young man took a swig of ale and raised his mug. "To the Prince of the Ohio. I never thought to see you in person."

Uncomfortable, Noah merely shrugged him off and sat down at the table with his back to the room. Hunter slid onto the bench across from him.

"You doing all right?" Hunter wanted to know. He leaned across the table, watching Noah carefully.

"Yeah. I hate all of that, though."

"I figured you did. Been feeling all right?"

Noah nodded. "Great." How did a man explain a heartache that would never kill him—just make him hurt morning, noon, and night? He had thought that time and distance would have driven Olivia out of his mind, but it had only intensified his feelings.

Jemma brought out a plate heaped with ham and beans and biscuits and gravy and then made the rounds of customers. As Noah dug in, Hunter was content to let him eat without any more questions. They settled back into the easy, quiet comradery they had always shared. Finally, when Noah had finished most of the meal, Hunter shook his head.

"Something's on your mind."

Why deny it, Noah thought. "Yeah. A couple of things."

"Such as?"

Noah lowered his voice, leaned toward the center of the table. "You're going to think I've lost more than my eye."

"Go on."

"You're going to think I've lost my mind."

"Why don't you get to the point and let me be the judge of that?"

"Water talks to me."

Hunter laughed until he realized Noah was perfectly serious, then sobered and scratched his head.

"Water talks to you?"

"Yeah." He rubbed his hand over the back of his neck.

"What in the hell does it say?"

"It doesn't really speak in words so much as it gives me a notion of where it's going and what's hidden beneath it."

Hunter frowned. "That's how you knew to warn that other pilot? The *water* told you?"

Noah was sorry he had said anything at all. If Hunter did not believe him, no one else would. He was beginning to understand why his mother had left her clan behind to live in isolation.

"How long has this been happening to you?"

"A few weeks."

"I don't know what to say, Noah. I never heard anything like it." As if he did not want to hear anything else about talking water, Hunter changed the subject.

"You said you had a couple of problems. Maybe I can help with the other."

Noah doubted it. At that point, Jemma came back into the tavern with a bright-eyed child riding her hip. The boy was a miniature version of both of them, complete with thick blond hair and sky-blue eyes. He had Jemma's dimples and smile. Suddenly, Noah envied his friend something that until now, he never knew he wanted.

Jemma walked up beside Noah. The toddler popped his fingers into his mouth and stared down at him.

"This is Derek Noah Boone," she said proudly. "Derek, say hello to your uncle Noah."

The boy drooled but did not utter a word. Jemma tried to hand Derek over to Noah, but the child kicked and squirmed, wanting nothing of the sort. She gave him to Hunter instead and went back to work. Noah watched Hunter jostle the baby to a comfortable position and pull his empty mug over so that Derek could play with it.

"Are you happy, Hunt?" The question was out before Noah could call it back.

Hunter looked over at him as if he had not heard right. "Am I happy? What do you mean?"

"All this," Noah said, gesturing around the tavern. "You told me once you weren't going to live in one place any longer than you had to, and now here you are with a wife and a family."

A contented smile slowly spread across Hunter's face. "Yeah, well, that was before Jemma O'Hurley ran into me in New Orleans and changed my mind." He considered Noah carefully. "Somehow, I get the feeling your other problem involves a woman."

Noah shrugged.

"It's about time," Hunter said, sounding relieved. "Tell me about her. Where did you meet her?"

"I found her."

"Don't tell me the water led you to her."

"No. She was lost in the swamp where I live now, which is another long story. I helped get her back to her family in Shawneetown."

"And now?"

"She's still got a lot of things to settle."

"You love her."

"I want her. All the time. Is that the same?"

"Does she want you?" Hunter's expression darkened to an angry scowl. "If she's the kind of woman who would let that eye patch stand in the way—"

Noah shook his head. "Nothing like that. It's just that she's been hurt. It'll take her some time."

Noah was not a talker to begin with, and uttering such confidences was nearly choking him. As he collected himself, he watched Derek grab Hunter's shirtfront, pull himself up to a standing position on his father's thigh, and take hold of a handful of Hunter's hair. Hunter easily extricated himself, sat the boy down and began to bounce him on his knee. Derek proceeded to pound the tabletop with his fists.

"You've had nieces and nephews, Hunt. A family. What do I know about being a husband or a father? I saw my father only a few weeks a year. I don't know how to hold a child, let alone talk to one. Even if she wanted to be with me, Olivia deserves more, especially after all she has been through.''

Derek started banging the wooden trencher against the table. Hunter tried to talk over the noise.

"They don't come better than you, Noah. You think I would give Derek just anybody's name?"

Payson Bond, Susanna, their boys, the struggling farm, the crude cabin, Olivia—all of them were never far from Noah's mind. Neither were his doubts.

"How do you do it?" he asked his friend. "How does any man stay no matter what happens?"

"If you have to ask, then you aren't really in love," Hunter said, with such surety and conviction that Noah began to doubt himself.

"But how will you know what answers to give your boy when he starts asking you questions? How can you even let yourself love him without being scared to death every minute of the day that something might happen to him? How do you face ever losing Jemma now that you have given her your heart?"

"Noah—"

"How in the hell do you know what to do?"

Hunter sighed. His gaze roamed the room until he found Jemma, watched her for a long moment, and then looked back again.

"Every family faces loss. There is not a father, mother, brother, sister, cousin, or friend that has not lost someone. No one is spared the death of a loved one—unless, of course, he chooses to hide himself in a swamp for his entire life and never know another living soul. But death has already touched you, Noah. Your father deserted you. You lost your mother and survived.

"As to having a family, there are no lessons on how to be a good husband and father, at least nothing written down like those guidebooks the emigrants from back East carry around with them. I just do the best I can. That's all any man can do. I know you well enough to know that you would do just fine."

Noah was still about as confused as he had been when he walked in.

Hunter straightened Derek's long shirt. "If you love her, Noah, don't let her go because you can't foresee the future. Just take one day at a time," he said.

Noah thought of Olivia, of all she had yet to settle within herself, of the fear that never left her, of her deep commitment to her family. He wished things were easier.

Derek was tired of the mug and began to squirm and fuss. Hunter shifted him to his hip. Before he stood up, he leaned across the table.

"Noah, if I were you?"

"Yeah?"

"I wouldn't tell anyone else about the talking water."

Shawneetown

Olivia ignored the incessant chatter of the young Scottish girl beside her as they headed into town accompanied by Little Pay and Freddie. There might be but a year's difference in their ages, but Molly MacKinnon seemed centuries younger. Two weeks ago, Molly had appeared at the cabin door without a word of explanation or apology, begging to have her fetch-and-carry job back, promising Payson that she wasn't about to run off again. She was willing to work for room and board, but when he told her that Olivia was with them, that they would no longer be needing her, Molly had stood on the threshold cussing a blue streak, not at him, but at herself, for ruining the opportunity to enjoy three meals a day.

As bemused by the girl's spunk as she was moved by the obvious signs of poverty in Molly's ragged, soiled gown, her bare feet, and her need of a good sudsing, Olivia had interceded for her, convincing her father that she could certainly use the extra help. Besides, she had added, Noah had already put by enough venison and ham to feed all of them *and* Molly.

Her father readily agreed, as Olivia knew he would.

Since she had been home he was more than willing to take any suggestions. She knew he was trying to assuage his guilt, and in Molly's case she let him. A few times she had almost told him what had happened in New Orleans, but then she would look around the humble cabin or see him struggling in the fields and, knowing all he faced and all he lost, she simply could not bring herself to add to his burden. They continued to dance around the truth and some days it was hard to ignore, almost as if something as big as Bob Carver's ox had wandered into the cabin and no one wanted to admit it was there.

Venturing into Shawneetown today had been the last thing Olivia had wanted to do, but when her father told her that he needed to have a day at home alone with Susanna, there was nothing she could do but agree to take Little Pay, Freddie, and Molly into town. Over the past few weeks she had watched Susanna grow stronger in both mind and body. Just as before the attack on the river, loving looks and gentle touches passed between her father and stepmother. No matter how reluctant Olivia still felt about going into town, she could not deny them the time alone they desperately needed.

Besides, she reminded herself earlier, it had been months since she had escaped from Darcy. Surely by now he had already taken in another virgin. Surely by now he had forgotten all about her. In a way, taking the boys and Molly to town with her was a godsend, for she would not be as vulnerable as she would be if alone. Sooner or later she would have had to get out into the world again. Letting go of her fear would help her turn her back on the past.

It had taken them over an hour to walk the two miles to town as both she and Molly carried baskets of vegetables to trade at the store. Freddie and Little Pay had run ahead, their dirty bare feet flying as they zigzagged back and forth across the field and along the footpath through the woods.

Molly had chatted on and on beside her. Olivia caught the Scots girl talking to herself so often that she did not think Molly cared if she listened to her or not.

"So ye see, it was my father's grand design to send me

here to America, but och, there's many a day I wish I was back in Scotland again.''

"Do you know where the store is, Molly?'' Knowing that waiting for the girl to take a breath was futile, Olivia cut in.

"I sure do. It's just over there.'' She pointed toward Nu Way Dry Goods, Ern and Faye Matheson's store.

Little Pay came running up to Olivia. "Can we go to the landing, Livvie? Can we go see the flatboats?''

Olivia scanned the street, taking note of the wagons, the horses, the churned mud that filled the wide lane between the two rows of buildings, the main thoroughfare of Shawneetown.

"I think you should stay with me.''

"I don't mind watching the little fellows, Livvie,'' Molly volunteered. "I surely don't. We can drop these baskets by the store and then I'll keep them busy while ye look around a bit.''

Olivia thought Molly as scatterbrained as the boys, but when she saw how eager her half-brothers were to see the riverfront, she decided to give in. She took a deep breath and silently swore that there was nothing to fear, that Molly could see to the boys, and that she was perfectly capable of taking care of herself now.

Freddie had run back to join Little Pay and the two of them started begging to go on ahead like magpies.

"Don't forget the red cloth,'' Freddie reminded her. They had both been wanting shirts like Noah's. It had been ages since she had sewn anything, but she had promised them, deciding that two small shirts was as good a place to start again as any, and not a great extravagance.

"I'll get it,'' she assured him. "Walk with us to the store and then Molly will take you to the river.''

"Hey!'' Freddie grabbed her by the elbow and started jumping up and down beside her. He pointed down the crowded street. "Hey, lookit! It'th Noah! There'th Noah, Livvie, crothin the threet.''

He flew off as if shot from a cannon, his short legs churning, his feet kicking up mud. Little Pay was hot on his heels and quickly passed his brother by as they raced along.

"Do they mean the man who built the smokehouse?" Molly asked, reminding Olivia she was still there.

Olivia nodded, unable to find her voice until she spotted Noah: heart-stoppingly handsome, his skin darkened by the sun, his strong features shaded by his hat brim. He was using the ragged red strip of turkey cloth as an eye patch and carried his pack and rifle, looking much the same as the day he left, except that now he led a sorrel horse.

The boys had stopped him in his tracks. She watched him greet them, then quickly scan the surroundings until Little Pay pointed in her direction and Noah turned her way. She faltered, almost tripped, then caught herself.

"Jeezus, now he's a fine handsome devil," Molly said.

Olivia instantly bristled. "He is that." She glanced over at the auburn-haired girl, assessing her shining blue eyes, her glowing cheeks, and the dusting of freckles spattered across her nose. She had never known jealousy before, so the experience was a new one, especially since she knew she had no right to claim Noah after turning him away.

Down the street, his long strides were eating up the distance between them. He handed the reins to Little Pay and now both the boys were running in his wake, trying to keep up.

Olivia's heart was pounding so hard she felt light-headed, but she found herself smiling for no reason at all, save one.

Noah.

Olivia smothered the urge to run to meet him. She straightened the skirt of her plain violet dress, raised a hand to her hair and decided it was too late to do anything about the way she looked.

Noah's mouth was set in a grim, determined line. They had not parted on the best of terms, but surely there was no reason for him to frown so.

"Noah, what a surprise." Even to her own ears, the greeting sounded inane.

"What are you doing in town by yourself?"

chapter
14

"I'M NOT ALONE," SHE SAID. "I'M WITH THE BOYS. AND Molly."

Noah dismissed the girl beside her with a glance.

"Not much protection," he said.

"From what?"

"I would think you know that better than I do."

Her heart was hammering so hard she could barely hear herself think. Seeing him there on the street, she knew for a certainty that time and distance could never erase what he had come to mean to her. She saw with blinding clarity that she more than cared for him. She loved Noah LeCroix. No matter how long he might stay away, no matter how many times she sent him home, she would always love him, but she would never be good enough for him, either.

Fighting to mask her feelings, she tightened her grip on the basket handle. "What are you doing here?"

He looked over her head, toward the path that led in the direction of the homestead and sidestepped her question with one of his own. "Where's your father?"

"I'm Molly MacKinnon," the Scottish girl suddenly piped up.

Noah ignored Molly. He asked Olivia again, "Where's Payson?"

"At home with Susanna. I'm perfectly capable of taking

care of myself and the boys." She handed her basket to Molly.

Little Pay and Freddie, leading Noah's horse, had finally reached them.

"Noah'th got a new horth." Freddie, as usual, proudly announced the obvious.

"He's taking us for a ride," Little Pay added.

"Why don't the two of you go down to the waterfront with Molly? _Now_," Olivia suggested.

They were both outraged. "Because we wanna stay with Noah," Little Pay told her.

Noah looked pained, but made no protest.

"Noah has things to do, I'm sure," Olivia told them, wishing them away for a few blessed moments of peace.

"No, I don't," he said.

The boys started jumping up and down.

"Your problem is that you are too honest," she told him.

Noah reached out and lifted a lock of her hair, rubbing it between his fingers. For an awkward moment, Olivia thought he might carry it to his lips. He let go and it dropped onto the bodice of her gown. The movement was open and spontaneous, as intimate as a kiss. Olivia went weak in the knees.

Blessed Molly chose that instant to set both baskets on the ground beside Olivia and announce, "My arms are breakin'. Come on, boys, off we go down to the river. You'll have a chance to talk to your friend Noah here in a while. How about we let him use those muscles of his to help Livvie carry the vegetable baskets to the store?"

Somehow the girl managed to persuade both boys to go with her without much fuss at all, and she even took it upon herself to tell Noah that they would tie his horse up at the hitching post outside the store.

Noah was still watching Olivia. She could feel his gaze on her as surely as if it had the warmth and power of his touch.

"How are things with you, Olivia?"

"Fine. Little Pay hasn't had any more accidents. The whole episode at the pool seems to have shaken Susanna out of herself. She's still not the way she was before, but she's let go of some of her sorrow and is up and about a little more. Molly's the girl my father had hired who ran off before. Everything seems to be getting better, little by little.''

"You speak of your family, but what of you? Have you told your father yet? Have you settled things between you?"

She caught her bottom lip between her teeth and looked at the ground. "There hasn't been a good time."

"Still having nightmares?"

The nightmares had started up again the night he left, but she wasn't about to admit it.

"No." She looked up and knew he had caught her in the lie. "Well, not so often, really."

He reached down for the baskets, picked them up, and waited for her to make the next move. Olivia started down the street and he fell into step beside her.

"What are you doing here?" She hoped her feelings did not show in her eyes. "Where did you get the horse?"

"I took a job piloting a boat downriver. Went as far as Natchez. Came back and picked up another one, went down again. In between I stopped off to see a friend in Kentucky who was looking to thin out his herd. I thought I'd give it to your father."

She stopped walking. "That's too generous," she said, unwilling for her family to owe him any more than they already did.

"I bought it as a favor to a friend. What am I going to do with a horse? Can you see it up in the treehouse?"

She found herself laughing for the first time in days. All too soon they reached the store. Now and again a passerby would stop and stare at Noah and then move on. At least no one started singing.

"Why don't you go on in, do what you need to do. I'll walk you and the others home," he suggested.

She wanted nothing more than to linger with him, but tried to change his mind. "I'm sure we can handle the horse, if you don't want to go back with us."

He stared back.

"All right," she said. "When I finish I'll find the boys and Molly and meet you here in an hour."

Noah walked into a tavern, a log structure filled with men on the move who needed a respite from the rigors of life in the West. He had been in the area for three days now, long enough for the townsfolk to become accustomed to him. The curious still stared.

His needing a drink was rare, but after seeing Olivia he decided a shot of whiskey might settle his nerves. He couldn't feel any worse.

Unless he took Hunter's final words of advice and came right out and asked her to marry him, this would be the last time he might ever see her.

He ordered a whiskey and carried the glass over to a table on the far side of the room. From there he could watch the door. He had to sit elbow-to-elbow with a group of blackjack players at the table beside him, but after the usual once-over and expressions of recognition, they paid him no mind.

With his pack on the floor beside him and his rifle propped against the wall, Noah forced himself to sip the whiskey slowly, hoping it would give him all the courage he needed.

The vegetable baskets were pounds lighter now that only a bit of red fabric, some buttons and thread were inside. Olivia stood outside the store, looked toward the river, and hoped tracking down the boys wouldn't take long. Shawneetown was more crowded with emigrants on the move than townsfolk.

After the isolation of the homestead, it was a joy to be out among people again, even though her heart was heavy. She walked along wondering how long it would be before she had to tell Noah good-bye again.

She stood in front of the hotel, watching a ferry crossing the river. On the other side of the Ohio, wagons, horses, and travelers on foot were lined up, prepared to wait for hours to cross into Illinois.

A flash of sunlight on a man's light blond hair caught her eye. The familiar tilt of his head momentarily paralyzed her. She could hear her heart beating in her ears. Bile rose up in her throat and for a moment she was afraid she might actually swoon. She put a hand against the side of the building to brace herself and stepped back into the shadows. As if a terrible nightmare were unfolding before her eyes, she watched Darcy Lankanal and a man she had once seen at the Palace in Darcy's office. They were strolling along the waterfront in heated conversation.

Her mind cried out for her to run, but her legs would not obey. Then, Darcy raised his head, as if he heard the terrified tattoo of her heart and sensed her presence. He slowly turned and surveyed the crowd milling about around him. As Olivia watched, helpless as a fly tangled in a spider's web, he turned his gaze on her.

The instant he recognized her, his expression froze. Then he smiled, a slow spreading smile on a too-handsome face. She was drawn to him, forced to step out of the shadows and walk toward him, not out of any mutual sense of attraction, but like a pet trained to obey.

She watched him say something to his companion. The older man looked at her with a smug smile and walked away. Olivia stood there trembling, hoping Molly and the boys wouldn't choose that exact moment to appear, wishing there were a way she could escape the inevitable, knowing there was not.

Overwhelming fear, not for herself, but for Noah, came over her. If he saw her with Darcy and guessed who the man was, there was no guaranteeing what he might do.

Darcy was upon her, smiling a smile that did not reach his eyes.

"So, Olivia, we meet again. I knew I would find you eventually."

She lifted her chin, feigning confidence she did not possess, daring him to try anything in broad daylight.

"Now that you have, you can turn right around and go back to New Orleans."

"Not without you," he said.

"I'm afraid things have changed, Darcy."

"Nothing has changed. I still own you."

"I'm no slave."

"Nor are you free. I paid good money for you, a small fortune in some men's eyes. You still owe me."

"I was *stolen* from my family and you know it."

He shrugged, a slow, lazy movement, a slight rise of the shoulder, barely perceptible. "I have no proof of that."

Her family lived so near, was so vulnerable.

He reached out, tried to draw her to him. She resisted, stepped back, but he was stronger.

"Relax, Olivia. Just relax and remember how good it can be between us."

It was no use to try to fight him physically, so instead, she tried to win at his game. She leaned into him, raised herself on tiptoe and pressed her mouth to his. Nothing moved inside her, nothing stirred except revulsion, but through the thin fabric of her calico gown she felt his immediate arousal and let him kiss her, kissing him back without feeling, and yet provoking him, teasing him. Then, once he was off guard, she broke the kiss and stepped an arm's length away.

Surprise and then anger swept across his finely drawn, aristocratic features.

"I'm not that woman anymore, Darcy."

"Yes, you are. If you were smart you would admit it and come with me. Now." He glanced around at the bustling crowd on the street as people streamed through the town. "We can do this nice and easy, Olivia, or we can do it the hard way, but I'm going to have you."

"Never again."

"You grew used to my touch, Olivia. What happened? Did the half-breed hurt you? Has he made you hate men?"

The half-breed.

So, he already knew of Noah, of Noah's connection to her. How? Had he seen them together earlier?

"I don't know what you are talking about."

"I've been here for two days, asking around about you and your family, finding out all I could. I've even seen your one-eyed hero, Olivia. I could have killed him by now, you know. The only thing that's kept him alive is the idea that I thought I might have needed to use him as bait to lure you in. I figured as long as he was strutting around town that you would show your face sooner or later."

She swallowed bile again. Darcy had been in town for two days, walking the same streets as Noah, watching him from afar. One bullet, one thrust of a knife and Noah might have been dead already. His blood would be on her hands, his only crime loving her.

"Leave me alone, Darcy, leave Noah alone, or I swear to God I'll go right to Ern Matheson, the keeper of the peace, and tell him everything. It'll be my word against yours."

He laughed. "You'll tell him *everything*? You'll tell him how you learned to like it when I made love to you? How you screamed every time I came inside you, Olivia? Will you tell him how much you begged for release?" He folded his arms across his brocade vest. "Go ahead and tell him everything. I'm sure your family will find the details inter-esting—even if they know the whole sordid story already."

Her palms were damp. She could barely breathe.

"You have plenty of other girls, Darcy. You don't need me."

As if he could see right through her clothing, he stared at the front of her gown. "Oh, but I do, Olivia. I do need you."

"Even you wouldn't stoop to murder."

"You think not?"

"Yes."

"Why don't we just see about that?" He was looking over her shoulder now. "Looks like your hero is on his way."

Ern Matheson had walked up to Noah in the tavern and took him aside, told him that a slick-looking gambler from

New Orleans had been in town a couple of days asking questions about the Bonds. Seeing as how Noah was close to the family, Ern said he thought Noah ought to know. The minute Matheson was through, Noah set down his empty whiskey glass, picked up his rifle, shouldered his pack and hurried out the door.

And discovered he had not moved fast enough.

The fine hairs on the back of his neck were bristling as Noah walked down the street toward Olivia and the tall, hatless stranger by the river. The cut of the man's clothes were far superior to those of the farmers and homesteaders milling around the flatboats or driving down the street on wagons loaded high with their possessions. The sun glinted off the man's light hair and the front of his shining satin waistcoat.

No one had to tell him that man was Darcy Lankanal. He could see it in Olivia's stance, in the look on her face. Why didn't she walk away? What was holding her there?

Noah saw Darcy Lankanal glance up. The gambler said something else to Olivia that suddenly made her stiffen. Noah picked up his pace and reached them in five long strides. Olivia whirled around. She said nothing. He stepped up beside her and stood close enough to feel her shaking like a leaf in a high wind. Compelled to let her know she was safe, he slipped an arm around her shoulders.

Darcy Lankanal's mouth hardened into a grim line. Noah silently challenged him with a look. He could see that the man was hard put to control himself. The gambler stood with his feet apart, braced to attack, his hands fisted at his sides. The last thing Noah wanted was to have to fight this man, especially in front of the whole town.

"Ah," Lankanal drawled. "You must be the famous Noah LeCroix. The flatboat pilot." He had a way of pronouncing every word as if it were profane.

"That would be me." Noah acknowledged him with a nod.

"Noah, please. Let's go," Olivia whispered.

She was shaking so violently that he feared she wouldn't be able to keep her feet.

"Does he know about you?" Darcy asked her, ignoring Noah for the moment. "Does he know about us?"

"I know *all* about her and what you did to her, Lankanal. None of that matters to me."

"I see my name and reputation proceeds me, too," Darcy smiled. "Hounds are used to scraps. They'll welcome another man's leavings. Now me, I'm particular." He focused on Olivia. "Remember what I told you, Olivia. You *will* see me again." Then he looked at Noah long and hard before he turned back to her again. "It's just a matter of time."

Darcy marveled at his own strength when he turned and walked away, for there was a deep darkness clouding his mind. When Telford Betts rushed up to join him, he still could not concentrate on anything but Olivia.

Even dressed like a pauper, she was more beautiful than any woman he had ever known. He could not remember feeling this way before; certainly he had never expected such a jolt when he saw her again. He shook his head, trying to fathom what had come over him.

Threatening LeCroix's life had not been enough to persuade her to come along with him. After seeing the way she had looked at the man, he knew why. Obviously, Olivia had somehow deluded herself into thinking that she was actually in love with the half-breed. The way she had stared at LeCroix, glowing and radiant despite her obvious fear, had been a kick in the gut. One thing was certain. There would be no having her as long as LeCroix was around.

Betts was practically yelling in his ear. Darcy stared down at his hands. He had never killed a man. The threats he had voiced had been for Olivia's benefit, but after seeing the way she had gazed up at LeCroix, he could almost consider killing.

Betts put his hand on Darcy's sleeve and tugged hard. Darcy stopped walking. They were almost back to the hotel.

"*What*, man?" When he realized he was yelling, Darcy lowered his voice. "What in the hell do you want?"

"My money." Betts's voice was hushed but furtive. He

flushed beet red, his neck oozing over a too-tight collar.

"Not until I have her." Darcy tried to walk away. The land agent held onto his sleeve, wrinkling the expensive material. Darcy tried to uncurl the man's fingers one by one.

"I held up my end of the bargain," Betts whined.

"When I get her, you'll get paid. For now, shut up, Betts."

"But—"

Darcy turned on the man. "Shut up! I'm thinking."

Betts backed down but matched his stride as they went through the door of the hotel.

If he couldn't get to Olivia, Darcy decided he would go to her father. The very idea that she would choose to live here, in this backwoods mudhole, dressed in a plain dress with a mud-stained hem, wearing the moccasins of a savage instead of silk slippers, was beyond him. She could be living in grand style in New Orleans, where he would dress her like a queen, give her the finest of everything.

As they entered the hotel, the odor of boiled cabbage hit him. He had not seen very many people around who did not look as poor as church mice. Maybe Olivia's return had been viewed by her family as nothing more than a bad penny turning up again. Perhaps she was just one more unwanted mouth to feed and her father would not hesitate to sell her. After all, he had given her away before. Darcy decided all he had to do was offer the man what a settler would consider a small fortune and he'd have Olivia again.

He nearly collided with Jewel McGuire, the proprietor of the hotel, a whiskey barrel of a man who reeked of liquor. He sidestepped the man, lost in thought, unable to forget the way Olivia had looked up at Noah LeCroix. He could not get the memory out of his mind.

He had to get to her father, right away, before she went whining to him for protection. How long would she and LeCroix be in town?

Walking upstairs, Darcy stopped so abruptly that Betts ran into him.

"Come with me," he said, turning around, heading down

again. "I want you to watch my back while I rent a horse at the livery."

Betts's upper lip was coated with sweat, his florid face nearly purple. "Where are you going?"

"To make a poor man an offer he can't refuse."

After she watched Darcy walk away, Olivia turned immediately to Noah and was amazed at his transformation. Gone was the caring, sensitive man who had given her sanctuary. She could feel his anger, so strong it almost made her recoil; she knew that if she did not act quickly, he was going to take it upon himself to see that Darcy never bothered her again. If that happened, she hated to think of the outcome.

She was cursed. She had to be. Since the attack on the river, trouble followed her everywhere. This time she had led it straight to Noah in the form of Darcy Lankanal. Her past and her present had just collided.

Dear God, she thought suddenly, what if Darcy had been watching the homestead? What if he knew the boys on sight? She became frantic to find them.

"I have to get home." She voiced her immediate thought aloud. "We have to find the boys and Molly and head back."

Noah grabbed her hand, forcing her to turn and look at him.

"Olivia, you have nothing to fear from him. Trust me."

She shook her head. "You don't know him. I don't want you anywhere near him. Please, promise me you won't do anything, Noah. Give me your word."

He pulled her in the direction of the wharf. "Let's find the boys."

She tugged on his hand, trying to get him to listen. "Noah, *please*." Her voice caught, broke. "Please say you'll ignore Darcy. He'll go away. I know he will." She had to think of something fast; there had to be a way to keep everyone safe.

Noah continued to lead her along the waterfront. As silent as a prairie grave, he made no promises, and his silence scared her to death. She needed to put time and distance between him and Darcy, send him on his way back to Heron Pond. She could not have his death on her hands.

It took them precious time to find the boys, who had made their way back to the store and charmed penny candy out of Faye Matheson. By the time they tracked them down, Olivia was about to come out of her skin. Sensing her irritation, Molly rounded up the boys. Noah settled them both atop the gelding and told Molly to start walking them down the trail toward home.

With Noah as untalkative as a stone, conversation was out of the question. Olivia tried, but could not bring herself to make small talk either, not with the image of Darcy here in Shawneetown so clear in her mind.

When they reached the edge of the homestead property, he stopped and watched Molly lead the horse across the field to the cabin.

"Come with me to my campsite, Olivia."

She could tell by his tone it was not a request—it was a demand.

"I really should get back and you should be on your way."

"You really think I would leave you now?"

"Yes. Because I'm asking you to."

"As if I were one of the boys?"

"Noah, don't."

"Come with me, Olivia. Now. We have to talk."

She put her hands to her temples. Determination, fear, anger at Darcy, love for Noah—all of it was pulling her apart.

"There's nothing more to say."

"Yes, there is," he told her. She knew by his tone that he was not going to budge until she heard him out.

Olivia sighed and looked across the field. The sun was going down behind the treeline. Deep blue shadows gathered against the trees. The cabin looked like a doll's house from where they stood, with yellow-gold light framed in the windows and white smoke curling up out of the rock chimney. A picture of peace and serenity. Within, her father and Susanna were putting their lives back together.

What would happen to them when she told them about Darcy? Surely she must confess all before the night passed. He was too close, too much a threat to all of them now. She had to tell her father. She had to warn him that the wolf was almost at the door.

And Noah? Noah was waiting for her, and she knew by the look on his face that he was not about to be denied this time.

There had to be some way to persuade him to leave, some way to be certain that he was out of harm's way for good. Even now, Darcy might be plotting to get her back through Noah.

She did not think he would act before morning. Darcy Lankanal did things at his own convenience. No one made him jump. She was convinced that he would toy with her awhile, let her stew and fret and worry about when he might appear. She truly doubted he would go so far as to ride out to the homestead.

No doubt he would have the best dinner money could buy him in Shawneetown and let her worry through a sleepless night.

The delay would give her time to find the courage to tell her father everything, as well as to convince Noah that she wanted him gone.

Olivia took a deep breath.

"All right, Noah. We'll talk."

chapter
15

DARCY LOOKED INTO PAYSON BOND'S VULNERABLE BLUE eyes and hated him on sight. The man bore no resemblance to Olivia in temperament or features. Here, Darcy thought as he introduced himself to the slightly built farmer, is the man who sold his daughter to river scum. A man not worthy of having such a treasure. From the looks of the poorly appointed cabin, the ragamuffin little boys and his sad-eyed younger wife hovering in the background, Darcy figured that Payson Bond would be easily bought.

"I'm looking for Olivia," he said.

"Come in, sir. Welcome." Bond eyed him curiously, but ushered him in politely nonetheless. Obviously the man had no idea who or what he was to Olivia.

The two sticky-faced, dirty imps came running across the room. He gave them a cursory glance and no more.

"Would you like to sit down?" Payson shooed the boys away and pointed to the table and benches.

Darcy would rather have been boiled in oil than sit anywhere in the crowded, messy room. "Thanks, but I'll stand."

Something rustled in the loft. He glanced up, half expecting to see Olivia, but it was an auburn-haired young girl with sparkling blue eyes whose face appeared over the edge. She stared down at him curiously. He dismissed her and concentrated on Bond again.

"Olivia's not here?"

Payson shook his head. "No. She's off with Noah somewhere. They sent the boys on ahead."

"You let her go off with a half-breed?"

The man immediately bristled. "I take offense to that remark, Mr. Lankanal. Noah LeCroix has been a true friend to this family and I trust him. Now perhaps you should state your business. What do you want with Olivia?"

LeCroix had obviously wormed his way into Bond's favor, which only infuriated Darcy more, so much so that he wanted to strike out and hurt someone.

"I want Olivia back, is what I want. I invested quite a sum in her in New Orleans and she's yet to pay me back in full."

Bond blanched white, which surprised Darcy, given the circumstances by which Olivia came to him in the first place.

"Explain yourself, sir." When Payson Bond recoiled and took a step back, Darcy smiled.

"After you sold her to Colonel Sullivan, he brought her to New Orleans and charged me an exorbitant sum for her. Since she was still a virgin, I gave in and paid the amount he demanded. In gold, I might add."

Bond's face drained of color. Darcy watched the farmer turn to the little boys, but it was a moment or two before he found his voice. "Go up to the loft, Little Pay. Take Freddie with you."

"Aw, Daddy. Why can't we stay?"

"Go!" Payson shouted.

Both boys moved quickly, the elder shepherding the younger up the ladder to the loft, where the girl was still staring down over the edge of the floor. In the farthest corner of the room, Bond's wife was sitting on the bed, leaning back against the wall with her eyes closed. Darcy did not know if she was listening or not, nor did he care.

Once the two boys were out of sight, Bond lowered his voice. "I did no such thing as *sell* my daughter to those men. We were ambushed on the river. She was kidnapped.

If you think I would sell her, for any price, you are mistaken.''

"She still owes me and she knows it. I'm taking her back with me so she can work off what I've invested in her."

Payson Bond looked around the room, his eyes searching frantically, almost as if he thought help might jump out of any corner.

"Tell me where she is. I'll be willing to make a deal with you," Darcy said.

"I'd sooner deal with the devil."

"You just might be, Mr. Bond," Darcy laughed. "I'm sure all the bible-beating Baptists around here would think that he was already standing in front of you." He smoothed his hand down the front of his vest, proud of the way the shining fabric caught the candlelight's glow. "I'm not just a gambler, Bond. I run the best whorehouse and saloon in New Orleans."

"Get out, Mr. Lankanal."

"Tell me where she is and I'll pay you enough to pack up and move back to wherever it is you came from. You can build a mansion, buy a few slaves to make your life easier. Hell, Bond, you can even buy some fancy clothes for your wife and some decent shoes for those two hellions of yours and still live like a king. What do you say?"

Payson never felt like more of a failure. He had always prided himself on being a man of logic and letters, a man who could recite poetry and the classics, draw pictures with words and make them sing with life. When his father-in-law wanted to give him land and slaves, he had refused outright. He did not believe in slavery, nor would he take anything he had not worked for.

He now knew for certain what had put the shadows in Olivia's eyes and why she cried out in her sleep. The man who had put her through hell was standing in his home, and he had not even marshaled the strength to throw Lankanal out. He was so shaken that he couldn't even recall where he had last seen his rifle.

Please, God, he prayed, *don't let Olivia come home yet.*

He had no idea where she and Noah were, but anywhere was better than here. She should not ever have to face this scoundrel again. And Noah? Payson was certain that Noah would not deal kindly with any man who dared to slander Olivia's name.

"What do you say, Bond?" Darcy Lankanal asked again. "I can hand over the money right now."

Money, the root of all evil. The thing that had driven him out of Virginia to begin with. He heard Susanna stir behind him. Surely she knew he would not betray Olivia again, even if it meant his death.

"What about you, Mrs. Bond? Wouldn't you like to live better than this?" Lankanal waved his hand, indicating the cabin.

"I *have* lived in far better surroundings, sir." Susanna crossed the room, moving up beside Payson. He held his breath, wondering what to expect. Could Susanna be tempted? Would she ask him to give Olivia up to this man, just as she had begged him to give her up once before?

"Susanna, don't," Payson whispered.

She slipped her hand into his and at that moment Payson knew he had never loved her more.

"I stand with my husband, Mr. Lankanal. I want you to leave our home and take any notion that our Livvie owes you anything else along with you."

"I don't think you know who you are dealing with." Darcy Lankanal leveled his gaze on Payson again.

Footsteps treaded softly in the loft overhead. There was a sound of wood against wood, then of metal against wood. Lankanal's eyes followed the sounds. Payson looked up as well.

Molly was hanging over the edge of the loft with the old rifle aimed straight at the gambler's heart.

"The Bonds been askin' ye to leave, mister. Me, I'm not so polite, I'm afraid. Maybe poor Mr. Bond there can't hit the side of a barn with this thing, but I'm one o' the best shots in Gallatin County. I don't know ye, but Mr. Bond here, he doesn't like ye, so I've nothin' to lose, ye see, by blowing yer head off yer body and if ye think I won't, yer foolin' yerself.''

If the situation had not been so dire, Payson might have laughed. Instead, he watched the gambler weigh her threat. Finally, the man smiled at Payson, his eyes cold as his expression turned to ice. In that instant, Payson had a terrible glimpse into what the last year must have been like for Olivia.

"I'll be back for her, Bond. You can count on that. But I won't be making this good an offer again."

Outside, darkness was gathering. When the door finally closed behind Darcy Lankanal, Payson sank down heavily onto one of the benches beside the table. Blindly, he reached for Susanna's hand and pulled her down beside him. Then he buried his face in his arms and wept.

From the moment he had first seen Olivia on the street with Lankanal, Noah knew that he had to propose, even if she turned him down. It was time for him to feel, to become part of not just the natural world, but of the world of feelings and family. He would open himself up to love and loving. He had been isolated too long, numb too long.

When he had stood with Hunter on the dock on the Mississippi to say his good-byes, his friend had advised, "Ask her, Noah. All she can do is turn you down."

If Olivia did turn him down, she might just as well rip out his heart and do a jig on it, but Noah had decided he had to ask.

The sunset was late in coming for it was not yet solstice. The days were long and warm, the fireflies thick in the forest. They walked in silence toward his camp, each lost in thought, side by side. He adjusted his long stride to her shorter one. Soon they reached his old campsite. The stone fire ring had not been disturbed, but he knew the Bond boys had been playing in his lean-to when he noticed a pile of sticks and an empty bird's nest inside.

He dropped his pack and set down his rifle. Olivia was gazing off at the rays of light and color radiating from the horizon. She had hardly spoken on the walk from town, and the once or twice that he had gotten her to speak, she had been very distracted, but not as frightened as he thought she might have been after seeing Lankanal. He walked up behind her, tempted to reach for her, but he did not dare.

"Olivia . . ."

When she did not respond, he touched her on the shoulder. She started, whirled and stared at him in such a way that he knew that her thoughts had been on Lankanal again.

Noah took a deep breath.

"I want you, Olivia."

Too fast, he thought. Too sudden. He wanted to call back the words at the first sign of sadness in her eyes and the regret. He was racing headlong toward disaster but could not stop now that he had begun.

"I want to keep you safe. Come with me to Heron Pond. I won't let him near you, ever."

Hunter's parting words slammed around in his head.

"Tell her you love her. For some damn reason, women need to hear it."

His need for her was overwhelming. He was sure that no other man would have been foolish enough to have waited so long to have the woman he loved. He had tarried so long that her past had caught up with her. Slowly, so as not to frighten her, he reached out to touch her hair.

"I love you, Olivia. Marry me." He spoke so softly that he doubted she even heard.

She reached out, touched his lips. "Don't say that," she whispered, "Please don't."

He grabbed her wrist, took her hand away from his mouth. He would make her hear, make her believe.

"I love you," he said again and found it far easier this time.

A sob tore its way from her throat. He was shocked but relieved when she threw her arms around his neck and held him tight.

So simple, he thought, amazed. *Thank you, Hunt.*

He wrapped his arms around her, felt her hands at his waist. He reached for her chin, tilted her face up, covered her mouth with his, afraid he was going to explode. He had to make her his, take her away with him, make her his wife. He would help her forget that Darcy Lankanal had ever existed.

She framed his face with her hands and held him while her tongue teased and explored, searching, tasting, delving. When her breasts flattened against him, he longed to move inside her, against her. He slid his hand up her body and cupped her breast, kneading it. Needing her.

They drew apart. Her breath was warm against his cheek. He knew if he did not bury himself inside her soon that he would go out of his mind.

Her hands were at his waist, frantically tugging his shirt out of his waistband, pushing it up until his midriff was bared. Her fingers scrabbled with the ties of his buckskin pants. She moaned in frustration, so he replaced her hands with his, quickly untying his pants. They fell around his ankles.

His shirt dropped around his hips when she let go of it and took him hot and hard into her hands. Noah buried his face in her hair, inhaling the rich scents of soap, fresh air, Olivia. He shuddered, strained to hold back and not spill his seed over her hands. He could barely breathe, let alone think.

"I love you, Olivia," he whispered, marveling at how easily the words flowed now, as if he had opened the floodgates to his heart.

As if it were the most natural act in the world, she cupped him, gently massaged him until he wanted to scream, the pleasure-pain was so excruciating. He reached down and gathered the fabric of her dress in his hands and bunched it up to her waist. He cupped her buttocks, kneaded her until she threw her head back and moaned his name where it rose on the warm, still air and hovered there, echoing in his ears, matching the beat of his heart.

Olivia was his again, miraculously in his arms again, filling not only his hands, but his heart. She wound her arms tight around his neck. He grasped her thighs, lifted her, impaled himself in her in one sure, swift move.

A muffled cry escaped her. She pressed her mouth to the

side of his neck and he thought he might have done her harm, until she began to move her hips, sliding along his shaft, pumping wildly with her arms and legs clasped so tight around him that they melded into one being under the stars.

Pressing her hips against him, he pinioned her there. She shuddered, sobbed out his name again and he felt her convulse around him as if her entire being demanded his own release.

He buried his face against her shoulder, overcome by the power of their wild joining, at one with her, just as he was with the water, sensing her every move, knowing that this was good and right and true and meant to be forever. He drove into her one final time. She cried out and came around him and he poured his seed, his heart, his soul into this woman that fate had led to his door.

Swaying a bit as if he were rocking her, Noah felt the night settle back into place. The first stars of the evening were glimmering against the deep purple sky. Fireflies winked against the black forest shadows closing in. Far off across the field, light shone in the cabin windows.

Olivia lifted her head and loosened her hold. He held her thighs and braced her against him, but he could tell she needed to move when her legs opened. As he withdrew, a deep sense of loss swept him and he tried to shake it off. There would be many nights once they were married, a lifetime of lovemaking, he reminded himself. There was no reason to feel so sad, so empty.

Slowly, he lowered her to the ground until she was standing. Her dress fell down around her ankles. Before he could move, she bent down, drew his pants up for him and then turned and walked a few feet away while he tied them up.

Noah hurried. Even in the gloaming he could see that she had turned inward, wrapped her arms around her midriff as if she ached inside.

How long would it take, he wondered, until she no longer felt shame or blamed herself for something so right, so natural between them. Would a preacher's words and a wedding ceremony be enough to release her of her guilt?

By the time he walked the half-dozen steps to where she stood, she had dropped her arms to her sides and turned to face him again. Her head was high, proud. For that he was grateful—until she said with cold finality, "Thank you very much, Noah. I got what I wanted."

A cold sense of dread, cold as winter waters, eddied about him. "What are you saying, Olivia?"

"Seeing Darcy again brought back everything he and I shared. But the only other man I've ever known is you, so I . . . I had to find out which of you I prefer. I can't marry you, Noah. Now or ever." Her voice sounded strained, not like her at all. The words pounded into his heart. "Darcy is a far more experienced lover. Besides, he can give me everything—clothes, jewels, horses." She reached up, grabbed a handful of her wild mane, and pushed it back off her face.

Things that she and Darcy shared?

"Olivia, you ran from him. What did he give you before? Fear? Terror? Imprisonment? I don't believe you." Shock rocked him.

Noah grabbed her wrist and pulled her up against him, expecting her at least to fight, to try to pull away, but there was no reaction from her whatsoever. Whatever passion had been there before they had made love was gone. He could feel her warmth, but nothing deep or lasting communicated itself to him. He might as well have been holding a doll.

She stared him in the face, held herself rigid. "Listen to me and listen well. There is nothing to understand. I am saying that your safe little world isn't for me, Noah. Go back to your treehouse and your swamp and forget about me. Tomorrow I'm going to New Orleans with Darcy."

Olivia started back across the field alone, dazed by her pain, drawn by the light in the cabin windows, willing herself not to look back at the man who would own her heart forever and never even know it. With a throat so full of unshed tears she was choking on them, she stumbled, barely saving herself from falling to her knees, from the humiliation of having Noah see her go down.

If she fell, could she get up? Or would she lie there in her father's field amid the rows of corn, in the dirt where she belonged?

Halfway home, she saw the slight figure of a woman run out of the front door. Molly was headed across the field toward her, carefully picking her way over the ruts and rows, through the knee-high corn.

"Molly, over here." So as not to frighten the girl out of her wits, Olivia called out softly. Her voice was that of another woman, certainly not her own, for she had just given up the final essence of herself, whatever remnant or grain of goodness, whatever speck had once been good and true in her—she had given it to Noah and left it with the lie she told him to save him, to save them all.

When Molly reached her side, the young Scots girl's burr was thick as porridge, a sure sign she was upset.

"Oh, Miss Livvie," she stopped to catch her breath. "There was a handsome man came to the door, sayin' terrible things to yer father. He wanted to buy ye, but yer father would have none of it and tried to throw the man out. I had to get the rifle and threaten him myself before he'd leave."

Olivia grabbed Molly's hand and held tight, but dared not speak, fearing that she would betray herself. She thanked God for the cover of night.

"Your father was so upset he actually broke down and cried. I wanted to run and get ye right away, but he 'ad me wait until he was sartin the man was gone and ye and Noah were safe. Now yer father wants ye home, Miss Livvie."

So, he had come already. Found the farm, found her family. Darcy was more desperate than she thought. He had actually seen her father, offered him money. For her. Her humiliation was complete, but with it her resolve hardened. Obviously Darcy would stop at nothing. He would kill Noah, and her father. Perhaps even Susanna and the boys' lives were in jeopardy.

Before she took another step, she braced herself for what

she had to say and do, and most of all for how her father might react. Then she let go of Molly's hand. She shook out her hair. The smell and taste of Noah was on her. His seed filled her womb. Would the others know what happened between them? She did not know or care, so long as it would not give her pretense away.

"Let's go, Molly."

She struck out again, across the field, toward the light. Outside the cabin door she pulled herself together, pasted a smile on her face and stepped inside. When Olivia walked through the door, they all looked at her, but said nothing. Most unlike themselves, the boys were sitting wide-eyed and silent, staring at their father, who looked as if he had just walked through the jaws of hell.

Susanna was beside Payson, her arm around his shoulder. She brushed his hair back off his forehead.

"Molly tells me Darcy Lankanal was here." Olivia fought to appear calm, as if she had been expecting the visit. Then she pretended to notice her father's distress for the first time.

"Daddy," she went to him, sat beside him on the bench. "What's wrong?"

His eyes were red-rimmed, a bright, watery blue that stood out in stark relief in his ashen face. "Oh, Livvie." His unshed tears actually stung her to her soul. "Livvie, he said horrible things, spoke of what you had to endure in New Orleans."

"Oh, Daddy." Feeling shallow and conniving, she actually found the will to smile as she reached over and hugged him quickly. She sat back, kept up the charade. "Darcy would say anything to get me to go back with him."

Payson whispered, "Don't try to make light of it to spare me."

Olivia glanced at Susanna. Her stepmother had not left Payson's side. She was watching Olivia very closely. If anyone could discern her lie, it was Susanna.

"What's a whore, Livvie?" Little Pay was as sober as

she had ever seen him as he leaned his crossed arms on the tabletop, expecting an answer.

Olivia blanched, then quickly recovered. "Why don't you boys go on up to bed and I'll be there shortly?"

"But . . . we just got back down."

"Go on." She gave him her sternest look. He sighed and nudged Freddie, who was almost asleep anyway, and the two of them trudged back up the ladder.

When they disappeared over the edge of the loft, Olivia slid onto the bench beside Payson. She took his hand and traced the blue veins that stood out against his worn, sun-burned skin.

"Did he tell the truth, Livvie? Did Lankanal buy you from those men?"

Unable to meet his eyes, she kept tracing her finger over the back of his hand and nodded, her mind racing ahead to put together a story, something, anything that would convince him that things were definitely not the way Darcy had said.

"He did, but he saved my life by doing so. Who knows what Colonel Sullivan and his men would have done to me if *they* had kept me? Darcy is very rich, Daddy. He kept me like a queen. I had everything I wanted."

"Why did you run away?"

"Because . . . I wanted to see all of you, but Darcy, well, he can be very possessive. One day we argued about me coming home for a visit and I was so mad that I . . . I ran. It was a childish thing to do, I know, but I wanted to see all of you and let you know I was all right. I . . . found a couple to travel with, but we became separated not far from here. Noah . . . found me and was kind enough to bring me home, as you know."

She felt Susanna's gaze on her, but could not meet her eyes. Instead, she forced herself to look at her father. He had such a hopeful, yearning expression on his face. He wanted so desperately to believe her that she could hardly bear to continue the lie.

Trying to give the story credibility, she added, "Did he offer you money for me?" She tried to laugh when Payson nodded, but a strangled, odd sound came out instead. "He told me he was going to do that when I saw him in town today, but I didn't think he would dare."

"You saw him today?" Payson looked down at their joined hands.

She nodded. "Yes. He came to Shawneetown to get me. I told him I wasn't entirely certain I wanted to go back with him and asked him to give me until tomorrow to decide. I wanted to be able to break the news to all of you first. I see he could not wait for me to tell you on my own—"

"Tell us *what*, Livvie?" Susanna spoke for the first time.

Olivia felt Molly move up closer to the table from where she had been standing in the shadow of the open door, listening.

"I've made up my mind," she said with bold finality and false bravado. "I'm going back to New Orleans with Darcy. Susanna is back on her feet and Molly is here to help you. Noah has gone back to Heron Pond. You'll all be fine."

Her father was staring at her as if she had grown another head.

"Are you doing this to punish me, Livvie? Are you doing this because I was too weak to save you before? Are you trying to pay me back by going off with Lankanal? By living with a gambler, a whoremonger?"

Up in the loft, Freddie's not-so-soft whisper echoed against the ceiling. "What'th a whore, Little Pay?"

Sick to her stomach at what she had brought into their home, Olivia let go of her father's hand. She stood and drew herself up with all the dignity she could muster.

"I have never whored for Darcy, Daddy. Whatever I did, I did willingly." She thought of the days and nights she had spent with Lankanal, never willing, never wanting to give in, holding back as long as she could, fighting her release until she could fight no more. Each time, although her heart never did, her body would betray her and Darcy would win another victory in their sensual battle of wills.

Susanna finally stirred. With a wistful stare, she watched

Olivia for a moment, then turned away, walked to the fireplace and stared down into the fire with her back to them.

"What about Noah?" Susanna asked without turning.

Olivia started, then looked at her stepmother's back, at the soft fall of her blond hair against the once-becoming day dress that was far too fine for a farmer's wife to own. Her shoulders were set in a stubborn line. If Susanna suspected her of lying, why didn't she challenge her? Olivia's heart skipped a beat. She shrugged and feigned nonchalance for her father's benefit.

"Noah is nice enough, but Darcy can give me everything I've ever wanted. I didn't realize how much I missed him until I saw him today in town."

"Where *is* Noah?" Payson glanced around the room as if he expected Noah to appear.

"Gone." Olivia willed her voice not to break. "Gone home. When I told him that I chose Darcy over him, he didn't take it very well."

"If you have intentionally set out to hurt me deeply, Livvie, you have succeeded." Payson spoke so softly that she barely heard.

"Of course I didn't, Daddy."

"Yet you'll give yourself to this man again, for things he can *buy* you? He bought *you* and yet you want to go back to him. Why? Just tell me why."

She looked down at her hands. "For love."

The words were like poison in her mouth, a poison she would willingly swallow to save all of them.

"Don't do it, Livvie." Payson was begging her now. "Don't go with him."

She was so afraid she was about to cry that she abruptly stood up and paced over to the window, past the open door, then back to the window. The floor was hard-packed dirt but uneven, with well-worn, gentle dips and rises. She stopped and stared out into the deepening night.

It was warm June weather, but she felt a need to rub her arms and fight back a shiver. When she had collected herself, she faced her father again. He was still seated at the table, as if he had lost the will to stand. His thinning hair

and the lines etched around his eyes reminded her that he
was no longer a young man.

"Please don't argue with me, Daddy. It won't do any
good. I have to go."

"Tell me why, for God's sake. *Why*, Livvie?"

"I told you. For love."

chapter
16

Shawneetown

Not only did the entire lower floor of the hotel smell like pork and cabbage, but plaster hung off the walls, the finish was cheap, the floors bare. Darcy thought the place a disgrace, but there was no other choice of lodging in Shawneetown.

Knowing he probably wouldn't get an hour's sleep in a sty like this one, he hurried across the lower floor to the stairs, went straight to Betts's room and knocked on the door. He hoped for Telford's sake the man was there. He had told the land agent to wait for him until he returned from the Bonds' place and wasn't in the mood to go searching for him.

Holding a fried chicken leg in one hand, a napkin tied around his neck, Betts opened the door a crack and stared out at Darcy.

"Open the door, you idiot, it's me." Darcy shouldered his way through, gave the man a disgusted glare, and then sat in the only chair in the room. Betts closed the door behind him, yanked the napkin off his neck and set the chicken leg back on a plate with a wistful sigh.

"Did you get her?" After wiping his greasy mouth on the napkin, Betts wadded the linen up and tossed it aside.

"Not yet. I have a job for you, Betts."

"When do I get my money?"

Darcy slipped two fingers into a slim pocket in his vest, snagged a gold piece and tossed it across the room with a flick of his wrist. "Here's a little advance. Now stop harping."

As Betts caught the coin and pocketed it, Darcy studied himself in an oval mirror above a small side table, smoothing his hand over his already neatly combed hair.

"What do you want me to do?" Betts slowly walked over to the bed and sat down. The bed ropes groaned and the husk-filled mattress crackled and sagged beneath his weight.

"I want you to hang out in the local establishments, keep an eye out for the half-breed. Keep him busy when he shows up looking for me."

"How do you know he'll come?"

Darcy smiled, thinking of the things he'd told Payson Bond, remembering the respect he'd heard in Bond's voice when he spoke of the stinking half-breed.

"Oh, he'll come all right. He'll only be too happy to try to make me pay for what I told that hayseed farmer." The man was obviously Olivia's self-appointed watchdog. Involuntarily, Darcy frowned, still haunted by the look that had passed between Olivia and LeCroix earlier. The way she had stepped close to the man for protection rankled him. Had LeCroix sampled her yet? Had he been between her soft, pale thighs?

Wondering brought Darcy to his feet. He began to pace the room. Olivia had wild blood and, whether she wanted to admit it or not, she liked what a man could do to her. Her needs were as strong as any man's. Darcy paused beside a glass tumbler on the table. He picked it up, felt the weight of it in his hands, stared into the emptiness of it.

Any man would gladly take what the hot-blooded little minx offered. Surely the half-breed had. Darcy looked over at the mirror again and then heaved the tumbler at his image. The mirror and the glass exploded, raining sparkling shards of silver over the table beneath it.

Betts jumped to his feet. "What'd you do that for?"

Darcy turned on him. The man's face was florid; his heavy lower lip quivered.

"I felt like it. I always do what I feel like doing, Betts. Don't forget that. Now, why don't you go on downstairs and peruse the town for LeCroix. If anyone asks, say that you haven't seen me all day and you have no idea where I am or when I'll be back. I'll stay right here so that if he goes looking in my room, he won't find me."

"But—"

"You'll get your money tomorrow, Betts. All of it and a bonus for keeping LeCroix away from me. I'm going back for Olivia tomorrow at first light and we'll all leave for New Orleans."

"If you're lying, Lankanal—" Betts's threat went unfinished. Both men knew he would do nothing to back it up.

With nothing left to lose, Noah slipped up the back stairs of the hotel with his pack on his back and his rifle in his hands and walked up to room number four, the one the owner told him was registered to Darcy Lankanal. With no idea of what he was going to do, he stood there staring at the number, his hand clenched around the stock of his rifle.

If Olivia wanted Lankanal, she would have him—but only after he was finished with him. Noah started to knock, then thought better of giving his rival fair warning. His hand closed over the knob and he tried it, slowly twisting the brass beneath his palm.

"Here, what are you doing?" The whiskey-soaked proprietor had followed him, fumbling up the stairs, weaving on his feet. "Did you knock? Maybe Mr. Lankanal doesn't want to be disturbed."

Noah turned on the man with a red wash of rage surging through him. He tried to focus on the heavy, drunken man. Somewhere in the back of his mind, years of honor and reason whispered to him, held his temper in check, kept him from lashing out.

"He told me to meet him here. Maybe you better open the door, see if he's all right." Noah held his breath, waited as the man slowly measured him with rheumy eyes, judged the worth of his words. A touch of fear and doubt warred with the awe in the man's eyes. He knew who Noah was, had called him by name downstairs.

Finally the slovenly man slowly nodded and took a ring of keys out of his pocket. He knocked and called out Lankanal's name twice before he fitted one into the lock.

Noah stood ready, damning Darcy Lankanal, itching to feel the man's neck between his hands.

The door swung inward. The room was dark, but the glow from a lamp in the hallway illuminated the bed with a ring of pale light. The room was empty.

"Sorry, Mr. LeCroix. He ain't here. Like I said, I ain't seen him since around midday. You might find the man he come in with, a Mr. Betts, and ask him where Mr. Lankanal is. I saw Betts leave a few minutes ago."

Doubting the man would even remember he had been here on the morrow, Noah turned on his heel and walked out. Determined to find Lankanal before his rage cooled, he hurried along the hall, took the narrow stairs two at a time and hit the street.

The taverns were crowded. Settlers, pilgrims, hunters, saline miners, one or two other half-breeds, and a handful of women of questionable backgrounds stood cheek to jowl in the first such establishment Noah entered. He hated being cooped up with so many people in one room, hated the stares that focused on him and held as he walked through the door. When he walked over to the bar and turned his back on the room, conversation started up again.

He ordered a whiskey, tossed it back, and put a coin down on the bar. The barkeep was short. The bar came almost to his chest. Loath to move on, the man kept wiping a rag in a circle in front of Noah.

"You seen a man named Betts in here? Gent from New Orleans? Or a gambler name of Lankanal?" Noah asked him.

Thrilled to be able to help the Prince of the Ohio, the barkeep nodded toward the back wall. "Lankanal hasn't been in all day, but that's Betts, back there in the corner eating steak and potatoes."

Noah nodded his thanks and began to thread his way through the crowd toward Betts. By the time he reached the table, Betts sensed all eyes turned in his direction. He swallowed his last bite of steak, wiped his mouth on a napkin, and was on his feet by the time Noah reached his table.

"Where is he?" Noah demanded when he reached Betts's side. Overweight, sweat-drenched, and flushed, the man posed no threat to him, and yet Noah did not relax his stance. He could feel anger rolling off him in wave after wave.

Betts swallowed hard. "Who?"

"You know who," Noah said softly, his voice devoid of emotion. "Lankanal."

"I haven't seen him all day. He went out looking for some little whore."

Noah's rifle clattered to the floor. The crowed parted around them as he lunged for Betts's throat. He grabbed the man by his shirtfront. Despite the fact that Betts outweighed him by a good fifty pounds, Noah was taller and stronger. He hefted him up and shook him hard. The man struggled and grabbed Noah's wrists but couldn't break the hold.

"Where is he?"

"I told you. He's not here. He said we were leaving at dawn. I don't expect him back until then."

Nothing was making sense to Noah anymore, not Olivia or the words coming out of the fat man's mouth. Was Lankanal at the Bond homestead then? Had he been there all the time, waiting for Olivia while she was making love to him in the woods? While she had been riding him, testing him? Comparing him to the handsome, golden-haired gambler?

Had the two of them planned to meet each other at the homestead when they spoke earlier in town?

What in the hell was going on?

The red haze of anger deepened with his confusion. Noah's hands tightened on the man's shirt. Betts' skin oozed over the top of the collar. Spittle was flying out of the land agent's mouth as he tried to form words of protest and squealed for help like a stuck pig. His legs pumped and his knees hit Noah in the thighs. Betts's hand came up, pulling off Noah's makeshift eye patch. A collective gasp was followed by hushed silence and suddenly Ern Matheson was there, his hand on Noah's arm, his voice ringing in Noah's ear.

"Put him down, LeCroix, before you kill him. Let him go, you hear me, boy? If you push this any further, I'll have to take you into custody and I got no place to lock you up."

Noah heard the constable's voice through his anger and fought his way back to the edge of reason, trying to surface. Finally, he managed to loosen his hold on Betts. The man dropped to his feet with a heavy thud and grabbed at his collar. His lips had gone almost blue.

Shaking his head as if he had just broken the surface of deep water, Noah stared at Betts, then at Ern Matheson, trying to remember where he was, what he was doing. Noah stared at Betts, watched the man's bug eyes staring back at him, saw his fear, felt himself ease off. He had no argument with this man, no clear idea why he had overreacted. His mind was befuddled. He felt as if it were filled with dense fog, the kind that hovered in the low-lying grasses and reeds in the dips and hollows along the riverbank.

"Mind telling me what's going on here?" Ern gestured to the crowd to get back to whatever it was they were doing before the altercation.

"He was asking me about Darcy Lankanal, the gambler I came up here with on business. I told him I didn't know where Darcy was and he went crazy." Telford Betts's voice sounded gravelly, ill used.

Noah watched the sweat trickle down the man's temple. Betts was shaking, gasping for breath like a dying fish pulled from the river. Betts's earlier words came back to him in a rush.

"He went out looking for a little whore."

Lankanal and Olivia. They were together. Somewhere.

"LeCroix?" Ern Matheson's hand was still on his shoulder. He gave Noah a shake. "LeCroix?"

Someone handed Noah his rifle. Betts was looking at the floor between them. Noah turned to Ern, trying to put the words together, but everything was a jumble now. He had to get out of the tavern, out into the street where the air was not heavy with the scent of too many bodies in a room, where it was free of tobacco smoke and the odors of stale food and whiskey.

"I'm sorry." Noah shook his head. He didn't mean the words—they were hollow and empty as his soul—but they seemed to be expected of him and so he said them.

"Why don't you take yourself out of here and lay off the whiskey. You know you people can't handle it."

Without trying to discern what Ern meant, Noah looked at Telford Betts. The man had gone down on one knee and was bent over, fumbling, one hand on the floor. Noah dismissed him and turned to go. The crowd parted like the Red Sea as the Prince of the Ohio walked away.

Noah went straight to the river, his feet and his heart taking over now that his brain had ceased to function. It wasn't until he stood on the edge of the Ohio, was back in his element again, that some of what had happened to him that evening began to come back in a rush of sensation and a blur of pain.

Olivia in the woods, desperate to touch him. He had taken her standing up; she had not fought him. She had even made him believe she had enjoyed it until—

"Thank you very much, Noah. I got what I wanted."

He had told her he loved her.

He had proposed marriage.

"Darcy is a far more experienced lover. He can give me everything."

Noah put his hand to his scarred temple. His head was throbbing. He longed for the sounds of the river to soothe him, the whispering voices to calm him, but the water was silent. She had run from Lankanal, had escaped him in New Orleans. She had feared the man. Her year with him had given her nightmares that had never ended. Yet now, after seeing him in town, she had chosen to go back to New Orleans with him again.

Had she been lying to him about her relationship with Lankanal all along?

"There's nothing to understand. Your safe little world isn't for me, Noah."

She was leaving Illinois with Darcy Lankanal in the morning. It was over. All of it.

Heat lightning cracked in the distance. There was a ring around the moon, a sure sign of rain. The air was thick with humidity. Noah started to walk along the muddy riverbank. His mocassin slipped in the ooze. He sat down hard beside the water, laid his rifle down beside him and shrugged off the pack. The water was deep and dark, rushing headlong toward its confluence with the Mississippi and on to New Orleans.

He should have listened to his gut and never left the swamp. Never come out among people again. Instead, he had fallen in love and played the hero for Olivia, brought her back, listened to the words of praise and songs about his skill on the water. He had fallen for the glamour of being a legend on the river.

It made the humiliation all that much greater, knowing it was all a lie. He was no hero, not to Olivia, not to anyone. He was a fool who heard voices in his head, a half-breed with a scar over half his face, that was all. A man who could not even pleasure a woman well enough to keep her.

He hadn't felt this low since the day Hunter had pulled him out of the river and he had realized he had lost his eye. He had wanted to die that day, to give up on life and living.

But tonight, death seemed too easy. It would be a more fitting end to have to suffer living out his life knowing what a fool he had been to ever love at all.

Darcy lay in the dark in Betts's room with his hands stacked beneath his head, staring up at the ceiling, listening to the occasional sounds of horses going by on the street outside, the drone of conversation from the dining room below, and the not very discreet, distinct sounds of two people making love in the room next door.

He lay there rock hard, wondering if he was going to

have to waste a perfectly good erection. The thought of finding a whore to service him had entered his mind—surely the town had one someplace—but then he reckoned that if the looks of the room and the sparse, bare necessities in the other establishments in town were any indication, he decided he'd rather stay randy. Besides, he had waited months already. Tomorrow he would have Olivia again and he was willing to wait one more day. She knew what he liked and how to satisfy him better than anyone.

When the door opened without warning and light from the hallway illuminated the silhouette of the man that filled the doorway, Darcy lunged to a sitting position, rose to his feet and backed into a darkened corner.

"Lankanal?"

The pent-up air rushed out of him when Darcy recognized Betts's voice.

"Get in here and shut the door," Darcy ordered as his heartbeat settled back to normal.

"Why are you sitting here in the dark?" Betts shuffled in and fumbled with the lamp. There was a sound of glass upon glass, the smell of sulfur and a flare of light. As Betts replaced the chimney and turned the wick down, Darcy settled himself on the bed again.

"Well?"

"You almost got me killed, Lankanal. It's time you pay up," Betts told him. The man's color was worse than ever, his face pale, his brow and upper lip coated with sweat. His hand shook as Telford reached into his coat pocket, pulled out a rumpled kerchief and mopped his brow.

"You found LeCroix?"

"He found me. He was looking for you. I think the man's mad," Telford said, pouring himself a glass of water from a pitcher standing on a listing chest of drawers near the only window in the room.

"Where is he now?"

"I don't know and I don't care," Betts told him. He set the empty glass down, rubbed his hand across his midriff, and then began to pace the room. "He had murder in his eye when he grabbed me."

"He accosted you?"

"Hell, yes. In a room full of people at the tavern. He didn't care who saw it. He nearly choked me to death. If one of the locals hadn't walked up and stopped him when he did, I'd be a dead man. No one else in the room took it upon themselves to stop the damn Prince of the Ohio from killing me."

Darcy threw back his head and laughed.

Telford Betts turned on him and paced over to stand at the foot of the bed.

"You think it's funny, Lankanal? I've had it. I'm telling you, pay up or else."

Darcy got to his feet again in one swift, fluid move. "Or else what, Betts? I've a good mind to choke you myself. You bring that out in a man, you know."

He expected the land agent to back down. Instead Betts stood there quivering like a huge mass of jellied consommé, his eyes bulging, his pallor gray.

Darcy walked over to the chair where he had carefully folded and draped his coat. He reached into an inside pocket, withdrew a folded wad of bills, peeled off the agreed-upon amount and handed them over to Betts. The land agent's gaze greedily followed the extra money as Darcy repocketed it.

"Don't get any ideas."

"This will keep me happy," Betts said, rolling the notes and opening his coat to put them away. "Look at this, will you?"

As Darcy waited, Betts drew a long, lethal-looking knife from inside his coat. Darcy had seen plenty like it before; the "Kaintucks" and backwoods men who came down to New Orleans all carried skinning knives with fine-honed blades that could slice the flesh right off a man before he knew it was gone. This one had a highly polished bone handle with a fierce-eyed wolf's head carved on it.

"Where'd you get that?"

"That's the best part," Betts smiled, but the expression looked pained. He rubbed his midriff again. "It's Le-Croix's. I must have kicked it loose in the scuffle. Saw it before anyone else knew he lost it and bent down to get it right away. I figure somebody might be willing to pay a pretty penny for a knife that once belonged to the Prince of the Ohio.''

Darcy liked it a hell of a lot better than the one he kept hidden in his boot.

"I need a whiskey," Telford said, his voice weakening. "I can't believe the shit I had to put up with tonight.''

"You look like hell.''

Once again, Betts wiped his forehead with his kerchief. He started toward the door with LeCroix's knife in his hand. Then he suddenly stopped and turned around again. Facing Darcy, Betts opened his mouth to speak but only a strangled gurgle escaped. He reached for his throat, tugged at his collar, then his eyes rolled up in his head and he pitched forward and hit the floor.

"Betts?''

Darcy jumped to his feet and rolled Betts over.

"Betts? Get up.''

The man had hit the floor like a dead weight. His nose was bleeding profusely and his eyes were open and unseeing. Darcy quickly unfastened the button at Betts's collar, felt his neck for a pulse, and then laid his head on his chest. There was no heartbeat, nothing to indicate Betts was alive.

Darcy sat back on his heels and stared down at the land agent's body for a moment before he reached inside Betts's coat pocket and pulled out the money he had just paid the man. As he started to stand, the handle of the skinning knife on the floor beside the body caught his eye. The snarling wolf's head stared back as the sharp blade caught the light and reflected it back. Darcy reached for LeCroix's knife, thumbing the honed edge of the blade.

Deadly sharp, the knife would go through a man's flesh like a whisper through the air. Maybe, Darcy decided, there might be a way to turn Betts's death to his advantage. He stared at the body again and thought of using the half-breed's knife to cut Betts's throat, but there would be too much blood, too much of a mess. He hated to risk staining his fine clothes.

He turned the knife over and over in his hands, slowly formulating a plan as he stared down at Telford Betts's corpse. A crowd in the tavern had seen LeCroix attack Betts. Now, the land agent was dead and LeCroix's knife was in his possession. Darcy rolled the blade over again, took the carved bone handle in his palm, measured the weight.

Threatening a man's life was one thing, but of all the underhanded things he had ever done, murder was not one of them. He stared at the heavy man's body. If Darcy carried out the plan he had just formulated, Betts wouldn't feel a thing and LeCroix would be out of the way for a good while, if not forever. If the flatboat pilot was arrested and hanged, there would be no chance of him ever coming after Olivia.

Darcy stood and walked over to the table, where the lamp still burned low. He cupped the top of the chimney, blew out the flame, and walked back to where Betts lay sprawled on the floor. He knelt beside the body.

As heat lightning flickered in the distance, he took the knife handle in both hands, holding on tight. When the lightning flashed again and the room was awash in silver-blue light, he raised the blade directly over Telford Betts's heart.

Bond Homestead

Olivia knelt in the stuffy loft beside the nest of bedding where Little Pay and Freddie lay sprawled out side by side like two exhausted puppies. The little boys were dead to the world, sleeping the innocent sleep of children, the only time they were ever still. She held each of them by the hand, made circles on their baby-soft skin with her thumb as she stared down at the two towheads, memorizing every detail.

She had no tears to shed today. She had made her decision and she ·was determined to live with it. Everything was clear to her now that she could see there was only one thing to do. So many things were clear to her now.

Olivia held the boys' hands a moment longer, then glanced over to the high window beneath the eaves. It was still dark out. The night had been a long, hot, miserable affair filled with thunder and lightning, then rain beating down on the roof, which was just a few feet above them. She had not slept for even a moment of it. She had heard her father moving restlessly downstairs for hours, but thankfully, an hour or so before dawn, she heard him begin to snore.

While everyone slept, she planned to be on her way before any of them stirred awake and caught her. Payson had tried to argue with her for hours, but there was no changing her mind. She let go of the boys' hands, leaned over and gently placed a kiss on each of their foreheads with a whispered good-bye.

Crawling across the space too small to stand in, she skirted Molly MacKinnon, who lay with her arms up beside her face, her lips slack, mouth open. The Scots girl did not stir. When she reached the trunk that held her clothing, Olivia opened the lid without a sound and then sat down beside it. Folded on top was the lovely embroidered shawl. Beneath that, the soft, perfectly cured doeskin dress. She ran her palm over it and admired the suppleness for the last time. Closing her eyes, she recalled the day Noah had given them to her, then thought of the day he had decided to accompany her to Shawneetown. The beginning of the end.

If only she had known then what she knew now, would she have done anything in her power to stay with him? If she had, what of her family? Would they have survived without her and Noah this summer?

Quickly she unlaced the moccasins she had worn all summer and stacked them one atop the other. She lifted the dress and shawl and carefully laid them beneath it. Feeling around in the contents below, she touched a pair of stockings and then found some sturdy leather shoes she had worn in Virginia, pulled them out, slipped them on.

She had braided her hair sometime during the night, while sleep eluded her. She was determined to take nothing of this life with her except the clothes on her back when she went to Darcy, not even her hairbrush.

She knew him well enough to know he would not find anything she valued worthy of his suite. He would only throw her things away as he had done once before. Just as someone might do for a precious child, or doll, or puppet, he would choose the clothes and jewels she wore, down to the silk undergarments, not once asking her preference or her opinion, for he would be dressing her for his own pleasure, not hers.

Without looking at her half-brothers again, she scooted past Molly and shimmied over the edge of the loft. Her toes found the top rung of the ladder. Careful not to make a sound, she climbed down slowly, holding her breath. When she glanced over at the bed, she could see her father sleeping soundly beside Susanna. Her stepmother lay on her side with her back to the room, her shoulder rising and falling in the deep, rhythmic breath of sleep.

When she reached the floor she paused, closed her eyes and pressed her forehead against a rung of the ladder. She took a deep breath, inhaling all the scents that would remind her of this home she had known for so short a time: the lingering aroma of beans and bacon, the hickory ash in the fireplace, the close humid air, the damp coolness of the earthen floor beneath her feet.

Olivia opened her eyes and straightened, making her way easily and silently through the darkened interior of the cabin, sidestepping the butter churn near the end of the table.

The door always creaked a bit on its leather hinges; it did so now, but she opened it quickly so that the sound was short lived. Outside, the horizon was barely tinged with light, the rest of the sky darkened by the low clouds. Far off in the distance, lightning still flickered, too far away for her to hear the thunder roll.

Darcy would be coming from the direction of town when he came for her. She would cross the muddy fields, enter the woods and hopefully head him off. There was no reason to hope he would not come. Not after what he had told her father last night, what he had threatened her with yesterday.

She did not look back at the cabin, nor did she allow herself to think of Noah at all, for if she did, she would be forced to remember the last time they made love and all of the terrible things she had said to him. It was far easier to keep her mind blank, her heart numb.

Olivia stepped away from the cabin and started across her father's cornfield for the last time.

Susanna waited until Livvie was out of the house before she carefully slipped out from beneath the sheet and slid out of bed. She stood there with her hands pressed atop one another over her heart, feeling its rapid beat beneath her long nightgown. As Payson slept on, Susanna picked up the hem of her gown and, barefooted, ran on tiptoe across the cabin and out the door.

Livvie was a few yards away already, too far to attract her attention without calling out, so Susanna began to run after her. The ground was soft and wet. Mud squished between her bare toes. It had been so long since she had even gone walking that she was out of breath in a few strides. By the time she was a few feet from Livvie, the girl whirled around, alerted by the heavy sound of her ragged breathing.

"Susanna, what are you doing?" Olivia looked over her shoulder at the cabin. "You have to go back before Daddy wakes up."

Susanna grabbed her stepdaughter's hand. "I won't let you do this, Livvie," she cried. "I won't let you break Payson's heart. He's been through enough."

Olivia tried to twist out of her hold. "I've made my choice, Susanna. It's Darcy. Now go back and stay quiet until I'm well away."

"No, I won't. I know you can't possibly love that terrible man who came here last night, Livvie. I know you love Noah. It's as plain as the nose on your face whenever you look at him. Where is he? Where has Noah gone? Why isn't he here to stop you?"

Olivia looked as if she were about to fly out of her skin at any moment. She frantically kept searching the front of the cabin for signs of life. Susanna ignored her and forced her to answer by refusing to budge.

"I sent Noah away. I told him that I made my choice and it's Darcy. That's what I'm telling you. Now once and for all, let me leave before Daddy wakes up."

"Not until you tell me the truth." Susanna clung to her the way a drowning man clings to a lifeline. She had let Livvie go once, lost the girl in order to save her boys. She wasn't about to let it happen again or she would never forgive herself. Payson would never forgive her either.

Olivia took a deep, frustrated breath, then let it out in a rush. She was so angry that her cheeks were blotched with color. She twisted her wrist out of Susanna's grasp but did not run away. Her shoulders were rigid, her feet planted in a wide stubborn stance.

"Fine, Susanna. I'll tell you why I'm leaving, but first you have to swear to me on your baby girl's grave that you will never tell Daddy the truth."

Susanna blinked, hurt to the quick. "I swear," she whispered. Now that it was forthcoming, she was afraid to hear the truth, sorry that she had to make such a promise.

Olivia spoke to her slowly, as if she were nothing but a witless child. "If I don't go with Darcy, he will kill Noah."

Susanna gasped. "Livvie, he wouldn't—"

"Oh, yes, Susanna, he would. Maybe he wouldn't commit murder himself, but I'm convinced he would never hesitate to have it done for him. And he won't stop with Noah, either. If Daddy were to stand in his way, Darcy would kill him, too. If I refused, he wouldn't stop there, but he would hurt you, and the boys. Everyone I love will be in harm's way unless I go back to New Orleans with him."

"How did you talk Noah into leaving?"

The sadness that filled Olivia's eyes was almost too much for Susanna to see.

"Oh, I was very convincing," Olivia whispered. She looked off toward the woods, where Noah's camp once stood. Her eyes filled with tears. Susanna's heart broke for her.

"Livvie, there has to be a way. We can go to town and talk to Ern Matheson."

"Do you honestly think *Ern* could stop a man like Darcy?"

"There has to be some way."

"There is no other way," Olivia said with solemn finality. She reached out, took Susanna's hands in hers and squeezed them.

"Someday, when the time is right, when I've been gone long enough for him to think about forgiving me, will you tell Daddy that now I understand what he did that day on the river and that I forgive him?"

"And me? Do you forgive me, Livvie?"

"Of course I do." Olivia slipped her arms around her, hugged her tight and then let go. "I couldn't say anything to Daddy last night, not without telling him all of it, but after I saw Darcy in town and I realized he had tracked me this far, I knew what I had to do. There is no other choice. I have to go with Darcy to save Noah and Daddy. Just like that day on the river when Daddy had to give me over to the colonel and his men to save you and the boys. There *was* no other choice he could make. I know that now. I know he did it out of love, not because he loved me any less or you and the boys any more, but to save three lives by sacrificing one. I survived Darcy before. At least this time I *know* where I'm going. I *know* what I have to do."

"But, Livvie. Will we ever see you again?"

One of the tears Olivia struggled to hold back escaped. Susanna reached out to wipe at a single droplet that had slipped over Olivia's lashes.

"I pray that we will meet again someday," Livvie whispered. "Now, please let me go, Susanna. Go back home and keep Daddy there until Darcy and I are well away. Promise me."

The edge of the horizon was lighter; the sun was creeping upward through a few remnants of blue-gray clouds. The air was close and still. Huge drops from a passing cloud spattered the field around them.

The promise was one that she was loath to make, but she

finally nodded to Olivia. Before Susanna could say good-bye, Olivia began running across the field.

Shawneetown

Darcy made a great show of rousting the hotel manager out of bed so that he could settle his account and leave. He asked if Telford Betts had checked out, then told the man that he had heard the half-breed pilot Noah LeCroix had a run-in with his business associate in the tavern the night before and that he was concerned. He added that as far as he knew, Betts had never returned to the hotel last night.

He thanked the man, paid him in full and gave him extra for his trouble, then sauntered out of the place as if he hadn't a care in the world.

Despite the foul summer weather, Darcy's spirits were lighter than they had been in months. It was just a little after sunup and, riding the nag he had rented at the livery, he would be back at the Bond homestead in no time. Very soon, if things worked out right, Noah LeCroix would be facing the end of a rope.

He retrieved the rented mount from the livery, saddled up, and rode out of town without a backward glance. After asking around, he decided it wouldn't hurt to take Olivia farther down the Ohio before renting a flatboat and heading south. It wouldn't do to have her hear about LeCroix's ''crime'' and have her decide to try to do the noble thing and cry foul.

Not when he had her just where he wanted her. By now she must know he had stopped by the cabin last night and told her father everything. She had to know that he would make good on his promises. If he had her on the run, she should walk right into his arms.

It hadn't been light an hour when he rode past a stand of switch cane and saw her walking alone on the trail, headed toward town. Smiling to himself, he pulled rein, crossed his arms, and leaned on the pommel, content to watch her walk the last few yards. The naturally seductive sway of her hips and the swell of her high, firm breasts beneath the cheap yellow calico stirred him in a way no other woman could, even one adorned in French silk and lace.

He felt himself quicken and thought about taking her right there in the middle of the trail, until he remembered that the ground was wet and that it would probably be covered with insects and droppings and filth, and he thought better of it. There would be plenty of time to savor her—the rest of his life if he so desired. Tonight, somewhere along the river, would be soon enough. He could wait that long.

When she walked up to him and stood in silence beside his horse, meeting his eyes with a challenge in hers, he could almost swear she was looking right through him.

"I see you took me at my word. How did you know I'd be here?" he asked.

"When I heard you had come to see my father last night, I knew that you meant every word you said yesterday. You are a bastard, Darcy. Why did you do it? Why did you tell my family what I've been? What you made me? You didn't have to go that far."

"Everyone in New Orleans knows I'm a bastard, darlin'." He thought of the love for LeCroix that he had seen in her eyes. "I thought I'd better show you how easy it would be to get to your family, how easy it was for me to to find them. Your father surprised me by turning down a small fortune for you. I'd pictured him as quite a different sort of man."

She didn't answer, just stared up at him with blank, unfeeling eyes.

"Where were you and that half-breed last night when I came by, Olivia? Did you bed him in some smelly teepee in the woods? Are you getting used to doing it on the filthy ground?"

She flinched, but didn't look away. "That's exactly what I was doing. You taught me so well, I made sure he'll remember last night for the rest of his life."

Anger got the best of him. In the time it took her to

blink, Darcy reached down and grabbed her by the hair, yanked her head back, and turned her face up to his. He covered her lips, forced a kiss on her mouth until she began to fight him in earnest. Only then did he let go of her hair.

"It's time we got started," he said.

She stared at him for a long, cold minute, then offered him her hand. He reached down for her arm; she jumped and he swung her up behind him. When he kicked the horse into a gallop, her arms went around him involuntarily. Darcy followed the trail until it forked south and east and then headed toward the Ohio.

"Boys, go outside." Payson shooed Little Pay and Freddie out the door, unwilling to talk to Susanna with the boys in the room, afraid he was not going to be able to hold his temper.

The day had gotten off to a bad start when he overslept, and it had continued to spiral downhill ever since. Susanna had been moody and silent when he awoke, her face streaked with tears, her thoughts so far away that he was afraid she was slipping back into her vale of depression.

Until Molly and the boys had come down to breakfast asking after Livvie, he had not even suspected his daughter was already gone. Realizing that was the reason for his wife's tears, that Susanna had known Olivia had already left them, he had demanded to know how she could let the girl go.

Susanna stood, walked out the door and refused to answer.

Finally the boys had been fed, and now Payson ushered them outside so that he might get the truth out of his wife. Molly was bustling about the table, clearing dishes, tossing them into a wooden bucket filled with soapy water.

"Molly, go milk the cow," Payson told her.

"Och. I hate that cow." She turned back to the dishes, ignoring his order.

"You want to keep your job? Go milk the cow, Molly. Now."

The hired girl tossed the cutlery into the dishwater and

stomped out grumbling, "Someday I'll be a fancy lady and no one will dare treat me this way ever again."

Susanna had slipped back in while the boys were eating. She sat on the bed mending the appliqué quilt they had brought from Virginia. He joined her in the shadowed interior of the cabin, wondering how she could see to sew.

"How could you let Olivia leave without trying to stop her, Susanna?" Had she secretly wanted the girl gone? Had she even tried to keep Livvie from going with the odious gambler who wanted her for his whore?

"How can you ask me that, Payson? Because of what happened before? Because once I begged you to save the boys? Do you think I would let Livvie go because I actually wanted her gone?"

He was ashamed. She had read his thoughts so easily.

Susanna looked away, keeping her eyes on her mending. Her needle didn't miss a stitch as she spoke.

"I tried to stop her. I begged her to stay but she told me this was her choice. She said she had to go."

"Well, I'll never believe it. There isn't an evil bone in that girl's body, Susanna, and you know it. I cannot imagine her choosing such a life." He ran his hand over his eyes, still tired from a restless night and two hours of sleep. Any real farmer worth his salt would have been in the field by the time the sun touched the sky.

"I'll never believe what that man said about my Livvie." His voice dropped to a whisper. "Never."

"Daddy!" Freddie came racing through the door. "You gotta come out here."

Payson was still watching Susanna. She appeared relieved by the interruption.

"Not now," Payson yelled back, stopping Freddie in his tracks.

"But, therth thom men here," Freddie whispered.

Payson sighed. He walked over to his younger son and put his hand on the boy's head. He could count the times he had yelled at his sons on one hand. Most of those times had been over the last few hours.

"Sorry, Freddie," he sighed. "What next?"

Payson followed Freddie out the door.

Ern Matheson had just dismounted. He accepted the dipper of water that Payson offered from the rain barrel at the side of the house.

"Came to ask you a few questions, Payson. I know your daughter is a friend of LeCroix's, that she came into town with him the day he first turned up and she was seen with him again yesterday afternoon."

Payson nodded, wondering what the man was getting at. "Noah LeCroix is a friend to this family, I'm proud to say. What about him?"

"Your girl Olivia here? Can I talk to her?"

Payson looked off toward the wood. Shook his head. "No. She's not here right now. She took off this morning."

"Damn. That don't look good," Ern mumbled. "Not good at all."

Payson's heart sank. "What do you mean?"

Ern sat down heavily on the chopping stump beside the woodpile, took off his hat, ran his hand over his bald head, and shoved his hat on again. Susanna came out of the cabin and stood in a swatch of shade.

"You know why LeCroix would want to kill a man named Telford Betts?"

"Never heard of him," Payson said. "Who's Telford Betts?"

"A land agent who's been in and out of here a dozen times in the past couple of years. Comes up from Louisiana to purchase land for clients of his who are speculatin'. He came into town a few days ago with a gambler name of Darcy Lankanal."

Susanna walked into the sunlight to stand beside him. When she took his hand, Payson felt her trembling.

Ern nodded at Susanna and went on. "LeCroix had a set-to with Betts in the tavern last night. Damn near choked him to death. I broke it up, sent Noah on his way. This morning, Jewel McGuire damn near had a heart attack when he found Betts dead in his room at the hotel. LeCroix's skinnin' knife was stuck through his heart. We ain't been able to find Lankanal at all and I'm just hoping we don't have two murders to try LeCroix for."

"Noah couldn't have done anything like that," Susanna cried, surprising Payson with her vehemence. "He's a quiet, gentle man."

Ern doffed his hat and rubbed his freckled, bald head again.

"Well, you're partly right about that, ma'am. He can be. He can also be the meanest son-of-a-gun you ever seen, which is just the way he was actin' last night. He's either the bravest man walking or the stupidest, 'cause he'll head right down the river when no other man would dare. That's why he's a legend from here to New Orleans."

"Noah LeCroix?" Payson stared at Ern, trying to comprehend what he had just heard.

"Our Noah?" Susanna sounded just as credulous.

"Hell, there's even been songs written about him. They call him the Prince of the Ohio."

"Noah is a legend?"

"In his own time," Ern laughed and then quickly sobered. "That's why some folks just can't believe he did this, and others—well, there's always those who like to see a legend fall."

"Are you looking for him?" Torn, Payson didn't know if he could turn in the man who had saved Little Pay's life. Even now Noah might be asleep at his campsite across the field.

"Oh, we already got him," Ern said. "We picked him up this morning down at the river. Just sat there all through the rain last night. He was soaked through. He was surprised to find his knife was missing, but he didn't have an alibi, nor did he put up any resistance at all."

Payson tried to picture Noah under arrest, being held somewhere. The image did not fit any more than the idea that the man he thought he knew might have committed murder.

"Did he confess?"

"No. But then he didn't even try to offer an alibi, either. I told him he'd most likely hang," Ern volunteered.

"Oh, my God," Susanna cried.

"He actually looked relieved," Ern added with a shake of his head.

"He didn't kill Lankanal," Susanna told Ern. When she let go of Payson's hand, she took a step closer to Ern Matheson. Her face was intent, her mouth set in a firm, determined line. "Noah did not kill Darcy Lankanal," she said again.

"How do you know that, ma'am?"

She turned to Payson, imploring him with her eyes, silently urging him to tell the man how they knew Darcy Lankanal was still alive. He hesitated. If he told Ern Matheson that Olivia had gone off with Lankanal, he would have to tell him why. Eventually it would all come out, where Olivia had been living, what she had done, what she was doing with the gambler.

"Payson, *tell* him," Susanna whispered. "You have to tell him."

He had no choice. Noah's life was far more important than Olivia's good name. He knew what Olivia would have him do if she were here. She would tell Ern everything herself in an effort to save Noah's life.

"Lankanal left town this morning with my daughter. They've gone to New Orleans."

"You say your gal took off with the gambler? When?"

"Sometime this morning," Susanna admitted, when Payson could not speak.

Ern's forehead folded into lines as he concentrated. "Did LeCroix know she was going off with Lankanal?"

Payson shrugged.

"Olivia told him last night," Susanna said.

"So, maybe in a rage, he came into town and stabbed Betts." Ern stood up and stretched, rubbing his hand over the back of his neck.

Payson stared at the ground between his feet, thinking aloud. "But that makes no sense. Why would Noah kill Betts?"

Ern speculated, "Because he couldn't find Lankanal. No one saw the gambler at all last night."

"He was here early in the evening," Susanna said. "He

came to see Olivia, but she was with Noah.''

When Payson looked up, Ern was concentrating on Susanna.

''You know anything more about any of this, Mrs. Bond?'' Matheson asked.

''Susanna?'' Confused, certain now that she knew far more than she was saying, Payson took her hand. ''Susanna, what's going on?''

''I have to go into town.'' Her eyes pleaded for understanding before she turned to Ern. ''I have to talk to Noah.''

chapter

17

NOAH HAD NEVER THOUGHT HE WOULD END HIS LIFE trussed up like a ham, but as he sat in the dirt in the dark on the floor of Ern Matheson's smokehouse, that's just how he felt. Not that it mattered. Nothing mattered anymore.

When they had come for him beside the river that morning, he had been surprised, but welcomed his arrest. At least now his muddied future was clear. He would end it hanging in a noose.

The hard dirt floor of the smokehouse had numbed his butt the way Olivia's rejection had numbed his heart and soul. He drew his legs up, propped his bound wrists on them, and rested his head in his hands. Ern had chinked the logs of the smokehouse good and tight so that not even a sliver of light filtered through. When they led him inside this morning, Noah had counted four hams hanging inside. At least he wouldn't starve to death in the meantime.

Ern's talkative wife Faye had brought him a cup and a bucket of water, and promised him some sugar cookies later in the day. He expected her to add, "If you're a good boy." Without a doubt he would give them no trouble. They were doing him a favor.

Once in a while he would hear whispers filtering through the wooden walls, disembodied voices of the curious standing outside.

"He's in there," someone said. "Noah LeCroix. Killed a man."

"Stabbed him in cold blood with a skinning knife."

"Prince of the Ohio's nothin' but a stinkin' half-breed after all."

"I heard tell he scalped Betts."

In the darkness, Noah had smiled at that. Betts didn't have enough hair on his head to bother with.

He felt as if he were shut up inside his head, sitting there in the close, confined space, unable to see his hands in front of his face. When they opened the door to put him in, he got a glimpse of the inside of his makeshift prison and expected he would go crazy in no time at all, but so far he had found the solitude comforting, a dark netherworld where he could drift in and out of his thoughts, reliving over and over the last time he had seen Olivia.

Her words echoed in the canyons of his mind, fell like boulders against his heart. The more the memory of it came to him, the more he recalled the way she had been almost frantic, even desperate during their lovemaking.

Something about her actions, something in her voice nagged him, prodded him to dwell on the exchange while another part of him tried to stop the madness.

She had made her choice. She was gone. What difference did any of it make now?

But the woman who had stepped away from him, the one who coldly pulled up his pants and turned away dismissing what had happened, the woman who said she was going to choose Darcy over him, was not the same Olivia he had found in the swamp, not the same girl who had awakened terrified and trembling, suffering memories of the man in New Orleans she had been desperate enough to escape without even a pair of decent shoes or a penny in her pocket.

Why? he kept asking himself over and over. Maybe she did not want him, he would grant her that, but *why* would she go with Darcy Lankanal?

What did he, Noah, know of pleasuring a woman? He had only made love to Olivia twice, and each time she had taken the initiative. There was no doubt that Lankanal was a better lover.

Over the past few months, had she gradually forgotten the hell Darcy had put her through in New Orleans? Had time tempered her memory? Had she truly come to miss the luxuries Lankanal could give her? The bleak cabin, the hard work and lack at the homestead might have worn her down.

Surely she knew that she would never want for anything if she went with him to Heron Pond. She would have everything he had the power to give her, but she would never have the fine things Lankanal could buy.

Noah had never set foot in a fancy whorehouse, but he doubted the kind of a life she would have to live there would suit her for very long. The thought of Olivia letting anyone touch her, lie with her for money sickened him, but since Olivia truly believed that Darcy Lankanal had soiled her for life, she might have finally convinced herself it was the only life she deserved.

There were people outside his small jail again; this time though, he recognized Ern Matheson's voice. "LeCroix's in here."

"You put him in the *smokehouse*?"

Noah's head went up when he heard Payson Bond.

"Well, hell, the jail fell apart after one of the last floods. This is the only place I got with a good latch on the outside."

The door swung open. Noah slammed his eye shut against the sudden light that filled the interior.

"Get up, LeCroix." Ern took his elbow and helped him to his feet. "You got yourself some visitors."

His leg muscles were cramped from sitting. He shuffled like an old man to the door of the smokehouse. Raising his hand to shield his eye from the light, Noah squinted around them and saw Payson and Susanna standing in front of the door. Behind them a crowd had gathered: women in leghorn bonnets, the usual onlookers and gossipmongers from farmers to merchants. The butcher had stepped outside and still had his blood-smeared apron tied over his clothes.

"Let's go on in the house and get away from all this.

Damn place is startin' to look like a prayer meetin' out here.'' Ern turned to the assemblage. "Go on home now folks, the show's over.''

"When's the hangin'?" the butcher wanted to know.

"I'll post a sign," Ern shouted back. "Now move on." He kept ahold of Noah's elbow as he led him across the yard to the back door of the dry goods store. Once inside the rooms upstairs where he and Faye lived, he had Noah sit on a spindly-legged chair with a fine embroidered seat.

Noah noticed that Susanna never took her eyes off of him, almost as if she were silently begging him to read her mind. Payson stepped into the parlor, took off his hat and politely stood near the door. Finally Susanna sat on the edge of a settee near Noah's chair.

"I brought these folks up here because they wanted to talk to you, LeCroix," Ern said.

Susanna turned to the peacekeeper. "Can I speak with him alone?"

Ern shook his head. "Anything you got to say to him you say in front of me."

She looked down at her hands where they were folded in her lap, then up at Noah. He saw the desperation in her eyes. Something was tearing her apart.

"What is it, Susanna?" he said softly.

"Did you do it, Noah? Did you kill that man?"

Payson stepped away from the doorjamb. "Susanna!"

Her gaze flew to her husband. "I had to ask, Payson. He had good cause."

Noah saw Payson flinch. "What is it you know, Susanna? What have you chosen to keep from me?" Olivia's father's voice had hardened; his features were taut, more than worried. He had aged overnight.

"Did you, Noah?" Susanna pressed.

Noah shook his head. "No."

She let go a sigh of relief. "I made Livvie a promise this morning," she said, her voice quivering. "I promised on my little girl's grave that I wouldn't break that promise, but my baby's already dead. What I have to say won't hurt her anymore, but it might save Livvie and it might save you, too,

Noah. I know Olivia would want me to help you.''

Payson visibly relaxed, crossed the room, and hunkered down beside his wife. He took her hands in his and stayed there beside her, lending her his strength. ''I'm sorry, Susanna. I didn't know what was said this morning, only that you were shutting me out again.''

Susanna's eyes were bright with tears when she laid her hand in Payson's. Then she looked at Noah and told him, ''Livvie went with Darcy because he told her that he would kill you, Noah, and you, Payson, if you stood in her way. He even threatened me and the boys . . . all of us, if we kept him from having her. She went with him out of fear.''

Noah felt the hot, killing rage come over him again. He fought it off, focusing on Susanna, on Payson. On the fact that his wrists were bound and he was already being held for a murder he hadn't committed.

''Wait a minute,'' Ern said. ''How is a gambler from New Orleans connected to your daughter, Bond?''

The color drained from Payson's face. Susanna spoke before her husband could even collect himself. ''Don't try to get it out of me, because that's a long story that I'm not even going into because you don't need to know all of it. That man threatened to kill Noah and took Olivia with him. Maybe Lankanal killed Betts—I don't know. I do know that I believe Noah when he says he didn't do it and I think you do, too.''

Ern looked directly at Noah now. ''How did your knife end up in Betts?''

Noah shrugged and shook his head. ''I don't know. I must have lost it in the tavern. Betts was kicking at me. He probably knocked it out of the sheath. I didn't even know it was gone until you arrested me this morning. *Someone* picked it up.''

''And killed Betts with it,'' Payson finished.

''Who'd want him dead?'' Ern turned to Noah. ''Why did you go after him in the tavern, anyway?''

Because Olivia had just ripped my heart out.

Because I was stupid enough to believe what she told me instead of believing in what had just passed between us.

"I was looking for Lankanal. Olivia had just told me she was going back to New Orleans with him. I'm glad I didn't find the gambler or I might have killed him. Someone else killed Betts and made it look like it was me."

"So you were mad enough to kill," Ern was watching him closely.

Noah nodded. "Maybe."

Payson and Susanna both protested. Finally Susanna won the floor and said to Ern, "Lankanal forced Olivia to go with him. He seemed like just the sort of man who would kill Betts to make certain Noah took the blame."

Payson gave Susanna's hands a squeeze and stood up. "Turn Noah loose, Ern." When he looked down at Noah, there was trust, friendship, and an unspoken promise in his eyes. "Let him go so he can bring my girl home again."

It took another twenty minutes of talking to persuade Ern Matheson to release him. The peacekeeper told Noah that he would hold Payson Bond personally responsible if he did not come back with Olivia and Lankanal and prove that he hadn't killed Betts. Afraid the town would want his head for letting a suspected killer go, Ern made Noah wait until dark when he could slip out unnoticed. For now, only the Bonds, Faye, and Ern would know that Noah was free. They all agreed to keep up the pretense that he was still incarcerated in the smokehouse for as long as possible.

With his rifle back in his hands and a new skinning knife on loan from the dry goods, Noah left by the side door, mounted up on the horse he had bought for Payson, and headed out of town overland. He kept to the less-traveled trails, heading due south along the river until he could somehow manage to beg, borrow, or steal a flatboat. He was already suspected of murder by almost everyone in Shawneetown. What did a little thievery matter?

*Cave in Rock
On the Ohio River*

Outside the glow of the fire, the dark walls of the cave loomed around them. Even in the heat of midsummer, the cool stone walls exuded an oppressive dampness, and the smell of mildew permeated the ground. Cave in Rock had sheltered man for centuries—Indians, river pirates, weary travelers.

As Olivia watched the firelight undulate over the rock walls, she was reminded of something tucked in the back of her memory, something illusive and lost to her now. She looked across the fire and shivered waiting for Darcy to return down the steep incline that led to the mouth of the cave.

They were alone here; the farmer who had carried them down the river on his way to market had only pulled in to let them off, directing them to the cave high on the bluff. Tomorrow Darcy intended to go overland to Golconda, where he would buy passage on a keelboat all the way to New Orleans. He chose to mix both river and overland routes in case her father, as he put it, "took it in his head to come after them."

Olivia knew her father would not come. Not after last night. Not after she convinced him that she would rather whore herself for trinkets than stay with the family. No, Payson Bond would not come after her. She had seen as much on his face, in the sadness reflected in his eyes.

Tonight she was alone with Darcy, here in the dark, hollow belly of the cave, sheltered by the cool sandstone walls on the bluff above the river. Little Pay, Freddie, Susanna, her father—they were all part of her past now. There was no going back.

And Noah? She still could not bring herself to even think his name, or she would shatter into countless, worthless pieces.

She heard the ring of Darcy's boots against the rocky floor as he made his way back down from the wide mouth opening of the cave, guided by the firelight. They had finished the food the farmer had sold them: chicken, pickles, and some bread, all wrapped in a piece of checkered cloth. Darcy had been hungry enough to eat what he called farmer's fare without much complaint, but sleeping on the ground with nothing between him and dirt but a thin wool blanket was keeping him awake.

He stood opposite her, deciding whether to sit or not.

"This place certainly isn't up to your usual standards," she told him. She was beyond caring if she made him angry.

"I told you I would go to any length to have you, Olivia. Even this, although I would much prefer a bed and clean sheets." He walked around the fire, hunkered down beside her and reached for a lock of her hair. When he rubbed it between his thumb and forefinger, the movement was so reminiscent of Noah that she had to close her eyes and tried to pull away.

He held tight, until her eyes stung with tears. Finally, he let go and her hair bounced back into a curl. She brushed it over her shoulder, lest he be tempted again. Ignoring him, she stared down into the white-hot flames of the fire that crackled and devoured the firewood beneath it.

Darcy hated her this way—resigned, compliant, the fire in her extinguished. He got to his feet and walked to the opposite side of the fire ring, lowered himself to the ratty blanket he had bought from the farmer, and concentrated on Olivia. He knew he was making her nervous by not touching her, by staring at her. She was so transparent it was pitiful. Let her try to avoid looking at him, let her try to ignore him. With very little effort and hardly any cost at all, he had her back in his possession. Soon, he would take her body again, but first he would heighten his need by watching her, owning her with his eyes.

Payson Bond came to mind, and Darcy felt his lip curl almost involuntarily. He tried to recall any similarity between the slight, tired-eyed farmer and Olivia's vibrant, flashing beauty. Thankfully, there was none. How could she really want to live a life of such bare existence, working herself to the bone, growing old before her time like her stepmother? It was beyond him.

Looking at her now, he could see that her hair wanted trimming; her chafed, reddened hands and feet needed to be manicured and rubbed with perfumed lotions and oils. How long had it been since she'd had a sensuous soak in a steaming, scented bath?

He had rescued her none too soon.

He shifted on the hard ground, propping his head on his hand. She glanced up and he caught a flash of emerald eyes before she dropped her gaze and her lashes swept her cheeks. His loins tightened, his pulse jumped. He began to reconsider waiting. Maybe he would have her before they returned to the Palace and he cleaned her up.

"What is it you want from me, Olivia? Say the word and I'll give it to you." The offer escaped him on its own. Since he could not call it back, he watched and waited to see what she would say.

Except for an almost imperceptible shiver, she did not respond at all.

"How about a miserable cabin in the dirt? Countless tubs of laundry to wash?" He thought back to the two little urchins he had seen at her father's place, the two towheads with traces of sticky candy around their mouths, with muddy feet and matted hair. He remembered having seen them in town before he found Olivia, although back then he had not even known they were her kin. Both of them had been sucking on penny candy, licking it off their dirty hands, laughing and rolling around outside the dry goods store.

"Did you have your heart set on a passel of children? Years of poverty?"

No response.

"If that's what you want, Olivia, I'm truly sorry that you will have to suffer with the best money can buy instead."

Finally, her head shot up and she glared at him, wild, beautiful rage on her face at long last. Anything, he thought. Anything to replace the resignation, the lethargy.

"The best money can buy for as long as you keep me for your pet, Darcy? Afterward you will set me up in my own little room and make me service, oh, how many men a night? Just to line your pockets?"

"And your own."

She laughed, a cold bitter laugh, and shook her head. "As if that were important. I won't be able to buy my soul back with tainted money." Her voice dropped to a whisper. "Or what I have lost."

He swung his legs under him, sat up and leaned close to the fire. "And what is it you think you have lost, Olivia? Your one-eyed, half-breed watchdog?"

The thought of the scarred half-breed putting his filthy hands all over her, putting himself inside her, made his blood boil.

"Don't tell me you *loved* him?" He laughed and the sound echoed off the walls of the cave. "Is that what you want? Love? Would that make it all better, Olivia? Would that make it worth it? Do you expect me to *love* you, to keep you with me forever instead of turning you into a whore like the others?"

He had been thinking the same thing lately, considering keeping her for himself, for always. He had gone through enough trouble to get her back, more than he would have done for any of the other girls. Those he would have given up without a chase. Olivia, he could not forget.

She shook her head, setting her dark, glistening curls rippling over her shoulders and down her back. He could almost feel her hair enveloping him. His hands itched to touch her, but he chose to torment himself with verbal foreplay, to stoke his need a while longer.

"Maybe," he mused, lowering his voice, hoping to stroke her, calm her, "maybe I do love you, Olivia, but I just don't know it. Maybe that's why I'm so obsessed with having you. Maybe that's why I never gave up and continued to track you down all these months."

"You don't know what love is, Darcy. If you did, I wouldn't be here."

"What is *that* supposed to mean?"

She irritated him by giving him a cool, small, knowing smile. "If you loved me, you would not force me to do anything. You would let me go."

"That's the most ridiculous thing I've ever heard." He laughed and the sound echoed off the cave walls.

"Of course it is, to someone like you."

The deep overwhelming sadness in her eyes caused him an intense tug of emotion that he had never felt before, one so foreign that he reacted to it with anger.

The memory of those grubby boys in the cabin flashed into his mind again, but it was quickly replaced with one of Olivia moving close to the half-breed, cozying up beneath the shelter of his arm on the street. Now, as he sat there staring at her, he watched Olivia slip back into her own private thoughts as she watched the fire.

What *did* he know of love? Some quirk of fate had led his mother to keep him when she found herself with child. He was raised at the Palace, coddled and nurtured by a bevy of whores. They dressed him up in velvet, in satin pants and top coats, clapped and laughed and gave him pennies and treats whenever he sang or danced or flashed his dimpled smile for them.

They were the only family he had ever known, those soft-skinned, fancy women of every hue who lived surrounded by clouds of perfume, powdered and painted, draped in loose silk and satin.

Olivia was right, of course. There was no way he could understand the kind of devotional, familial love she was talking about, the kind of love that would keep a man tied to the life he had glimpsed last night in Payson Bond's cabin.

Why would any man want that kind of life? Or any woman, for that matter?

As the firelight played off the soft turn of her cheek, bounced back off the highlights in her hair, shadowed the contours of her chin, her long throat, Darcy silently had to agree with her. If that was love, then indeed, he was ignorant of it.

He did not know that kind of love. Nor did he care to.

"If you loved me you would let me go."

Of one thing he was certain. To love was to possess, to

control, to own. In that way, he did care for her. More than any woman he had ever known.

The night was clear, the moon full, casting shadows on the water as Noah alternately steered and then paddled his way down the Ohio. He was alone in a dugout canoe for which he traded his hat and Payson's newly acquired horse to an old, toothless Shawnee who was fishing along the shore a few miles south of Shawneetown.

Navigating the river at night was not only foolhardy, it was dangerous, even under the full moon. There wasn't another craft on the water large or small; still, he was careful to keep the canoe close to the bank of the river where the shadows from the trees darkened the water. Whenever he passed a smaller settlement or homestead near the water, he would lift the paddle to make certain no one heard him drift by—not that anyone in his right mind would be expecting someone to be on the water at night.

The harmonic voices whispering in the water were back, murmuring to him, guiding him, telling him where to turn, when to drift with the current, what places to avoid. The stars shining above and the moonlight glistening off the water added magic to the hushed sounds that filled his head. Even more curious than the voices was an imprint on the water, one that he could feel rather than see, one that convinced him that Olivia had passed this way earlier. After the first hour on the water he was sure the river was guiding him to her. The water whispered her name.

As he came around a wide bend in the river, an inner knowing tugged at him, urging him to pull in to shore. Just to be certain, he let the canoe drift on past the spot for a quarter mile until the feeling that Olivia had been this way slowly faded. He stopped, turned the canoe back upstream, and hugged the bank where the water was shallow and the current weak. He waited, puzzling over the odd sensations.

Should he trust the voices or was he only losing his mind? He paddled back upstream until the feeling hit him again. Olivia was near. Olivia had definitely come ashore here. He beached the canoe, stepped out, and pulled it up across the muddy riverbank, hiding it beneath some overhanging branches. Standing there beside the river, he looked around. The land rolled gently upward and ended at a high sandstone bluff. There were no tracks in the moonlight and now that he stood on solid ground, the voices were still.

He closed his eye and took a deep breath. A slight, hardly detectable scent of smoke came to him on the still night air. Hiking a few yards away from the water, he headed toward the bluff until he found what he was looking for. There, almost disembodied in the face of the bluff he saw the faint, far off glow of a campfire. The moon was so bright that it was almost impossible to distinguish the firelight or the trail of smoke.

Cave in Rock. Of course.

It was the perfect hiding place, a natural cave in the sandstone bluff. Most recently, bands of river pirates had used it to lure unsuspecting emigrants to shore. It was a fitting place for the gambler and whoremonger to spend the night, but not with Olivia.

Noah began to climb with a purpose. How long had they been there, he wondered?

What had Olivia already endured?

"Darcy is a far more experienced lover."

He stopped to take a deep breath, to adjust the second red headband he had torn from his quickly vanishing shirttails and fought back the lingering hint of doubt that had not left him all day.

Susanna had told him that Olivia had left with Darcy to save him, to save her family, but the words Olivia had said after the heat of their passion had branded themselves indelibly on his heart. Didn't she *know* he could save himself? That he didn't need her to sacrifice herself to Lankanal for him? With such soft hands and fair skin, with such perfect, handsome features, Lankanal had probably never fought another man in his life. He was not the type to dirty his own hands fighting or killing. He would have someone else do it for him.

Lankanal, in and of himself, was no threat.

But how was Olivia to have known?

Noah realized she truly believed she was protecting him and her family. There had to be only one reason she would make such a sacrifice. She loved him as much as she did Payson, Susanna, and the boys.

Noah tightened his grip on his rifle and began to jog across the sandy soil, weaving his way through the trees, hoping he was not too late.

chapter
18

OLIVIA SAT HUDDLED WITH HER LEGS DRAWN UP AND HER arms wrapped around her knees, watching the firelight flicker on the walls of the cave, trying to shake the haunting sense of having been here before. Darcy lay across the fire ring, striking a casual pose that was marred every time he looked at the ground around him in disgust and made certain his clothes were not touching the dirt.

After the sleepless night before and the emotional upheaval of lying to Noah and her family, Olivia was so exhausted now that she could barely keep her eyes open.

For whatever reason, Darcy had chosen to verbally toy with her, prolonging the inevitable. She did not even dare to hope that this night would pass without his taking her on the floor of the cave.

Suddenly it came to her with aching clarity that she had seen this same scene before in a dream, a dream that had begun as a nightmare the night that she and Noah first made love in his cabin high over the swamp. That night she had dreamed of being enclosed in the stone walls of a cavern with firelight writhing on the walls just the way it was now. A tall, broad shouldered man had come to her, a dark angel who had taken away the fear and the pain. The angel had gently loved her, had given of himself, brought her joy and light. Noah. She had awakened in his arms and discovered that her dream had become reality.

But that was almost a summer ago, a lifetime. There would be no dark angel this time. She had banished him from her life, sent him home without her; the only consolation was knowing that he was safe.

"Thinking of your half-breed lover?"

Darcy's voice startled her. She gazed over at him, tried to pin him with a cool, even stare.

"Actually, I was." She watched him blanch. Anger hardened his perfect features, but he no longer inspired fear. There was nothing he could do to her that he had not already done before, aside from kill her, and she was beginning to think that death might be a welcome escape. In fact, Olivia thought, as she stared back into his cynical blue eyes, perhaps ending her life and taking Darcy with her might be a way to save a number of other young girls from suffering the same fate at his hands.

"What were you thinking about him?" Darcy's voice was low, even, deadly.

"I was just comparing the two of you, and you come up wanting, Darcy. You aren't even fit to walk the ground he's walked on."

She expected him to come up off the blanket, to explode in a rage. Instead he only looked into her eyes and laughed.

"Fine talk coming from a whore."

"I never said that I was worthy of him." She propped her chin on her knees. Unwilling to take her eyes off of him, she was ready for him to quit toying with her and pounce. "In fact, I had to spend most of the summer convincing him that I was not good enough for him. That's what made it easier to give him up and leave with you, Darcy. You see, I love him. I would do *anything* to see him safe, even stay with the likes of you."

She had struck one chord too many. He was on his feet, rounding the fire, on her in an instant. His fingers bit into her upper arms as he grabbed her and pulled her up. She yelped in pain when her hair became tangled beneath his grasping hands. The pressure on her arms let up when he released them, but he found purchase at the neckline of her calico gown. She grabbed his wrists, but was no match for his strength.

The fabric tore with a ragged sound, exposing her only piece of underclothing, a light muslin chemise.

"God, I hated that dress." He pushed it down around her hips until it slid to the floor and pooled around her feet and ankles.

His hands closed over her breasts. He began to knead them painfully. His eyelids were half closed, his breath coming hard and fast. She had never seen him like this. He had never physically hurt her before. Olivia winced, but refused to give him the satisfaction of crying out.

She threw her head back and stared at him, willing him to open his eyes, to look into hers.

"I'll kill you, Darcy. I swear it. Have me now and enjoy it, but be warned, I'm going to kill you one day if it's the last thing I do."

She knew she was well and truly lost then, that she had sunk as low as she could go. He had taken all of the good left in her, for now she could smile coldly back at him and actually think of killing him. Her soul was damned. She might just as well rid the world of the both of them.

Her feet tangled in the fabric of her gown as he began to push her back toward the stone wall behind them. When she tripped and started to fall, he jerked her up, pressing her back with one hand on her breast. With the other he grabbed a handful of her hair and wrapped it around his wrist. He pulled her head back until her face was tilted up to his and she had no recourse but to take the kiss he forced upon her.

Darcy was squeezing her breast, thrusting his tongue in her mouth, rubbing up against her. To think of Noah now was almost a sacrilege, but her mind retreated of its own volition, hiding in the memory of him, of Noah's hands, Noah's kiss, Noah's gentle, healing touch.

The beautiful recollections succeeded in making Darcy's attempts to have her, to reach her, very pitiful in comparison. Not only her body, but her mind rebelled with loathing and she began to fight him in earnest, in a way she never had before. She could not allow his touch to defile and replace Noah's. Where once he might have eventually overcome her body, this time nothing happened. Instead of stoking her passion, he only succeeded in firing her determination to fight him off for as long as she could.

She tried to escape his hold by twisting away, but he pulled her hair so hard that she cried out against his mouth, kicked him in the shins, struck out at him with her fists. Stunned, he lifted his head. She slapped him hard across the mouth, so hard she split the corner of his lip.

"You really mean it, don't you?" He blinked, stunned.

Swiping off blood with the back of his hand, he stared down at his ruffled white cuff and the blood that stained it.

"Damn it, Olivia." He stared at her in shocked disbelief. "I've never had to rape a woman in my life. Women *love* me."

"Forcing me is the only way you'll have me, Darcy, because I loathe you. I'd rather sleep with the devil."

"I don't want it to be like this. I've chased across the country after you, Olivia. Doesn't that mean anything to you?"

"Darcy, I can't give you what you want anymore, not willingly."

"I want you to look at me the way you looked at him."

There was actually remorse in his tone, a hint of pleading, something that she never in her life expected to hear. He actually sounded sincere, as if he were truly sorry, as if he had no idea how to have her, or any woman, except by owning her.

Olivia shook her head, sadness swelling inside the hurt.

She whispered, "I'll never look at you the way I looked at Noah. I loved him."

Just then, she caught a glimpse of movement on the dark incline across the fire. One of the burning branches in the fire ring popped and split and fell into the ash, sending up sparks that swirled in the heat of the flames like minute starbursts.

She saw a figure in the deep black shadows, watched a tall, broad shape move from boulder to boulder, faster now, heading toward the light, toward her. Coming out of nowhere like an avenging angel, the man's shape grew larger, his shadow curving upward, hugging the walls of the cavern.

"No," she whispered. "Oh, no." She shook her head, wincing against the tug of Darcy's fist in her hair.

"Oh, yes," Darcy whispered. With his back to the entrance of the cave, it was impossible for him to know what was about to befall him. "Make it easy on yourself, Olivia. I swear, I'll make you like it as much as you used to. I promise." He bent his head, forcing her face up to receive his kiss.

The man in the shadows stepped into the ring of light. Olivia bit her lip to keep from crying out to him, from giving his presence away. She had to keep Darcy from turning around, from seeing Noah. Her nightmare had come to pass, but this time, instead of a gentle coming together at the end of the dream, the lovemaking, the ending would be all wrong. Nothing good or true or wonderful would happen this time.

"Let her go, Lankanal." Noah's strong voice rang against the stone. Magnified by the curvature of the walls, it echoed around them.

Noah's hand tightened on his rifle. The old Hawken was primed and ready to fire. All he had to do was squeeze the trigger and rid the world of Darcy Lankanal.

Behind the gambler, Olivia leaned against the stone wall, panting; her chemise was torn, exposing the swell of her breast and the purpling finger marks on her fair skin. Her hair was a wild black nimbus around her head, her eyes huge in the ivory oval of her face.

Noah had been outside climbing the hillside when he heard her cry out. Knowing it could only be Olivia's cry, knowing Darcy had his hands on her, was hurting her, spurred him on. Afraid of what Lankanal might be forced to do if he discovered that he was trapped, Noah had stealthily entered the cave and covered the last few yards down the incline without a sound.

The cost of his silence was that he had to watch as Darcy manhandled Olivia. He had seen the gambler grab her breast, pull her hair, and humiliate her before he could reach her.

What other atrocities had she suffered? How much damage had Lankanal done before he arrived?

"Olivia." Noah was shocked at the sound of his own voice. Emotion choked him so that he sounded rusty, like an old, old man. He cleared his throat and tried again.

"Olivia, are you all right?"

He saw her nod, watched her try to cover her breasts with her hands and arms. She slunk along the wall behind Darcy, edging away from him, moving toward the fire where her dress lay in a tangled heap of calico.

Lankanal was bleeding from a cut on his lip. Noah smiled as his finger caressed the trigger.

"I'm not armed," Lankanal warned him. He wiped his lip with his coat sleeve, frowning at the blood spot and then at Noah.

"What chance did you give Betts before you put my knife in his chest?"

Noah heard Olivia gasp as she knelt by the fire trying to cover her near-nakedness.

"He was already dead," Darcy told him. "Keeled over dead without any warning. All I did was use his body to make it look like you killed him."

"You left me to hang for a murder I didn't commit."

Darcy shrugged as if it were nothing. "I had a feeling that if you weren't out of the way, you would eventually come looking for Olivia and I didn't want that." He took a chance, glancing over at her. "She has that effect on men." He shrugged his shoulders, straightened his swallow-tailed coat and ran his hands down the front of his shirt. "I swear to God, I didn't kill Betts."

Noah found himself believing the man, although he desperately wanted not to. Now that Olivia was safe, the urge to kill Darcy had ebbed away, his code of honor too great to overcome, even when faced with the likes of Darcy Lankanal. Noah looked at Olivia again. She had slipped her dress on and was holding the bodice bunched in her fist.

"Come here, Olivia," Noah said softly.

She scooted around the fire and slowly walked up beside him. He lowered his rifle and took an instant to smile over at her, an instant of time that was long enough for Darcy to bend over and reach inside his boot.

Noah caught a flicker of movement out of the corner of his eye. Shoving Olivia out of harm's way, he took a step toward Lankanal. There was a flash of silver. Before he could react, he realized Darcy had thrown a knife. As the weapon flew with deadly accuracy, Olivia screamed.

Pain slammed into Noah's shoulder, pain that sent him reeling back. He squeezed the trigger a moment before dropping his rifle. The charge went off, the ball ricocheted against stone, hit no one.

"Noah!" Olivia screamed and ran toward him.

"Get out," he yelled back. "Run to the river. I'll meet you there."

"No. *I'll not* leave you," she cried. "Not again."

Her words lent him strength. Noah pulled out the knife, rising to his feet in time to meet Lankanal as the man launched himself at him. The weapon went flying as Noah took the brunt of the gambler's weight on his injured shoulder and both of them fell to the ground. They were well matched in physical stature, but Noah could tell immediately that Lankanal's life had made him soft. His own shoulder wound evened the match.

The way the gambler was carefully aiming each blow told him not to underestimate his opponent.

Olivia watched Noah and Darcy rolling and punching one another with her hand pressed to her lips to keep from crying out. In the fire's glow, Noah's torn red shirt could not conceal the dark, spreading stain quickly covering his shoulder and upper sleeve. The wound was bleeding fast. Noah was favoring his right side and Darcy was wise enough to aim many of his blows there. Somehow, when Darcy made it to his feet, Noah shakily rose to meet him.

With a blow to the face, Noah opened a cut over Darcy's

eye that began to bleed profusely, hampering Darcy's vision. The leveling seemed to fuel Noah with newfound energy and he began to pound Darcy in earnest, knocking him to the ground, hammering him in the face, the jaw, the temple.

When she saw Darcy lose his grip on Noah's shirtfront, falling to lie there senseless, Olivia knew she had to act. She ran across the cave, reached for Noah. He did not hear her, did not stop pounding Darcy with his fists. She took hold of his shirt and began to shake him.

"Stop, Noah! Don't kill him. Please, let him go."

Noah might as well have been swimming in deep water. He could hear Olivia calling to him but her voice was coming from somewhere far away, tugging at him, demanding attention. He tried to shrug it off, but as the tugging became more insistent, Olivia's voice became louder until he realized they were connected, that she had knelt beside him in the dirt and was pulling on his shirt. He blinked and looked over at her, slowly surfacing, coming back to the moment, coming into himself. Shaking his head, he tried to clear his vision. Blood droplets flew, spattering her cheek. It wasn't until he saw the bright red blood against her pale skin that he settled fully into himself and realized where he was.

Darcy Lankanal lay sprawled on the floor beneath his straddled legs. The gambler's once-handsome face, so flawless, so perfectly angelic, was a mass of cuts and ugly welts. His left eye was the size of a goose egg, swollen shut.

"Don't kill him, Noah," Olivia begged again. "Please."

Noah realized those were the same words he had been hearing, that she was kneeling in the dirt beside him begging for mercy—for Lankanal.

"Don't kill him?" he whispered. He looked down, finding it hard to believe he had nearly beaten the man to death already.

She took his battered hands in hers, held them, smoothed her fingers over his torn knuckles.

"Don't do it, Noah. You will regret it for as long as you live."

He blinked, trying hard to understand. She gave up trying to keep her ruined gown closed. It gaped open, exposing her chemise and the bruises on her breasts.

"You want him to live?" Noah tried to understand, but his mind was so muddied. His shoulder was on fire. He ached all over.

"I don't want you to kill him." She nodded, speaking slowly, carefully, as if he had forgotten the English words.

He shook his head, still trying to clear it. "You do love him, then?"

"Oh, no, Noah. I don't love him." She reached out and smoothed his matted hair off of his face, straightening his headband so that it covered his scar. "I just don't want you to have his soul on your conscience for the rest of your life."

"But . . . he hurt you." As long as he lived, he would never forget seeing her suffering Darcy's abuse.

She nodded. "Let him go. He's not worth it."

Noah put his hand to his head, trying to think clearly. It was hard, with his brain still rattling around. "If we let him go, he will always be out there somewhere. He will keep coming back, again and again." His thoughts were coming faster now. The fog was slowly lifting. "He is obsessed with you, Olivia. He tried to blame a murder on me, tried to get me out of the way, to be certain that I hung."

Noah looked down at the gambler. Olivia followed his gaze. Darcy was conscious and staring up at both of them through his bloodshot eye.

Olivia put one hand on Noah's good shoulder and leaned over Lankanal.

"Listen to me, Darcy, and listen well. *It's over.*"

Even semiconscious, Darcy realized that he would have to throw away his very expensive, very fashionable, French-tailored swallowtail coat.

The idea of ever wearing it again was disgusting him more than the pain in his head, the throbbing cut over his eye, or the fact that Olivia's half-breed was still straddling him, pinning him to the dirt. He should have never worn the coat to Illinois. None of the local dirt farmers, saline miners or emigrants had even recognized it for the fine article of clothing that it was.

"Darcy? Did you hear me?" Olivia was leaning over him, looking radiantly pale—an impossibility, he reminded himself. He would have smiled at the jest, but his face hurt.

"Hear what?" he tried to whisper. He swallowed and tasted blood.

"It's over. Go back to New Orleans and leave me alone," Olivia said.

"I can't hear you with him sitting on me like this," he complained.

She looked at her lover and nodded. "Go ahead, Noah, kill him."

Darcy raised his hand to ward off a blow. "Wait!"

Looking up at the two of them kneeling above him, Darcy saw them exchange a look that excluded the rest of the world—and he suddenly realized how Olivia could still look so lovely, so openly joyous, even though she was kneeling there in the dirt in her soiled, ruined dress.

It was love that glowed in her eyes. Love for the man beside her. Earlier, before LeCroix had burst into the cave, she had declared her love for the legendary river pilot openly. With a sinking feeling, Darcy had known that nothing would extinguish her love for the half-breed. Nothing. He knew it as sure as he knew that the nose on his face was broken and he would never wear his fine coat or shirt again.

She had been willing to destroy them both; he had seen it in her eyes when she had pledged to kill him. If he did not give up his obsession and let her go, he would be forced to watch her destroy herself—and perhaps himself in the bargain.

Now, after seeing her face-to-face with LeCroix, after knowing she would never submit to him again, no matter what he offered, no matter where he took her, how long he kept her, he knew his only alternative was to let her go. Let her be and forget her.

"All right. It's over," he mumbled.

"What did you say?" Noah LeCroix's hand tightened on his collar.

"It's over," he said as loud and clear as he could through busted lips. "But I'm not doing this for you, LeCroix. I'd sooner you killed me." He looked over into Olivia's deep green eyes, sincere in every word. "I'm doing this for you, Olivia, because I know that you will never care about me the way you do him. It's too late for that. Maybe if we had met another way, another time, perhaps it would have worked out." He shrugged, "But now all I can do is let you go."

He tried to smile. His mouth felt like a pulpy mass. Then he looked up at LeCroix and had the satisfaction of seeing that the man's face was bruised, his shoulder bleeding. It would be a long time before the Prince of the Ohio forgot Darcy Lankanal.

"Do you think you can get off me now?" He asked LeCroix.

As Olivia helped her lover to his feet, Darcy lay there watching them, wishing he had learned something about true love a lot sooner.

chapter
19

THEY LEFT DARCY LANKANAL IN THE CAVE FOR THE night, propped against the wall with his hands bound, the fire burning low. Assured of the resignation and the defeat in Lankanal's eyes, Noah believed the man when he gave his word not to pursue Olivia anymore and would have let him go, except that in order to clear his own name he had to take the gambler back to Shawneetown and explain things to Ern Matheson.

At the base of the hill, beside the river, Olivia washed Noah's wounds and bound his shoulder by moonlight. Although the knife wound appeared to be clean, he had lost a lot of blood. It took some talking to convince Olivia that he felt better than he looked. For a while, they sat by the bank, each lost in thought, both holding their silence. Noah found it impossible not to think of the scene he had come upon in the cave, nor could he forget the bruises on Olivia's upper arms or her breasts, any more than he could forget what had happened the night before, when they had made love and she had sent him away.

His shoulder was hurting like hell. He could only watch her, keeping his own silence. Her long hair hung loose down her back; her ruined dress had slipped off one shoulder. She had to be more exhausted than he, and yet she was wide awake, staring at the dark water of the Ohio as it flowed south.

Noah looked over at the canoe he had dragged on shore and thought of the proud old man to which it had belonged, of the way the toothless Shawnee had rubbed his palm over the black felt hat before he put it on, the way his chest swelled with pride when he led Payson's horse away.

If only they could climb into that canoe and go back to Heron Pond, leave everything and everyone behind, move back to the seclusion and safety of the swamp, where they would not have to look back. Instead, they faced hauling Lankanal back to Shawneetown to clear his name and to let Olivia's family know that she was safe. Would Olivia go with him if he asked again? Did she love him enough?

"Noah? Are you all right?" Her soft voice, so full of concern, gently drew him back to reality.

"I'm fine." It was a warm night. Outside the dank cave, they needed no fire. He knew he was too tired to eat, but he wasn't sure about Olivia.

"How did you find me?"

He looked at the river, the dark, swift moving water dappled with milk-white moonlight. She had been through too much. He was not going to tell her how the voices in the water had led him to her. Perhaps, someday, if they had any future together, he would tell her about them, about his mother and the voices in the wind, but not tonight.

"I saw the light from the cave," he explained, sidestepping the truth.

She shook her head. "Did they . . . did you really go to jail?" Looking up at him from where she sat clutching her ruined dress together, she reminded him of a lost little girl.

"Nah. I went to the smokehouse."

"The *what*?"

"There is no jail. Ern Matheson locked me in his smokehouse. It wasn't so bad."

"How did you get away?"

Carefully, feeling every muscle in his body, he lowered himself to the hard ground beside her. "Susanna and your father came to town. She told Matheson and Payson that the reason you really went with Lankanal was because he threatened to harm me, and them, and the boys."

She whispered, "She promised me. She gave me her word that she would not tell anyone."

He reached over, gently cupped her chin in his hand, met her eyes.

"She did it to keep me from hanging."

A shudder ripped through her.

"Thank God. What I don't understand is why in the world anyone would think you wanted Betts dead. You had no cause."

"He came into town with Lankanal. I was upset after you sent me away. I was no better than Lankanal that night."

She shook her head vehemently. "Not you, Noah. Never you. You have more honor in your little finger than Darcy will ever have in his entire body."

"It was almost as if I had stopped thinking. I went looking for Lankanal, but I ran into his friend Betts first, in the tavern. I guess I frightened him pretty bad. Ern said I almost choked him to death."

"I can't bear to hear what I have done to you. I can't bear it." She hid her face in her hands.

"Stop it." He reached for her wrists and slowly drew her hands away from her face. In the moonlight, the tear streaks on her cheeks glistened silver.

"I'm so sorry, Noah. I'm sorry for all of it. Because of me, you might have hanged. And tonight, Darcy nearly killed you."

"Haven't you heard yet?"

"What?"

"It'll take more than a fancy-dressed gambler to kill me. I'm the Prince of the Ohio."

She sniffed and wiped her eyes again, this time with the hem of her dress.

"This is no laughing matter, Noah." Despite her tears, she had to smile. Olivia touched his cheek.

In the silence, they could hear the river lapping against the shore. The air was close and heavy. Not a leaf moved, not a blade of grass. Somewhere an owl hooted.

He still wanted her, now and forever. Wanted to make

her his in every way, wanted to ask her to marry him, but he was more scared of asking and being turned away again than he had been facing Darcy's blade back in the cave.

Ask her. He could hear Hunter's bold laugh. *Ask her.*

The words stuck in his throat.

He reached for her and slowly opened the ragged edges of the gown, exposing dark bruises on ivory skin bathed by moonlight.

"Now he has marked me on the outside, too," she said with a broken sigh.

As tenderly as he could, he traced her bruises with his fingertips, wished he could erase them with a touch. He was afraid to move, to touch her the way he wanted, to take her in his arms and make her forget Darcy and all that had happened. The moonlight illuminated the tears shimmering in her eyes.

She slipped her arms around him and pressed her face against his neck. He tilted her face to his, touched his lips to hers and felt her melt. She kissed him full and deep, urging him to kiss her back, opening to him, teasing him with her tongue.

He wanted to communicate his love to her through his touch, tried to tell her all the things he could not say, but he was still haunted by something she had said to him at the campsite.

"I keep wondering," he whispered against her cheek, "about what you told me about Darcy pleasing you. I know you spoke those words to make me angry enough to leave you, but I can't get them out of my head."

Olivia went perfectly still. She hated knowing how much she had hurt him, how the things she had said to save his life still made him doubt himself. Hugging him close, she smoothed her hand down his spine, resting it in the hollow at the small of his back.

"Noah, I said those things at the campsite to keep you safe, to make you so angry that you would go home and forget about me. Never, ever, think that Darcy is better than you . . . at anything. His touch made me feel filthy and sick inside. Yours gives me life. When you touch me, you make me feel whole and pure and good again. Never, ever doubt yourself.''

"Then let me help you now," he whispered. "Let me help you forget *this* night."

She knew that what she was doing was wrong, that she should stop him before it was too late, but she could not stop herself any more than Noah could have turned the direction of the current of the river behind them. Darcy's attack had left her shaken; her own thoughts of killing him and herself had left her feeling bleak and empty inside. Noah was offering the one thing she knew would redeem her, if only for a while.

His touch was gentle, hesitant. He was not asking for any more than she was willing to give. She wanted him in every way. She wanted him to take her and make her his again, to tell him that she was ready to take back everything she had ever done to hurt him, that if he would only ask again she would go with him to Heron Pond.

For a brief second before he kissed her, she thought perhaps he was going to say the words she longed to hear, but the moment passed. She had no right to expect any more than this, for she had wounded him deeply one too many times. Perhaps she had finally convinced him that she was only good enough for this sharing of desires, these stolen moments of passion, and nothing more.

When his hand slid up her thigh, she held perfectly still. When he brushed the fabric of her gown up her legs, she felt the warm kiss of the night air on her skin and shivered. Always the more honorable one, he hesitated before he touched her intimately, seeking permission. She sensed his reservation.

"Please, Noah," she breathed, no better than what Darcy had made her, no worse than a woman in love.

He took her then, his hands sure as they found her center. His fingers slipped into her honeyed warmth, slowly, deliciously moving gently until she clung to him and cried out his name. His damp hair swept her cheek and then her breasts, cool against her fevered skin as he moved down her, kissing her breasts, suckling her until she writhed with pleasure against the soft summer grass beneath them.

Gentle and yet masterful, he moved down her, worshipping her, caressing her, cleansing her of the past, of all she was before until she felt new and whole, treasuring each and every breathtaking sensation, every word and touch and sigh.

His hands were sure as he parted her. There was no doubt or hesitation as he moved between her legs, rose and entered her, holding himself back, thinking of her pleasure, taking her little by little. She felt herself stretch for him as he filled her. Slowly they began to move together. There was no frenetic rush, not like the last time at his campsite, when she thought that his life was in jeopardy, that she was leaving him for good, forever. Tonight, there was all the time in the world.

There beneath the moon they made slow, tender, burning love as the night air caressed them and fireflies danced against the backdrop of trees like fairies come to celebrate with them. There was healing. There were silent promises and unspoken vows.

Bond Homestead

Illinois in summer. The air was close and humid, thick as a hot wet towel. Payson walked to the open cabin door and stared out over the field where the stalks of Indian corn had grown taller by the day, but he did not see the corn stalks as he stared absently across the field. Nor did he see the clear blue sky above. All he had been able to dwell on for the last two days was Olivia, of what she had endured and what she might even now be enduring at Darcy Lankanal's hands.

He leaned against the doorjamb, idly scratching his shirtfront. No words came to him, nothing the poets had written that could fill the void of Olivia's leaving again; nothing could replace his own self-loathing. Because he had been too afraid to pursue her about the details of where she had spent the last year, because he had been able to fool himself into thinking that he would ask her when the time was right, he had made them all vulnerable. He had left the door open for Darcy Lankanal to waltz right in.

He heard Little Pay shouting at the side of the cabin. The boy's words were indistinguishable, something about boats and pirates. He and Freddie had been running at full tilt all morning, chasing each other in and out and around the cabin. Without warning, they appeared around the corner of the house and ran straight at Payson, hooting and hollering. Each of them wore an identical swath of red fabric tied around his head and down over one eye. They tried to duck past him.

"What are you two doing?" He was sorry he had given them so little of his time of late.

"We're playing Noah and the river pirates." Little Pay stuck out his narrow chest and proudly pointed to himself. "I'm Noah."

"An I'm Little Noah," Freddie quickly informed him. They ran inside, disappeared up the ladder to the loft and in what seemed like two minutes were climbing back down again.

They came and went and Payson did nothing to even slow them down. Because they did not comprehend the full weight of Olivia's departure, the boys carried no burden of worry. Nor should they have to, Payson thought. Let them play, he told himself. He wanted them to be young and carefree for as long as they could.

Behind him, Susanna set down a bowl of cornmeal and walked across the room. She reached out to him when she got to the door, slipped her arm around his waist and leaned into him. Together they stared out at the same field, the same clear sky.

"He'll find her, Payson. Noah will bring Livvie home again."

"You think so?"

"He will go all the way to New Orleans if he has to, and it won't be just to clear his name."

He stood away from the doorjamb, his arm around her

shoulders. "Susanna, I keep asking myself why I didn't talk to her sooner, why I didn't sit her down and make her tell me what happened. I saw such sorrow in her eyes when she first came back to us that I just could not bear to dredge it up for her again. Why didn't I act?"

"To what end? What could you have done?"

He sighed. "I could have prevented all this. I could have been on the lookout for Lankanal. I would have already known what she had been through. I could have thought more clearly. I would have come up with a plan to keep him from her. Susanna, when he told me all those things, about buying Livvie from the colonel and his men, I was in such shock that I couldn't think clearly. If it hadn't been for Molly—"

"Who could blame you?"

When he turned and looked down into her eyes, there was such suffering reflected in his that it made her ache for him.

"Certainly not you, Susanna, although you have every right to blame me for all of this. I should have listened to your father—"

She put her fingers to his lips to silence him. "Never say that, Payson. You would have never survived living under my father's roof. I know that now."

"But can we survive out here? Look at all that's happened. It was my place to protect you and Livvie and the boys. I failed on our journey West. Without Noah's help this summer, I could not have provided for all of you for another winter. Now I've failed Olivia again."

"She understands now that you did what you had to do that day on the river. The last thing she told me before she left was that she wanted you to know that she forgives you, Payson. She said that she realizes now that sometimes one has no choice. Livvie knows you only did what you *had* to do last summer. She told me that she survived once and she will again. When she went with Lankanal, she was doing what she thought she had to do because she loves us . . . and Noah."

Payson frowned. "But Noah can defend himself. How

she thought Lankanal could best him, I'll never know."

"I'm sure Livvie didn't want Noah put to the test."

"But she knew *I* was wanting. Even Molly knows that I can't hit the broad side of a barn with a rifle. Livvie knew that, too. She must have sincerely doubted that I could protect myself from Lankanal. But I could have warned Ern about him, I could have gotten help, if only I had known about him. I could have asked the neighbors to stand with me. I could have been ready for him, if I'd only had the nerve to make her tell me the truth."

"But could you have told anyone in town *why* you needed help against Lankanal? Would you have wanted all of it to come out? I think that you would have wanted to keep Olivia's past a secret, for her sake." She stepped away from him, returned to the table and started to pour the hoecake batter into a skillet. She felt him watching her.

He left the open door and crossed the room to be near her.

"Do you really believe it, Susanna? Do you think Noah will bring her back?"

She looked up at him and smiled. "Yes."

"When he does, I'm taking you all back East. This is a wild place. It's too hard on all of you. The boys are turning into hellions and you have suffered enough. You deserve the finery you had before you married me, the help, a grand house." He sighed, looked at his worn hands. "Lord knows, I'm not a farmer. I'm a teacher."

Susanna reached up to him and smoothed his hair back behind his ear. There were new lines at the corners of his eyes, lines carved by the sun and the wind and endless hours outside. She traced them with her thumbs as she cupped his face.

"We can't leave here now, Payson. Not now that you have a good crop coming in. We've enough put by for the winter and . . . I'm on my feet again." She looked out the window toward the treeline, where the small wooden cross stood all alone. "We've invested a child into this land, Payson. A baby. Your sweat and blood, too. Our tears. We can't just walk away now. And you *will* teach again. Did you notice how much the town has grown, just in the year since we first arrived? Soon there will be a church and a school and folks around here will be looking for a teacher.''

Excited by the direction of her thought, a grand new idea came to her right there over the hoecake batter.

''This fall, after the corn is in, why don't you think about calling on the families closest to us, ask them if they wouldn't like to send their children over here for lessons a few hours a week? Our own little hellions could certainly use some tutoring.''

She saw a light flare in his eyes that had not been there for a long, long while.

''I don't deserve you, Susanna.''

''You stood by me when I was locked inside myself. You stayed.'' She leaned into him. ''I love you for that and so much more.''

''I love you, too, Susanna.''

He looked out the window at his fields and beyond. ''Maybe,'' he said softly. ''Maybe I will teach again. But I can't even think about anything of the sort until Livvie comes home.''

Shawneetown

Much to Darcy's intense shame, the local hayseeds lined the main thoroughfare of Shawneetown as Noah and Olivia led him bound at the wrists from the edge of town all the way to Ern Matheson's Nu Way Dry Goods store. By the time the humiliating little parade reached the front door and they walked into the dark interior, cooler than the bright sunshine, rich with the smell of tobacco, spices, and citrus fruits brought up from the South, the speculative nature of the curious had turned into the surly catcalls of a crowd on the brink of becoming a mob.

''I was beginning to think I was never gonna see the likes of you again,'' Ern Matheson said to LeCroix.

Darcy watched the storekeeper reach for LeCroix's hand and pump it up and down. The man would have started thumping the half-breed on the shoulder if LeCroix had not quickly shrugged him off. Then Matheson noticed the bloodstain on Noah's shirt and his bandaged shoulder beneath.

"What the hell happened to you?"

"Lankanal happened," Noah told him, nodding at Darcy.

Ern turned toward Darcy, staring at the bonds that held his hands tied together at his wrists. Darcy didn't even try to straighten and present himself, what with his good clothes torn and filthy, his face looking like a map with purple bruises marking the hills and valleys.

"We brought him back to clear my name, but he says he didn't kill Betts either," LeCroix told the peacekeeper.

Ern wiped his brow with the back of his hand. "Folks around here are expectin' a hanging. Where the hell have you been? When you weren't back in two days' time I had to tell folks what Susanna Bond told me and how I let you go. Now here you are claiming this man didn't kill Betts either?"

"I didn't," Darcy said. There was no way he wanted to provide the entertainment for the populace of Shawneetown at a hanging.

Ern turned on him. "I suppose Telford Betts shoved that knife into his own heart?"

"No, I did, but—"

"But you didn't kill him? Betts looked good and dead to me. He didn't let out a peep when we buried him," Ern groused. "Hell." He started to spit on the floor, thought better of it, and swallowed. He looked at Olivia, stared at the front of her torn dress, eyed LeCroix carefully, too, and finally looked back at Darcy.

"I guess you all got a *real* good explanation?"

"Betts was already dead when I stabbed him. He just keeled over." Darcy thought that the honest-to-God truth sounded lame even to his own ears. Ern Matheson stared back at him in outright disbelief.

Darcy looked at LeCroix. He had tried to tell the half-breed that no one was going to believe him, that they should have let him go back to New Orleans, but LeCroix had needed his own alibi and unfortunately, he was it.

"Yeah, and I can fly like a bird on a good day, too." Ern was looking at all of them as if they had lost their minds. "Tell me you don't believe him," he said to Olivia and her lover.

"Why would he want Betts dead? The man was just a land agent. He's the one who brought Lankanal here," the river pilot argued in his defense.

"This man tried to frame you for murder, Noah."

Darcy decided it was up to him to plead his own case. "The idea didn't even come to me until after Betts died," he told Ern. "He had picked up LeCroix's knife after the fight in the tavern. When I saw that, I figured I'd get LeCroix out of the way once and for all."

"So you could take the girl?"

Darcy looked at Olivia. "Yeah. So I could have Olivia."

Over the past couple of days, while he had been traveling back upriver with Olivia and LeCroix, he had slowly become somewhat accustomed to seeing them together. For the most part, they hardly communicated when they were in earshot of him, but he noticed they did not need words. That Olivia loved the half-breed, there was no doubt.

He remembered thinking, *Let her go on and marry the man and have a passel of grubby little candy-faced children.* He had wasted the spring and most of the summer tracking her down. It was time to get over her, to get on with his life—if he could just save himself from a hanging.

Suddenly a middle-aged woman appeared on the stairs that led to the second floor. When she saw the three of them she came flying down the steps, her brown eyes wide behind her spectacles as she began fussing over Olivia.

"Oh, you poor thing, what happened to you?" The woman, whom Darcy took to be none other than Matheson's wife, pulled Olivia into her embrace and then brushed her tangled hair off her face.

"You come upstairs and let's get you out of that ruined dress."

Darcy stared at the floor as Matheson's wife clucked over

the torn bodice. When he looked up again, the peace-keeper's wife was pinning him with a knowing glare.

"What are you going to do about this, Ern?" Without waiting for an answer, she turned to Olivia and then Noah LeCroix. "You two look like you could use some decent food and rest."

Darcy watched her bustle around, collecting some items from the shelves. Matheson's wife stopped a few inches away from him.

"Is *this* that fancy New Orleans gambler?" Her hair was pulled back in a severe bun, and her dark eyes snapped as she inspected him from head to toe.

"That's him," Matheson told her. "Darcy Lankanal."

"What are you gonna do with him, Ern?" She was eyeing him over her spectacles.

"Put him in the smokehouse, I reckon. Claims he's not guilty, so we gotta hold off the hangin' and bring the circuit judge in."

Darcy closed his eyes, fighting to stay on his feet. He was hurting, hungry, and tired. He wanted a bath and a change of clothes and he wanted to get the hell out of Illinois. He thought of his grand suite in the Palace of Angels, of the beautiful women there who would give anything to sleep with him, pamper him, and cater to his every need. He tried not to imagine how good it would feel to soak his aching bruises and muscles in a deep, warm, scented bath, to slip into a silk dressing gown and light up an expensive cigar. He tried not to think at all, but he was facing impending doom. Suddenly Ern Matheson's last statement registered.

"You're putting me in the smokehouse? Like some . . . some . . ."

"Ham." Noah LeCroix stepped up to him and actually smiled. "It's not as bad as it sounds, Lankanal. You'll get used to it."

chapter
20

The Mathesons fed them fried catfish and beans, lent them clothes, and promised to keep Darcy Lankanal locked up right and tight in the smokehouse until the circuit judge could be summoned. Ern extracted a promise from Noah that he would appear at the hearing. Insisting she wanted to get back home before another night fell, Olivia easily convinced Noah they should walk the two miles back to the homestead. A tense silence accompanied them. She had no idea what he was thinking, or how long he would stay this time. Certainly he would be here until the hearing was over.

They were almost home, at the last bend in the road, when she suddenly stopped walking and let go of Noah's hand. A war whoop cut the air, a high shrill sound that had Noah going for his gun and Olivia's heart racing.

Little Pay and Freddie suddenly appeared beside the trail, scratches on their arms from the low bushes, dirt rubbed into their faces. Each of them had strips of turkey-red cloth tied over one of their eyes, Little Pay's right, Freddie's left.

"Thurprithe!" Freddie called out, oblivious to the fact that Noah might have shot them both if he had not hesitated. Little Pay ran up to Olivia and threw his arms around her waist.

"Boy, Livvie, is Daddy ever gonna be glad to see you. He's been waitin' by the door and looking out the windows since you left."

She felt her heart quicken and looked over at Noah. He was frowning as he stared down at the two boys.

"Why are they wearing those rags?"

"Why do you think? They are pretending to be you."

Noah looked down at the boys a few seconds longer, then went down on one knee. In an unexpected show of affection, Freddie threw his arms around Noah's neck before the man could get a word out. Noah winced, but did not pull away.

"Be careful of Noah's shoulder," she warned them.

"Thankth for bringing Livvie home again, Noah," the child said softly. "Daddy wath worried, but Ma didn't doubt for a minute but what you wouldn't bring our Livvie back." Freddie's inflection was so much like Susanna's that Olivia smiled.

Noah looked uncomfortable with Freddie's nearness, but then he reached out, touched the swath of red cloth the boy wore, and smiled.

Noah said nothing, but he hauled Freddie up in the crook of his arm on his good side. Little Pay bounced around them, demanding equal attention. When Noah turned to her, she could not read his expression.

"Let's go, Olivia. Your family is waiting."

They crossed the cornfield together. She thought the stalks must have grown a foot since they left. So great was her happiness that the sky seemed bluer, the forest around the homestead richer and greener, the cabin warm and welcoming and hardly shabby-looking at all. She knew then she was coming to think of the place as home.

Little Pay ran ahead to announce their return, calling out at the top of his lungs, tripping on clods of rich, dark soil, waving his arms over his head. Freddie was content to walk beside Noah and hold his hand, trying to match the man's stride.

Payson appeared in the open doorway. Olivia watched

her father wave at them, take two steps out the door, and then stop to watch them cross the field.

It was all so reminiscent of her last homecoming, she thought. This time, even though there were no dark secrets left to hide, the future was still uncertain.

When she reached the yard before the cabin, she left Noah and Freddie and walked straight into her father's embrace.

"Oh, Livvie," he said, holding her close. "Thank God Noah found you."

She put her arms around him and patted him gently on the back. Compared to Noah, he was so much smaller that he seemed almost frail. With shattering insight she realized that in many ways she was far stronger than her father ever was or would be. If she had not been tested over the past year, she would never have known how very much she could endure and survive.

Susanna hurried out of the cabin to join them. Molly came to the doorway and stood there watching the exchange. Olivia smiled over her father's shoulder at the serving girl. Payson finally let her go.

"Livvie, please forgive me. I had to break my promise," Susanna appeared troubled, sorry she had broken the trust.

"I know," Olivia said, taking Susanna's hand. "But since you did it to save Noah, I thank you." She looked over her shoulder and saw Noah making an effort to converse with Little Pay and Freddie. Her heart stumbled.

"It's finally over." Payson shook his head as Susanna moved up beside him.

"Not quite yet." Olivia hated to darken the mood. "There's still Darcy's trial. We had to bring him back to clear Noah's name. He admits Noah didn't kill Mr. Betts, but he says that he didn't either. He claims the man died of heart failure."

"But Noah's knife—"

By this time Noah had joined them. The boys flanked him like bookends, hanging on his every word.

"Ern Matheson said that as soon as the circuit judge is

located, we'll be called back to town for the hearing," Olivia told them.

"Is Noah safe?"

"Darcy's admitted to stabbing Betts with Noah's knife. Ern talked to as many folks as he could while we were gone and they know Noah's reputation. Darcy, on the other hand, is a complete stranger with no alibi. He may be found guilty because there's no one to vouch for him or his word."

"What do you think?" Payson asked her.

"Although he used the man's death to frame Noah, we don't think he killed Betts," she said.

"There's nothing we can do until we get word from Ern, so right now, why don't we all go in and have something to eat? Come, Noah, come join us at our table again." Payson called out to Molly. "How about helping dish up some of those beans and hamhocks for everybody?"

Molly lingered in the open doorway. "Where is Mr. Lankanal now?"

"Ern put him in the smokehouse," Noah said.

"I'm sure it's an experience he'll never forget," Olivia added, thinking of the quality of the accommodations Darcy was used to.

"The beans, Molly," Susanna reminded the girl gently.

"Get the beans. Milk the cow. Ye'd think that's all a body had to do around here was work." After Molly grumbled her way back inside, the rest of them followed.

Noah's frustration mounted as the afternoon came and went. Everyone wanted Olivia's attention, from Susanna, who was more lively than Noah had ever seen her, to the little boys who alternately wanted to play with him or were begging Olivia to tell them a story. Payson, relieved and happy to have his family together again, took a book down from one of the shelves and sat in a corner, content to read. He looked up occasionally and watched them all. Even Molly would not leave Olivia alone. She begged to hear the story of the harrowing trip downriver, asking about every detail.

Restless and bored, Noah began to wonder if Olivia was hiding behind her family's attention. He needed to talk to her alone, to speak of all the things in his heart, but there was no time. As the afternoon and evening wore on, he was plagued with the ache in his wounded shoulder. Finally, after they had eaten a light evening meal of corn bread and milk, during which he hardly took his gaze off her, he concluded that Olivia was purposely avoiding him. He stood up at the table and announced he was going back to his old campsite to spend the night.

At that, Olivia quickly looked up, but he still could not read the expression on her face. Was it disappointment or worry? The boys sat on each side of her, watching him intently.

"Can we sleep out there with you, Noah?" Little Pay asked.

"We'll be real, real quiet," Freddie added.

Noah shook his head, looked directly at Olivia. "What I need is some sleep."

A look passed between Susanna and Payson, and they suddenly stood up. Olivia's father went back to the rocking chair as Susanna silently began helping Molly clear the dishes.

Olivia's gaze shot to the loft where she, Molly, and the boys slept, already crowded together. Then she met his gaze for the longest time since they had entered the cabin.

He thought for a moment she was about to say something, but she fell silent, quickly casting her eyes down at her hands where they rested on the tabletop.

"Olivia?"

She shook her head, a nearly imperceptible movement. "We'll talk tomorrow," she said.

All day he had been trying to marshal the courage to ask her to marry him and go back to Heron Pond. Seeing her with her family again gave him doubt, but he held on to his hope. He wanted her to step outside with him so that he might see what she was thinking and feeling, but obviously she did not want to be alone with him tonight. If he did propose, would she turn him down again?

His shoulder ached, he was dirty and tired, and he wanted nothing more than to wash up at the creek, put his head down and sleep. His own indecision was making him crazy. His patience finally snapped.

"Have a good night then, Olivia." It was said more harshly than he had intended. He stood up, bid everyone else good-night, and walked out of the cabin without looking back.

Olivia waited until everyone was asleep, then took her moccasins out of the trunk, slipped them over her bare feet, and climbed down out of the loft. Without making a sound, she left the house. The moon was not yet up, but the darkness no longer frightened her.

Across the field she hurried, then quickly walked along the woodland path. She halted at the edge of the clearing around his lean-to. The fire had reduced itself to glowing embers and white ash within a ring of stones.

She crept closer, gliding across the grass. Noah slept on his side, his wounded shoulder up, his back to the clearing. When she reached the low lean-to, she knelt down, tempted to reach for him, to touch his hair. She longed to lie down beside him, to be there to watch the sun come up, to see him awaken, to smile at his surprise when he found her there, but a few stolen moments was all she would allow herself.

She saw that he had bathed in the pool. His long straight hair was still wet where it lay against his cheek, covering his scar. Ern had given him a shirt to replace what was left of the one torn during the fight, the same shirt whose hem Noah had ripped off to make new headbands. His new brown calico shirt was unbuttoned down the front, revealing his smooth, hard chest. She longed to lay her palm against his bare skin, to feel his heart beating beneath her touch.

She added some wood to the fire to keep away the predators that roamed the woods; then, as carefully as she could, she lowered herself to the grass beside him. He was so exhausted that he did not even stir. She decided to stay and keep watch while he slept, for this might be one of the last times she was alone with him.

As she stared down at the sleeping man, she thought of the many times he had offered her his love and protection, of the way she had hurt him, the times she turned him away. He was a strong man, a proud one, too. He would not ask again.

She sat beside him late into the night, alternately dozing and then listening to the sounds of the fire crackling in the fire ring, the hoot of an owl perched high in the tree above them. She sat beside him until the first stars began to fade. Then with a touch as light as a butterfly flitting across a summer meadow, she leaned forward and pressed her lips to his cheek. Stiff from sitting on the grass, she finally stood up and left him to finish his dreams alone.

Darcy was escorted to the trial in chains, chains that Ern Matheson had to borrow from the local blacksmith. The heavy, oily iron rattled and clanked as he was marched to the tavern instead of the courthouse, which had been damaged in the spring floods. No liquor would be sold this morning while the place served as a courtroom. The tables had been rearranged; one had been set up apart from the others for the circuit court judge.

Chairs were lined up in uneven rows, the extra tables stacked in the back of the room. The windows were all open but the air was hot, muggy, and still. The place still held the fetid smell of a tavern, reeking of whiskey and ale, tobacco and unwashed men.

When they left him standing just inside the doorway with a guard, Darcy slowly perused the room. There was no comparing it to the Palace of Angels with its crystal chandeliers, imported carpets, gilt-framed mirrors, and silk wall coverings. He only hoped to God that he would live to see the Palace again.

In a matter of seconds, Ern Matheson was back at his side. The yokel peacekeeper was puffed up with importance, smiling and nodding as folks streamed through the door. The man had even donned a clean shirt for the occasion, which gave Darcy pause. The townsfolk all seemed to be taking his trial very seriously. Probably nothing else of such import had happened here in years.

"Come on, Lankanal." Ern took his arm, letting him set his own pace because the heavy chains tangled and dragged from his waist, down his legs to the shackles at his ankles. He pulled out a chair behind a table and motioned Darcy to sit.

Before he did, Darcy scanned the room. The Bonds and the half-breed had not yet arrived. He felt a moment of fear when he thought that they might not come. He tried to shove his panic aside. LeCroix and Olivia were the only ones who could testify on his behalf, and they owed him nothing. She hated him. He saw that with the clarity of a man who had just spent hours alone chained up in a dark smokehouse ruminating over his own past. He had gone mad for a while, lost his mind over a woman who certainly was lovely, but wasn't worth losing everything it had taken both him and his mother a lifetime to build.

He should have toasted Olivia the day she escaped the Palace, found himself another virgin, and forgotten Miss Bond had ever existed. But if there was one thing he knew for certain now, the view back is far clearer than the road ahead.

The room was filling up fast with townsfolk, men and women both. Some of the women held squirming children. Others even brought along older ones with them. Everyone was curious, probably just as eager to see him hang. Raising his head, he slowly looked around the room, staring back at the crowd, giving them what they wanted—a chance to look at an accused killer. Some turned away quickly; others stared back unabashedly. A woman in the front row shivered when he met her gaze. She blanched and closed her eyes. When he thought she might faint, he smiled at her.

There was a commotion at the door that drew his attention, along with everyone else's. Darcy watched as Olivia's father stepped through the door. His wife came along after him, her good looks surprising. The night he had visited the cabin to offer to buy Olivia, he had thought her a pale, tired woman. Today Payson Bond's wife's cheeks were bright, her eyes shining. She had washed her shining blond hair and in the pale blue gown she was wearing, she actually looked much younger and quite fetching. The two little towheaded hellions ran through the door behind her and raced to take seats in front. The younger one smiled and waved to the crowd, and when he caught Darcy looking at him, he stuck out his tongue.

Darcy braced himself for Olivia's entrance when she walked in with the half-breed. Head high, her cheeks flaming, she wore a long doeskin dress, Indian garb adorned with fringe that swayed provocatively with her every step. Her long black hair curled riotously, almost to her waist. He had to hand it to her—she looked stunning and untouchable with the huge man beside her.

LeCroix appeared formidable in a clean white shirt with full sleeves, his ragged red eye patch a bold statement that only exaggerated his "Prince of the Ohio" image. If the man's shoulder wound still bothered him, he did not let on as he stood there beside Olivia, daring anyone in the room to approach her.

As he stared across the room at Noah LeCroix, Darcy thanked his lucky stars that the heavier, well-built man had not killed him at Cave in Rock. At least now he would still be able to tell his side of the story to the judge and hopefully save his own neck.

Spending almost twenty-four hours in the smokehouse had given him time to prepare his own defense. He just hoped his ability to charm the skin off a snake had not totally evaporated. His failure to win over Olivia was a setback that still shocked him, but this was no time to give in to doubt. His future depended on his ability to convince the justice of the peace and the crowd that he was innocent of Betts's murder.

LeCroix stared over at him as he escorted Olivia to her chair. A murmur rippled through the crowd. The last of the Bond entourage to enter was the young serving girl who had threatened Darcy with the rifle. There was an undeniable flash in her eyes and a bounce in her step that any warm-blooded man would be hard-pressed not to notice. She was ready for a tumble, and advertising in not-so-subtle ways. He found himself wondering what she would look like in silk, with those thick auburn curls done up in style, when Ern stepped up to the judge's table and rapped it with a wooden spoon. On the way over there had been much discussion about a missing gavel. Faye Matheson had volunteered to run back to the store and grab a substitute gavel when they promised that they wouldn't start without her.

"Hear ye, hear ye. Time for this honorable court to come to order."

The whispering and shuffling of feet against the wooden floorboards stopped. An expectant hush fell over the room.

"The honorable Elihu Richmond will preside." Ern Matheson took his role to heart, standing straight as a poker, chest out, shoulders back.

Darcy stared at the slight, crooked figure coming through the door. Elihu Richmond was old as dirt, nearly bent double over a wooden cane. In his other bent, gnarled hand he carried a worn leather satchel. As he shuffled along, his feet never left the ground. His back was so crippled that he could barely lift his head and look up. He reminded Darcy of an old turtle, with wisps of white hair sticking out of large ears that bracketed a bald, freckled pate.

Ern helped him into his chair. The justice took his time hanging the cane on the edge of the table and arranging it just so. Then he dug through his satchel and made a great show of sorting through a pile of wrinkled papers, then tried to smooth them flat with his arthritic hands. Finally his head came up a fraction of an inch and he rolled his eyes to scan the crowd.

Elihu Richmond cleared his throat and rasped. "Well, let's begin."

Ern stood and gave an official, long-winded version of what had happened; he told of finding Betts's body at the hotel and how he recognized Noah's distinctive knife, of Noah's arrest, of Susanna Bond's statement that her stepdaughter had gone away with Darcy because he had threatened all of their lives if she did not.

Susanna Bond was called to give her statement again. There was much shifting on the hard-bottomed chairs as she swore to tell the truth on the bible, but during her testimony, the place was quiet enough to hear a pin drop.

Darcy knew when his time came, he had better make the story good.

Olivia stared straight ahead, refusing to look at Darcy even once. She had donned Noah's mother's dress as a talisman and hoped that it would offer her protection. Butterflies were amassing in her stomach, for she knew that when it was her turn to cross the room alone and stand before the wizened old judge, she would have to tell the truth—and the truth would mean the whole story. She would have to tell why and how Darcy had come into her life, and then the town would know that she had been his captive whore for over a year. No matter that none of it had been her choice. Most of these stouthearted, God-fearing people would see it as an indelible black stain upon her soul.

Noah surprised her by reaching over to take her hand and giving it a squeeze. When she looked at him, he smiled and, despite the circumstances, the crowd, the fact that Darcy was only a few feet away, she felt warm and safe, as if they were the only two people in the world.

Ern was conferring with Judge Richmond, who kept yelling, "What'd you say?" every time Ern whispered in his ear. Finally Ern yelled back, "I said LeCroix is a half-breed," and a murmur rippled through the crowd.

"Then I'm not allowin' his testimony," Richmond shot back.

Olivia glanced up at Noah. He was staring straight ahead at the bright sunlight beyond the open door, toward the river. She straightened, lifted her chin. Her hand tightened in his. The judge said something she did not hear over her deep concern for Noah's pride.

"Miss Livvie?" Ern finally caught her attention. He was across the room, waiting expectantly for something. She realized she had finally been called to speak.

She closed her eyes and took a deep breath to calm herself. The judge's table was only a few steps away and yet it seemed like miles as she crossed the room. The fringe on the doeskin dress swayed with a whispering *hush-hush* sound. The touch of the rich cured skin against her flesh gave her courage and she thought of that other world, the swamp, and the day Noah had given her the dress. Finally she faced both the judge and the room at large.

Beside her family, Noah was staring up at her from his seat in the front row. He looked so natural there, so much a part of them that she was afraid she was going to cry. She glanced at Susanna, who smiled back, although her eyes were suspiciously bright. Payson looked nervous as he sat with his hat on his knees. He nodded at her and mouthed, "We love you, Livvie."

And she knew that he did love her, that her family would always love her no matter what the rest of Shawneetown thought of her once the story had been told.

She could not bear to look at the boys. Molly sat beside them, watching her intently. Even the serving girl appeared nervous for her. Molly sat there twisting her hands in the worn material of her homespun skirt and glancing around the room.

Ern Matheson touched her arm, had her place her hand on the cracked, black leather cover of an old bible and swear to tell the truth. He advised her to speak up good and loud. Then he nodded to Richmond. When the judge asked how she came to know Darcy Lankanal, she quickly glossed over the raid by the river pirates and then told of how they had sold her to Darcy in New Orleans. Just as she expected, the crowd lost control. It took Ern much pounding of the wooden spoon and yelling for quiet before things simmered down.

"So Lankanal bought you?"

"He did."

"And then what happened?" For the first time, Elihu Richmond seemed truly interested in the testimony.

"He kept me locked up in his place of business for over a year."

"His place of business?"

"Yes. The Palace of Angels. A gambling saloon and house of prostitution in the French Quarter."

A woman in one of the chairs near the back actually swooned. There was much commotion as she was carried out like a fallen doe hanging limp between two men while her bonnet dangled by its ribbons from her neck.

"Go on." Richmond was leaning across the table toward her, his neck twisted so that he could look up at her. "What did you do there?"

The room was hushed. Olivia's face burned and her heart hammered in her chest. Everyone in the room was leaning forward, intently staring at her from the edges of their seats, anxious to hear every sordid detail of the time she had spent with Darcy. The air was close and hot and still, and for a moment she thought that she was going to faint. She took a deep breath and then another. Flashes of memory assailed her, days and nights locked in Darcy's suite. The first few weeks he had not given her any clothes, kept her nude to prevent escape.

He had never brutally harmed her, certainly not the way he had done in the cave. His patience and skill always paid off, and eventually he would win over her traitorous body, if not her mind. How could she put any of it into words? How quickly did one die of shame?

A man near the door snickered. Chairs creaked. She looked to Noah again for strength and knew that was a mistake. His face was already dark with anger, his hands fisted on his thighs.

"Miss Bond, I asked you a question," Richmond said, licking his lips. "What happened while Lankanal had you in his possession?"

Olivia opened her mouth to speak but never got a word out, for Noah had jumped to his feet.

"Stop!" His voice echoed around the silent room. His footsteps were heavy as he strode to her side. He was shaking with rage.

"Enough, Olivia. We're leaving."

chapter
21

PANDEMONIUM BROKE OUT. EVEN RICHMOND STRUGGLED to his feet. He ignored the wooden spoon and took to pounding on the tabletop with the worn bible.

"Sit down, sir!" he hollered. "Sit back down and be quiet or I'll have Ern toss you out."

Noah tugged on Olivia's hand. "Come on."

"Oh, Noah." She touched his cheek and smiled up at him. "I have to do this. It's all right, really."

"I won't have you humiliated, not for him." He indicated Darcy with a lift of his chin.

"I have to do what is right. I can only tell the truth. My concern before was in telling my family, but now they already know all there is to know and they still love me anyway."

He looked over the crowded tavern, at the men and women with their heads together, conferring with each other in hushed whispers, pointing, staring at the two of them, at Darcy and at Olivia's family.

When he looked into her eyes, her heart lodged in her throat.

"I love you too, Olivia. I will always love you."

Upon hearing the words she had never thought to hear from him again she closed her eyes, took a deep breath, and willed her tears not to fall.

"Then please, go back to your chair, Noah. I'll be fine."

He hesitated a moment more. A wave of relief went through her when Noah finally let go of her hand and slowly walked back to his seat. He stared down the crowd with every step.

"Are you ready now?" the judge asked. "Any more theatrics?"

She shook her head. "No, sir."

"Fine. Then go on."

Olivia finally looked at Darcy. "Mr. Lankanal locked me in his private suite and kept me there for weeks. Eventually, he let me move about the place, but not often, and never alone. I devised a way to escape by hiding in a pile of laundry, stealing one of the house slaves' dresses, and slipping out."

She told of hiring on for the trip up the Mississippi with the Marlboroughs, but left out the rest of the sordid details.

"After I was separated from the Marlborough family, Noah LeCroix found me and led me here, to Shawneetown."

Finally she allowed herself to look at Noah again. Although he was sitting very still, she knew him well enough to see that he was seething. She concentrated on his tender, public profession of love and knew she could bear anything now.

"I thought I was safe until I saw Darcy Lankanal here in town. He told me that I still owed him the money that he paid the river pirates for me. He claimed that I had not worked off my time yet. He used that to blackmail me and made threats that led me to believe that he would kill Noah and my family if I didn't go back to New Orleans with him. After everything he had already done, I believed him. When I left with him, I had no idea he would try to frame Noah for a crime he never committed."

"But now you believe Mr. Lankanal did *not* kill this man Betts?"

"Yes."

"Why?"

"Because he said he didn't. He's not one to let an opportunity go by, so when Betts collapsed, he took advantage.''

''After all he did to you, you believe him? I find that pretty hard to swallow, little lady.''

The room was stifling, the air too close for comfort with so many people crowded together. Olivia looked at Darcy again.

Gone was his bold, arrogant demeanor, his overbearing confidence. His once high-glossed boots were muddy and scratched beyond repair, his swallowtail coat torn and stained. The leg of his trousers was ripped at the knee. He looked wrinkled and tired and disheveled. His face was purple with bruises, his lips cut, his eye still swollen. In the courtroom, surrounded by all the others he looked smaller, his once-threatening presence diminished by all that had happened. He was watching her intently without a trace of fear for his life, only regret.

He had tried to have her and had failed. He had also made her a promise to go back to New Orleans and leave them all in peace. She could not explain why, but yes, she believed him.

''I think I know him well enough to know when he's lying, and I'm certain he is telling the truth about Betts.''

The judge's hands stopped fidgeting with his papers. He stared at her through rheumy hazel eyes. The room fell silent as a tomb.

''But yet before, you truly believed he would have harmed your family?''

''At the time I did.''

The judge let out a long-suffering sigh and shook his head.

''You forgive him, girl, for all he did to you?''

Olivia looked at Payson. Her father was on the edge of his seat, staring at Darcy. She had seen the same expression on her father's face often enough; it was one he wore when he was trying to come to terms with some new philosophy he had just read or when he was wrestling with the words of a new poem.

Beside Payson, Noah sat watching her. She could almost

feel him willing her to be strong, to ignore the whispers and expressions of distaste and condemnation on the faces of the crowd. She knew that he would try to fight them all if she gave him even the slightest indication that this whole affair was getting the best of her, so she was careful not to look into his face for too long.

"I asked if you can forgive Lankanal, girl?" Richmond repeated.

Certain of her answer, she turned to the judge.

"I do, sir. I forgive him."

"And why is that? Because you have some lingering feelings for the scoundrel?"

"The only thing I feel for him is loathing. But I am ready to put the past behind me, once and for all, and in order to do that, I must forgive him."

At last she looked over at her father. He was watching her with pride, his eyes bright.

A stunned silence hung over the room until the judge finally said, "Thank you, then, Miss Bond. You may sit down."

As Olivia once more took her seat beside Noah, Elihu Richmond turned his watery gaze on Darcy and squinted across the space that separated them from the rest of the room.

"I suppose I ought to hear your version of the story, Mr. Lankanal, afore I pass judgment. So step on up here and tell it."

Darcy stood and made his way, chains dragging, across the floor.

"Ern, get those things off that man," Richmond instructed. "He don't look like he could outrun a child the shape he's in anyway."

Ern quickly freed Darcy, who politely thanked the judge for his compassion.

"Don't think that means you still aren't gonna swing, young man. Now get on with it."

Darcy turned to face the room. Intentionally, he did not straighten to his full height. He played up his cuts and bruises, turning the most battered side of his face toward the crowd. He scanned the crowd of farmers, merchants, miners, and pilgrims, the fortunate souls able to get a seat in the crowded room, and reminded himself to raise his voice so that the old judge heard every word.

"How far would any of you men go to have the woman you loved by your side? Would you track her down? Would you hire men to find her? Would you let her go without a fight?"

He could see that his opening caught them off guard, and waited while the stunned audience mulled over the questions he had put to them. "If so, then you would be guilty as I am. I was obsessed with a woman." He nodded at Olivia. "When she left my . . . protection—" He cleared his throat, knowing that he was stretching the truth a bit too far, but the crowd was with him. "When Olivia Bond left my protection I was hell-bent on getting her back any way I could. Months went by. I couldn't find her. Finally Telford Betts came to me and told me he'd seen her here in Shawneetown. I did come here and I *did* threaten her family, it's true. I threatened to harm Mr. LeCroix. But I knew Olivia well enough to know that the mere *threat* of harm to them would be enough, that she would go with me to save her family."

The judge toyed with the wooden-spoon gavel. A fly buzzed around the cuts on Darcy's face. He brushed at it, winced when he moved, and made certain the crowd noticed his terribly pained expression.

"Nice little tale, Lankanal, but get to the murder. Why did you kill Betts?" Richmond was obviously tired and irritable. It had been a long, hot afternoon for everyone, and Darcy figured even longer for someone as old as Methuselah.

"I swear I did not kill Telford Betts, as I have said before. He dropped dead in his own room. I had gone there early to wait for him, but he took so long getting back that I fell asleep on his bed. When he walked in, he told me how LeCroix had accosted him and had even tried to choke him. During the scuffle, LeCroix had dropped his knife and

Betts picked it up. He was pretty proud of having snuck it into his coat without anyone seeing him do it. He was very nervous and riled up over everything that had happened, and pressing me to pay him off for leading me to Olivia. Suddenly, he turned red and fell to the floor. I thought he had passed out, but he was dead.

"When I looked down and saw LeCroix's knife on the floor beside him, it dawned on me I could make certain that the half-breed didn't follow me and Olivia back to New Orleans."

The onlookers began to murmur to each other. Somewhere in the back of a room a baby fussed. Darcy waited while its mother quickly skirted between the chairs and hurried from the room. The sound of crying faded down the street.

"Are you telling me that you stabbed a *dead body*?" The judge cupped his hand around his ear.

"Yes, sir," Darcy shouted. "I stabbed a dead body."

Richmond nodded sagely. He pursed his lips, sucked in the bottom one, and shoved it out again. "Damnedest story I ever heard," he muttered.

"Thank you, sir," Darcy smiled.

Richmond said, "But if anyone doesn't have anything else to say, you have no proof, Mr. Lankanal. All I have is the word of a fornicator, a flesh peddler, a gambler and the word of his former whore. You really expect me to believe either of you?"

Noah was on his feet again, his face filled with rage. Olivia grabbed his arm and pulled him back down.

Richmond looked over the audience. "If nobody else can speak for you, then I'll have to declare you guilty and set the hanging for dawn tomorrow."

Darcy's heart fell to his toes. He grabbed the edge of the table, not certain whether he could stay on his feet. Tomorrow at dawn he would die.

Ern jumped to his feet. "Elihu, maybe . . ."

The judge blinked and looked up at Ern. "Dawn might be a bit too early. Let's make it noon, then." He opened his satchel and started shoving papers back into it.

Darcy felt the urge to run, knowing there was nowhere to go, no way to escape, even if he was capable of running. Suddenly he saw the auburn-haired girl who worked for the Bonds leap to her feet.

"Ye can't hang 'im, sir. Not 'til I get to tell my part."

Darcy frowned. What was her name? What could she possibly say that would save his neck from the rope?

"And what might you know relative to this case, missy?" Elihu's gnarled hands stilled on top of his papers.

Before his legs gave out from under him, Darcy made it back to his chair. He sat down heavily and watched as the Bonds' serving girl walked directly over to the judge's table without a bit of hesitation.

"What's your name, girl?"

"Molly MacKinnon. I'm the Bonds' fetch-and-carry girl."

She smiled down at Richmond with the same bold, impudent smile she gave everyone, but she soon sobered when Ern swore her in. Like a schoolgirl at prayer, she clasped her hands in front of her and then, in a voice loud enough for all to hear, she began.

"Mr. Lankanal came out to the cabin to threaten Mr. Bond. He said lots of bad things about Miss Livvie and finally, Mr. Bond asked him to leave, but Mr. Lankanal wouldn't go, so me bein' the best shot of the lot, I persuaded him. Soon as everyone was asleep, I slipped out of the loft and snuck into town. Ye see, I was gonna ask Mr. Lankanal to take *me* to New Orleans instead of Miss Livvie, for I always been wantin' to get me a better life."

"You say you sneaked into town the night of the murder?"

"That's right," she nodded, with a swift glance at Darcy.

At this point Darcy could only wait, dumbfounded like the others, to see what she was going to say. He was going to be condemned to swing for murder. Why would she want to drive the nails into his coffin?

"I saw him at the hotel, saw him go into Mr. Betts's room and close the door. I made sure nobody saw me while

I waited around in the hallway until I didn't hear a sound inside and then slowly opened the door.''

At that point she looked down at her hands. Her shoulders drooped and she let out a long-suffering sigh. ''My life ain't been all that good since I come to America with me uncle. I thought if I could just get Mr. Lankanal to take notice of me, he'd forget about wanting Livvie back. She had no need of him, and I did.''

''I think I'm beginning to see where you are headed, young lady.'' Richmond reached up and scratched his freckled head with yellow nails in need of trimming.

''Aye, sir, and though I'm not proud of myself, I've got to tell the truth of it. Mr. Lankanal was asleep on Mr. Betts's bed. I slipped over and was about to wake him when I heard footsteps in the hall. I run to the wardrobe, climbed in and hid.'' She shot a glance at Darcy. He straightened up on his chair. Her next words would either save or condemn him.

''Then it all happened just like Mr. Lankanal said. Betts came in, they talked and the man got all excited. He fell dead after showin' Mr. Lankanal the knife. Then Mr. Lankanal, he tried to wake up Mr. Betts. He rolled him back and forth and laid his head on the man's chest to listen to his heart. Then he waited a while to be sartin the man was dead before he picked the knife up and stabbed Mr. Betts.'' She paused, shook her head and set her curls bobbing. ''Stabbed Mr. Betts's *body*, that is,'' she quickly added. ''He was already dead. I seen the whole of it, I did, and it was just like Mr. Lankanal said.''

The crowd erupted again. Darcy could only sit dumbfounded and stare at Molly MacKinnon. She was either the best actress in the world, or she really had been there, watching the whole thing. Right now, he didn't give a tinker's damn if she was lying or acting. Right now she was his only hope, the only thing standing between him and a hanging at noon tomorrow.

Richmond was pounding the wooden spoon again, demanding order. His gravelly voice was going hoarse. Finally everyone settled back down.

"This certainly puts a new light on things, doesn't it, Ern?" Richmond looked absolutely stunned, almost disappointed.

Ern Matheson merely looked perplexed. "Yes, sir, it does."

"You swear you're tellin' the truth, girl?"

Richmond crooked his finger and motioned the serving girl closer. Darcy held his breath. Would Molly MacKinnon stick to her story, or would the judge wear her down?

The room was hushed and quiet. Sweat beaded Darcy's upper lip but he did not bother to wipe it off.

"Well, girl? Is it true you saw Betts fall dead before Lankanal stabbed him?" Richmond wore a fierce expression as he stared up at the serving girl.

Molly never blinked, nor did she hesitate. "He turned blue as a Scottish lake and then white as a sheet. He was clearly dead, sir, a long time before Mr. Darcy let 'im have it with the knife."

The judge rubbed his head again, sucked his lower lip in and out, then looked over at Darcy.

"You're one lucky son of a gun, Lankanal, what with all these folks ready to testify in your defense, even the ones you wronged." He stared Darcy in the eye. "But I'll tell you right now, if I ever see you standing before my bench again, I'll hang you just for the hell of it because I think you're getting off too easy." Then he banged the spoon on the table. "Not guilty," he shouted. "No hanging. Court's closed. Ern, help me stand up and get me outta here. I gotta take a piss."

For Noah, it was over too soon. Darcy Lankanal would not hang, but there was still one more thing he wanted, something that he had to do before the hateful, nearly deaf old man behind the table cleared the room.

"Wait!" Noah shot to his feet, swept up by the moment and his lingering outrage. Beside him, Olivia gasped. He felt her tug on his sleeve, but he shook free and crossed the room before she could stop him. Ern was trying to help the judge out of the chair when Noah reached the front table.

Both Richmond and Ern turned to him, the peacekeeper with a question in his eyes, the judge clearly afraid.

"You would not let me speak before, but now I'll have my say." Noah felt the hush fall behind him, turned and saw that not one person had left his or her chair.

"What now?" Richmond sighed as he sank back down. Ern let go of the judge's arm but remained beside him.

"I wish to speak for this woman, and to her. There are things that have to be said, and I refuse to be silenced."

Noah cursed himself for waiting, but he had to speak now, while nearly the entire town was assembled. He refused to be intimidated by the crowd, so he looked down into Olivia's eyes, knowing that whenever he did, all else faded away.

"Oh, Noah, what are you doing?" Olivia whispered, and yet he heard her.

All eyes were upon him—a host of strangers, along with Payson and Susanna, Little Pay and Freddie, Molly, Lankanal, the Mathesons, and the judge. The only one who mattered was Olivia.

"I have heard all of you whispering, felt the condemnation in the room as Olivia Bond told her story. The judge would not let me speak before, because when he looks at me he sees only a half-breed. He doesn't know me, doesn't know that I am a man of my word. Most of you know of me. You call me the Prince of the Ohio. You feel free to sing songs about me, to tell stories. So now, I'll ask you to listen. You owe me that much.

"I want to speak for Olivia Bond, for she left out much of her own story to spare her family, but just as she said, they will love her anyway. I want to say what she could not. When I found her, she was afraid of her own shadow. Her eyes were haunted by what Lankanal had done to her. She had been bought and sold like livestock, held against her will for over a year. Her only offense is that she did what she had to do in order to survive. Is that a sin? Did she do anything more or less than any one of you would have done? How can any of you condemn her for that?"

He looked to Olivia again where she sat frozen, like a spring blossom hit by the last frost of winter. Her lovely green eyes glistened with tears.

"She has forgiven Lankanal. She should be forgiven for whatever wrong anyone might *think* that she committed in order to survive. Today she is going to be my wife."

"But Noah—" she protested.

He was beyond arguing. He was doing what he should have done long ago, what Hunter had advised he do the minute he saw her again. As if they were the only two people in the room, he spoke directly to her.

"I won't hear that you are not good enough, because I don't believe it and I won't take no for an answer anymore. Enough is enough, Olivia."

"Impossible." Like him, she ignored the crowded room of onlookers and her family. The time had come to say what was in her heart. "Do you think I can ever forget what I have done, even if *one* of these good people finds it in her heart to overlook what I have become?"

"Moment by moment you'll forget because I'll be there to help you. I don't know how to be a husband, certainly not a father, but I promise I will try to do the best I can. I'll give you all the love that I have to give and I will learn to be a good husband and a loving father to our children, because I love you with all my heart, Olivia. Isn't that enough?"

"Oh, Noah, it's *more* than enough, but I still can't do this to you." Her voice broke. She stood up.

He looked over at Payson and thought of something that might convince her.

"You've forgiven your father, Olivia. You've forgiven Darcy. Can't you find enough love in your heart to forgive *yourself* for what happened in New Orleans?"

"What are you saying?" she whispered.

"Forgive yourself, Olivia. Forgive yourself and let me love you."

He was not about to leave the room before their future together was assured; he turned to Elihu Richmond next.

"You have the power to marry people?" Noah kept his voice even, trying not to shout in order to make himself heard by the old man, but he would yell the roof off if need be.

Richmond squinted up at him. "This just gets better and better." Then he nodded, "Yes, I can marry people."

"Good. Then you will marry us." Noah turned and found that Olivia had taken a step toward him. Ever so slightly she shook her head no when it dawned on her what he was about.

"See here a minute," Richmond protested. "I've done enough for one day."

Noah turned on him, made use of his greater height by bending over the table, leaning close to the old man until they were nose to nose.

"You'll marry us now. Today."

Ern touched the old man's shoulder. "You can spare another five minutes, can't you, Judge?"

Richmond grumbled. "I still gotta piss."

Olivia had stopped halfway between her family and the judge's table, as if she were afraid to go forward and yet unable to go back. Noah turned and held out his hand.

"Will you marry me *now*, Olivia?"

chapter

22

OLIVIA WAS SHAKING LIKE A LEAF WHEN NOAH TOOK HER hand and enfolded it in his. She had survived river pirates, Darcy, and now public humiliation, but Noah's tender, heartfelt profession of love had almost brought her to her knees. Standing beside him there before the judge's table, she felt whole and strong and free. Strong enough to hold her head high and ignore the crowd while her family moved up to encircle them. The boys started to argue, vying for the privilege of who would get to stand closest to Noah.

"Well, Judge?" Ern leaned over Elihu Richmond, who was still glowering up at Noah.

"I still gotta take a piss."

Faye had moved in alongside Ern. "Why don't we all go on over to the store. There's plenty of room for the whole family and anyone else who wants to witness the happy occasion and the judge can . . . take care of his . . . personal business."

Judge Richmond smacked the table with the wooden spoon. "Court's adjourned." He finally smiled at Olivia. "I'll be performing a wedding within the hour over at Faye and Ern's store."

Ern looked relieved, but not as much as the judge. The peacekeeper helped the old man to his feet, juggled the satchel and the man's elbow, and slowly led him away from the table.

Susanna was the first to hug and congratulate Olivia, while Payson pumped Noah's hand and beamed.

"We'll take the boys and go on over to the store ahead of you, in case there's anything you want to say to one another in private," he told them.

"Thanks, Daddy." As Olivia hugged him, she wished her knees would stop shaking. Then she turned to Noah. He had not taken one step away from her side.

"Thank you, Noah."

"For what?"

She could see that he had said his piece and had no wish to draw further attention to himself. He was watching Darcy, who was still seated across the room. Her former captor looked as if he were trying to gather the strength to stand and leave the tavern.

"Thank you for standing up for me and for not giving up on me." She reached up and touched his mouth just below the end of his scar. "For the gift of you, your love, your life."

"We'll be happy, Olivia."

"Very."

"We'll have children."

"Many."

"We'll be late to our own wedding." He finally smiled.

"Do you really think that the judge would have finished his 'personal business' by now?"

Noah laughed. Olivia slipped her arm through his and was about to turn around to leave when Molly walked up and bid her wait. The girl showed no ounce of remorse or regret for having gone to Darcy's room alone, or of getting up in front of the whole town and telling everyone about it.

"Can I talk to you alone, Livvie?"

Olivia gave Noah's arm a squeeze. "Why don't you go on ahead?"

He glanced at the emptying room, at the remnants of the crowd lingering outside, at Darcy, seated alone, and shook his head.

"No. I'll wait for you right outside the door."

As soon as he left the room, Molly took Olivia's hand.

"I hope ye ain't mad at me, Miss Livvie." The girl spoke quickly, in a hushed whisper. "But I was thinkin', that seein' as how ye didn't want Mr. Darcy Lankanal for yerself, that ye wouldn't mind if maybe I could have 'im? I didn't think I'd ever see any other way of gettin' out of here."

"Oh, Molly," Olivia took her hands. "You have no idea what you are getting into if you pursue this. No idea at all."

Molly shrugged. "Maybe not, but I know what I got now and I know I want more."

"I can't believe you slipped out and followed Darcy to town that night."

"I can't believe it either, but I'm glad the judge did." Molly's gaze kept sliding over to Darcy and back again.

"What you do is up to you, Molly. But please, go back to the homestead with my family." Olivia was more than anxious to put her nightmare behind her, but hated to think she was passing it on to someone else.

Molly hesitated, then shook her head with finality. "Tell them not to wait for me. I want to find my own way."

"I hope to God you will be all right." Olivia gave Molly's hand a squeeze.

Just before she stepped outside, Olivia turned and looked back at Darcy. He was still seated, but Molly was walking toward the empty chair beside him. Olivia turned her back on them, on the past terrible year, looking forward to sharing her joy with her family as she went outside to join Noah.

Olivia found him waiting by the door, just as he'd promised. A knot of people stood close by, watching them, yet unwilling to approach.

"Are you ready?" he asked when she reached his side.

"I wish we were already on the way back to Heron Pond."

As they started down the street toward Faye and Ern's store, he asked, "What about your family?"

"Susanna is so much stronger in mind and body that I

feel I can leave her now. The smokehouse is well stocked for winter, thanks to you. I hope we can come back to see them often, but I don't need to stay on here any longer. I can't let you suffer through any more of either Darcy or this town.''

Ignoring the crowd, he wrapped his arm around her shoulders and pulled her close. They walked in step down the street.

''We can stay if you want, Olivia.''

They were almost at the front door of the dry goods establishment when Little Pay came bursting out onto the street.

''Livvie, Daddy says you and Noah gotta get inside right now.'' Little Pay leaned over and planted his hands on his knees, making a great show of catching his breath. ''Faye said we gotta get the celebration started. She's even breakin' out the penny candy for us. Ma already had one whole glass of blackberry wine.''

Noah slipped his hand down to the small of her back and, just before they were about to step inside the door, Olivia looked up into his face and smiled.

''I love you, Noah LeCroix.''

''I know,'' he said softly. ''And I'm glad.''

''What makes you so certain that's true?'' She smiled. Knowing how serious he was, she wanted him to be sure that she was only teasing. She knew that he did love her. The whole town knew now.

Noah smiled back.

''I'm the Prince of the Ohio,'' he said. ''How could you resist?''

Darcy had glanced up in time to see Olivia and LeCroix leave, but found himself more intrigued by the serving girl, Molly, who had just slipped into the chair beside him.

''Were you really hiding in that hotel wardrobe?'' Darcy lowered his voice to a whisper so their words would not carry through the near empty room. Only the barkeep remained, and he was putting the place in order, pushing tables back from the wall, shoving chairs across the floor.

"Does it really matter to you, Mr. Darcy? You're not gonna hang now. The way I see it, whether I was or not, ye still owe me."

He hated owing anyone anything. He much rather people owed him. "What do you want?"

She nearly leapt on him. "Take me with ye. Take me to New Orleans."

He folded his arms. "How old are you, Molly Mac-Kinnon?"

"Twenty."

"Liar."

"Nineteen. Honest."

"Seventeen," he said, guessing.

"All right then, eighteen and a half."

Darcy couldn't help but laugh out loud, even though it hurt his battered mouth.

"The answer is no." He started to stand. She grabbed his torn sleeve and easily pulled him back down.

"I'll go to that old coot of a judge and change my story," she threatened.

"He's already found me not guilty."

"He *almost* found you guilty. You think he can't change his mind?"

"Not now. He's already passed judgment. But you, on the other hand, could be in very serious trouble for lying."

"Aye, but they wouldn't hang me, now would they?" She cocked her head and smiled up at him.

"So you want a trip down to New Orleans?"

She shook her head. "No. I want it all. I want everything I heard ye offer for Miss Livvie. The clothes and the jewels and the horses. I want money of me own and I want to live in a fine, grand place. A Palace of Angels."

Again he had a vision of her dressed in French silk, her hair bound up with pearls, her firm young breasts riding high above the indecently low neckline of a revealing gown. She had pale skin and a dusting of freckles that reminded him of the merest hint of nutmeg. She had spunk and a definite style of her own that showed through her rags. He was beginning to warm to her. So much so that he had to shift around to get comfortable on the hard-bottomed chair. He wondered if one man would ever be enough for Molly MacKinnon.

"I don't think you understand what working at the Palace entails," he told her.

"Oh, but I think I do," she said with a wink.

"Are you a virgin, Molly?"

"Do ye want me to be, Mr. Lankanal?"

For the first time in months the world seemed livable again. The heavy cloud of darkness that had come over him the day he discovered Olivia gone had finally lifted. In a surprising yet comforting way, her forgiveness had moved through him earlier, so much so that he now found himself looking forward to starting over.

He was free again, of both the charge of murder and of his obsession for Olivia. He was master of his world.

But most of all, after one long look into Molly Mac-Kinnon's adoring eyes, he knew his old charm was back.

Darcy carefully straightened what was left of his coat. He ran his hand over his hair and tried to ignore the throbbing above his eye.

"How long will it take you to pack, Molly? I think we might be able to catch a ride downriver this very afternoon if we hurry."

She stood up, holding her arms open wide. "Everything I own ye see right here before ye, Mr. Lankanal." Then she smiled, leaned close and whispered, "But the best part is *under* me dress."

With Olivia beside him, Noah stepped inside the dry goods store and waited for his vision to adjust. The afternoon sunlight that filtered in through the front window barely reached the center of the room. Lamps had been lit along the back wall and the oil smell only added to the close, still air filled with the pungent scent of tallow candles, tobacco, and spices.

To his chagrin, the place was almost as crowded with people as the tavern had been earlier. Every inch of floor space was taken up with tables of merchandise, so folks wedged between them into every corner. Those who could not get through the front door were gathered on the street trying to peer through the windows. He had an urge to walk out, until he looked down at Olivia and found her watching him with an apology in her eyes. She squeezed his hand.

"I'm sorry, Prince," she whispered with a shrug, "but you're the one who went and proposed in front of the whole town."

She sounded as if she were teasing, but she looked so concerned that he wanted to raise her spirits, so he smiled for her sake and then sought out her family across the room.

"Follow me," he said.

The crowd parted to let them through. Most of those in attendance were curious, but others smiled as he and Olivia passed by and wished them luck. He did not see Ern or Judge Richmond, but the Bonds were waiting with Faye Matheson, who beamed from ear to ear as she smiled and nodded at familiar faces in the crowd.

Little Pay and Freddie had their mouths so stuffed with candy that they couldn't even speak, which greatly relieved Noah. He decided that Faye Matheson knew exactly what she was doing by giving them so much candy.

Olivia's father stood by looking proud, daring anyone to object to his daughter marrying a half-breed. Noah guided Olivia over to her family and, once there, found himself too nervous to speak. His stomach felt as if the Ohio were churning through it; he took a long deep breath and tried to imagine that he was outside and not in the close confines of the dimly lit store.

Susanna stepped up beside Olivia and smiled, reached out to smooth her hair for her, and then straightened the neckline of the doeskin dress. As the two women started talking in hushed whispers, every so often Olivia glanced around the room at the strangers around them. She looked as nervous as he felt.

"Do you feel all right, Noah?"

He nearly jumped out of his skin when Payson moved in close.

"Just fine."

"You're sure about all this?" Payson studied his face intently.

Noah nodded. "Very sure."

He was sure he wanted Olivia forever, but not quite sure whether he would live through the formalities.

When he heard Ern's voice booming in the stairwell and then saw the peacekeeper help Judge Richmond down the narrow stairs, he had an urge to run. His panic intensified when everyone in the room squeezed in closer, pressing forward so as not to miss a word.

Leaning hard on his cane, the judge made his way across the room with Ern at his elbow. Finally he stopped right in front of Olivia, craning his neck so that he could look up at her.

"Where's the groom?" His voice grated like an unoiled hinge.

Noah cleared his throat. "Right here." He took a step forward, stood beside his bride, and reached for her hand. As soon as they touched, a calm swept through him and he knew he would be all right.

Judge Richmond peered over his spectacles. "You sure you both want to do this?" He stared into Olivia's eyes.

She whispered, "Yes."

He glanced over at Noah. "Well?"

Noah nodded back.

Then Richmond looked over at Payson. "You sure you want to give your daughter to this man?"

Noah felt his face burn. Although he was certain Payson would not object, he realized he was holding his breath.

"I know of no finer man than Noah LeCroix," Payson assured the judge.

Noah barely heard a word after that. He had seen only one wedding ceremony and that from the edge of the forest, where he had hidden and watched Hunter marry Jemma. He had lost his eye only a few weeks before and back then could not think of showing himself and ruining their day.

He had little idea of what to expect of this ceremony and soon realized that if anyone were ever to ask him what the judge had said today, he probably would not be able to relate any of the details.

He did know that when he swore to love and to honor, to cherish and to keep Olivia until death parted them, that he meant each and every word of the vow. He knew, too, that the love in her eyes when she spoke her own vows was real, and true, and lasting. When she promised to love and obey, to cherish him always, to have and to hold him until death, that in that singular moment, he felt as if they were completely and entirely alone. The strangers, the curious onlookers, the Mathesons, and even the Bonds who loved them might well have been hundreds of miles away.

In that instant nothing else existed save the love they shared with one another, the memories they had already made and those yet to make.

Judge Richmond did not tarry over the words or the sentiment, he simply pronounced them man and wife without fanfare.

"There," he said, shoving his glasses up his crooked nose, reaching for the hat Ern held out to him. "That ought to do it. Now, I need to be on my way. Ern, you better come along and help me into my buggy before all that blackberry wine I had upstairs starts to take effect."

"Now what?" Little Pay shouted, breaking the silence as the adults around him laughed.

Not to be outdone, Freddie echoed, "Now what?"

"Kiss the bride!" a man hollered from the front of the store.

Olivia turned her face up to Noah expectantly, a slow, knowing smile on her lips. He couldn't believe they expected him to actually kiss her right in the middle of the crowded store.

He swallowed. Hard. He looked around and saw that everyone was waiting expectantly, most of all Olivia.

"You don't have to," she whispered. Her eyes told him differently. He closed his eye and leaned toward her, unerringly found her mouth and tried to shut out the rest of what seemed like the entire world. In two heartbeats he forgot they were not alone. He became lost in the taste and scent of her, in the moist softness of her lips, in the promise of the future.

Faye initiated a round of applause. Hoots and hollers started in earnest. Olivia pulled away, her cheeks ablaze, her eyes wide and startled as if she, too, had momentarily forgotten where they were. Payson took Olivia in his arms and hugged her. Susanna walked over to Noah and stood on tiptoe so that she could kiss his cheek. The boys each grabbed one of his hands and started tugging him in two different directions.

While Noah finally let them lead him to a counter where Faye had set out some cookies, candies, and glasses of rich, dark wine, he smiled at Olivia and watched as some of the women shyly stepped up to congratulate her.

Olivia stared into the sea of unknown faces, wishing Noah had not been so obliging to the boys and had stayed by her side, but she couldn't blame him for escaping. Faye had done her very best to muster up a wedding party because she had been determined, as she had assured Olivia in a whisper, to turn what had been an extremely trying day into a celebration.

Unexpectedly, one of the women suddenly handed her a folded sheet of paper. She appeared quite shy as she ducked her head in greeting.

"I'm Mary Ellen Walker," she said quietly. "An old friend of Faye's. I thought you might be needing these recipes." She held out the page. "They're three of my favorites. I'd 'a put down more, but I couldn't write any faster on such short notice."

Expecting nothing but censure after all she had revealed this morning, Olivia could only stare at the woman in surprise. When she finally managed to look down at the recipes carefully penned in ink, the letters blurred and wavered.

Pulling herself together, she looked up.

"Thank you, Mary Ellen. I'll treasure these recipes always and think of you every time I make calf's head or cider cake or persimmon pudding."

Another woman, this one older than Mary Ellen with a face lined and care-worn, her brow knit in a permanent frown from squinting in the sun, shoved a folded homespun cloth at Olivia.

"Here, this ain't much, but it'll get you started, I reckon."

As she carefully opened the piece, Olivia complimented the colorful pink and lavender petunias embroidered around the scalloped edges. Hard-pressed to find words to express her thanks, she stared up at the stranger in awe.

"It's a tablecloth," Susanna prompted. She stood at Olivia's elbow like a proud mother hen.

"Thank you," Olivia told the older lady. "I'll treasure it always."

A girl who looked younger than herself quickly slipped into the circle of women. She thrust an old, brass, long-handled combination strainer and ladle at Olivia.

"Congratulations, ma'am. I'm sorry we almost hung your husband."

Olivia had to bite her lips until she could calmly thank the girl. She then turned to Susanna and Faye.

"I don't understand," she said softly. "These women don't even know me."

Faye chuckled. "But they know the Prince of the Ohio, and after the way he stood up for you today, I'm certain everybody wants to make up for any ill thoughts they might have started to entertain."

"But—"

"Just smile and say thanks, honey," Susanna advised. "You don't need to fret anymore."

Not everyone in the room stepped up to personally wish her well, but by the time the last of the women had congratulated her, Olivia's arms were full of hand-worked pieces, various cooking utensils, lengths of cloth, homespun thread, and even a small basket of fresh brown eggs.

When Noah finally caught her eye from across the room, her heart swelled with joy.

epilogue

Bond Homestead

NOAH STOOD IN FRONT OF THE CABIN WATCHING THE Bonds, a family together for a few moments more. He delighted in watching his wife, his Olivia. Dressed in a lightweight muslin gown that would see her through the long walk home, she had packed a few of her essential things, only what they could carry this time. She made him proud when she included his mother's shawl and her doeskin gown.

She was ready to leave her family. This time there would be only tears of joy, not sorrow, except for Freddie's tears. He still could not understand why his sister had to leave again.

While Noah waited with Payson, Olivia tried to explain to the boy that they would both come back to visit soon. While they were talking, Susanna had disappeared inside.

"But, Livvie, I don't want you or Noah to go away." He locked his little arms around her neck and planted two loud wet kisses on her cheek, leaving a sticky peppermint-scented trail behind. When Olivia finally managed to escape his hug, she stood him on the ground and looked to Noah for help.

"We'll be back in a few weeks," Noah promised. "Olivia will need more clothes and some more of those presents she got today.''

Then he turned to Olivia. He cupped her cheek and traced her soft skin with his thumb, still finding it hard to believe that she was his wife, that she belonged to him forever. The meaning behind Hunter's words of advice came rushing back to him when he suddenly realized that he loved Olivia enough to stay on with her family if that would make her happy.

''If you want, we'll stay,'' he whispered. It wasn't until she shook her head no that he realized how much it meant to him that she truly was looking forward to going back to Heron Pond.

''I want to be with you, Noah, in your home. I want us to make our own way. But I would like to come back in the fall to help with the harvest.''

He smiled. ''I told you I am willing to learn what being part of a family means. And about loving.''

She reached up, drew his face down close to hers, and whispered softly, ''I'll teach you all there is to know.'' As she gazed into his eyes, he nodded in the direction of the boys, reminding her that they were not alone.

Just then, Susanna came back out of the cabin carrying a small bundle in her hands. She walked over to them and smiled up at Noah.

''I have a present for the two of you, something for luck.'' She handed the gift to Olivia.

Noah watched as his new bride unfolded a linen towel Susanna had wrapped around the gift—a small silver pitcher with a dent in one side near the handle. The significance was lost on him, but tears instantly wavered in Olivia's eyes.

''Why, this was the creamer to your silver tea service.'' Olivia tried to hand the gift back to Susanna. ''I can't take this. It belonged to your great-grandmother. Didn't you once tell me that it came from England?''

''You have to keep it. It's a remembrance, from all of us to the two of you,'' Susanna told her.

"But I thought the tea set was stolen by Sullivan's men."

Her stepmother shook her head as the boys and Payson gathered close and stared at the shining silver object in Olivia's hands, remembering.

Susanna spoke softly, reverently. "The scoundrels dropped this piece when they rode off. It's a little bit battered, but it survived."

Payson held a thin book in his hands. He was smiling at Olivia. "Weren't we all a bit battered? And didn't we survive? Take it, Livvie. And take this, too."

He looked over at Noah. "I hope on those long winter evenings when you have nothing to do, you might want to read to your husband by candlelight."

Susanna laughed. "I'm sure they will think of other things to do on long, cold winter evenings, Payson."

Olivia blushed. Noah cleared his throat, feeling more than a bit uncomfortable.

"Like what?" Little Pay wanted to know.

"Like what?" Freddie echoed.

Noah sighed and decided he had learned more than enough about the intricacies of family life for one day. He was ready to take Olivia home.

"Time to go," he told her. He reached for his pack, took the silver creamer that Olivia handed him and tucked it inside, then slipped the strap over his shoulder.

Olivia was looking down at the new book in her hand. "Percy Bysshe Shelley?"

Noah glanced over her shoulder. The words on the pages looked like nothing but dots and specks and lines to him. He did not see how the symbols held the power to bring tears to her eyes, but somehow they did.

Payson said, "It's a book of poetry. I thought you should have at least one book in your new home. I marked a special place for you in *Prometheus Unbound*."

Olivia turned the pages until she came to one where a small dried wildflower lay pressed inside. She carefully lifted the fragile flower and stared down at the words. Noah noticed that there were some lines drawn beneath some of the letters. He did recognize an H among them.

Olivia whispered. "To forgive wrongs darker than death or night; . . . To love and bear; to hope till Hope creates . . . is to be good, great, and joyous, beautiful and free."

"Oh, Daddy." She reached for her father and put her arms around his neck. "Thank you, so very, very much. I'll treasure this always."

Payson hugged her close. When Olivia finally drew back and looked up at her father, Noah was relieved by the bright smile on her face.

"You are already beautiful, Livvie. Now you must go and be joyous and free." Payson hugged her one last time. He turned to Noah and offered his hand, then changed his mind and hugged him, slapping him on the back. "Good luck to you, son. I know you'll take good care of her."

Noah watched Olivia brush Little Pay's hair back off his forehead with her fingers, a last touch, an unspoken, loving gesture of good-bye.

"If it gets any later, we might as well stay the night."

He sighed, shifting the weight of his pack as he picked up his rifle. He looked off toward the southwest, toward home.

When Olivia slipped her hand into the crook of his elbow, eyes dry and smiling, ready to go with him, Noah knew that no matter what the future held in store for them, they would face it together.

"I'm ready." Olivia smiled up at him.

"Then let's go home."

The cypress and tupelo swamp closed around the couple in the low, sleek pirogue as it cut through the water, guided by the sure, strong strokes of the man as he dipped the paddle into deceptively still water. Below the surface speckled with emerald duckweed, an unseen current flowed swift and sure, carrying fresh water through the swamp, ensuring purity, passing on ancient wisdom and all the secrets of the water, not only to the man, but to the tiny bud of life nestled in the woman's womb.

The woman looked up, through the thick canopy of leaves and branches, at the patches of sky streaked orange and gold with sunset. High above them, through the gathering mist, she saw the outline of a dwelling amid the trees and recognized the sturdy, well-constructed cabin and the wide wooden porch that surrounded it. The house was suspended in the branches of a tree that had grown old before the first inhabitants walked the land.

She turned to the man behind her and let her smile convey most of her thoughts, for there were no fitting words that she could use to express her love, her gratitude, her joy, save two.

"We're home."